KIM  ASHAM

Blood of the First Flame

The Moonborne Prophecy

Copyright © 2025 by Kimberley S Basham

All rights reserved. No part of this publication may be reproduced, stored or transmitted in any form or by any means, electronic, mechanical, photocopying, recording, scanning, or otherwise without written permission from the publisher. It is illegal to copy this book, post it to a website, or distribute it by any other means without permission.

This novel is entirely a work of fiction. The names, characters and incidents portrayed in it are the work of the author's imagination. Any resemblance to actual persons, living or dead, events or localities is entirely coincidental.

Kimberley S Basham asserts the moral right to be identified as the author of this work.

Kimberley S Basham has no responsibility for the persistence or accuracy of URLs for external or third-party Internet Websites referred to in this publication and does not guarantee that any content on such Websites is, or will remain, accurate or appropriate.

Designations used by companies to distinguish their products are often claimed as trademarks. All brand names and product names used in this book and on its cover are trade names, service marks, trademarks and registered trademarks of their respective owners. The publishers and the book are not associated with any product or vendor mentioned in this book. None of the companies referenced within the book have endorsed the book.

First edition

ISBN (paperback): 9798298864435
ISBN (hardcover): 9798298880183

Cover art by Kimberley S Basham

This book was professionally typeset on Reedsy. Find out more at reedsy.com

To my cousin Megan—
Your unwavering belief in me has been the quiet force behind every word on these pages.
You offered inspiration when I felt empty, motivation when I faltered, and a kind of love I never knew I needed.
This book exists because you never let me forget why I started.
Thank you, from the depths of my heart.

"I think fearless is having fears but jumping anyway"

- TAYLOR SWIFT

Prologue

Lucian's voice trembled as he whispered, "Don't look. I love you so much. Take care of our son." His words hung in the air like a fragile thread, binding him to his wife, Inez, who sat frozen on the sofa. Her hands clutched the fabric of her dress, her knuckles white with fear. Lucian stood tall, his back to her, shielding her from the horror that was about to unfold. He turned to the attacker, his eyes steady, his resolve unshaken.

The attacker's face twisted in fury, his grip tightening on the gun. He stepped forwards, his boots echoing ominously against the wooden floor. Lucian's heart pounded, but his expression remained calm. He knew this moment was inevitable. As the attacker closed the distance, Lucian's mind flashed through memories: his wedding day, the laughter that once filled their home. He closed his eyes, a single tear escaping down his cheek.

The attacker's rage boiled over. He lunged forwards, pressing the cold barrel of the gun against Lucian's forehead. The room seemed to shrink, the air thick with tension. Lucian opened his eyes, meeting the attacker's gaze. Recognition flickered between them, a silent acknowledgement of a shared past. Lucian's lips curled into a smile, a gesture of acceptance, perhaps even forgiveness.

"Do it," Lucian said, quiet but firm. The attacker hesitated, his hand shaking. But anger won out. He gritted his teeth and pulled the trigger. The deafening sound of the gunshot shattered the silence. Lucian's body crumpled to the floor, his lifeless eyes staring into the void. Blood pooled beneath him, staining the floor with the finality of his sacrifice.

Inez screamed, her voice raw and piercing. She scrambled off the sofa, her pink gown trailing behind her as she collapsed beside her husband's body. Her hands shook as she touched his face, his skin already growing cold. "Lucian, no," she sobbed, her tears falling onto his cheeks. She cradled him, rocking back and forth, her cries echoing through the room.

The attacker stumbled backwards, his face pale, his breath ragged. He stared at the scene before him, the weight of his actions crashing down like a tidal wave. He dropped the gun, the clatter breaking the spell of his shock.

Inez's sobs grew quieter, her throat hoarse from screaming. She pressed her forehead against Lucian's, whispering, "You're okay, wake up. Please, wake up." But there was no response, only the haunting stillness of death. She clung to him, her gown soaked with his blood, her heart broken beyond repair.

The attacker, realising the enormity of what he had done, froze as panic clutched at his chest. His breath hitched as he cast a frantic glance at the lifeless form of Lucian crumpled on the floor. The clock was ticking. He knew he had to act before she lifted herself from the corpse and caught a glimpse of his face. She wouldn't understand. How could she? The situation had spiralled beyond his control. His thoughts raced: he couldn't bear to add another death to his already stained conscience, especially hers. Especially not when she was carrying a life within her.

Composing himself, he moved silently, almost predatory, behind Inez. She was trembling uncontrollably, her fingers still clutching at Lucian's shirt as though her touch might anchor him to life. He leaned in close, the proximity making his stomach churn. His hands found her shoulders, gently at first, as though afraid she might crack under his grip. Slowly, he began to lift her from the floor. She was limp, her weight folding into him as though her grief had drained her strength.

He made sure to keep her turned away, his hands firm but not cruel. She couldn't see him. She couldn't see anything but Lucian. Her husband. The man who had been her anchor, her love, her protector. Her baby's father. The sight of his open, empty hazel eyes hollowed her out, the accusation floating in their lifeless depths. He was gone. Gone forever.

Tears streamed down her face, blurring her vision, but her focus never wavered from Lucian. Her mind screamed at her to wake up, to shake him, to do something. This had to be a nightmare. It couldn't be real. It simply couldn't. She was paralysed between disbelief and a grief so consuming it felt as though she might drown in it.

Little did the attacker know, her grief had locked her in a world where he didn't exist. Not yet. She didn't notice the shift in the air as he moved closer. She didn't register his presence fully, blinded as she was by the agony of loss.

But he was there. He was real. And as he guided her quivering form away from Lucian's body, he steeled himself. He had no other choice.

The attacker released one hand from her shoulder, his movements frantic as he rummaged through his pocket. His fingers brushed against the chloroformed cloth, a tool meant for Lucian, a plan meticulously crafted but now rendered useless. The situation had shifted, and he had to adapt. Lucian was supposed to be alive, carried out discreetly by his men. But that possibility had slipped through his grasp, leaving him with no choice but to improvise.

As he lifted the cloth towards Inez's face, his heart pounded against his ribs. She reacted instantly, her survival instincts kicking in with a ferocity he hadn't anticipated. Her body twisted and thrashed, her head jerking from side to side in a desperate attempt to evade him. Her movements were wild, fuelled by the primal need to protect herself and the life growing within her.

In the chaos, she found an opening—a fleeting moment of opportunity—and she seized it. Her teeth sank into the leather of his glove, her jaw clamping down with all the strength she could muster. The attacker recoiled, a sharp grunt escaping his lips as pain shot through his hand. He jerked away, his annoyance flaring, but he didn't let go. His grip tightened, his left hand pulling her closer, forcing her against his chest. He had to keep her still, had to stop her from turning, from fighting, from seeing him.

As she struggled, a scent wafted towards her, a smell that tugged at the edges of her memory. It was faint, elusive, yet unmistakably familiar. Her movements slowed, her mind trying to place it. Did she know him? Her confusion temporarily overrode her fear.

The attacker took advantage of her hesitation, pressing the cloth firmly against her face. Her vision blurred, the world around her dissolving into a haze. Her strength ebbed away, her thrashing reduced to weak, futile attempts. The scent of chloroform filled her senses, overpowering the familiarity that had momentarily distracted her. And then, everything faded to white.

The attacker lifted Inez into his arms, her unconscious form limp and fragile against him. He moved swiftly but carefully, his steps echoing down the dimly lit hallway. The weight of her body was nothing compared to the burden of what he had done. Each step felt heavier than the last, as though the walls themselves were closing in, suffocating him.

He reached the lift, the metallic doors sliding open with a cold, mechanical hiss. The silence inside was deafening, broken only by the hum of the lift descending. He adjusted his grip on her, his hands shaking slightly as he cradled her closer. Her face, streaked with tears, was a haunting reflection of the life he had destroyed. He couldn't let himself dwell on it. Not now.

The lift doors opened to the back of the building, where the van awaited like a predator ready to devour its prey. He carried her outside, the chill of the night air biting at his skin. His crew stood nearby, their faces in shadow.

"Go clean up and ensure nothing is left behind," he ordered.

They nodded in acknowledgement, their movements efficient as they dispersed to erase any trace of the chaos.

He turned back to Inez, his gaze softening. He wiped the tears from her cheeks, his fingers brushing away the evidence of her pain. Her hair, damp and dishevelled, was smoothed back with a tenderness that seemed out of place. He reached for the bag, his hands steady as he placed it over her head. The cuffs clicked into place, a cruel necessity to ensure she couldn't escape when she awoke.

He lay her on the back seat of the van gently, as though trying to shield her from further harm. Her body sank into the seat, her breathing shallow. He stayed for a moment, his eyes focused on her face before he turned away. Climbing into the driver's seat, he started the engine, the low rumble breaking the stillness of the night.

As the van pulled away, the building faded into the distance, swallowed

PROLOGUE

by the darkness. The attacker's grip tightened on the wheel, his mind racing with what had transpired. It was behind him, but the consequences were far from over.

1

The Enchanted Cup

A young couple lived in the city of light, their days painted with hope and excitement as they prepared for the arrival of their baby boy. Newly-weds Inez and Lucian Clarke, brimming with dreams of their future, had recently purchased their first apartment. It was a sanctuary they would call home. The location was a dream: close enough to the heart of the bustling city to enjoy the vibrant energy, yet tucked away just far enough to escape the chaotic stampede of workers. From their ninth-floor balcony, they could gaze at the river as it shimmered under the golden glow of sunset. The view was a daily reminder of the beauty and promise that surrounded them.

The apartment was everything they had hoped for: spacious, modern, and brimming with potential for the new chapter of their lives. With three bedrooms, it provided more than enough room for the growing family. As they stepped through the entrance, they were greeted by an immaculate expanse of white, from the gleaming floors to the pristine walls. The hallway stretched ahead, flanked by four doors—two on each side—leading to the heart of their home.

At the end of the hallway was the open-plan living room and kitchen, a space where the couple envisioned laughter, love, and countless memories. The front room's centrepiece was a stunning white marble electric fireplace, oozing warmth and elegance. Above it, a sleek flat screen television dominated the wall, poised to host cosy movie nights and shared moments of relaxation.

The seating arrangement was as inviting as it was stylish. A plush grey fabric three-seater sofa seemed to beckon one to sink in after a long day. An ottoman rested at one end, offering a perfect perch for tired legs. At the opposite end stood a coveted circle swivel chair, the source of light-hearted battles between them. Inez had unofficially claimed it as her own. Draped in a soft throw, it became her sanctuary, her drawing and reading nook. The chrome floor lamp that arched gracefully over it provided the perfect glow for her late-night escape into the worlds of words and sketches.

Their home was a blend of their personalities, tastefully decorated with modern touches. Glass vases filled with delicate artificial flowers adorned various surfaces, bringing a hint of nature's charm without the hassle of maintenance. Inez had decided long ago she wasn't one for the constant care real flowers demanded. Despite their lifelike appearance, they carried the beauty and elegance that complemented their surroundings.

Every corner of the apartment seemed to echo their love and anticipation. It was more than just a place to live. It was the backdrop of their unfolding story, a place where dreams would grow and the gentle pitter-patter of tiny feet would soon fill the air.

The kitchen was a study in sleek functionality. Its white gloss cabinetry reflected light with every movement, while the grey marble worktops provided a sophisticated contrast. At the centre, a matching island stood as the hub of activity. It was perfect for meal prep or casual breakfasts. The minimalist design was evident, from the streamlined appliances to the open, uncluttered surfaces. Yet it was a different world compared to the inviting sitting area, which was alive with personality and warmth.

Lucian's office was a space of focus, tailored to his needs as a web designer. It stood in stark contrast to the rest of the apartment's brightness, cloaked in dark grey tones that exuded a sense of calm. The room was immaculate, just as he preferred. It was a testament to his disciplined nature. In front of the floor-to-ceiling window sat a sleek glass desk, its surface reflecting the light from outside. His faux leather office chair was a throne of productivity, positioned perfectly to offer a view of the river behind him. It was a sight that often inspired his creativity, the flowing water a symbol of constant movement and innovation.

Nearest the door, a black metal bookcase added structure to the space. Its upper half, featuring glass shelves, held an assortment of carefully chosen items: books, awards, and tools of his trade, each meticulously arranged. The lower half was practical, with cupboard space providing storage for files and paperwork accumulated during long hours of work. Despite its darker palette, the room bore the same careful attention to detail that defined the entire apartment. It was Lucian's domain, a haven of order and calm.

This home, each corner infused with their distinct personalities, was not just a place to live. It was a canvas for their story—a story of love, dreams, and shared aspirations, waiting to unfold.

Following the living room to the balcony, a world of lights unfolded before you. It was a dazzling display of stars not from the heavens above, but from the glowing city below. The skyline stretched endlessly, punctuated by towering buildings and famous landmarks that shimmered against the night. The view from their balcony was breathtaking, a panorama that encapsulated the vibrant heartbeat of the city of light. It was no wonder Inez had made this space her artistic haven, setting up her easel where the boundless beauty inspired her to capture it on canvas. She often found herself here, brush poised in hand, as the city offered its stories to those who paused long enough to see them.

From that vantage point, it was easy to understand why anyone would want to paint it. But Inez's love for this life wasn't borne from the skyline or the bustling charm of the city. It was borne from Lucian. She'd never wanted much before meeting him. Simple things had sufficed, but after Lucian walked into her world, everything shifted. Together, they built a life filled with quiet joys and shared dreams.

Their story began years ago, on a snowy afternoon when fate led them to a humble coffee shop tucked away at a crossroads. It wasn't much. A modest shop with frosted windows and an aroma of roasted beans greeted every visitor. For Inez, it had been the perfect place to escape and recharge.

She'd often come here to sketch out ideas for the art studio she worked in or simply to unwind. At that time, her artwork was private, tucked away from the world as she focused on showcasing others' creations. The role wasn't ideal, but she saw it as a stepping stone to something bigger.

That day, the sunlight had streamed through the window, casting a golden glow on her warm, ivory skin. It danced along her perfectly cut jawline and illuminated the mid-length brown hair that sparkled subtly against the snowy backdrop. Sitting on a wooden barstool by the window, she was fully immersed. Her camera captured the magic of the day: the snowman beside the red post box, the rhythmic dance of black cabs navigating the streets, and the tender kiss of an elderly couple beneath mistletoe. The scene was perfect, peaceful, and filled with the kind of beauty that makes an artist's fingers itch to create.

The spell was broken by the call of the barista. "Inez, large caramel hot chocolate," the server announced, bringing her back from her reverie. She hurried to the oak counter, tucking her camera away in her bag, and reached for the recycled cardboard cup. But as she spun around, her footing betrayed her. In a heart-stopping moment, the hot drink splashed out of her grasp and onto the gleaming black loafers of the man standing behind her.

Her cheeks burned with embarrassment, turning a shade of crimson that rivalled the post box outside. Words tumbled from her mouth in a flurry of apologies. She dared to glance up—and froze. He was tall, with dark hair and striking hazel eyes that locked onto her almost-grey ones. There was an ease to his smirk, a warmth in the way he extended a steamy cup from the counter to her trembling hands.

"Luckily, I also ordered a caramel hot chocolate," he said, his voice low and smooth.

Inez stuttered in response, "Oh, I really couldn't. I... I'm so sorry."

"It's not a problem," he replied effortlessly, his lips curling into an amused smile. "I have another anyway," he added, shifting the second cup between his hands, his fingertips pulling back slightly from the heat. Before she could protest further, he leaned in, his hand lightly squeezing her shoulder as if to steady her, his hazel eyes sparkling with playful confidence.

"Have a lovely day. Enjoy the drink, Inez," he said with a cheeky grin.

Her name on his lips sent a jolt through her as she tried to process the encounter. When she finally glanced at the puddle on the floor, her reflection stared back at her from its rippling surface. She rolled her eyes at herself, letting out a quiet groan. Then she looked up and, as if he were nothing but a mirage, he was gone. The only evidence of his presence was the cup in her hand. Written on it, in bold letters, was a single name: Lucian.

2

Canvas of Destiny

Inez returned home, her mind still buzzing with the events of the day. As the evening settled around her, she powered up her computer and began scrolling through the photos she had taken at the coffee shop. The memories of the snowy afternoon came flooding back, and she felt the warmth of the caramel hot chocolate and the flurry of emotions as vivid as if it had happened seconds ago. Her fingers clicked idly through the images, until suddenly, she stopped. One photo called out to her, stopping her in her tracks.

The ice-white snow stretched across the screen, pristine but not untouched. A single footprint punctuated the purity of the scene, its edges slightly raised, hinting at the crunch that would have echoed as the pedestrian moved forward. Across the street, the glow of the shop windows bathed the snow in golden light, creating a dreamy contrast against the cool shadows cast by bare tree branches. There was a depth to this image, a sense of stillness paired with quiet motion, that captivated her. It wasn't just a photograph. It was a story waiting to be told.

Inez wasted no time. She dug out her canvas, sharpened her pencils and began to sketch the composition with precision and care. Every stroke felt deliberate, as though this moment had been waiting for her to bring it to life. When the time came to paint, she felt her brush move effortlessly, as though guided by the memories and emotions tied to that winter afternoon. The exhibit deadline loomed. She barely noticed. She was engrossed, completely lost in the process of creation.

As the weeks passed, she poured her heart into the artwork, perfecting every detail, every nuance of light that had struck her when she took that photograph. Yet her thoughts strayed to the man she had met that day. Lucian. His name was etched in her mind as she stared at her nearly finished masterpiece. She flushed at the memory of spilling the drink, her cheeks burning with the same embarrassment as before. Her eyes sparkled too, reflecting the warmth of the encounter that had left an indelible mark on her.

The day of the exhibit arrived, bringing both excitement and nerves. Inez stood before her finished work, now hanging against the stark white wall of the gallery. Her breath caught in her throat as she looked at the painting. It was the culmination of years of dreams, hard work and perseverance. For the first time, her art was on display for the public, her very first piece to claim its place in a gallery. It was overwhelming, bittersweet even. While it should have felt perfect, she couldn't help but wish she had someone to share it with. The absence of family and friends weighed heavily, a familiar loneliness that had followed her throughout her life.

An orphan who had spent her childhood bouncing between homes, Inez had struggled to make lasting connections. Her focus on work and her artistic pursuits had filled the gaps. Tonight, as she stood amidst strangers dressed in black tie, the emptiness felt acute. She distracted herself with small, repetitive actions, touching her loosely curled hair, glancing at her reflection in a compact mirror. Her red silk gown, backless and floor-length with a daring leg slit, drew glances from every corner of the room. None of them held her interest.

That was until she saw him.

He entered the gallery with an air of quiet confidence, his black suit perfectly tailored to his frame. He straightened his bow tie as he crossed the lobby, ensuring his cufflinks were secure. His movements were measured, as though preparing himself for an evening of significance. With a subtle shrug, he adjusted his blazer into place, rolling his shoulders before descending the three steps into the main hall. For a while, his gaze was fixed on the ground, his polished loafers catching the light. But then, he looked up.

The room seemed to fall away as his hazel eyes found hers. Inez's heartbeat quickened. He stood there, poised and striking, as if he owned not just the space but the very air around him. And in that moment, there was no doubt in Lucian's mind. She was the most beautiful woman there.

As they locked eyes across the crowded gallery, a whirlwind of thoughts flooded Inez's mind. The questions came rapid-fire, each one colliding with the next. Should she be the first to speak? Should she thank him for the drink from that snowy afternoon? Should she apologise again for spilling hers? But no, perhaps saying nothing was the better choice. Her heart pounded as she watched him raise his head in acknowledgement, his effortless movements commanding the attention of everyone around him.

He began walking towards her, the crowd parting instinctively as though making way for someone of importance. Her nerves danced on the edge as he stopped before her, his aura magnetic. He took her hand gently but decisively, lowering his head to kiss it. As his lips met her skin, his hazel eyes flicked upward to meet hers, lingering on her perfectly symmetrical face, with the exception of the small, charming spot gracing her cheek.

"Wow, finally meeting the amazing Inez Weston," he said, his voice smooth and warm, yet laced with a quiet admiration that took her by surprise.

"Inez," she corrected softly, blinking in shock. "And... you know my name?" Her voice faltered slightly as she stumbled over the realisation, her surprise mounting with each word.

Lucian smiled, his gaze steady and unwavering. "I've been following your work for weeks now," he began. "Ever since I saw it listed on the exhibit schedule and added to the event website. I couldn't help but wonder... have you ever considered starting your own site? Somewhere to showcase exhibit dates, new artwork, events?"

Her mind raced as she processed his words. How had he seen her work? How did he know her surname? She hesitated, her puzzlement clear in the furrow of her brows.

Lucian immediately caught on to her confusion. "Ah, apologies," he added with a small laugh. "I should introduce myself. I'm Lucian Clarke, web designer and promoter. I designed the website for this event, and your painting..." He trailed off, his smile deepening. "It stood out to me the most. Reminded me of a little coffee shop I used to visit sometimes. They serve the best..."

"Caramel hot chocolate," they finished in unison, their voices overlapping with excitement.

And just like that, the barriers between them seemed to dissolve. What followed was hours of laughter, conversation and shared passion for hot chocolate, artwork and their inspirations. They talked until the gallery began to close its doors for the night. As the event ended, they exchanged numbers and promised to meet again—this time over dinner and drinks.

That evening, Inez arrived home with a dazed smile painted across her face. Her feet ached from the long day, but she barely noticed as she kicked her shoes off and collapsed onto her bed. She didn't even bother to change out of her gown, her thoughts consumed by the man she'd met. Lucian. The name hung in her mind, sparking a flutter in her chest that she couldn't ignore. Staring up at the ceiling, her lips curled into a dreamy grin. Had she met the man of her dreams? Could this be her second chance?

But then came the worry. What should she wear for her first-ever date?

Fast-forward three years, and Inez's worries over outfits were long gone. Their dates had turned into milestones, each one cherished more than the last. The most significant of them all had been their wedding day, a celebration that cemented their love in the presence of those closest to them. Now, their shared life was expanding once more. With just five months until their baby boy's arrival, the couple was consumed with preparations for his nursery. The debates were never-ending, from furniture styles to colour schemes, to the choice of a name. A decision that had them clashing for months.

Finally, they settled on warm white paint and a simple white crib, favouring a neutral palette that felt timeless. When Lucian called Inez into the nursery to see the finished room, her heart swelled as she took it all in. Everything was pristine, perfect. But there was one last touch. As Inez lifted the dust sheet covering the crib, her eyes widened. The headboard bore an engraved lion with the name "Leo" inscribed beneath it.

Leo. The name she'd cherished since childhood. The name of her late foster father. He had been her guiding light, helping her pursue her artistic dreams by buying her an easel and camera, the tools that had set her on her path. Lucian had always teased that the name was too short for a baby, but in truth, he'd understood its significance all along. This surprise was his way of honouring her and the memory of the man who had supported her at her lowest.

Inside the crib lay a perfectly made bed, ready to welcome their little prince. And every prince needed a loyal companion. Leo's was a stuffed lion teddy bear. Inez's heart overflowed as she admired the toy, noticing the extra touch Lucian had added. A voice recording rested within the teddy's heart, a thoughtful suggestion from the specialist Lucian had ordered it from. The gesture was perfect, a reflection of the care Lucian poured into their life together.

One stormy night, lightning streaked across the sky like wild, luminous whips. Thunder roared through the air like a pride of lions, shaking the quiet city streets as rain cascaded to the ground. The weather's ferocity kept Inez awake, each flash and crash pulling her from sleep. She debated whether to get up and capture the storm's beauty, a scene worthy of her canvas, but knew she needed rest more. Turning towards Lucian, she reached out to hug him, hoping the comfort of his warmth would lull her to sleep. But instead of finding him, she saw his pillow indented and his duvet crumpled in the corner.

Rising, startled, she walked through the hallway to find the office light glowing. There he was, her husband, slumped over his desk, his eyes heavy as he worked tirelessly on a project for a high-paying client. Inez gently lifted him, coaxing him back to bed, and though her heart ached at seeing him so burdened, she admired his drive and dedication.

As she drifted to sleep, Lucian pulled her close, his whisper brushing against her ear. "Are you still awake?" he murmured. She turned to face him, and he began rubbing her four-month-old bump, voicing his worries about money and fatherhood. He confessed that this big job, a website, pop-ups and a set of leaflets, had consumed him, but its reward could secure their future. Despite the tight deadline, he couldn't let the opportunity slip away.

Their journey was far from easy. But together, they faced every challenge head-on, ready to welcome their little prince and the life they were building for him.

The next afternoon unfolded under a sky that seemed to mirror the turmoil brewing within. Pitch-black clouds churned aggressively, their edges illuminated by flashes of lightning that split the heavens with raw power. Rain lashed against the windows, creating a rhythmic patter that filled the apartment with a sense of isolation. Inside, the couple found solace in each other's arms, cocooned on their comfortable sofa. The warmth of caramel hot chocolate in their hands and the soft glow of the television at odds with the mayhem outside.

Lucian sat at one end of the sofa, his legs propped up on the ottoman, while Inez stretched out beside him, her head resting on his chest. Her breathing slowed as the film reached its conclusion, her eyelids fluttering shut in peaceful slumber. Lucian smiled, careful not to disturb her as he shifted. He gently lifted her head, placing a pillow beneath it, and draped a blanket over her sleeping form. For a moment, he waited, watching her serene expression before retreating to his office to finish his work.

The storm outside seemed to echo his urgency as he completed the final design for his client. His fingers moved swiftly across the keyboard, crafting the email that would deliver the completed web link along with a detailed breakdown of its functionality. He ensured the payment information was included, setting up the process for immediate transfer. Once the payment was received, he prepared an envelope containing further documents and his business card, which bore his name, address and contact details. The notification of payment arrived within seconds, and Lucian wasted no time heading down to the lobby to hand the envelope to the front desk clerk.

The lift was out of service, a detail that struck him as odd. Maintenance hadn't sent any emails about repairs, yet the lifts were unavailable. Shrugging off the thought, he took the stairs, his footsteps echoing in the empty stairwell. As he ascended to the ninth floor, a strange sensation prickled at the back of his neck. A feeling of being watched. He glanced over his shoulder, his movements cautious, but the stairwell was empty. Shaking his head, he dismissed the unease and continued to his apartment.

Lucian entered quietly, careful not to wake Inez. He removed his shoes and jacket, the rustle of fabric the only sound in the room. Inez stirred, her eyes fluttering open as she woke peacefully. Lucian greeted her with a kiss on the forehead, his touch gentle and reassuring. He moved to the kitchen to prepare another drink, returning to the sofa where they settled in to choose their next film.

As Inez cradled her mug, the warmth of the caramel hot chocolate seeped into her hands. Her thoughts drifted to the day they'd met, a memory that brought a nervous giggle to her lips. "Imagine if I never spilt my drink on you that day in the coffee shop," she said, full of playful nostalgia.

Lucian's brow furrowed in confusion. "What coffee shop?" he asked, his tone genuine.

"Don't mess with me!" she replied, her grin faltering slightly. "There wouldn't be an us if it weren't for that day. After that, I couldn't stop thinking about you. That's why I painted the coffee shop where we met, because of how you made me feel." Her voice softened, her gaze searching his face. "You recognised the location in my painting, and the cup you handed me said 'Lucian' on it."

Lucian's expression shifted, his confusion deepening. "Babe, I have no idea what you're talking about. We met for the first time at THAT exhibit. I recognised the painting because it's a café I go to with…" His voice trailed off, his eyes widening. Fear flickered across his face.

Inez's heart sank as she saw the truth in his eyes. "Who was it then?" she asked, her voice trembling. "Who did you go with?"

Lucian exhaled heavily, his shoulders sagging under the weight of the unspoken answer. "Well…"

Before he could finish, the front door exploded inwards with a deafening crash. Splinters of wood scattered across the floor as the force of the kick reverberated through the apartment. The thunder seemed to roar in unison, lightning illuminating the figure standing in the doorway. The man's menacing silhouette was stark against the flashes of light. In his hand, the unmistakable outline of a gun glinted in the storm's glow.

Lucian rose instinctively, his body shielding Inez as she cradled her pregnant belly. "Don't do this," he pleaded, his voice steady despite the terror coursing through him. He took a step forwards, his hand pressed to his chest in a gesture of surrender. "You want me, not her. Please don't hurt them," he begged, his other hand extended protectively towards his wife. "Please."

The room hung in tense silence, the tempest outside a chaotic backdrop to the unfolding nightmare.

3

The Faceless Man

Inez began to stir, her senses slowly returning as she drifted out of unconsciousness. Everything was hazy, her surroundings blurred and disjointed, as though she were trapped in a nightmare she couldn't wake from. Confusion gripped her, and her mind struggled to piece together the fragments of what had happened. Then, like a dam breaking, her emotions and memories flooded back, overwhelming her with their intensity.

The sound of Lucian's body hitting the floor replayed in her mind, a sickening thud that echoed. Her heart clenched as she envisioned the scene over and over, unable to escape the horror of it. Tears streamed down her face as guilt consumed her. She should have fought harder, should have done something, anything, to stop the attacker before he struck. But it was too late. Her beloved husband was gone, his life stolen in an instant as he defended her and their unborn child.

Her thoughts spiralled, dragging her deeper into despair. Just hours ago, their life had been perfect. They had been cuddled up on the sofa, sipping hot chocolate and watching a film, their world filled with warmth and love. And now, everything had been ripped away. In mere minutes, her life had been turned upside down, leaving her widowed and her baby fatherless. The weight of it was unbearable.

Images of the aftermath haunted her. The pool of red blood on the floor, thick and glistening, was seared into her memory. She could still feel the panic that had gripped her as she stared at her reflection in the blood dripping from her hands, the crimson liquid slipping between her fingers. The attacker had picked her up off the floor, his movements cold and mechanical, and she had tried desperately to make out his face. But all she could see was the black silhouette of the man who had shattered her world. Everything had happened so quickly, yet it felt like an eternity had passed.

The more she thought about it, the more certain she became, this wasn't random. The attacker hadn't chosen them by chance. He had wanted to hurt Lucian. The way Lucian had spoken to him, as though he knew him, wouldn't leave her mind. Questions swirled, each one more painful than the last. Who was this man? What had Lucian done to make someone hate him enough to do this?

Suddenly, Inez's awareness sharpened as she regained full consciousness. Her head throbbed violently, vibrating with pain as it banged against an unknown object. She tried to move, but her vision was obscured by blackness. Occasionally, a blinding light pierced through the tightly woven sack covering her head, disorienting her further. She squinted, trying to make sense of the outlines around her, but the shapes were unfamiliar, alien. Wherever she was, it was cold and unyielding.

The numbing chill of metal cuffs bit into her wrists and ankles, their edges rubbing raw against her skin. She fidgeted, aching to free herself, but the restraints held firm. Her hands felt sticky, and as she moved her fingers, she realised the source, it was Lucian's blood. The realisation hit her like a physical blow, and she began rubbing her palms against her lounge wear, trying to rid herself of the dried blood. Flakes of crimson fell onto her lap, a grim reminder of the nightmare she was trapped in.

Inez's thoughts were a chaotic jumble of fear, grief and anger. She didn't know where she was or what was going to happen next, but one thing was clear, she had to survive. For herself. For her baby. And for Lucian.

Inez's mind was racing uncontrollably. Why had they come to their home? What did they want with her, or worse, with her baby? What would happen to Lucian's body? The questions clawed at her, each one more agonising than the last. Her heart ached as she tried to make sense of it all, but the answers eluded her. The van jolted violently as it sped over road bumps and potholes, throwing her body into the air and slamming her back down onto the cold, unforgiving metal seat. The twists and turns of the seemingly endless road caused her to slide around in her bloodied robe, the sticky fabric clinging to her skin. She hugged her stomach protectively, her thoughts consumed by the worst night of her life.

Uncertainty loomed over her like a dark cloud. How long would her life last now? Seconds? Minutes? Days? The attacker's intentions were a mystery, but the dread of what he might do next was suffocating. Why hadn't he killed her at home? What was his plan?

The sound of her movements caught the attacker's attention. His eyes flicked to the rear-view mirror, observing her with a cold, calculating gaze. "You're awake?" he said, his deep, husky voice cutting through the silence like a blade. The suddenness of his words made Inez jump, her body recoiling instinctively.

"Who are you? Why did you do this? What do you want with me?" she demanded, her voice cracking.

"One question at a time," he replied, dripping with mockery. "Your dear husband didn't comply."

Inez gasped with confusion, his words hitting her like a physical blow. Before she could respond, he continued with a sinister smirk. "You, on the other hand, are one of many."

One of many? The phrase echoed in her mind, its meaning elusive yet terrifying. What did he mean by that? She tried to make sense of his cryptic statement.

Suddenly, the van screeched to a halt, flinging Inez forwards along the metal seat. The abrupt stop left her disoriented, her body aching from the impact. The driver's door opened, and the van shook slightly as his weight shifted. A loud bang on the side of the van followed, the sound reverberating through the confined space. Inez strained to hear the muffled conversation outside, the attacker's voice mingling with two others. Their words were unintelligible, but their tone was intimate, conspiratorial.

Desperation surged through her as she scanned the van for any means of escape. She tugged at her cuffs, the metal clanking loudly as she struggled against them. The noise drew the men's attention, their conversation abruptly stopping. The back doors of the van unlocked, the sound chilling. She crawled into the farthest corner, her body trembling as the doors swung open violently.

Through the starch-scented potato sack covering her head, she could make out the silhouette of a short, chunky man. This wasn't the attacker from last night, his outline was different, unforgettable. Was it even last night? Inez couldn't be sure how long she'd been unconscious before waking up in the van.

"Grab her," the shorter man commanded. Another man, his face obscured by a bandana, leaned into the van and grabbed the cuffs around her ankles. He yanked her towards the edge, removing the metal restraints with practised efficiency. Inez thrashed wildly, her movements frantic and uncoordinated, like a fish out of water. Her mind was consumed by thoughts of her baby, of Leo, and the horrors that might await them both. In her struggle, she kicked something solid, the impact reverberating through her foot.

The man dragged her out of the van, her body hitting the rough, pebbly ground with a painful thud. The chilly air bit at her exposed legs, sending shivers coursing through her body and raising goosebumps on her skin. Terror gripped her as she tried to make sense of her surroundings, her eyes darting through the woven holes of the sack in search of anything recognisable.

The attacker drove away in a different vehicle, the sound of burning rubber filling the air. Pebbles flicked up from the tires, stinging her legs as they scattered across the ground. Her heart pounded furiously, the fear of abandonment mingling with the dread of what was to come.

A hand reached towards her face, its grip firm. The other hand held her cuffs, ensuring she couldn't escape. The sack was yanked off, strands of her loosely tied hair pulling painfully as it was removed. Her vision cleared, revealing two men standing before her.

One was tall and imposing, his muscular frame clad in a black T-shirt and black combat trousers. He exuded power, his presence intimidating and unrelenting. The other was shorter but equally formidable, his deep-set eyes framed by rounded glasses perched at the end of his large, prominent nose. He wore suit trousers, a shirt and a white doctor's coat, his appearance incongruous yet chilling.

Inez stared at them, her mind filling with questions. Who were these men? What did they want with her? And most importantly, how would she survive?

Inez flicked the tangled strands of hair out of her face, her movements shaky and disoriented. The blinding floodlights pierced her vision, making her squint in pain. She turned her head away from the lights, her gaze shifting towards the van. And then, she saw it, the object she had kicked. Her heart sank instantly as she realised it was a body covered in black tarpaulin. Dread took hold of her like a vice as the first thought tore through her mind: it must be Lucian. The anguish rose inside her, suffocating her as she bowed her head and let out a choked cry.

The tall man nudged the cuffs towards the van, letting the restraints around her wrists clatter loosely onto the metal. He tilted his head towards the vehicle, silently signalling his approval. Inez stumbled backwards, her legs weak beneath her, and tried to steady herself. But her balance faltered, and she collapsed to the ground, the jagged pebbles cutting into her bare knees. Pain shot through her, but it was drowned out by the swelling fear in her chest.

With her hands still in cuffs, she leaned into the van and took a deep, shuddering breath. Her lungs burned as she inhaled, bracing herself for the worst. Slowly, she reached for the edge of the tarpaulin, her fingers hesitant as they closed around its fabric. The image of Lucian's lifeless face was already haunting her, playing out in her mind like a cruel prophecy. She pulled the cover back.

Her scream tore through the air as her eyes locked onto the face beneath. It wasn't Lucian. Instead, it was a tall, slim blonde woman. The woman's fringe were matted with blood, a single gunshot wound to the forehead marking the end of her life. Inez's shock turned into fleeting relief, her husband wasn't lying there, but the sight of the woman's corpse reignited memories of her own tragedy. The blood, the violence, the unbearable loss of Lucian, it all came rushing back, drowning her once again in grief.

Where was Lucian? Why wasn't his body here? What had these people done to him? The tall man moved without hesitation, covering the body again as though her torment was unworthy of his time. He grabbed her cuffs and yanked her off the floor with a force that sent fresh jolts of pain through her knees. The floodlights burned her skin as she stumbled forwards, trying to regain her footing.

"We must get a move on," the doctor ordered. His voice was devoid of empathy, cold and calculating. He turned towards the dilapidated building, reaching for the door as though this grotesque spectacle were routine. Inez's terror surged as she met the eyes of the man pulling her along. "You can let me go," she pleaded. "I won't speak, I can't even see your face, please."

The man grunted, his grip tightening as he dragged her forwards. Her plea fell on deaf ears. He pulled her towards the building.

The doctor stopped briefly, his eyes sweeping over her with sickening detail. His eyes lingered on her belly, and his lips curled into a sinister chuckle. "We most certainly will not be letting you go," he said with malice.

Inez froze, her entire body trembling. She had never seen these men before, yet their presence was suffocating, their intentions terrifying. Her thoughts raced, not just about what might happen to her, but the fate of her unborn child. She hugged her stomach protectively, willing herself to stay strong. The tall man yanked her arms, forcing her to walk towards the building. The effects of the chloroform were still present, making her movements sluggish and uncoordinated. Her feet dragged through the dirt, leaving a trail behind her like a human snail.

The building loomed ahead, a beaten and dirty husk of its former self. The once-white concrete walls were now a murky brown, streaked with grime and covered in ivy that crept upwards like veins. To the right of the door, the remains of a light-up sign hung lifelessly, its red lettering long extinguished. On the roof, a larger sign stood weathered and faded, its words barely legible. Inez squinted through the darkness, her fear and fatigue clouding her ability to make sense of it.

As they passed through the entrance doors, the reception area unfolded before her like a snapshot of decay. A long oak desk stretched across the room, its surface caked in dust. Behind it, certificates hung crookedly in oak frames, their glass cloudy from neglect. Oak key boxes lined the walls, though many keys were missing, leaving their slots empty. The air was heavy with the stale stench of abandonment. It was clear the building had been left to rot for years.

She was dragged through reception, her legs struggling to keep up as they entered a long, dark, narrow hallway. The atmosphere pressed in on her. At the end of the corridor, a wooden door with a small glass window stood illuminated by a single light shining through. The men guided her towards the glow, their shadows stretching ahead of them like ominous warnings.

Inez's eyes darted around as she passed the old hotel rooms. The interiors were wrecked, their oak tables overturned and grey fabric beds torn apart. Dull-coloured curtains hung in tatters, some splintered by wooden shards, others faded and stained. Newspapers were plastered against the windows, yellowed and brittle with age. Doors were missing or hanging precariously by a single hinge, their frames sagging under years of neglect.

The building was a graveyard of its former self, and Inez's terror deepened with every step. Her surroundings were desolate, her captors relentless and her fate uncertain. But one thing was clear, she would have to endure this nightmare, for her baby and for the hope of survival.

The buzzing of struggling filament bulbs filled the air, their light flickering erratically behind metal cages. As they approached a door, her heart raced with uncertainty. The tall man calmly swiped a card, the kind used for hotel room access, and the door clicked open. Without hesitation, they descended a flight of stairs, the dim lighting casting long shadows on the walls. The hallway they entered mirrored the previous one, narrow and dark. But unlike before, there was no door at the end, only a room.

Inez stepped inside, her confusion mounting. The room looked identical to the others she had passed. What made this one so special? Her eyes darted around, searching for answers, until the man moved towards the lone piece of furniture standing in the room, a pine wardrobe. He opened it with care, revealing a heavy-duty, fire-resistant metal door hidden within. The door was imposing, its surface gleaming under the fluorescent lights. The only way in or out was through a fingerprint and retina scanner, a level of security that made her stomach churn.

As the scanner verified their access, the door slid open to reveal a starkly different hallway. Unlike the previous two, this one was brightly lit, its pristine condition almost jarring. The tan tiles reflected the light, their surface spotless and gleaming. The air was thick with the scent of bleach and lemon, so potent it stung her nose. The hallway reminded her of a psychiatric ward, with its sterile cleanliness and secured doors. Each door was reinforced like the entrance.

Inez's gaze wandered as she tried to make sense of her surroundings. The silence was deafening, broken only by the faint hum of the lights above. Suddenly, the sound of another door opening snapped her attention back. Before she could react, the tall man shoved her inside a room, his forceful push sending her stumbling forwards. Her bound hands made it impossible to steady herself, and she fell against the cold, hard floor. The door slammed shut behind her, the sound echoing in the confined space.

Panic surged through her as she scrambled to her feet. She turned to face the door, banging her metal cuffs against it with all her strength. Her screams and pleas for mercy filled the room, her voice raw. The buzzing sound returned, followed by a sharp click that signalled the door had been secured remotely. Her heart sank as the tall man opened a small hatch in the middle of the door. "Put your arms through," he demanded, cold and commanding.

Inez hesitated but knew she had no choice. She extended her arms through the hatch. The cuffs were removed with a swift motion, the relief of freedom tempered by the bruises that had already begun to form on her wrists. The hatch slammed shut before she could catch a glimpse of anything beyond it. She cradled her wrists, massaging the tender skin.

Her blood-soaked gown clung to her body. She looked around the room, taking in every detail. A metal bed stood against the wall, its surface covered by what appeared to be a blanket serving as a makeshift mattress. At the end of the bed, fresh clothing awaited her. A plastic green bowl filled with warm water sat on a chair by the sink, accompanied by a towel. It was a small mercy, but one she couldn't ignore.

Inez moved towards the bowl, her hands trembling as she picked up the cloth. She dipped it into the water, wringing it out until it was no longer dripping. As she scrubbed her skin, the blood began to spread, staining her further before she could remove it. She emptied the bowl multiple times, the water turning red with each rinse. The process was painstaking, but she persisted until her skin was clean. Finally, she turned her attention to her face and neck, scrubbing away the remnants of blood. She looked up into the mirror above the sink, her reflection staring back at her. Her wedding ring caught her eye, its presence a painful reminder of Lucian.

Tears welled up as she thought of him again, the memories threatening to overwhelm her. She shook her head, forcing herself to focus. Taking a deep breath, she whispered a pep talk to herself: "I can do this. Just do anything they say, and they will let us go." She hugged her belly, her resolve strengthening as she thought of her baby.

She removed her gown and changed into the fresh clothing. The light grey joggers and knitted white hoodie were basic, devoid of pockets or any means of concealment. She felt exposed, vulnerable, but knew she had no choice. Her mind raced with thoughts of escape, but for now, survival was her only goal.

4

Beneath the Boards

She sat on the cold, metal bed, her legs crossed, cradling her swollen belly as her tears fell silently onto the joggers she wore, fresh and clean. Inez felt the crushing weight of loneliness press down on her. There was no one who even knew she was missing, no family, no close friends to raise an alarm. Her absence would be unnoticed, forgotten. She had booked time off work to prepare for the baby's arrival, leaving her free of deadlines for months. That decision, which once felt like a gift of time, now left her isolated, adrift, with no tether to the outside world.

Her sorrow gave way to restlessness. She circled the small room several times, her eyes scanning every corner, running her fingers over every surface in search of something, anything, that might offer a clue or a means to escape. But the room revealed nothing. The monotony of its pale walls and sparse furnishings mocked her, stripping her of hope. Refusing to give in, she approached the heavy door and began to scream, her voice cracking under the strain. "Help me! Is anyone there? Can anyone hear me? Help!" Her pleas bounced off the unforgiving walls, the sound swallowed whole by the emptiness.

"Shhh, you'll make them mad," a voice called out, muffled yet distinct. The sound came from the wall beside her. Inez froze. Dropping to her knees, she pressed her palms against the gritty floor and leaned towards the grate in the wall. Her heartbeat quickened, a flicker of hope igniting within her. On the other side, she could make out the outline of a woman.

Inez gasped, the realisation hitting her, she wasn't alone. "Who are you?" she asked urgently.

"I'm Lara," the stranger replied. "You'll meet everyone else soon enough. We get time together daily." A single tear slipped down Inez's cheek as relief mixed with dread. There were others. She wasn't the only captive. The attacker's cryptic words from the van resurfaced in her mind, "One of many." Her stomach churned as she whispered the phrase aloud.

"What did you say?" Lara asked, puzzled.

"Oh, nothing," Inez replied quickly, brushing away the thought. "Just remembering things. I'm Inez." The desire for answers burned within her. "Do you know where we are or what this place is?"

Lara hesitated. "Someone said it looked like a beaten-down hotel, but they have a surgical room. We all get routine testing done."

Inez gasped. "Testing? What kind of testing?" Fear gripped her as her thoughts turned to her unborn child.

"It doesn't hurt, don't worry," Lara assured her.

The reassurance did little to calm Inez's racing mind. "Did you have anything on you? They'll take it all away in the night with your old clothes," Lara warned.

"I have my rings," Inez said, faltering as she glanced at the wedding and engagement rings glinting on her fingers.

"Before they take them," Lara advised, "there's a loose tile under the right foot of the bed. There's space to store stuff."

Inez grunted as she dragged the bed across the floor, the frame scratching noisily against the tiles. Straining, she managed to access the hiding spot Lara had described. She lifted the tile, her hands quivering as she uncovered two other rings, a wedding band and an engagement ring that were not her own. The sight made her heart sink as she contemplated the unknown fate that awaited her. Reluctantly, she slipped her own rings off and dropped them into the hole. She replaced the tile and pushed the bed back into place.

Climbing to her feet, Inez returned to the grate. "Lara?" she called softly.

"Yes?" Lara responded.

"What is going to happen to us?" Inez asked, her voice thick with worry.

There was a pause before Lara answered, her tone quiet but firm. "Go to sleep for now. You'll need it; they wake us early for breakfast."

Lara's words settled heavily on Inez's chest. She pulled herself away from the grate and climbed into the metal bed. The mattress was thin, the wires beneath it digging into her sides uncomfortably. She curled up, hugging her belly as exhaustion tugged at her, though sleep felt impossible.

Her thoughts were consumed by Leo, her unborn child. She worried no end about the stress she was under, was it harming him? Was he okay? She tried to push the thoughts away, but they clung to her. Every time her eyes closed, Lucian's lifeless gaze haunted her, his hazel eyes staring into hers as if frozen in time. The memory was unbearable, a cruel loop that played over and over in her mind.

Eventually, fatigue overtook her, and she drifted into a restless sleep. But it didn't last. A loud banging on the door jolted her awake, her heart racing as terror gripped her. The sound transported her back to the moment Lucian was shot, the horror replaying vividly in her mind. She scrambled to the back of the bed, hugging her knees tightly, her body trembling as she tried to steady her breathing.

The banging stopped, replaced by the sound of a hatch sliding open at the bottom of the door. A canteen dinner tray was pushed through, its contents unrecognisable, a mound of mashed-up, greyish food that looked anything but appetising. Inez hesitated, her stomach churning at the sight. She knew she needed to eat for Leo's sake, but the thought of consuming the mush made her gag.

"Just hold your nose for the first few times," Lara's voice called out from the room next door. "Trust me, you'll regret not eating it."

Inez clung to Lara's advice, pinching her nose as she forced herself to eat. The taste was vile, the texture even worse, but she swallowed as much as she could, focusing on Leo rather than the food. Each bite was a battle, but she knew she had no choice.

Time passed, how much, she couldn't say. The hatch opened again, and this time, a pack of playing cards slid into the room. Inez leaned over to pick them up, her confusion growing. "They give us something different each day and take it at night while we're asleep," Lara explained, sensing Inez's questions. "There isn't much else to do here. What did you get?"

"Playing cards," Inez replied flatly.

"Better than me," Lara said with a laugh. "I have a crossword book. I hate crosswords. Solitaire is the best way to pass the time with playing cards."

Lara's voice was a lifeline, her words offering comfort and companionship in the bleakness of their situation. "Thank you," Inez said, her gratitude genuine.

5

The Registry

Later that day, the buzzing noise returned, followed by the familiar click that signalled the door's lock. A voice crackled through the speakers, its tone cold and clinical. Inez recognised it immediately, it was the doctor. "Exit the room and go to the hall for lunch," he instructed.

Inez hesitated, her fear mounting as she slowly opened the door. She stepped into the hallway, her movements cautious, and followed the other women towards the hall. The main door locked behind them, the sound echoing ominously. As Inez entered the room, she felt their gazes. Every woman turned to look at her, their expressions unreadable. And then she noticed something, every single one of them was pregnant, just like her.

Her legs felt weak, and she began to shake her head in disbelief. Why were they all pregnant? What was the purpose of this place?

"Inez, you're next to me," Lara called out, waving with a smile. Her warmth was a small comfort in the sea of uncertainty. Inez forced herself to move, sitting down at the canteen table beside Lara.

"Sorry to be so upfront, it's nice to finally put a face to a name, I'm Lara", she reached out her hand and Inez shook it with a tender smile.

Inez's eyes fell on the tray in front of her, a meal far nicer than the grey mush she had been given earlier. A name tag with her name sat beside it, a detail that felt oddly personal in such an impersonal place.

"This is the best meal of the day; they mix it up. Monday is Chicken Roast.

Tuesday is Tikka Masala—"

"Do you know what day it is?" she asked, gripping Lara's arm in panic.

"Yes, it's Thursday, Beef Hotpot Day," Lara replied, keeping the tone light.

Inez froze as she worked through the calculations. "I woke up at 3 p.m. on Wednesday after my nap," she murmured, thinking aloud. "And I slept here last night." Her voice wavered as she turned back to Lara. "Do you know what time we went to sleep?"

Lara shrugged lightly. "Going by the time I had dinner, about 9 p.m.," she responded matter-of-factly.

"Okay," she muttered, her eyes darting downwards as she pieced it together. "I was in their van for about an hour, max, which means we're roughly four to five hours from the city." She sighed, the uncertainty bearing down on her. "But they could've driven around in circles just to confuse me."

Lara gave her a gentle pat on the back. "Eat your food," she encouraged. "We don't get long together."

Taking Lara's advice, Inez dug into her meal, each bite easing the hunger that gnawed at her. Despite the heavy thoughts clouding her mind, it tasted like the best meal of her life. She let herself eat without reservation, focusing on the nourishment her baby desperately needed.

After finishing their meals, the women gravitated towards an empty table covered with board games. They talked and shared pieces of their lives, their conversations weaving a fragile connection. Inez listened intently, but her curiosity got the better of her. "Where is Maggie?" one of the women asked suddenly, breaking the light chatter. The group fell silent, their eyes dropping to the floor as they shook their heads. No one seemed to know where Maggie was or what had happened to her.

Inez hesitated but eventually leaned closer to Lara, her need for answers outweighing her apprehension. "How long have you been here?" she asked.

Lara's expression darkened, her usual cheer dimming. "We don't ask things like that," she replied softly. "There have been so many before, we just try to forget what this place is."

Inez's heart sank at the unspoken truth in Lara's words, but she pressed on, in need of hope. "But surely we get to leave," she whispered.

Before Lara could respond, another woman sitting in the corner spoke up, her tone flat and chilling. "No one leaves unless it's in a body bag."

Inez felt her stomach twist as the words settled over her. Her gaze darted from woman to woman, searching for some sign of disagreement, some flicker of hope, but there was none. "Surely this cannot be the only way," she said, terror lacing her voice.

Names began to echo through the speakers one by one, breaking the tense silence. Each time, a woman would leave the room through the door, not to return until later in the day. Lara leaned over to explain in a hushed tone. "That's for routine testing," she said. "They'll run checks in that room, then send you back to your room for a few hours until dinner. It's the same thing every day."

Inez swallowed hard. "Who is Maggie?" she asked finally.

"She was another mum," Lara replied, her expression softening. "She was charming, had beautiful long blonde hair."

Inez's mind flashed to the woman in the van, the slim, blonde figure with a fringe and a gunshot wound to the forehead. Was that her? The thought was unnerving. The other mothers were right, no one left this place alive. But what about the babies? What would happen to them? Dread curled in her chest.

The names continued to be called, the line of women shrinking until only four remained. Inez's name echoed through the speakers, making her flinch. She felt Lara's reassuring hand on her arm as the woman nodded encouragingly. "I'll see you soon," Lara said.

Inez forced herself to stand and walk towards the door, her legs trembling beneath her. She glanced back one last time, Lara's smile giving her a fleeting sense of strength. The door clicked shut and locked behind her, the sound reverberating like a final sentence.

She scanned the room, her eyes falling on a metal chair in the middle. The speaker sputtered to life, startling her. "Please sit," the voice commanded.

Inez moved cautiously towards the chair, her heart pounding with each step. She lowered herself into the seat, her hands gripping the cold metal as a door opened behind her. She stiffened as the doctor entered, his presence casting a shadow over her. Without a word, he restrained her to the chair.

"Just going to check the baby and run some blood work," he said, tilting his head and peering over his glasses. His tone was unsettlingly calm.

He worked efficiently, taking her temperature, checking her heart rate and running an ECG. When he performed the ultrasound, the volume was turned up, and the sound of Leo's heartbeat filled the room. The rhythmic thudding sent a jolt through Inez, bittersweet memories of Lucian flashing through her mind. The last time she had heard that sound, Lucian was holding her hand, his face alight with joy when they discovered they were having a boy.

"A boy," the doctor commented, observing the screen. "Lovely."

The moment was short-lived as the doctor continued his examination, drawing blood from one arm and inserting an IV into the other. The red fluid flowing through the IV made Inez uneasy. "What is that?" she asked, her voice shaky.

"Just vitamins and nutrients," he replied smoothly, as if her concern were unwarranted. "To ensure you and the baby are getting everything you need."

After finishing, he unfastened the restraints and led her back to her room without another word. Inez sat down heavily on the bed, her thoughts racing as she waited for Lara to return.

The days that followed fell into a pattern. Each day was the same, a cold, repetitive routine that stripped her of hope. Meals marked the passage of time, her only means of counting the hours in a place where sunlight never reached.

She saw the doctor daily, his presence a constant reminder of her captivity. The blood work, the checks, the IV, all were now routine, though they did nothing to ease her fear. Lunches with the other mothers became her only solace, the thread of companionship helping her cling to sanity. But with each passing day, she felt the walls closing in.

6

Drain in the Room

After a few weeks, one of the mothers entered the room for her routine tests and didn't return. It was just like Maggie on Inez's first day. The absence hung heavy in the air, a question no one dared to voice. Everyone was puzzled, their unease growing with each passing hour. There was no warning, no explanation for the disappearance, and no one knew where the missing women were taken, or if they had made it out alive.

But Inez couldn't afford to lose hope. Not after everything she had endured. Not for herself, but for Leo. She clung to the fragile belief that there was still a way out, that she could protect her baby from whatever horrors this place held. Yet, as the weeks dragged on, the disappearances became more frequent. One by one, the mothers vanished, leaving behind only their empty rooms and the echoes of their fear.

The oddest part was the state of the women before they disappeared. They were unwell, exhausted and unable to sleep, vomiting but not from morning sickness, and growing alarmingly thin. Their faces became gaunt, their movements sluggish. Deep down, everyone knew something was wrong. The mothers complained of stomach aches and cramps in the days leading up to their disappearances, their pain a grim prelude to whatever fate awaited them.

Inez began to notice a pattern. It seemed to happen to those who were due soon or those who had grown too unwell to continue. The group dwindled until only three remained: Becca, a quiet woman who kept to herself; Lara, who had become Inez's closest confidante; and Inez herself. If her theory was correct, Becca would be the next to go. But not for a few weeks.

Her prediction proved accurate. Another few weeks passed, and Becca was gone. Now, it was just Inez and Lara. The weight of their isolation pressed down on them, the silence of the empty rooms around them a clue to their dwindling numbers. One night, as they lay in their respective rooms, they spoke through the grate, their voices low and filled with dread.

"I'm next," Lara whispered. "It will be tomorrow. I don't want them to take me or the baby. I can't do it." Her words broke into sobs, the sound raw and heart-wrenching.

Inez's heart ached for her friend. "You'll be okay," she said, trying to sound reassuring even as anxiety clawed at her own chest. "You may be free after this."

"I won't be," Lara replied, heavy with resignation. "They're going to kill me."

Lara's pain was evident. She continued to vomit, her body wracked with cramps that left her doubled over in agony. Inez felt helpless, unable to do anything but offer words of comfort. "Are you okay?" she asked softly, though she already knew the answer.

"I can't take this pain," Lara admitted, her voice barely above a whisper.

They spoke for hours, their conversation a fragile lifeline in the darkness. Eventually, they fell silent, each retreating into their own thoughts. Inez lay awake worrying about Lara.

A sudden crash from Lara's room jolted Inez upright. Her heart pounded as she called out, "Lara? Are you okay?" But there was no response. Panic surged through her as she scrambled to the grate, pressing her face against the cold metal. What she saw on the other side made her blood run cold.

Lara lay on the floor, her wrists slit and a shard of broken mirror clutched in her hand. Blood pooled around her, flowing steadily towards the drain in the centre of the room. Inez's breath caught in her throat, and tears streamed down her face as she screamed for help. "Help! Please, someone, help Lara! Help!"

The hatch in Inez's door slid open, and a man appeared, ready to reprimand her. But before he could speak, Inez pointed frantically towards Lara's room. "Help her!" she cried, her voice breaking.

The man hesitated, then left the hatch open. Inez watched in horror as two men and the doctor rushed into Lara's room. "She's gone," the doctor said coldly, devoid of emotion. "Get her to the surgical table now. The baby may be spared."

The men lifted Lara's body, leaving a trail of blood through the hallway as they carried her away. Inez's sobs grew louder, her chest heaving with grief and helplessness.

The doctor paused outside her door, his face calm and detached. "Do not worry," he said through the hatch, his voice eerily soothing. "She was weak-minded. Just sleep, you have weeks." With that, he closed the hatch and walked away, leaving Inez alone with her despair.

The silence that followed was deafening. Inez sat on the floor, her body shaking as she hugged her knees. The image of Lara's lifeless body was burned into her mind. She couldn't let this be her fate. For Leo's sake, she had to find a way to survive.

Inez didn't sleep well that night. She was awake long before the food tray slid through the hatch, her body stiff from the restless hours spent tossing and turning. She forced herself to eat the mush, the bland taste doing little to ease her nausea. Sitting on the edge of her bed, she waited for the day's activity, the routine that had become her only marker of time. But it never came.

Instead, the doctor arrived, his presence oppressive. "I'm going to come in," he said through the hatch in a composed tone "We can do this pleasantly, or I can restrain you."

Inez nodded, her movements slow and resigned. She sat cross-legged on the bed, clutching her pillow tightly as he entered. The doctor took a seat on the chair by the door, his gaze fixed on her. For a moment, he said nothing, simply observing her as she fidgeted with the pillow in her lap.

"So, you are aware you are the last," he said finally, cutting through the silence like a blade. His eyes locked onto hers, unyielding and cold.

Inez looked up from the pillow, her face pale and drawn. She nodded, her throat too dry to speak.

"If you become weak-minded like that one last night, you will not be the last. Do you understand me?" His words were a warning.

She nodded again, her movements mechanical.

"Speak," he ordered, his voice rising slightly. "Tell me you understand."

"Yes, I understand," Inez replied, flat and devoid of emotion. She knew her fate. She had been here for months, and it was only a matter of time before he took her. There was no point in fighting it.

The nice meals had stopped. With no one else left, there was no need for luxuries. Her breakfast now consisted of mush and a single piece of fruit, a small concession that felt more like a mockery than a kindness. As her day approached, the doctor asked her what she wanted for her last meal. The offer was meant to be a privilege, but Inez felt nothing. She didn't care. She just wanted it to be over.

The next morning arrived, and with it, the feeling of inevitability. She expected the day to follow the usual routine, breakfast, lunch and then the testing room. But it didn't. Her breakfast was different: poached eggs and avocado on toast. The sight of the meal was almost jarring, its presentation far too pleasant for the circumstances. What she didn't know was that it had been laced with a non-lethal dose of medication, just enough to make her groggy and compliant.

The buzzing noise returned, followed by the familiar click of the door unlocking. Two men entered, their movements brisk and purposeful. They grabbed her under her arms, lifting her from the bed and dragging her towards a wheelchair. Inez's vision blurred, each blink feeling like an eternity. The stiff wheel of the chair scratched loudly against the tiles as they wheeled her down the hallway, the sound grating.

When they reached the testing room, the men lifted her again, placing her into the metal chair at the centre. They began to restrain her, their hands moving quickly to secure her arms and legs. Inez fought with all her might, her screams echoing through the room as she tried to protect herself and her baby. But her body betrayed her. The medication dulled her movements, reducing her struggle to weak flails and soft whimpers.

"Thank you," the doctor said to the men. "You may now leave."

The men exited without a word, leaving Inez alone with the doctor. He carried out the routine checks, his movements methodical and detached. He took her temperature, checked her heart rate and performed an ECG. When he conducted the ultrasound, he turned up the volume, allowing the sound of Leo's heartbeat to fill the room. The rhythmic thudding was both comforting and devastating, a reminder of the life she was fighting to protect.

"He's perfectly healthy," the doctor said, his voice tinged with surprise as he looked up at the large glass panel on the wall. Inez followed his gaze, her eyes widening as she saw the silhouette of the attacker standing behind the glass, watching her.

"Why is he here?" she asked, her voice shaky with fear.

"This is his institution," the doctor replied, a smile spreading across his face. "And you are a wonder."

Inez's heart raced as she continued to scan the room, desperate to find a way to escape. Every detail felt magnified, every shadow a potential threat.

"Inez," the doctor said, pulling her attention back to him. She turned to face him, her body tense. He placed a mask over her face calmly. "Let's begin," he said before he started counting back from ten.

7

The Silent Scar

When Inez awoke, the world around her was unfamiliar and foreboding. The room smelled the same as the rest of the building, cold, damp and metallic, the odour clinging to the back of her throat. This new cell lacked the sparse comforts she had grown accustomed to. The wire-framed bed with its pitiful mattress was gone, replaced by a thin blanket spread haphazardly across the bare concrete floor. The walls were blank and stifling, and, notably, there was no grate, no means of hearing another voice or clinging to the fragile lifeline of human connection. She was entirely alone.

Her body felt heavy, and her thoughts were muddled. The haze of the anaesthesia remained, clouding her mind as she rubbed her eyes in an attempt to wake fully. The effort only made her nausea worse. As the sickly wave overtook her, she rolled onto her side and vomited on the floor, her body convulsing with the effort. Weak and shaky, she wiped her mouth with the sleeve of her already dirty sweatshirt. Too drained to sit up, she sank back onto the cold concrete, staring at the cracked ceiling above.

Her mind swirled with questions. *Why am I still alive? Is everyone else alive? What happened?*

Her eyelids grew heavy again, the pull of exhaustion overpowering her. She slipped back into a fitful sleep, her body longing for rest.

Hours, or perhaps just moments, later, Inez jolted awake, her stomach lurching violently. The nausea was unrelenting, and she barely managed to lean to the side before vomiting again. The acrid smell filled the room, mingling with the damp stench of the walls. She lay there trembling, unsure of what to do. Her body felt like it was betraying her, weighed down with drowsiness that made every movement an effort.

The rattling of keys startled her, snapping her out of her fog. She sat up slowly, her limbs aching as she propped herself against the wall. The door creaked open, and the doctor entered, filling the small room with an air of authority. He carried a chair and placed it near the door before sitting down. His expression was almost casual as he surveyed the room.

"Someone clean this up now," he commanded as his eyes flicked towards the vomit on the floor.

A man entered silently, broom and bucket in hand. The scrape of the bristles against the concrete filled the air as he swept up the mess, his movements quick and efficient. He then poured bleach over the spot, the chemical scent stinging Inez's eyes and throat. She coughed, her vision blurring with tears.

"Enough. Leave us," the doctor ordered curtly. The man bowed his head in acknowledgement and left the room, closing the door behind him.

Now alone with Inez, the doctor adjusted his chair, leaning forwards slightly as he studied her. His gaze was piercing, taking in every detail of her dishevelled appearance. Inez clutched her knees to her chest, her body tense under his scrutiny.

"You're still alive," he began, his voice measured, as though he were commenting on the weather. "I'm sure you're wondering why."

Inez didn't respond, her dry throat making it difficult to speak even if she'd wanted to.

"The others didn't get to see this concrete grave you now occupy," he continued. "Consider it your final resting place. But you should be grateful. You're still breathing, for now."

The words sent a chill down her spine, her pulse quickening. She wanted to scream, to demand answers, but her voice felt trapped.

"Rest," the doctor said, standing from his chair. "You'll need your strength for what comes next."

"Inez, unfortunately, you, like the other mothers, started to get rather ill," the doctor began, his voice clinical and detached. "The IV was no longer effective, and both you and the baby were deteriorating. You were going to die."

Inez's head snapped up with fury and disbelief. "You said I was perfectly healthy. I remember!" she interrupted, her hands tightening over the pillow she held to her chest.

The doctor's eyes narrowed, his tone sharpening with irritation. "Do not interrupt me. That is rude. Did your parents never teach you manners?" The callous remark stung, though he had no idea of the painful truth, that Inez had been an orphan with no parents to teach her anything. Without pausing, he continued. "It was a matter of survival for both of you. And ultimately… just you."

His gaze flicked downwards, landing on her stomach. The words landed like a blow. "We did what was necessary to save you," he added coldly, "but the child has died."

Time seemed to freeze. Inez began to shake, her breathing erratic as the room spun around her. The walls felt like they were closing in, her heart hammering against her ribs. Her hands instinctively cradled her stomach, but all she could feel was emptiness, the cruel absence of Leo. Tears welled in her eyes as his words settled over her.

Her face grew ashen, her skin icy cold. The quiet trickle of tears quickly became an uncontrollable flood. She had lost the last piece of Lucian, the one thing connecting her to him. The sobs wracked her body as her grief consumed her.

With shaking hands, Inez flung the loosely knitted blanket off herself and made an attempt to stand. Her legs buckled beneath her, and she stumbled to the wall for support. Slowly, she lifted her shirt, revealing her once-rounded belly, now flat and scarred. The stitches stretched across her abdomen, the surrounding skin raw and bruised. Red inflammation marked the edges of the cuts, and the sight made her stomach churn.

She pulled her top down, her body shaking as her tears suddenly stopped.

Her sorrow solidified into anger, pure, blinding rage. She spun on her heel, her eyes blazing as she faced the doctor. Staggering towards him, she placed her hands on either side of his chair, leaning over him as fury radiated off her.

"Where is he?" she demanded, her volume rising. "I want to see him! I need to see my baby boy! He's all I have left!" She pushed herself back from the chair, bowing her head as one hand clutched her scarred stomach.

The doctor regarded her with a calmness that bordered on cruelty. "You shall not see him," he said, heavy with mock sorrow. "He's gone. We disposed of him immediately. It would be too hard for you."

The words hit her like a punch to the chest. Disposed of? Her baby? Leo? Her hands clenched into fists as she turned away from him, her head spinning with the enormity of what she'd just heard. Her anguish gave way to an explosion of emotion. She whipped back around, her face contorted with grief and anger, and let out a primal scream that echoed in the small room.

The doctor, anticipating such a reaction, moved swiftly. Before Inez could lash out, she felt the prick of a needle in her neck. Her body immediately began to weaken, her limbs losing their strength as the sedative spread through her veins. She slumped forwards, barely aware of one of the men entering the room. He caught her before she could hit the ground, steadying her as she sank to the cold concrete. The man draped the thin blanket over her trembling form before stepping aside.

The doctor stood, his work done, and exited the room without another word. The man followed, dragging the chair with him. The sound of the keys rattling as the door locked behind them was the last thing Inez heard before the fog of the sedative dragged her into unconsciousness.

When Inez eventually awoke, she found a cup of water and a tray of grey mush beside her. Her stomach growled loudly, the hunger overpowering her revulsion. Weak and drained, she dragged herself across the floor, her hands scooping up the mush. She no longer cared about the vile taste or texture; she devoured it quickly. She downed the water in one long gulp, letting out a deep, ragged breath as she finished.

Tired and cold, she crawled back to her corner, pulling the blanket tightly around herself. The chill of the concrete seeped through the thin material, sending shivers through her body. She sat in silence, her mind too overwhelmed to think. Hours passed, at least, they felt like hours, but eventually, the quiet became unbearable.

She couldn't take it any more. Slamming her fist against the door, she shouted, her voice cracking. "Help me! Is anyone there? Let me out!"

To her surprise, a voice answered. "I'm here. You're not alone."

8

What Might Have Been

Inez froze, her heart leaping at the sound. "Who are you?" she called back, hoarse but hopeful.

"You don't need to shout," the voice replied gently. "I'm Maris. I've been here forever. I haven't met any other women here before. Who are you?"

The exchange sent a pang of déjà vu through Inez, reminding her of when she had first met Lara. "I'm Inez," she said, softening. "There were loads of us, but I'm the last one. Or at least… I thought I was."

She pulled the blanket closer and retreated to her spot on the floor, her voice fading away. The faint connection with Maris brought a flicker of warmth, but Inez couldn't shake the feeling of isolation. Despite the presence of another person, the crushing weight of her loss was heavier than ever.

Hours passed as Inez and Maris continued to talk, their voices weaving through the silence of their cells. Maris revealed that she had been in this place for about six months, though she admitted she had lost track of time. Her last clear memory was from the day she arrived. Inez couldn't help but worry, was this going to be her life too? The thought gnawed at her.

"Were you pregnant?" Inez asked hesitantly.

"Yes," Maris replied, surprised. "How did you know?"

"We all were," Inez said, her sorrow clear. "My baby died."

Maris's voice dropped, her words heavy with grief. "They killed mine. He was a little boy."

"Killed?" Inez echoed, her heart sinking further.

"Yes," Maris confirmed. "They said he wasn't made for this world."

The horror of Maris's words hung over her like a dark cloud. "Did no one look for you?" she asked, barely above a whisper.

"The dad didn't know," Maris admitted. "He thought I was away at work. I was going to tell him, but then… this happened."

The two women continued to talk, their shared pain forging a bond between them. They spoke of their lives before captivity, their hopes and dreams, and the devastating loss of their baby boys. The connection brought Inez a small measure of comfort, a flicker of humanity in an otherwise inhumane existence.

Days turned into weeks, and Inez lost all sense of time. The meals came randomly, always the same grey mush, and the monotony of her days was suffocating. She had finally stopped being sick, but the emptiness of her routine left her feeling hollow. The only thing that kept her going was Maris. Their conversations were a lifeline, though Maris wasn't always up for a chat. Sometimes she would ignore Inez entirely, leaving her to assume Maris was simply sleeping to pass the time.

One day, as they spoke through the wall, Maris noticed something different about Inez. "What's wrong?" she asked, filled with concern.

"I can't do this any more," Inez admitted, her voice shaking. "This is not the life for us. We need to get out."

Maris's response was immediate and resolute. "My thoughts exactly. Let's do it."

Inez was taken aback by Maris's determination. "I have a routine check today," Maris continued. "I'll get it set up."

"Set up?" Inez asked, confusion flickering across her face.

"The chair," Maris explained. "All you have to do is remember the cuffs."

"Will they be doing a check on me, too?" Inez asked apprehensively.

"No," Maris replied. "When I'm back, I'll tell you. That's when you let loose."

"Let loose?" Inez repeated, her confusion deepening.

"Flip your room," Maris instructed. "Throw the food, make a mess, so they have to come and get you."

"You think it will work?" Inez asked, doubt creeping into her voice. "What will happen after?"

"Just remember the cuffs," Maris said firmly. "The rest is up to you. If you set a fire, all the doors will open, and we can escape. We'll leave together."

Maris's words ignited a spark of hope in Inez, though the plan seemed fraught with risk. Could they really pull this off? The thought of freedom was tantalising, but the fear of failure loomed large. Still, for the first time in weeks, Inez felt a glimmer of possibility. Together, they might just have a chance.

Inez allowed herself a rare moment of hope, a flicker of light in the darkness that had consumed her for months. She drifted into sleep peacefully, no longer haunted by nightmares. When she woke, the sound of Maris's voice reached her through the walls. "I'm going now. See you soon," Maris said.

The words lingered in Inez's mind as she stared at the food tray left for her breakfast. She didn't eat, her stomach churned with anticipation, and her nerves made the thought of food unbearable. Instead, she busied herself with small, anxious movements, picking at the skin around her nails as she waited for Maris's return, hoping the plan would still be viable.

What felt like hours passed, but finally, Maris's voice cut through the silence. "Go," Maris said firmly, charged with urgency. "Remember two things: cuffs and fire. I'll meet you outside. Don't come for me."

"I can't leave you," Inez replied, heavy with worry. She couldn't imagine escaping without Maris, the only friend she had in this nightmare.

"We're far from the doctor's room," Maris explained, her tone unwavering. "The fire will spread too quickly. I saw a way out for me, just go through the double doors and down the hall. It's the way you came in." She paused, softening just slightly. "Now GO."

Inez felt torn, her body trembling with hesitation. But Maris's firm resolve snapped her back to focus. She nodded to herself, steeling her nerves as she prepared to follow the plan.

She started by throwing her food tray against the wall, the grey mush splattering across the surface. She tore her bedding apart, ripping the fabric into shreds and scattering it across the room. The mirror didn't stand a chance, it shattered under the force of her food tray, the glass shards scattering across the floor. Inez screamed at the top of her lungs, the rawness of her voice echoing through her cell. Her cries were wild, loud enough to draw attention.

Moments later, she heard movement outside the door, the creak of the handle turning. Someone was there. Inez clenched her fists, preparing to fight with whatever strength she had left. She had nothing to lose any more. Maris was counting on her, and she refused to fail.

But then, something caught her attention. From the corners of the room, a low hissing sound began to emerge. Inez's heart sank as she turned towards the noise, her eyes widening in fear. The room started to fill with a suspicious gas, the cloudy substance spreading quickly. Her lungs burned as the air thickened, and she began to cough violently.

"No!" she screamed, her voice hoarse as panic set in. "Maris! Maris, the room it's filling with gas!" she yelled louder, but there was no response. The silence from the next room was deafening, her cries swallowed by the gas that was suffocating her.

Inez staggered towards the wall, her hands fumbling to find the grate that connected her to Maris. But there was nothing, no sound, no movement from the other side. Her vision blurred as the gas took hold, her strength ebbing away with every breath. Desperation consumed her as she clawed at the wall. Maris had given her hope, and now that hope was slipping away.

9

The Rings on the Table

Inez slowly came to, her head pounding as her senses returned one by one. Her vision was blurry, her surroundings hazy as she blinked rapidly to clear the fog. As her eyes adjusted, she saw the outline of a woman in the distance. The voice was unmistakable, it was Maris. "Cuffs and fire. Look at the cuff," the apparition said firmly, her words resonating in Inez's mind.

Before Inez could respond, the shape faded away, leaving her alone once more. She blinked again, searching for Maris, but the room was empty except for herself and the chair in which she was restrained. The testing room felt colder than ever, the steel walls reflecting a dull, lifeless light. The dirty, cracked tiles on the floor and walls added to the oppressive atmosphere, each imperfection a silent witness to the horrors committed here.

Next to her, the doctor sat casually, his presence unsettling. He was fidgeting with something small and reflective, the gleam bouncing off its surface and catching Inez's eye. She squinted, her heart skipping as the bright light flashed into her vision.

"Ah, yes. I found them," the doctor said with a smirk, holding up the rings he had undoubtedly taken from the hiding spot beneath her bed. "The scratch marks on the floor were obvious. So, which set is yours?" His tone was dripping with sarcasm.

Inez felt her stomach twist as she stared at him. She exhaled heavily in defeat. "The gold ones, please. They're all I have left," she said, her gaze dropping to the floor.

The doctor rose from his chair. He placed all the rings on the worktop near the double doors, pausing for a moment before exiting the room without another word. The sound of the door clicking shut echoed in Inez's ears, snapping her out of her daze.

Maris's words reverberated in her mind. Cuffs. Inez's eyes darted downwards, her pulse quickening as she realised the left cuff was looser than it had ever been before. This was her chance, she had to act quickly, before the doctor returned.

She began pulling against the strap. The pressure was agonising, the material biting into her skin. Her hand grew hot, the flesh reddening and swelling as blood pooled beneath the surface. The burning sensation spread up her arm, her body screaming for her to stop. But she couldn't. She couldn't let this opportunity slip away. She gritted her teeth, her determination outweighing the pain, and pulled harder.

Suddenly, she heard a loud bang echoing down the hallway. Her heartbeat thundered in her ears. The sound was a stark reminder of the urgency of her situation. With adrenaline coursing through her veins, she made one final tug, and just like that, she was free.

Her left hand slid out, her wrist throbbing and purple from the strain. She wasted no time, freeing her other hand with trembling fingers. As soon as her arms were unbound, she leapt up, her eyes scanning the room for anything she could use. Her gaze landed on the cupboard, and she rushed towards it.

Flinging open the doors, she rifled through the contents, her movements frantic. Among the items strewn across the shelves, something caught her eye, a scalpel. She grabbed it without hesitation, gripping it tightly in her hand. Maris's voice echoed in her mind: *It is up to you to escape.*

Inez knew this was her chance. Her chest heaved as she steadied herself, her grip tightening around the blade. Whatever was waiting beyond the double doors, she was ready to face it.

Inez pressed herself against the cold metal of the multiway door, her breath shallow and her heart pounding. The frosted glass cut-outs offered a distorted view of the room beyond, but she remained hidden. The sound of footsteps echoed down the hallway, growing louder with each passing second. The doctor entered, his silhouette framed by the doorway. He paused, his head tilting as he scanned the room, puzzled by her absence.

He stepped further inside, his movements cautious but confident. As he turned to survey the space, Inez moved silently behind him, her body pulsing with fear and rage. The scalpel gleamed in her hand, catching the light as she raised it. "Get in the chair," she yelled, sharp and commanding.

The doctor froze, his hands slowly rising in surrender. His eyes locked onto hers, a flicker of amusement dancing in his eyes despite the situation. He began to step backwards. "Alright, alright," he said, calm but calculated. As he retreated, one hand lowered towards his pocket.

Inez's eyes darted to the pocket, her pulse quickening. She realised too late, he had a weapon. The rage that had been simmering within her erupted, consuming her entirely. With a guttural cry, she lunged forwards, grabbing the back of his neck with one hand and driving the scalpel into his abdomen with the other. The blade sank into his flesh, and she pulled it out only to stab him again. And again. Each thrust was fuelled by the pain and loss she had endured, her grief transforming into a violent storm.

Finally, she paused, her chest heaving as she stared into his wide eyes. With one final motion, she plunged the scalpel into him slowly as she whispered, "That's for my baby boy."

The room fell silent, the weight of her actions like a suffocating blanket. She stood frozen, her hand still gripping the scalpel as the doctor's body slumped to the floor. Time seemed to stretch, each second dragging on as she stared at the lifeless form before her. She had killed him in cold blood, and the realisation hit her like a tidal wave.

When she finally looked up, her eyes landed on a wardrobe in the corner of the room. Needing something, anything, to ground herself, she rushed over and flung the doors open.

Inside, she found rows of identical jeans and T-shirts in various sizes. The uniformity was jarring. She grabbed a set in her size and quickly changed, shedding her blood-stained clothes. The fabric felt foreign against her skin, but she didn't have time to dwell on it.

Dressed and slightly steadier, Inez began to search the room for a way to escape. Her mind raced with thoughts of what she had done and the consequences that might follow. The image of the doctor's lifeless eyes haunted her, but she forced herself to focus. She couldn't afford to falter now, not when freedom was so close.

Her eyes darted around the room, searching for anything flammable. The clock was ticking, and she knew she had to act fast. The fire was her only chance.

What she needed was a lighter. She began tearing through the drawers, yanking them open and sending their contents flying. Her movements grew more frantic with each failed attempt, the pressure mounting with every second. Finally, in the fifth drawer, her fingers closed around a small box of matches. Relief flooded her, but it was short-lived. She still needed something to ignite.

Inez stood in the dark room, clutching the box of matches. Her hands twitched, Maris's plan pressing heavily on her shoulders. Maris's voice echoed in her mind: *Set a fire, and all the doors will unlock.*

She scanned the room once more, searching for something flammable. The shelves were lined with chemicals, their labels unfamiliar and intimidating. Inez hesitated, knowing the danger of mixing them without understanding their properties. She couldn't risk harming herself or jeopardising the plan. Her gaze shifted to the pile of clothes in the wardrobe. She crouched down, gathering the scraps of fabric into a small pile in the centre of the room.

Inez struck a match, the tiny flame flickering to life in her hand. She stared at it for a while, the light casting shadows across her face. This was it, the moment that would decide her fate. She lowered the match to the fabric, her breath hitching as the flame caught. The fire spread slowly at first, the edges of the fabric curling and blackening. But as the flames grew, the heat intensified, and the room began to fill with smoke.

She coughed, her eyes watering as the acrid smell of burning fabric filled the air. The fire crackled and hissed, the sound both terrifying and exhilarating. Inez backed away, her body pressed against the cold metal wall as she watched the flames consume the pile. The smoke thickened, curling upwards and spreading through the room.

The heat was unbearable, the smoke suffocating, but she couldn't stop now.

She noticed a long glass window at the top of the room. There was his silhouette again, the attacker, watching her become a murderer. Rage once again filled her, and she let out a scream and threw the closest chemical on the flames.

The fire surged high, roaring like a beast unleashed. Its glow bathed the room in a violent, fiery hue briefly before suddenly dying down. Inez stared at the smouldering pile, her heart racing with anticipation and dread. Was it enough? Would the alarms, the high-pitched screeching that signalled her last shred of hope, finally go off? Her hands trembled as she waited, the seconds stretching into hours.

And then, the piercing sound of the alarms broke the silence, cutting through her thoughts like a knife. The noise reverberated through her body, startling her despite her anticipation. The sound travelled along her spine, electric and overwhelming, and suddenly she felt the cold spray of water hit her face. It was working. Inez leaned back, letting the water wash over her, droplets mingling with the sweat on her brow. It felt like a miracle, her first taste of relief.

The metal door began to hum, its gears groaning as it came to life. The sound reverberated down the hall, a mechanical symphony that startled her again. Inez froze, unable to believe her eyes as the automatic door slowly slid open. It worked. The fire had triggered the release mechanism, and she was free, or at least, the way to freedom had been unlocked.

Her eyes swept across the room, taking in the chaos left behind. She glanced back at the window to the sitting area where she had last seen him, the attacker. But he was gone. She took a step backwards, only to knock over a medical trolley behind her. The clang of metal utensils hitting the floor echoed loudly, and the crack of glass shattering pierced the air.

10

Smoke and Sunlight

Inez stumbled, her foot catching on the fallen trolley, sending her sprawling forwards. She landed hard on top of it, the edge of the frame digging into her ribs. Pain shot through her side, and she let out a small, anguished whimper. A single tear slipped down her cheek as the sting of her ribs compounded the emotional weight she carried.

Pushing herself onto her hands, she turned her face towards the ground to steady herself. Her gaze landed on a strange sight, a pile of red dust from a smashed beaker and a burst IV bag, the crimson liquid pooling on the floor. The vibrant red was stark against the cold grey tiles, almost glowing in the weak light. Struggling to get up, Inez felt the warmth of the fire creeping closer. The flickering flames licked at the air behind her.

Turning to look back at the fire, she realised she didn't have much time. She groaned loudly, pushing herself up despite the sting of glass embedded in her skin. Her face was damp, dripping with the fluid from the IV bag, but she couldn't let herself falter.

Inez staggered towards the door, her legs shaky but resolute. Her hand fell onto the worktop as she passed, her fingers finding the rings she thought she had lost forever. Relief flooded through her as she slipped them onto her finger, the familiar weight grounding her.

With the rings secured, she took a deep breath and faced the open door. Her path to freedom was clear, but the fight wasn't over yet.

Finally reaching the staircase, Inez paused, her body shaking with exhaustion and pain. She tilted her head back, looking up at the flight of stairs spiralling above her. They stretched on forever, a cruel test of her endurance. She gritted her teeth, pressing a hand to her aching ribs as she struggled to regulate her breathing. The ache in her side burned with each inhale, and she wheezed as she drew in a deep breath to gather her strength.

Grasping the metal bannister tightly, she hauled herself upwards, one agonising step at a time. The weight of her body felt unbearable, but she pushed forwards, her willpower outweighing the pain. Her injured leg dragged slightly with each step. When she finally reached the top, she flung the door open with all the strength she could muster, the sudden rush of fresh air hitting her like a wave.

Inez stumbled outside, the brightness of the daylight overwhelming her senses. After months of darkness or artificial light, the sun's brilliance was almost blinding. She shielded her eyes with one hand, squinting against the glare. The warmth of the sun caressed her skin, a sensation she had almost forgotten. She paused, tilting her face towards the sky, allowing the sunlight to cleanse her. For a fleeting moment, everything else melted away. The pain, the terror, the loss, they all seemed distant under the sun's embrace. A soft sigh escaped her lips as a sense of peace settled over her.

But it didn't last. The harsh caw of a crow pierced the silence, startling her from her fragile daydream. She flinched, her head snapping towards the sound. The bird perched on a crumbling piece of rubble nearby, its black feathers glinting in the light as it screeched again. The noise jolted her back to reality, the reality of her situation crashing down on her once more.

Inez turned back to the building, her heart twisting painfully in her chest. She couldn't leave, not without Maris. With one arm wrapped protectively around her ribs and the other shielding her eyes from the sun, she hesitated, torn between the urgent need to escape and the unbearable thought of abandoning her friend. How long should she wait? Should she go back in for Maris?

Steeling herself, Inez made her decision. She began to limp back towards the building, each step a battle against her own battered body. Maris had helped her escape, and she couldn't leave her behind. Just as she neared the entrance, a deafening explosion filled the air. The force of it sent her flying backwards, her body slamming into the ground as rubble and shards of glass rained down around her.

The impact left her breathless, the pain in her ribs flaring to an unbearable level. She lay motionless, unsure of where she hurt most. Everything ached, her body screaming in protest as she struggled to move. Finally, she managed to push herself up onto her elbows, her vision swimming as she turned to look at the building.

Flames roared hungrily from the structure, thick black smoke billowing into the sky. The heat was intense, waves of it radiating outwards and scorching the air. Inez's heart dropped as she stared at the inferno, her mind unable to process what she was seeing. "MARIS!" she screamed. "MARIS!" The name tore from her throat, each cry more anguished than the last.

Staggering to her feet, she shielded her face with her arms as she stumbled closer to the wreckage, her eyes frantically scanning for any sign of Maris. But the flames were relentless, consuming everything in their path. The smoke choked the air, making it impossible to see more than a few feet ahead. The realisation hit her like a punch to the gut, no one could survive this.

A guttural sob escaped her as she sank to her knees, tears streaming down her face. Her grief was crushing her, the loss of Maris a fresh wound that cut deep. She buried her face in her hands, her body shaking with the force of her cries. The thought that Maris, who had been her only companion in this nightmare, was gone forever was too much to bear.

As the flames roared on, Inez cried for her friend, for the life they could have escaped to together, and for all the hope that had been stolen from her.

Inez turned around and blinked rapidly, trying to regain her vision. The acrid smoke enveloped her, mixing with the glare of the afternoon sun, stinging her eyes. The air itself seemed hostile, suffocating and heavy, making every breath a struggle. She staggered slightly, overwhelmed, and shielded her face with one hand. When her sight finally cleared, the scene before her sharpened: a navy-blue car stood conspicuously among the commotion, its glossy surface marred by flecks of ash. On the roof, she spotted a pair of keys glinting in the sunlight like an invitation, or a trap. Was this the attacker's car? Could he still be inside? Or had he fled into the shadows, leaving behind this strange clue?

Summoning courage, Inez approached the car, her senses heightened and her body tense. Her fingers brushed against the handle, and she hesitated for a beat. Then, with a swift motion, she climbed in, her instincts urging her to move. She flipped down the sun visor and gasped as she caught sight of her reflection in the vanity mirror. Jagged shards of glass were embedded in her skin, tiny but unmistakable, sparkling like cruel gems against her flushed face. They were superficial wounds, merely piercing the outermost layer, but they left her shaken. Carefully, methodically, she brushed them away, each shard tinkling as it hit the floor of the car. Miraculously, her skin remained unscarred, untouched as if the ordeal had been nothing more than a nightmare.

Her gaze drifted downwards, settling on her hand clutching the steering wheel tightly. The sunlight caught her ring, a simple band of gold, and its reflection danced across the cabin like a fleeting beacon. The brightness dazed her, a hypnotic pull that trapped her in a momentary trance. Time seemed to stretch and warp, the world outside fading to a muted hum. When she finally snapped out of her reverie, a wave of anxiety crashed over her, leaving her breathless. She exhaled deeply, as if expelling the fear that gripped her chest, and twisted the key in the ignition. The engine roared to life.

With a final glance at the scene behind her, she pressed her foot to the pedal and eased the car forwards. The dirt path stretched ahead, winding between towering trees that intertwined to form a natural tunnel. The oppressive heat of the sun filtered through the canopy, casting fragmented beams of light onto the dusty road. Every turn she took felt like a step towards salvation, or perhaps an escape into the unknown. Inez drove on, her mind replaying the events like a fractured film reel, her resolve hardening with each passing mile.

11

The Dream Question

Inez drove on, her hands gripping the steering wheel tightly, her knuckles pale against her skin. The dirt road stretched before her, winding through a forest full of secrets. The trees stood like solemn sentinels, their shadows flickering over her face as sunlight pierced through the canopy. She had no idea where she was heading, only that she couldn't stop. The engine's hum was her only companion, a monotonous comfort in the eerie silence.

After what seemed an eternity, she began to notice road signs scattered like breadcrumbs along the path. At first, they were nameless markers, but soon they began to show familiar names and symbols. Relief swept over her as she pieced together her surroundings. She exhaled audibly, the tension in her chest loosening as she realised she wasn't lost after all. By the time she reached the city limits, a clarity of purpose had returned to her mind.

Her heart quickened when she pulled up to her apartment building. She killed the engine and sat in the car, staring at the familiar façade, her hands still resting on the steering wheel. Her thoughts churned uncontrollably. Why am I here? What if he's still inside? What if I find Lucian's body... decayed and lifeless? The images flashed in her mind, vivid and unrelenting. She shook her head as if to dispel the thoughts, but the unease clung to her like a second skin. She let five long minutes drift by, her eyes fixed on the building's entrance, before finally summoning the courage to move.

Stepping out of the car, she walked briskly towards the entrance, her head low. The man at the concierge desk looked up, his expression indifferent, and she instinctively avoided his gaze. Her heart thudded as she slipped past him unnoticed and entered the lift. The mirrored walls reflected her pale, anxious face, the hollowness of her eyes betraying the terror bubbling beneath her calm exterior. As the lift ascended, floor by floor, her fear grew with each passing second. When the doors slid open on the ninth floor, she froze momentarily, gripped by an overwhelming sense of dread. Her legs felt heavy as she stepped into the hallway, her footsteps muffled on the carpeted floor.

She reached her apartment door and hesitated, her eyes falling on the red vase beside it. Slowly, she lifted it and retrieved the spare key hidden underneath. Her fingers shook as she slid the key into the lock and turned it. The click of the mechanism echoed, a sound that seemed impossibly loud. She took a deep breath, steadied herself and pushed the door open.

To her surprise, everything was as she had left it. The apartment was immaculate, untouched by violence. There was no body, no blood, no stench of decay, only the scent of stagnant air mingled with the faint trace of her own perfume from weeks before. Relief swept over her, but it was fleeting, shadowed by guilt. She had killed the doctor and possibly her attacker. *But who will look for me now?* she thought grimly. Perhaps here, in her sanctuary, she could find a semblance of normality.

Eager to reclaim her space, she opened the fridge, only to recoil at the rancid odour of spoilt food. The once-vibrant produce had turned to mush, and cartons of milk had bloated ominously. Grimacing, she gathered the expired contents into a rubbish bag and carried it downstairs. The motion of walking, the simple act of completing a task, gave her a fragile sense of purpose. Once the rubbish was gone, she slipped into the small corner shop next door to buy supplies. The familiar jingle of the shop bell startled her, and the sudden recognition on the shopkeeper's face made her uneasy.

"It's been so long!" the shopkeeper's wife exclaimed warmly. "You had the baby, congratulations!"

Inez froze, her heart lurching at the words. She forced a tight, worried smile and muttered, "Thank you," before hurriedly collecting her groceries. The interaction left her rattled. Why did it feel like every movement was under scrutiny?

Returning to her apartment, she unpacked the groceries, prepared a simple meal and collapsed onto the couch. She switched on the television, hoping to immerse herself in the mundane outside world. The news flickered on the screen, a torrent of images and sounds she had missed. As she ate in silence, she tried to anchor herself in the present. Yet, her mind wandered, reliving fragments of the recent past. Everything pressed down on her, but for now, she stayed put, determined to find a way forwards.

Inez drifted off to sleep on the worn sofa, her body aching. Her apartment offered no solace, only an eerie calm that felt foreign to her. She was startled awake by a sudden, loud bang, the sound of her neighbour's door slamming shut. Panic shot through her veins as she jolted upright, her heart hammering against her ribs. In her confusion, she thought she was back in the cell. Her eyes darted frantically around the room, searching for signs of captivity, but as her surroundings came into focus, she realised she was home. She held her head in her hands, trying to shake the nightmare. Was it all just a bad dream? Or had reality blurred into something else entirely?

Desperate for clarity, she rose unsteadily to her feet and made her way to Lucian's study. The room was silent, still and coated in a fine layer of dust. The sight of the neglected space tore at her heart, it was as if time had frozen the second he had disappeared. He was gone, and the void he left behind was palpable. Closing the door softly, she turned around and noticed Leo's nursery, its door ajar as if beckoning her inside. She pushed the door open wider and stepped into the room. The nursery, once vibrant and filled with warmth, now felt like a ghost of what could have been. Holding her flat stomach, she stood at the threshold, grief washing over her like waves crashing against a rocky shore. She walked over to the crib and ran her finger along the chiselled wood, tracing the engraved name that belonged to a child she never truly knew. The heartbreak was raw, visceral and overwhelming, searing through her like wildfire. Unable to bear her emotions, she picked up the lion teddy from the crib, clutching it tightly as she left the room.

Her thoughts turned to her body, the marks left behind from the past weeks, and she instinctively made her way to the bathroom. Flicking on the light, she stared at her reflection. Carefully, she lifted her shirt, expecting to find red scars and bruised skin, but to her surprise, the redness had vanished, and the scar had healed completely. She stared in disbelief, it was as though her body had erased the pain she had endured. Lifting her shirt higher to inspect her rib, she was astonished to see no discolouration or bruising whatsoever. Confusion clouded her mind, and doubt crept in. Had she imagined it all? Could it have been a dream... or was her sense of time truly warped?

Then it hit her, she couldn't stay here. This wasn't her home any more. Not without Lucian. Not without Leo. Resolute, she decided it was time to leave. She entered her wardrobe and pulled out her suitcase and duffel bag, filling them with the essentials: clothes, shoes, toiletries and food. She took a moment to stand in front of Lucian's side of the closet, running her hand over his clothing. The remnants of his scent remained, a bittersweet reminder of all she had lost. Tears pricked her eyes as she took in the emptiness that now defined her world. She couldn't bring herself to take any of his things, they belonged to the memories she was leaving behind.

Her gaze fell on his chest of drawers, and there, glinting in the light, was his wedding band. It stopped her cold. He had worn this the night he died, she thought, her mind spinning. How was it here? Did the attacker leave it behind as some sinister message? She looked down at her own hand, at the ring that symbolised their union, their love. Slowly, with a trembling heart, she removed her ring and placed it next to his. The symbolic act felt final, like closing the door on a chapter she could never revisit.

Inez exited the closet and flipped off the light, sealing the room behind her. She carried her packed bags to the front door and set them down, her movements purposeful yet heavy with emotion. As the day faded to night, she lay down on her bed, staring up at the ceiling for an indeterminate time. This would be her last night in the apartment, her last night surrounded by the echoes of a life she once knew. She closed her eyes, her breathing steady, and let the decision sink in. Tomorrow, she would leave it all behind.

Inez awoke with a start and heard Lucian's voice filling the room. It was rich, warm and achingly familiar. For one fleeting, blissful moment, she thought he was there, alive, calling out to her. She bolted upright and looked around the dimly lit room, her eyes darting in search of him. But the source of the voice was something else entirely. The glow emanating from Leo's teddy bear caught her attention, its soft light spilling across the room. She cradled it in her hands and realised Lucian had recorded his voice, ensuring their son would always hear him. Tears streamed freely as she clutched the teddy to her chest, its light illuminating the grief etched on her face. She cried until her body could take no more, her tears eventually lulling her back into an uneasy sleep.

When morning arrived, Inez stirred awake, the memory of the night before weighing heavily on her mind. She moved mechanically, preparing breakfast and finishing the last bits of packing. With the teddy still tucked under her arm, she surveyed her apartment one final time. She paused at the threshold, her heart constricting. Something inside her stopped her from stepping out. Turning on her heel, she retraced her steps to Leo's nursery. The room was cloaked in a heavy silence, as though it mourned alongside her. She approached the crib and ran her fingers over its intricate carvings, her touch lingering on the engraved name of the son she never got to hold. Slowly, she placed the teddy back in its rightful place. It felt like leaving behind a piece of herself, a fragment of her heart she could never reclaim. She stepped back and pulled the nursery door closed. The click of the latch felt impossibly final.

Inez blinked, fighting back the tears threatening to spill, but her surroundings shifted unexpectedly. She saw Lucian lying on the floor, his lifeblood pooling beneath him. The vision was vivid, wrenching and all too real. Her composure shattered, and tears cascaded down her cheeks as the memory surged forwards. She could almost hear his voice whispering to her, but when she opened her eyes again, the image was gone, leaving only the painful void in its place.

Shaking herself from the trance, she walked to the front door. She opened it, placed her suitcase in the corridor and slung the duffel bag over her shoulder. Before stepping out, she paused and glanced back into the apartment. Her mind painted a picture so vivid it was almost tangible: Leo and Lucian laughing and running around the living room while she stood in the kitchen, stirring a pot or lost in the pages of a book. The vision was bittersweet, a reflection of the life she had imagined, the life that had been stolen from her. A smile played at her lips as she basked in the warmth of what could have been.

Her gaze lowered to the spot where Lucian had lain in his final moments. *What would he have said to me that night?* she wondered. Would he have told her he loved her? That everything would be alright? Or would his last words have been filled with regret? She exhaled deeply, releasing the questions into the stillness around her. Turning back to the door, she flicked off the light, enveloping the apartment in shadow. She closed the door gently, knelt to place the key under the plant and straightened herself with quiet resolve.

The crisp morning air greeted her as she walked towards her car. She heaved the suitcase into the boot, placed the duffel bag on the passenger seat and climbed behind the wheel. For a while, she sat there, the teddy's absence unbearable. She unfolded a map, the edges worn from use, and scanned it for a destination. Her finger hovered over a random spot near the water before she made her decision. *That's the one,* she thought, setting her path in motion.

As the engine roared to life, she cast one final glance in her rear-view mirror. The apartment building stood quietly, its windows reflecting the morning light. In her mind's eye, she saw them again, Lucian and Leo, alive and laughing, their love filling the space she now left behind. A soft, wistful smile crossed her lips. She allowed herself to imagine happiness, even if only for a moment.

The city receded into the distance as Inez drove, her eyes fixed on the road ahead. The hours stretched on, the journey long and winding, but she was resolute. As the sun dipped low on the horizon, painting the sky in hues of amber and rose, she arrived at her destination. The water shimmered under the fading light, its vast expanse offering the promise of solace, or perhaps reinvention. She stepped out of the car, the cool breeze brushing against her skin, and took a deep breath.

12

Gone Without a Trace

Inez wandered through the small, coastal town, her eyes scanning for a hotel or a B&B, anywhere public where she wouldn't feel the suffocating solitude. The salty breeze from the ocean carried echoes of laughter and music from nearby beach goers, but the sounds felt distant, as though she were moving through a world she no longer belonged to. Eventually, her gaze landed on a recognisable hotel chain perched near the beach. It wasn't luxurious, but it was enough. She stepped inside, the cool air-conditioning brushing against her skin, and paid for two weeks upfront. This would give her a semblance of stability, a small window of time to regroup and decide what came next.

As she stood at the reception desk, the clerk handed her the room key with a polite smile. When he mentioned the date during the transaction, her stomach dropped. Five months. She had been in captivity for five long months. The realisation gripped her like a vice. How could so much time have passed? Panic travelled through her veins. Had no one noticed that she and Lucian were gone? But deep down, she knew the truth. No one knew the full story. No one knew he was dead.

Once in the safety of her room, Inez felt exhausted. Wanting to cleanse herself of the invisible filth clinging to her after those harrowing months, she headed to the bathroom. The tiles were cold beneath her bare feet as she stepped into the shower. Warm water flowed over her skin, but every sound, every car horn outside, every distant door slamming in the adjoining rooms, jolted her. Her heart raced wildly, her breath quick and shallow. Overwhelmed, she slid down the shower wall, her knees drawn tightly to her chest. There, on the floor of the stall, she let out the sobs she had been holding back. The hot water mingled with her tears. She stayed like that for a long time, her cries echoing in the small room. When she finally stood and shut off the water, it was almost 11 p.m.

Wrapping a towel around herself, Inez left the bathroom, still trembling. She went to the bedside table to grab a hairdryer and plugged it in, preparing to dry her hair. As she reached for the switch, a sudden, irrational dread swept over her. Her eyes darted to the door. She hurried towards it, her breath shallow, and checked the lock multiple times to reassure herself. The thought of someone entering the room while she was vulnerable, unable to hear over the roar of the hairdryer, paralysed her with fear. Satisfied the lock was secure, she returned to the device, picked it up from the floor and began drying her hair in quick, jerky movements. When she finished, she slipped into her pyjamas and stood in front of the mirror.

The fluorescent light flickered as she lifted her top to inspect the scar on her abdomen once more. It was gone. Not a single mark or trace remained. She ran her fingers over the smooth, unblemished skin. It was as though Leo had never existed, as though no one would ever know the depth of her loss. The feeling left her hollow, her grief momentarily replaced by disbelief and confusion. *Was it real?* she wondered. *Did I imagine it all?*

Inez climbed into the double bed and lay still, staring at the ceiling. The mattress was thick and plush, a far cry from the coffin-like box she had been trapped in. But every time she closed her eyes, she was back there, confined in the darkness, her breath catching as anxiety clawed at her. She opened the window in an attempt to ground herself. The cool breeze whispered into the room. She inhaled deeply, forcing herself to remember where she was. This was different. She had escaped. She was free.

Eventually, she fell into a deep, dreamless sleep. The sun was high in the sky when she stirred the next day, the clock reading 1 p.m. She had slept through the morning, her body demanding the rest it had been deprived of for so long. As she sat up, the weight of her memories felt lighter, dulled by the restorative sleep. She almost didn't recognise herself in the mirror as she brushed her hair and applied a light layer of makeup. She looked... normal.

Feeling slightly steadier, Inez packed a small handbag with essentials and slung it over her shoulder. She glanced around the room one last time before stepping out. The world outside awaited her, bright and full of life, though the scars on her heart remained beneath her composed exterior.

Walking down the bustling high street, Inez felt the rumble of her stomach, an unwelcome sound that startled her. She froze mid-step, momentarily disoriented. How long had it been since she'd eaten? Her energy waning, she glanced around in search of food and spotted a modest fast-food burger joint tucked between two shops. Relief swept over her. It wasn't glamorous, but it was affordable.

Stepping inside, she was greeted by the tantalising aroma of sizzling bacon and fresh fries. She ordered a bacon cheeseburger, extra pickles, chips and a Coke Zero. When her tray arrived, she wasted no time, tearing into the food like someone starved for years. The texture and taste were overwhelming, so unlike the mush she had endured during her months of captivity. She devoured the burger with an urgency that drew a few glances from nearby patrons. Their curious gazes made her feel exposed, and she forced herself to slow down, calming her nerves with deep breaths. She reminded herself to be inconspicuous.

With her appetite briefly satisfied, Inez wandered through the local shops, stopping occasionally to peer through store front windows. The walk, though mundane, felt surreal. She treated herself to an ice cream, a simple cone topped with a Flake, and found a quiet bench near the beach where she could sit and soak up the sun. Closing her eyes, she tilted her face towards the sky, letting the warm UV rays kiss her skin. It had been far too long since she felt the sun's embrace. For a moment, she allowed herself to forget the pain, the loss and the fear that had defined her existence for months.

Fatigue from the walk and the carb-heavy meal began to set in, and she decided to return to her hotel room. As she strolled back, her eyes darted to her surroundings, constantly checking over her shoulder. Paranoia whispered in her ear, what if someone was following her? Her heart thudded heavily with each glance, but the streets remained empty of pursuers. She exhaled in relief when she reached her hotel room safely. Once inside, she locked the door and sank onto the bed. The soft cushions welcomed her, wrapping her in comfort as she turned on the television. The images on the screen blurred together as she drifted into sleep.

Her dreams, however, were anything but peaceful. They played out with vivid clarity, each detail etched deeply into her mind. Inez found herself in an abandoned casino, its grand entrance imposing and mysterious. Twin spiral staircases framed the vast room, their once-glorious bannisters coated in years of dust. A broken stone fountain stood at the centre, its cracks weaving a tale of neglect. She ascended the staircase to the left, her fingers trailing along the bannister, leaving clean streaks amid the grime. At the top, she noticed a faint light emanating from a room in the back. Drawn to it, she pushed open the heavy door and stepped inside.

The atmosphere shifted immediately. Inside, she saw three figures, Zaire, a man with piercing eyes; Nadia, a gentle yet guarded woman; and Hunter, who exuded quiet strength. Strangely, their names burned brightly in her memory, as if they were etched into her being. The trio spoke as if they knew her, their words unravelling secrets she didn't fully understand. A sudden bang at the door snapped her attention away from them. Inez turned to see the attacker standing there, his presence suffocating and sinister. Terror gripped her, but Zaire shouted at her to run. The urgency in his voice propelled her forwards, and then everything went dark. She woke abruptly, her heart pounding, the dream hovering like a shadow.

Still unsettled, Inez decided to head out for breakfast to clear her mind. The ocean front was alive with activity, families and couples filling the air with laughter and joy. Children shrieked as they ran between rides, their parents struggling to keep up. She smiled at the young couples in the arcade, their playful rivalry unfolding as they challenged each other to basketball games and collected tickets. Nearby, older couples engaged in rounds of crazy golf, the husbands celebrating with exaggerated fist pumps each time they achieved a hole-in-one. Their wives rolled their eyes with amused smiles, humouring their partners' "pro" golfing antics.

Inez allowed herself to be swept up in the light-heartedness of the scene. On a whim, she decided to step into the arcade herself. The flashing lights, cheerful music and clattering of coins felt like another world, one that welcomed her.

Inez found herself drawn to the flashing lights and playful chaos of the games. Hours slipped by as she tried her hand at the two-pence machines, Down the Clown and even Skee-Ball, her favourite game, the one that always brought out her competitive streak. Memories of Lucian occupied her mind as she stood in front of the Skee-Ball machine, placing a pound coin into the slot. She could almost hear his voice beside her, teasing and cheering her on as they tried to outdo one another. Every toss brought a flood of nostalgia, her shots instinctively landing perfectly in the higher-scoring holes. The final ball sat in her sweaty palm, her determination mounting. She caught a glimpse of her reflection in the machine and froze. For just a fleeting second, she thought she saw Lucian standing behind her, his comforting presence, his encouraging smile. Her eyes widened in disbelief, but when she turned around, he was gone. The feeling of loss pressed on her chest, and she let out a long, quivering sigh. She tilted her head up to the ceiling and murmured, "This is for you."

The ball rolled off her fingers, bouncing against the rim of the elusive 100-point hole. It hung on the edge, teasing her, before it finally dropped in with a satisfying clink. She gasped, a mix of joy and bittersweet gratitude filling her as she felt the unexplainable nudge of an unknown force guiding it. She knew it was him, Lucian was still with her, in some way.

The machine erupted in celebratory noises as the jackpot poured out, thousands of tickets spilling onto the floor. Inez scooped them up, unsure what she would do with them. Then, out of the corner of her eye, she noticed a little boy tugging at his mother's jumper, pointing at her pile of tickets with wide-eyed wonder. Something stirred in her heart, and she approached them. Bending down to meet the boy at eye level, she asked gently, "Could you help me get something with these tickets?"

The boy looked up at his mother, seeking permission, and she nodded with a warm smile. "Go on then."

With an excited squeal, the little boy, Benjamin, darted towards the counter, clutching the tickets with as much enthusiasm as his small arms could muster. His mother turned to Inez, gratitude shining in her eyes. "Thank you so much," she said softly. Inez merely smiled, not seeing it as an inconvenience but a small act of kindness. In that moment, she imagined herself with Leo and Lucian, spending carefree days at the arcade, laughing and making memories. The image was so vivid, so real, that it brought tears to her eyes. But the sharp sting of reality hit her, it would never happen.

Overwhelmed, she turned to leave, her heart heavy, but Benjamin stopped her in her tracks. He wrapped his tiny arms around her in a hug and said, "Thank you, miss." Then, with the innocence only a child could possess, he handed her a small teddy bear and a lollipop. Inez accepted them, her throat tightening as she fought back tears.

She stepped outside, needing the cool sea breeze to steady herself. The salty air mingled with the scent of heavily salted chips she carried in a paper cone. Each bite was punctuated with a squint as the salt stung her tongue. The wooden fork helped her avoid getting the salt on her fingers, but by the time she finished, she rubbed her tongue against the roof of her mouth, trying to awaken her dulled taste buds. She rolled the paper cone up neatly and tossed it into the bin. As she turned to leave, a colourful sign caught her eye: *Fireworks Display Saturday at 7 PM*. Her heart skipped a beat. That was today, in an hour. She figured she was already there, so she might as well stay and watch.

Finding a spot on a stone wall, she observed the beach gradually filling with people as the display's start time approached. Thirty minutes remained, and the crowd grew denser, laughter and chatter punctuating the evening air. Wanting some solitude, Inez decided to take a stroll further up the beach. The sand crunched softly beneath her feet as she distanced herself from the crowd. She found a quieter spot just as the fireworks began, their first explosion reverberating through her chest. The vibration startled her, though she knew it was harmless. By the fifth burst, she had grown more accustomed to the rhythm, her gaze fixed on the vibrant colours lighting up the night sky.

   Her focus shifted to a building partially obscuring her view. With each explosion, the structure was bathed in hues of blue, green and red, its silhouette becoming clearer. Something about it tugged at her memory. She tilted her head, narrowing her eyes as she studied its form. A sense of familiarity washed over her, pulling her thoughts into the depths of the past.

13

The Trio in the Room

It was unmistakable, the building from her dream. Standing at the edge of the property, Inez felt her stomach churn. Had she glimpsed this place briefly when she arrived? That would explain why her subconscious had woven it into her dream. But it didn't feel coincidental. Something deeper gnawed at her, urging her to investigate.

Her steps felt heavy as she approached the casino. Torn 'WARNING: DO NOT ENTER' tape fluttered in the breeze, clinging to the corners of the door frame like faded remnants of forgotten warnings. Surrounding the property was a crude metal fence anchored in stone blocks. She noticed one section of the fencing had been pulled free, leaving an inviting gap large enough to slip through. Inez hesitated, staring at the loose fence. It felt intentional, an unspoken invitation. When her eyes landed on the door, she realised it was slightly ajar, as if the building itself were welcoming her. Curiosity consumed her, overriding caution. She stepped forwards.

The moment she crossed the threshold, the air inside shifted. The room was bathed in shadows, the deep red walls adorned with golden accents that glimmered in the feeble light. Twin spiral staircases framed the broken fountain centrepiece, its topper lying in crumbled pieces at its base. The sight struck her like a bolt of lightning. It was exactly like the dream. She froze, her eyes scanning every inch of the space, absorbing the uncanny details. It wasn't possible, her subconscious couldn't have conjured up an image of a place she had never entered before.

Taking a deep breath, Inez steadied herself and stepped forwards. The soft shuffle of her feet disturbed the silence, every creak of the floorboards amplifying her unease. When she reached the stairs, her fingers brushed against the handrail. The layer of dust clung to her fingertips, leaving a streak behind, just like in her dream. Her movements grew hypnotic, each step merging reality with fragments of her dream.

Suddenly, a shout echoed from upstairs, snapping her out of her trance. She startled, her head whipping upwards to the hallway. She paused, her body rigid, waiting for another sound. But the silence returned, heavy and oppressive. She glanced back at the dust trail on the handrail and resumed her slow ascent, the dreamlike state reclaiming her. Her heart thundered in her chest as she reached the landing. The murmur of voices grew clearer, their cadence pulling her forwards until she stood outside a room with the door cracked open. A sliver of golden light spilt into the hallway, its brightness overwhelming. She blinked rapidly, trying to adjust her vision. Through the gap, three indistinct silhouettes loomed on the cloth-covered furniture within. Holding her breath, she pushed the door open and stepped inside.

The room was eerily still, yet alive with energy. Her pulse raced as her gaze landed on the trio from her dream. Zaire. Nadia. Hunter. They were just as she remembered, every detail identical to her dream. It didn't make sense. How did she know them? How could her mind have conjured their exact likeness? She stumbled back towards the door, her instinct to flee colliding with her need for answers.

Her eyes flicked to Nadia first. Inez tilted her head, squinting in confusion as she moved closer, her curiosity overtaking her fear. Nadia's features were striking: long, curly brown hair framing her face, large brown eyes accentuated by thin black eyeliner that stood out against her warm complexion. Her tan jumpsuit added to her sleek, feline grace, giving her an aura of quiet confidence. She looked like a creature borne of mystery and elegance.

Next, Inez turned to Hunter, puzzled as she studied him. His blond hair and neatly groomed facial hair matched the vision from her dream. He had big brown eyes, their depth contrasting with the playful edge of his brow piercing. His casual cargo pants and baggy T-shirt gave him an air of approachability, yet, there was something in his stance that hinted at resilience.

Finally, her eyes fell on Zaire, and Inez froze in place. He was, without question, the most captivating of the trio. His fluffy light brown hair framed his piercing blue eyes, which seemed to radiate wisdom and intensity. His dark blue jeans, plain white T-shirt and black blazer gave him an understated elegance. Something about him drew Inez forwards as if an invisible thread connected them. Her breath shallowed, her movements slow as she approached him in a daze.

Just as she closed the distance between them, reality shattered with a deafening explosion. Another firework. The light spilt into the room, illuminating the trio in bursts of vibrant colour. Inez gasped, her trance broken as the loud boom resonated through her. She took a step back, her mind filling with questions that demanded answers.

They stared at her, confusion and suspicion clouding their faces. Hunter was the first to speak, his voice low and defensive as he stepped towards her, his chest puffed out in a show of authority. "How did you know we were here?"

Inez opened her mouth to respond, but no words came. Her mind was a whirlwind of conflicting emotions: distress at the surreal recognition of her dream matching reality, confusion over who these people were, and terror that the attacker might burst through the door at any moment.

The scene blurred in her mind, everything happening too quickly to fully process. The next thing she remembered was locking eyes with Zaire. His piercing blue eyes bore into her, filled with urgency and something else she couldn't place, concern, perhaps? He leaned towards her slightly, calm yet commanding as he said, "Run. If he gets you again, he won't let you go. Run now. Go out the window, there are ladders to the ground floor."

She wanted to demand answers, who was he talking about? How did he know this?, but there was no time. A sound echoed from downstairs, the click of the entrance door closing. Her head snapped towards the noise, her body seized with panic. She turned back to Zaire. "Thank you," she said before spinning on her heels and darting towards the window.

In her haste, she didn't notice the teddy bear drop from her grasp. Her focus was singular: escaping. She climbed through the open window and descended the ladder as quickly as she could, the rungs cold against her hands. She ran, her legs carrying her faster than she thought possible, not stopping until she reached the safety of her hotel room.

Once inside, she locked the door and leaned against it, her chest heaving as she tried to catch her breath. The terror slowly gave way to exhaustion, and she trudged to the bathroom, her body aching for warmth and solace. The hot water of the shower cascaded over her, soothing her raw nerves. Yet, as she stood there, fragments of what Zaire had said echoed in her mind: "If he gets you again, he won't let you go."

She gripped the wall for support, her nails digging into the tiles as her thoughts raced. *How does he know me? How does he know what I've been through?* No matter how hard she tried to piece it together, it made no sense. The events of the evening revolved in her mind like a disjointed puzzle, each piece more perplexing than the last. By the time she stepped out of the shower, she felt no closer to answers.

She dried her hair absent-mindedly, her reflection staring back at her from the bathroom mirror. She wrapped the towel securely around her chest and opened the door, and froze in place. Zaire was sitting on her bed, his intense blue eyes fixed on her.

Instinctively, she stepped backwards, her hand clutching the towel for dear life. "How did you find me?" she demanded, her voice trembling with equal parts fear and anger.

Zaire tilted his head, his expression unreadable. "I had a dream," he said simply. "I've never had these dreams before you. How do you do it?"

"What?" she said, squinting at him in disbelief. "How do you think I'm doing this to you?"

He stood up slowly, closing the distance between them in a few measured steps. She flinched, but he stopped short of touching her. "Come to this

THE TRIO IN THE ROOM

location tomorrow at 8.30 p.m.," he said, his tone calm but resolute. He handed her a folded piece of paper and the teddy bear she had dropped earlier.

Inez's gaze flicked to the paper in her hands. She unfolded it and read the words scrawled in a steady hand: *The abandoned library.* An address followed, but it was the first line that made her shoulders sag in exasperation. "Why is everything abandoned?" she muttered under her breath.

Before she could look back at him, the soft sound of the door closing filled the room. She turned sharply, but Zaire was gone, leaving behind nothing but questions and a sense of unease. She stared at the folded paper and the bear in her hands. She had to find out what was happening. She had to meet this mysterious man with those mesmerising blue eyes, even if it meant uncovering truths she wasn't ready to face.

14

Where She Dreamed

The next day was consumed by thoughts swirling in Inez's mind. She lay on the thick memory foam mattress in her hotel room, cocooned in the airy duvet, staring at the ceiling as questions flew at her. Why had she been handed over to another man who tortured her for months, stealing her unborn child in the process? The weight of it all pressed down on her, suffocating and relentless. She needed answers.

The only reprieve came when she ventured out to a local café for food, the brief distraction offering a momentary escape from her turmoil. But as soon as she returned to her room, the questions resumed their assault. Her gaze drifted to the note from Zaire sitting on her desk. It seemed to taunt her, its folded edges holding secrets she wasn't sure she wanted to uncover.

She sat up in bed, her body tense with indecision. Slowly, she walked to the desk, her bare feet brushing against the cool floor. She stared down at the note, reluctant to touch it, as though it might burn her fingers. With a frustrated huff, she turned and climbed back into bed, pulling the duvet over her head as if it could shield her from the choices she had to make. Closing her eyes, she tried to push the thoughts away, but instead, Zaire's face appeared in her mind. His piercing blue eyes stared back at her, filled with a strange mix of trust and urgency. She remembered the way he had told her to run, the way he had given her freedom. *Why would he let me go just to hurt me?* she wondered. The connection she felt to him was inexplicable, yet undeniable. It was as though she had known him for years, not seconds.

The thought grew stronger with each passing minute. *Should I go?* she asked herself. The answer came quietly but firmly: *yes*. The decision sent a surge of adrenaline through her, and she sat up abruptly, the sudden movement making her head spin. She steadied herself, her hands gripping the edge of the mattress as she waited for the dizziness to pass. Rising to her feet, she crossed the room to the mirror, her reflection staring back at her with determination and uncertainty. She glanced towards the bathroom, her mind shifting to practicalities. Turning her head slightly, she sniffed her shoulder, checking herself. The clock caught her eye, and she calculated the time. *I can have a quick shower*, she thought.

Without hesitation, she began to undress, slipping out of her soft satin pyjama shorts and matching vest. The fabric fell to the floor in a whisper, and she stepped into the bathroom, the warm steam enveloping her as she turned on the shower. The water washed away the remnants of indecision and fear. For a brief moment, she felt grounded, her thoughts quieting as the warmth soothed her. But even as she stood there, the note and Zaire's words stayed in the back of her mind, pulling her towards the unknown.

Inez couldn't shake the thought of him, how he had been there, sitting on her bed, his piercing blue eyes holding her in place like a lifeline. Every time she closed her eyes, those eyes haunted her. Her alarm jolted her back to reality. The loud beeping echoed in the room, startling her. "Shit," she muttered, leaping out of bed. She hurriedly threw on something more appropriate for an outing, anything better than the towel he had seen her wearing the night before. Her hands fumbled with the fabric in her haste, her nerves fraying as anticipation set in.

The evening air greeted her coolly as she stepped into the private car park reserved for hotel guests. The stolen car sat there, its navy-blue exterior dusty under the fading sunlight. Inez slipped into the driver's seat, her movements automatic as she entered the location of the abandoned library into the GPS. The route wasn't far, and she barely noticed the scenery flashing past as she drove. Before she knew it, the car came to a halt in the middle of nowhere. She glanced around at the desolate surroundings, gripping the steering wheel tightly. The clock read 8.25 p.m.

The minutes dragged as she sat in the car, her stomach churning. She closed her eyes briefly, praying that this meeting would be different, that it wouldn't spiral into yet another disaster. At 8.30 sharp, the sound of an engine broke the stillness. She watched as a car pulled into the clearing and parked beside her. The headlights flicked off, and Zaire stepped out, his movements confident and unhurried. He approached her window and tapped it lightly. His grin was lopsided, almost playful. "Nice wheels," he said, nodding towards her car. "Just like the boss's." He tilted his head towards the library, gesturing for her to follow him.

Inez hesitated, her heart hammering, before she opened the door and stepped out. She trailed behind him, her movements tentative as they ascended the broken porch steps. The wood creaked beneath their weight, the sound unsettling in the quiet night. As they entered the library, the musty scent of decay and neglect filled her senses. The place was overgrown and in disrepair, dust clung to every surface, and vines snaked their way through broken windows. Her eyes widened as she took in the scene.

The sight triggered something deep within her, flashes of the hotel coming to the forefront of her mind. Overturned furniture, doors hanging precariously from their hinges, books strewn about with their pages ripped and scattered, it all felt eerily familiar. Her chest tightened, and she stepped back, her instinct to flee kicking in. Every fibre of her being screamed at her to run and never look back. But then Zaire turned to her, his expression softening as their eyes met. There was something in his eyes, an unspoken reassurance, that made her stop. She let out a shaky sigh, her fear momentarily subdued.

They moved deeper into the library, stepping carefully over debris and fallen shelves. Zaire led her into a dingy where an old computer sat on a rickety desk, its screen cracked like a spider's web. The hum of electricity filled the air as he typed something into the keyboard. A sudden click, followed by a familiar buzzing sound, made Inez freeze. Her eyes widened, and her hands instinctively flew to her wrists, the phantom sensation of restraints digging into her skin. The noise was too similar to the one she had heard in the concrete coffin during her captivity. Her breathing quickened, and she looked around the room, disoriented, until her gaze landed on Zaire.

His eyes found hers, steady and calming, and for a moment, she felt as though the tumult inside her was suppressed. "It's okay," he said, his voice low and reassuring. "It's just the door opening." He extended his hand towards her, and after a brief hesitation, she took it. His touch was firm but gentle, grounding her in the present. He guided her forwards, leading her through the newly opened doorway. She glanced back over her shoulder, her instincts screaming at her to remain vigilant. But when she turned back to Zaire and met his eyes once more, the horror within her subsided slightly. There was something inexplicably trustworthy about him, and though she barely knew him, she felt a connection that defied logic.

Letting out a deep breath, Inez furrowed her brow in thought. Still holding onto his hand, she followed him into the unknown, each step carrying her closer to whatever truths awaited her.

Inez followed Zaire through the dark hallway, her steps hesitant and cautious. The air grew colder as they ventured deeper, the faint light barely illuminating the space ahead. When they reached the room, its design reminded her of a police interrogation chamber, several glass windows lined the walls, but all she could see was her reflection and Zaire's beside her. Her heart sank as unease prickled at the back of her neck.

She let go of Zaire's hand, stepping further into the room to survey its emptiness. The quiet was suffocating, and the pale lighting gave the space an eerie glow. *Why did he bring me here?* she wondered, scanning every corner in search of answers. The sound of a door clicking shut pulled her out of her thoughts. She spun around, startled. Zaire was gone.

Panic surged through her veins as she rushed to the door and tugged at the handle. It wouldn't budge. She pulled harder, praying that it would miraculously open, but it remained firmly locked. Tears began to blur her vision as she banged on the door. "Please, let me out! Don't do this, please!" Her screams echoed through the room, swallowed by the oppressive silence.

Exhausted and trembling, she turned her back to the door, scanning the room for something, anything that could help her escape. Just as she began to process her situation, the unmistakable sound of the door creaking open behind her froze her in place. Hope flickered in her chest as she whirled around, expecting to see Zaire. But the figure standing before her wasn't Zaire.

It was a man, dressed entirely in black. His bulletproof vest gleamed in the dim light, and his face was hidden behind a black face guard that only added to his menacing aura. He carried a hose in one hand and a stun gun on a long stick in the other, implements that sent terror coursing through Inez's body.

Her instincts screamed at her to create distance, and she backed towards one of the glass windows. Her hands pressed against the cold surface as she began banging frantically. "Someone help me! Let me out!" The pleas came tumbling out in a desperate cascade. She glanced over her shoulder at the man, who remained motionless, his presence looming over her. Inez's heart pounded erratically as she continued to cry for help, the walls around her feeling like they were closing in.

15

The Glass Barrier

Zaire stood on the other side of the glass, his silhouette etched against the weak glow of the observation room. The faint hum of machinery filled the space, a cold, sterile sound that matched the tension in the air. A man loitered in the shadows behind him, his presence disturbing and obscure. "You're not going to hurt her, right? Just test her limits," Zaire said, his voice firm but betraying a flicker of hesitation. He directed the words to the stranger, though his eyes never left the woman on the other side.

The man in the shadows gave a curt nod, raising his arm as a signal. Another figure, stationed by a panel of switches, responded without hesitation. His fingers moved with practised precision. The first switch clicked down, plunging the observation room into darkness. A second flick unleashed the static crackle of electricity, a stun gun spark dancing ominously in the gloom. When the final switch was thrown, the reality behind the glass came to life under a harsh, clinical light.

The sight left Inez frozen. Her gaze darted to the tableau now revealed, a quartet of businesspeople seated at a polished table, their expressions chillingly detached. Three men in impeccable suits and a woman in a pencil skirt, each holding bidding paddles in their hands. The scene felt surreal, a grotesque parody of an auction room. Their stares pinned her in place, their intentions veiled behind impassive masks.

Confusion and dread churned within her as her eyes sought Zaire's through the glass. She pressed her palm against the cold surface, her voice a whisper that barely rose above the stillness. "I thought I could trust you," she pleaded, her words heavy with betrayal. Zaire's expression flickered, a fleeting glimpse of conflict, but he stood unmoving, his silence deafening.

The man holding the stun gun stepped forwards. He grabbed a hose, twisting the nozzle until a stream of icy water erupted forth. The spray hit Inez with force, soaking her instantly. She squinted against the sting as droplets invaded her eyes, her body instinctively curling inwards to shield itself. The chill seeped through her clothes, biting at her skin, and she staggered backwards, retreating to the furthest corner of the room. Turning her face away, she tried in vain to escape the relentless assault of water.

The hose clattered to the floor as the man released it, his focus shifting to the frightened figure before him. Inez clutched her arm, her body shaking uncontrollably. Her voice cracked as she pleaded, her words echoing off the sterile walls. The woman observing from behind the glass rose abruptly, her chair scraping against the floor. Without a word, she left the room, her departure unnoticed by Inez.

The three men seated behind the glass leaned forwards, their postures tense with anticipation. Their eyes followed the man as he advanced towards Inez, the stun gun in his hand sparking ominously. The room seemed to hold its breath as he closed the distance, the hum of electricity growing louder.

Then came the first shock. Inez's scream tore through the air, a sound so visceral it sent shivers through everyone present. The stun gun struck her neck, then her arms, her legs, her abdomen, her chest, each jolt a fresh wave of agony. Her cries of terror filled the room, drowning out the mechanical hum of the stun gun. This was worse than the concrete coffin, worse than anything she had endured before. The man showed no mercy, his movements methodical as he continued the assault.

For a brief moment, the power flickered, and the pain Inez was feeling muted the stun guns hum. Inez collapsed against the wall, her soaked hair plastered to its surface. She slid down, her body folding into itself. Her sobs were ragged, her breath coming in shallow gasps. She begged him to stop, a broken whisper.

The businesspeople shifted uncomfortably in their seats, their faces turning away as the scene unfolded. The spectacle was too much, even for them. Zaire, unable to bear it any longer, surged towards the switches. His hand shot out, grabbing the man stationed there by the cuff of his shirt. With a forceful shove, he sent the man stumbling aside and reached for the controls.

Before he could act, a cold, metallic click froze him in place. The boss stood behind him, a gun pressed firmly against the back of Zaire's head. "Step away," the boss commanded, his voice low and unyielding. Zaire raised his hands in surrender, his jaw clenched in frustration. Slowly, he backed off, retreating to the far side of the room, his eyes burning with helpless rage.

Then, silence. The flickering hum of the stun gun ceased, and Inez's screams abruptly stopped. The sudden quiet was deafening, drawing every pair of eyes back to her. She was rising from the floor, her movements slow. Her soaked hair clung to her face, her eyes blazing.

The armed guard reacted rapidly, lunging towards her and dialling the stun gun to 25%. Inez flinched as he approached, her shoulders tensing in anticipation of the electric surge. But as the seconds passed and no pain came, she exhaled shakily, her body loosening. The guard, undeterred, turned the dial to 50%. Inez flicked her hair out of her face, her eyes locking onto the torturer with a defiant intensity.

The guard hesitated, glancing towards the boss for confirmation. The boss, intrigued, stepped closer to the glass, his silhouette looming. He nodded once, a silent command. The guard turned back to Inez, his hand quivering slightly as he cranked the stun gun to its maximum, 100%, a charge lethal enough to bring down a grizzly bear.

Inez's lips curled into a smirk. She raised her eyebrows, tilting her head mockingly. "Next move," she taunted, her voice steady despite the chaos. The guard faltered, stepping back instinctively. The boss slammed his fist against the glass, the sound jolting the guard forwards again.

Blue electrical arcs danced menacingly at the tip of the stun gun as the guard advanced. Inez's smirk faltered for a fraction of a second, her mind flashing to the agony she had endured moments before. *Not again*, she thought, steeling herself.

With a sudden burst of energy, she lunged forwards, grabbing the guard's wrist. In one fluid motion, she twisted around, positioning herself behind him. She forced him to face the others. Over his shoulder, she cast a cold glance at the boss before slamming her forehead into the guard's face. He stumbled back, the stun gun slipping from his grasp as he clutched at his face guard, now painfully misaligned.

Inez seized the stun gun, her knuckles white as she gripped it tightly. Her anger flared as she ripped the guard's face gear off, eliciting a pained grunt. He swung a fist at her, but she leaned back effortlessly, the punch missing its mark. Straightening, she met his gaze once more, her smirk returning.

Inez was unaware that the three businesspeople had begun placing their bids, their voices low and calculated. The boss, standing tall and composed, leaned towards his assistant, whispering instructions. The assistant nodded and approached the bidders, his expression unreadable. "The bidding is over," he announced, his tone final. The businesspeople exchanged glances, some of disappointment, others of quiet acceptance, before gathering their belongings and leaving the room.

The boss turned back to the glass and fixed his stare on Inez. She was a rare find, a gem unlike any other, and he had no intention of letting her go. He knocked on the window before raising his hand and rotating his wrist with a single finger in the air, a signal to end it. Zaire, standing nearby, felt his stomach drop. He leaned closer to the glass, his face pale with dread. He knew all too well what that gesture meant. But how had he missed the boss's true intentions? How had he not seen this coming?

Inez caught the motion through the corner of her eye, her anger flaring. As the guard turned to face her, she acted on instinct. Gripping the stun gun tightly, she drove it into his face, the prongs striking his eye with a sickening crackle. The guard screamed, clutching his face as he stumbled backwards. He turned towards the glass, his hand trembling as he pulled it away to reveal the damage. His eye was gone, reduced to a viscous liquid that dripped down his cheek. He collapsed to the floor, gasping for air, his body writhing in pain.

Inez stared at the stun gun in her hand. "What did I just do?" she whispered. The weight of her actions pinned her down. She dropped the stun gun. "Did I just kill someone else?"

The boss, unfazed, pressed a button beneath the window. The doors hissed open, and two guards entered. The boss slipped out through a side exit, leaving Zaire behind. Zaire hesitated, torn between his loyalty and his growing fear. He couldn't bring himself to leave her, not now.

One guard held a stun gun, its prongs sparking ominously, while the other carried a tranquilliser dart. Inez raised her hands, her palms open in a gesture of surrender. "Please," she said. The guard with the stun gun stepped forwards, his weapon aimed at her chest. But it was a ruse. The second guard raised his dart gun, aiming for the back of her neck.

In a blur of motion, Inez turned, her reflexes razor-sharp. Her fingers closed around the dart mid-air, catching it between her thumb and index finger. She smirked, the rage within her igniting once more. Without hesitation, she hurled the dart back at its sender, the needle embedding itself in his neck. The guard staggered, his eyes wide with shock, before he crumpled to the floor.

Inez's gaze shifted to the stun gun she had dropped. With a swift kick, she sent it flying into her hand. She turned to the remaining guard, her movements fluid and precise. The stun gun sizzled as she drove it into his side, the electric current sending him sprawling.

Zaire watched from behind the glass. *Who is this woman?* he thought, his confusion mingling with awe.

The room fell silent for a moment, the tension thick in the air. Then, a new figure entered, a man holding a small black controller with a single blue button. Zaire's eyes widened in recognition. Without a word, he turned and fled the viewing room, disappearing into the shadows.

Inez turned to face the newcomer, her body ready. But before she could act, he pressed the button. A wave of dizziness washed over her, her vision blurring. She stumbled towards him, her fists pounding against the locked door as he slipped out and sealed it behind him. Her strength waned, her body betraying her as she sank to the floor. Leaning against the door, she cast one last glance at the empty observation room. The world around her faded, the edges of her vision turning white until there was nothing.

16

Loose Strap

Tied once again to a bed, but this time not in a concrete grave or an operating room, Inez woke to the creak of a wired chair. Her eyes fluttered open, adjusting to the light, and there he was, Zaire, sitting beside her, his face a storm of guilt and hesitation. Her heart sank. The familiar feeling of leather straps on her wrists sent a jolt of panic through her. She tugged instinctively, the restraints biting into her skin.

"Zaire," she whispered. "What is this? Why am I here?"

He leaned forwards, elbows resting on the edge of the bed, his hands clasped tightly as if in prayer. "I never meant for this to happen," he said, his voice low and strained. "The boss promised me he wouldn't hurt you."

Betrayal clawed at her chest. "How can I trust you after this?" she spat, her pitch rising. "You saved me from that man just to hand me back to him? Do you even hear yourself?"

Zaire flinched, his eyes dropping to the floor. "You don't understand," he muttered. "The boss promised, he's never broken his word before. I thought…" He trailed off, words failing him under her glare.

"Promised?" she echoed, the word dripping with disbelief. "Do you have any idea what I've been through? What your precious boss has done to me?" She shook her head, trying to compose herself. "He murdered my husband. He gave me to that monster of a doctor. Do you know what it's like being left in a cell, being treated like… like nothing?"

Zaire reached out, his hand shaking as it hovered over hers. "I didn't know," he said quietly. "I'm so sorry, Inez. If I had known—"

"Don't," she snapped, pulling her hand away as far as the restraints would allow. "Don't you dare try to comfort me. You made this worse. You—" Her voice broke, and she turned her head away, tears streaming down her face. "Just leave me alone."

Zaire sat frozen, his hand still outstretched, his eyes wide with shock. "Inez," he began, but his voice faltered. He pointed instead. "Your arm."

She followed his gaze, her breath catching as she saw her wrist, free from the restraint, the leather strap still buckled but hanging loose. "How..." she whispered. "What's happening to me?"

Zaire's eyes darted between her face and her hand. "How long have you been able to do that?" he asked, the words tinged with awe and fear.

"I don't know," she said. "I don't know what's happening."

He moved closer, his earlier hesitation replaced by a strange determination. "We need to figure this out," he said. "Tell me everything, everything that's happened to you."

She hesitated. "It started after the fire," she said finally. "In the lab. I fell into a tray, there was something in it. I don't know what, but it hurt. It felt like my ribs were breaking. And then..." Her hand moved instinctively to her stomach. "That's why my baby died," she said, her voice breaking. "They did something to me. They changed me."

Zaire reached out again, his hand resting lightly on her shoulder. "We'll figure this out," he said. "I promise."

Inez sat up slowly, her head swimming with questions as Zaire knelt beside the bed. The broken beaker that had torn through her face barely left a mark, the pain an afterthought as she brushed off the remaining shards of glass like it was nothing. Her skin, which seemed to repel the stun guns electric shock, felt alien to her. It hadn't burned her flesh, not even left a scar.

"Quick reflexes, speed..." she muttered to herself, recalling when she dodged the dart that should have pierced her neck. Each revelation made her chest tighten. What was happening to her?

LOOSE STRAP

They sat in heavy silence, Inez's hands shaking as the reality of her transformation set in. "Omnipotent," Zaire finally murmured, his eyes scanning hers for answers.

"Omnipotent?" she repeated, the word hanging heavy in the air. "You mean... anything? Every talent? Every power?"

"It seems so," he said softly, his voice laced with unease. "But only when you need them. It's as though your body unlocks them the second you require them."

Inez shivered. "And then I... keep them forever," she whispered. A deep, guttural fear twisted in her gut, but there was no time to dwell on it. Zaire's expression shifted, his brows furrowing as the boss's plan became clearer.

"He's keeping you for a reason," Zaire said suddenly, rising to his feet. "Inez, I won't let him use you. I'll protect you, I swear."

"You don't even know me," Inez retorted sharply. But before Zaire could answer, the door swung open.

The perfectly matched duo, Hunter and Nadia, strode in with the kind of elegance and dominance that sent chills down her spine. Hunter greeted Zaire with a firm pat on the back, his eyes cool and calculating. He moved to the end of the bed, resting his hands on the footboard as his stare bore into Inez.

"You must be the infamous Inez," Hunter said with a smirk. "I like her," he added, chuckling to himself as Inez scoffed.

Nadia glided to Zaire, her manicured hands resting on his shoulders before she stepped back to stand beside Hunter. She folded her arms, rolling her eyes. "Well," she said drily, "is she the one we need?"

"Be nice, honey," Hunter teased.

Nadia huffed. "Why her? She's already caused problems," she said, glaring at Zaire.

Inez leaned forwards, her eyes narrowing. "What does she mean?" she demanded. "You need me? For what? How have I caused you problems?"

Zaire placed a calming hand over hers, the gesture both grounding and disarming. "One question at a time, okay?" he said gently.

Hunter grinned. "Oh, I like her fire. She's going to be fun." His words hung in the air, but their implication was anything but light-hearted.

Zaire uncuffed Inez's other hand gently. She rubbed her wrist, the skin red raw, and shot him a look of pure hatred. The intensity cut through him like a blade, and he recoiled slightly, his shoulders slumping under her disdain.

"Nadia," he said, his voice heavy with disappointment, "can I leave this to you? I have a feeling I'm not wanted here."

Nadia smirked, her confidence unwavering. "Yeah, I'll handle her," she replied, clearly amused. Zaire hesitated for a moment, his eyes lingering on Inez, before turning and walking out of the room with Hunter trailing behind him.

As the door clicked shut, Nadia turned to Inez, her expression softening slightly. "We'll take you to your new room," she said. "It's a lot nicer than this one, and you can decorate it however you want."

Inez narrowed her eyes, her confusion evident. "I'm not a prisoner," she said.

Nadia tilted her head, a sly smile playing on her lips. "Well," she began pointedly, "you can't leave unless it's for a mission or pre-approved. But I wouldn't use the word 'prisoner.'"

Inez's brows furrowed, her confusion deepening. "What does that even mean?" she asked, frustrated.

Nadia gestured towards the door, her movements graceful. "Come on," she said, her tone shifting to one of patience. "I'll show you your room. Your suitcase is already there, so you can freshen up. We'll come by later to get you for dinner."

Inez hesitated, her mind occupied by questions she couldn't yet voice. She followed Nadia reluctantly, her steps uncertain. The promise of a nicer room did little to ease the tightening in her chest.

17

The Light Beneath

Inez hesitated for a moment before opening her door, bracing herself for what lay on the other side. To her surprise, the room that greeted her was bright and immaculately clean. Sunlight streamed through a wall of square windows, casting golden patterns on the wooden floor. The room had a cosy yet modern charm. One wall featured three doors, hiding various amenities. She tried the first door and discovered a bathroom with gleaming white tiles. The second door opened to reveal a compact yet functional mini kitchen, complete with a kettle and a neatly stacked set of dishes. Behind the third door lay a spacious walk-in wardrobe, empty, waiting to be filled with her belongings.

In the centre of the room, a double bed adorned with a thick duvet and fluffy pillows beckoned her to sink into its embrace. At the foot of the bed, her suitcase sat waiting, a stark reminder of the journey that had brought her here. With a deep breath, Inez whispered to herself, "This might not be so bad," and got to work unpacking.

She opened her suitcase and methodically placed her clothing and belongings into the crooked wardrobe and slightly wobbly chest of drawers. She arranged her toiletries neatly along the bathroom counter, the colourful bottles adding a personal touch to the sterile space. With a sense of finality, she slid her empty suitcase into a corner of the room. Glancing at the bed, she pulled out an outfit for the evening, a deliberate choice, though she wasn't entirely sure of her plans yet.

Stripping off her travel-worn clothes, Inez stepped into the shower. The warm water cascaded over her, carrying away the fatigue and tension of the past weeks. She allowed herself to relax, her thoughts drifting to a different time, one filled with memories she was determined to leave behind. As the steam enveloped her, those memories began to fade, becoming nothing more than distant echoes. She exhaled a breath she hadn't realised she was holding, though she still felt a pang of guilt. Would Lucian disapprove of her moving forwards so easily?

Emerging from the bathroom, Inez wrapped herself in a fluffy towel, letting her damp hair fall loosely around her shoulders. She retrieved her hairdryer, letting its steady hum fill the silence as she carefully straightened her hair. With practised ease, she applied a touch of makeup, just enough to accentuate her features. The reflection staring back at her in the mirror seemed unfamiliar, lighter, freer. Donning a navy floral dress, comfortable white trainers and a well-worn denim jacket, Inez felt ready to face whatever awaited her. Well, almost ready. She couldn't leave without Nadia.

Her gaze landed on a glossy magazine on her bedside table, adorned with a vibrant sticky note in a bold, loopy script: *Pick out some stuff you would like, and I can explain how it all works later., Nadia.* A smile tugged at the corners of her lips. Perhaps she had found her first real friend in this unfamiliar place.

A sudden knock on the door startled her, causing the book in her hands to slip from her grasp and tumble onto the bedside table. Heart pounding, she took a calming breath before opening the door. To her surprise, standing there was a striking couple.

"Inez," Hunter greeted her with an easy smile.

"Ready for dinner?" Nadia chimed in enthusiastically, her hand reaching out to gently take Inez's.

Speechless, Inez nodded, finding comfort in Nadia's radiant energy. The three of them strolled down the softly lit hallway, their footsteps echoing off the polished wood floors. At the end of the corridor, Hunter pushed open a pair of grand double wooden doors, revealing an opulent dining hall. The space was a feast for the senses, with chandeliers casting a warm glow over rows of tables. At the far end, a sumptuous buffet awaited, the aromas tantalising. To the right, a drinks counter glittered with glasses and bottles, inviting the guests to indulge.

Inez felt a flicker of hope. Maybe this was the fresh start she so desperately needed.

"Come sit," Nadia said to Inez, patting the chair beside her with an inviting smile. Inez hesitated only briefly before taking the seat.

"Been demoted, I see," Hunter said drily as he dropped into the chair directly across from them, smirking playfully.

"Just ignore him, I do," Nadia quipped, the laughter that followed light and infectious. She rolled her eyes dramatically for effect, earning a chuckle from Inez. "Now go get us some food while I explain everything," Nadia added.

Hunter groaned in mock protest, rolling his eyes before standing. "You're impossible," he muttered under his breath as he trudged off towards the buffet.

Once he was out of earshot, Nadia leaned in closer to Inez. "I know this is all a bit overwhelming, but there's some stuff you'll need to know," she began. "Here, we earn credits by doing chores, jobs and missions. Those credits let us buy things, stuff for our rooms, clothes, even activities or treats. You follow so far?"

Inez nodded, intrigued but still unsure. "Yes, but... what kind of chores or jobs?" she asked, her brow furrowed.

"Jobs might be going out to collect food or supplies," Nadia explained matter-of-factly. "Chores are the basics, cooking, cleaning, that kind of thing. And missions... well, those are specific tasks the boss gives us. They can be a bit more... interesting." She winked mischievously, as though alluding to secrets she couldn't yet share.

"As you're new here," Nadia continued, "you'll get fifty points to start. You can use them to design your room. That magazine I gave you will tell you how many points each item costs, bedding is two points, a rug is five, and a desk is ten. Are you still with me?" she asked.

Inez nodded again, her interest piqued. "I think I've got it," she said, a small smile forming.

"Good," Nadia said, her grin widening. "Tomorrow, I'll meet you at nine for breakfast, and then I'll give you the grand tour," she added, her enthusiasm infectious.

As Nadia finished speaking, Hunter returned, balancing plates of food in each hand. He placed a plate in front of each of the girls before vanishing briefly to retrieve his own. "I didn't know what you liked, so I just grabbed a bit of everything," he said when he returned.

"Thank you, I really appreciate it," Inez replied sincerely.

Before anyone could begin eating, Zaire entered the dining hall. His presence was magnetic, and Inez couldn't help but notice the way his eyes locked onto hers for a fleeting, intense moment. Then, as though ashamed or unsure, he quickly looked down at the floor.

"You sitting here, pal?" Hunter asked, raising an eyebrow at Zaire and gesturing towards the empty seat at their table.

Zaire hesitated, his gaze flickering back to Inez. "If I'm welcome?" he asked.

"Please, join us," Inez said, offering him a gentle smile. Zaire relaxed slightly and slid into the seat, his movements careful, as though he didn't want to disrupt the delicate dynamic of the group.

The table settled into an awkward silence as they ate, the clinking of utensils the only sound. Finally, Hunter broke the tension. "So," he began, glancing at Inez, "any ideas for your room yet?"

Inez set down her fork and leaned back in her chair, a wistful expression crossing her face. "I was looking before dinner," she admitted. "There was this rug I used to have at home, green with diamond shapes on it. I had matching emerald-green bedding, an ottoman… I loved that setup. Oh, and I'd need a bookcase, reading is my escape. Maybe a comfy chair too. And plants… I love being surrounded by them. Honestly, I'd just recreate my old room if I could." She let out a laugh, though it was tainted with sadness, a bittersweet longing for the life she'd left behind.

"You'll get there," Zaire said quietly. "Just give it time. Eventually, this place will start to feel like home."

"Hunter and I always go for a run before lights out," Nadia said to Inez as she pulled on her jacket. "Are you okay with me leaving you? You know your way back?"

"Yes, no problem," Inez replied with a reassuring smile. "I'll see you in the morning. Thank you for everything."

"Anytime," Nadia said with a wink, and she and Hunter disappeared through the exit, their laughter fading into the background. The room fell noticeably quieter, leaving Inez alone with Zaire.

Not one to idle, Inez began clearing the table, stacking the dirty plates and carrying them to a nearby stand by the bin. Zaire, watching her from his seat, tilted his head and said, "You don't have to do that. Those are the cleaning chores we get paid for."

Inez turned to him, her expression firm but not unkind. "It's just good manners," she replied briskly.

Zaire blinked in surprise, then softened. "May I walk you back to your room?" he asked politely, rising from his seat.

She hesitated for a moment before nodding. "Sure."

As they walked side by side through the dimly lit hallway, Zaire glanced at Inez, his expression curious. "So," he began, "where did you live before?"

"In the city," Inez said. "Near the Isle Bridge."

Zaire's eyes lit up with recognition. "I know that area. What was the name of your building?"

"I live at 47 High Park Tower," she replied, her tone infused with nostalgia.

"Ah," Zaire said, nodding. "I know it well. There's a lovely park at the end of the road, perfect for clearing your head."

She nodded in agreement, a small smile tugging at the corners of her lips. "It is," she murmured, her mind momentarily drifting back to lazy afternoons spent under the trees of that very park.

Before she could ask Zaire about his own past, he glanced at his watch and frowned. "I have to go," he said apologetically. "Lights out in two minutes. I'll see you tomorrow. Sleep well, Inez."

"You too, Zaire," Inez said, watching him disappear down the corridor.

She entered her room and closed the door behind her, the quiet enveloping her instantly. As she leaned against the door, an unfamiliar fluttering sensation welled up in her stomach. Butterflies. She shook her head, brushing the feeling aside as best she could.

18

Walls and Woods

Inez awoke feeling as if she'd been gently cradled by the sunrise itself, refreshed, rejuvenated and quietly hopeful. In the cocoon of early morning, she marvelled at how her new life here already held the promise of change, even if it was only her first night in this unfamiliar haven. The new day filled her with a sense of serene possibility, a whisper that everything was exactly as it should be.

She rose slowly, savouring the warmth of her dreams as they dissolved into reality. With thoughtful deliberation, Inez changed into something more befitting the bright morning, a light, comfortable outfit. The fabric moved fluidly over her skin, and as she secured her hair into a loose ponytail, each strand fell perfectly into place, mirroring the calm that had begun to settle in her heart.

Stepping gracefully towards the door, Inez paused to appreciate the gentle light and shadow dancing along the corridor, a prelude to the day's adventures. Just as she reached for the worn brass knob, a familiar and cheerful knock echoed down the hall. Opening the door, she found Nadia standing there with her characteristic warm smile.

"Timing or what? Let's go," Nadia said, each word carrying a spark of possibility. In that moment, the simple act of opening her door felt like stepping into a new chapter.

They walked together to the breakfast hall, a spacious, softly lit room where the clink of cutlery and gentle hum of early conversation blended with the aroma of freshly prepared food. As they perched at a long wooden table polished by years of use, Nadia launched into stories of her and Hunter's exploits. With animated gestures, she described their latest training session, their playful competitions and even a few mishaps. Inez listened intently, her mind alight with curious wonder.

"So where is he now?" Inez finally asked, tilting her head as she sipped her tea, the rhythmic chatter of the dining hall momentarily pausing around them.

"He's in training right now; we'll pop by and see him soon," Nadia responded, smiling as though the mention of Hunter brought her joy. With that, they began their breakfast, a blend of robust coffee, freshly baked bread and delicate pastries, each bite punctuating the unfolding dialogue.

Mid-conversation, the tapping of footsteps signalled another presence. A woman crossed the threshold of the hall, a striking figure dressed entirely in black, her hair modestly veiled by a hijab. Even in the gentle light of morning, the meticulous precision of her winged eyeliner accentuated her hazel eyes, giving her an air of intensity and confident poise. Following closely at her heels padded a grey British shorthair cat, its sleek fur and alert gaze adding a mysterious charm to her entrance.

"Who's that?" Inez enquired, feeling a mix of intrigue and admiration as she took in the woman's formidable appearance.

"Megyn, and the cat is Qita," she explained, her voice layered with fondness. "She looks intense, doesn't she?" Nadia added, leaning towards Inez as if sharing a light-hearted secret. "But don't be deceived, she's a warrior at heart. And watch out for the cat; he's known to be as feisty as they come." With that, Nadia leaned back and returned her focus to her meal.

For a long time, Inez found herself locking eyes with Megyn. There was a silent exchange in that look, a challenge, perhaps, before Megyn's unwavering stare shifted away.

"Ready for the tour?" Nadia broke the moment with a cheerful interjection.

"Yep, let's go," Inez replied, anxious yet excited as they stepped away from the breakfast hall.

Later, as the two toured the sprawling compound, Nadia pointed out the intricate layout of the building. They began at the grand main entrance hall, a space marked by its grandeur and military-level discipline. Two imposing staircases ascended from either side. To the north lay the wing for ranked officers such as Zaire, a place where the weight of responsibility was reflected in the refined decor and personal touches of the living quarters. In contrast, the south wing, shrouded in a veil of exclusivity, was reserved for the boss, a space of mystery and authority.

Turning left from the entrance, they encountered the massive library on the lower ground. This quiet sanctuary, with its never-ending rows of books and carved wooden study desks, invited deep thought and silent exploration. To the right was the familiar dining hall.

Double doors flanked the main entrance, leading to long, narrow halls filled with dorm rooms, a testament to the many lives intertwined within these walls. At the very centre of the building, they arrived at the green, a sprawling communal area filled with vibrant plants, bubbling fountains and inviting benches designed for a moment of respite. Here, the natural beauty of carefully tended flora offered a stark contrast to the regimented interior.

At the end of the left hall stood the gathering hall, which doubled as the entrance to the training field, a zone where raw determination met disciplined practice. On the other side, the right hall ended at the infirmary, a necessary haven to mend the injuries from rigorous training. Tucked away in the back of the building was the large training room.

As Nadia continued to weave stories about each corner of this intricate space, Inez felt herself gradually enveloped by the life and energy that permeated every hall, every room, a life full of promise, battles won and lost, and the ever-present thrill of discovery waiting behind the next door.

As they stepped into the training room, Inez gasped. The space was nothing short of extraordinary, a testament to the resources poured into this facility. One entire wall was a series of floor-to-ceiling black square windows, offering a panoramic view of the sprawling training field beyond. The training field sprawled before them, bordered by a dense forest that seemed to hold its own secrets. It was clear they were in the middle of nowhere, isolated yet surrounded by nature's beauty.

The wooden flooring gleamed under the overhead lights, its polished surface interrupted by several black mats neatly arranged for training. Around the room, punching bags hung like sentinels, their surfaces worn from countless strikes. A rack of training katanas stood proudly against one wall, their blades gleaming. In the far corner, a sparring ring dominated the space, its ropes taut, inviting those brave enough to step inside.

"Hello, beautiful." Hunter's playful voice broke the silence. He leaned in, planting a sweaty kiss on Nadia's cheek, the evidence of his recent boxing session glistening on his skin. "Up for a round?" he teased, a mischievous glint in his eye as he winked at her.

Nadia smirked. "Go on then," she replied. As Hunter peeled off his shirt, revealing a physique honed to perfection, Nadia couldn't help but laugh at his theatrics. Together, they climbed into the sparring ring, the air around them charged with anticipation.

"This ring," Nadia explained to Inez, gesturing to the space around them, "it neutralises our powers. Forces us to rely on pure skill, hand-to-hand combat." Her voice carried a note of pride, a testament to her mastery despite her lack of supernatural speed or flexibility. She had learned to use her smaller stature to her advantage.

The fight began with a ferocity that left Inez wide-eyed. They moved with a fluidity that spoke of countless hours of practice, their strikes and counters a dance of power. Nadia landed a series of low jabs, her movements calculated and swift. A well-placed uppercut sent Hunter stumbling back, his head shaking as he tried to clear the dizziness.

"That's enough for now," Hunter declared with mock defeat. "Don't want to tire me out before Zaire gets here." His words earned a scoff from Nadia, who stepped out of the ring without so much as a bead of sweat on her brow.

"Don't worry," Nadia said, turning to Inez with a reassuring smile. "You'll learn too. Size isn't everything."

Intrigued, Inez asked, "How come he's sparring with Zaire?"

"They do it all the time," Nadia replied. "Hunter's got the strength, but he doesn't think ahead. Zaire, though, he's a strategist. Always five steps ahead. Drives Hunter crazy."

"I thought they were best friends," Inez said, her surprise evident.

"Oh, they are," Nadia assured her. "But sometimes, they're more like brothers. They were raised together, after all."

"What?" Inez's confusion was palpable, her mind trying to piece together this new information.

Before she could ask more, the doors burst open with a dramatic flair. Zaire strode in, his presence commanding the room. The crowd that had gathered seemed to hold their breath. Inez instinctively shrank back, blending into the crowd to avoid his gaze.

Zaire stripped down to loose gym shorts, revealing a sculpted physique. His chiselled abs and muscular arms were a testament to his discipline, while the intricate tattoo sleeve on his arm told a story of its own. The centrepiece, a majestic lion on his upper back, a symbol of strength and pride.

As the fight commenced, Inez couldn't tear her eyes away. Zaire's calculated approach versus Hunter's aggression. Every move was considered, every strike part of a larger plan. When Hunter landed a powerful punch, splitting Zaire's lip and sending a spray of blood into the air, Inez flinched.

"When does it end?" she whispered to Nadia, barely audible over the fight.

"When one is knocked out, taps out, or the timer ends," Nadia replied matter-of-factly.

Inez glanced at the timer, two minutes remained. Her sight shifted back to the ring, and for a fleeting moment, her eyes locked with Zaire's. She saw something in his expression, a flicker of understanding as he noticed her fear. Without breaking eye contact, Zaire glanced at the clock, then knelt and tapped out.

The crowd groaned in disappointment, their excitement deflating as they began to disperse. Conversations turned to lunch, and the room slowly emptied. "Go, baby!" Nadia cheered, her voice cutting through the chatter as she called out to Hunter.

"Let's go," Nadia said to Inez, and they exited the training room. The air felt cooler in the hallway, a welcome change after the intensity of the sparring session.

Hunter stayed behind, his eyes fixed on Zaire. "You could have lasted. Why'd you stop?" he asked, curious.

Zaire shrugged, his expression unreadable. "Nothing. Just had enough," he replied, though his eyes betrayed him as they flicked towards Inez.

Hunter smirked knowingly, slinging his bag over his shoulder. "Ohh, I get it. Thanks for the win," he said, tapping his back before picking up his shirt and strolling away. His confidence was clear as he caught up with the girls.

"Want to join me for a shower?" Hunter teased, wrapping an arm around Nadia's waist with a playful grin.

Nadia rolled her eyes but didn't resist his touch. "Go ahead. I'll find my way," Inez said, her smile warm as she reassured her new friend. She watched them disappear down the hall, their laughter echoing faintly behind them.

Left alone, Inez began to walk, her footsteps light against the polished floor. The hallway stretched ahead, lined with doors that seemed to hold secrets of their own. She was lost in thought when a voice called her name.

"Inez!" It was Zaire, his voice urgent. She turned to see him jogging towards her, his shirt flung casually over his shoulder. His chest glistened.

"Hi," Zaire said, slightly breathless as he reached her.

"Hi," Inez replied, her smile shy but genuine.

"How was the tour?" he asked casually.

"It's a lovely place," she responded sincerely as she glanced around.

Zaire's lips curved into a cheeky smile, his confidence shining through. "Well, with your room done, it'll feel more like home. Trust me," he said.

"I hope so," Inez replied softly. "I better have lunch."

"Yeah, and I'd better have a shower," Zaire said, his grin widening. "See you at dinner?" His words carried an unspoken invitation, and he kept his gaze steady as he waited for her response.

Inez nodded, her smile lingering as she turned to walk away. The moment hung in the air, a connection that neither of them acknowledged.

19

The Waiting Moment

After lunch, Inez made her way back to her room, enjoying the comforting feeling of the day. As she reached her door, she noticed a note pinned to it. The handwriting was unfamiliar: *I hope you like it*.

Like what? Curiosity bubbled within her as she pulled the door open, and instantly, a wave of familiarity washed over her. Her eyes travelled over the space. It wasn't just a room any more; it was hers.

The same rug from her home lay beneath her feet, its soft fibres grounding her in the past she had left behind. Beneath the window sat a small bookcase, now lined with her favourite reads. The window ledge was decorated with artificial plants that added warmth, a perfect contrast against the sleek black frames on the wall and the emerald-green bedding.

Her gaze moved further. A second bookcase stood proudly, a striking industrial-style piece, its shelves waiting to be filled. In front of it was a white fabric chair with a plush green cushion, accompanied by a matching circular ottoman.

And then, she noticed the chest of drawers, it wasn't just any chest, it was hers, the same one from her home. Every detail had been thought of. Her jewellery sat where it belonged; her books had all been placed neatly. Even her easel, the one from her old balcony, stood in the corner, waiting patiently for her to return to her art.

A slow, stunned smile spread across her lips. It was perfect. Every inch of the space reflected her, as though she had never left.

She took a deep breath, letting the emotions settle before heading to the shower to freshen up. Once clean, she grabbed a book, sank into her chair and lost herself in the familiar embrace of its pages.

Meanwhile, in the dining hall, Hunter and Nadia were already seated when Zaire walked in. He made his way to the buffet, grabbed a plate of food and took a seat beside them.

"How's your afternoon been?" he asked, keeping the conversation light.

"I haven't seen her since the tour," Nadia replied with a shrug.

"Is she coming for dinner?" Hunter asked, taking a sip of water.

"She said she was," Nadia answered, though a glance at the clock showed time was slipping by.

An hour passed, and eventually, Hunter and Nadia left for their evening run, preparing to wind down before lights-out. Zaire, however, remained seated, the uneaten plate of food before him now repurposed for a new plan.

Gathering the meal, he made his way towards Inez's room, the dimming corridor lights casting shadows along the walls. He knocked once. Waited. Knocked again.

The door cracked open, revealing Inez, her eyes heavy with sleep as she rubbed them groggily.

"You missed dinner," Zaire said, offering a small smile. "I didn't want you to have to wait until breakfast."

She blinked, registering his presence before her lips curved into a grateful smile. "Thank you. I fell asleep... guess I needed it," she admitted, taking the plate from his hands.

A beat of silence stretched between them before she gestured towards the room. "Would you like to come in?"

"I can stay for a little while," Zaire said, stepping inside.

She sat at the end of her bed, carefully balancing the plate on her lap, then glanced up at him. "Please, sit." She gestured to the reading chair.

He sank into it, taking in the space with quiet appreciation. "I love the room," he commented, his eyes moving over the thoughtful details.

"Same," she replied, glancing around with admiration. "I came back from the tour, and it was already like this. It's perfect."

She finished her meal, setting the plate aside.

"Wish I'd woken up sooner," she mused, stretching her arms. "I really want to stretch my legs."

"Come on then," Zaire said, standing with an easy smile. "I'm one of the upper ranks, you'll be with me."

She hesitated. "Is that okay?"

"Of course," he assured her, extending a hand towards the door. "Come on."

They strolled through the central green, their pace slow, their steps in sync as they admired the vibrant plants and the steady trickle of water from the fountain. The night air was crisp, carrying a scent of earth and fresh greenery.

"It reminds me of the casino," Inez murmured.

"The night we met. I remember," Zaire replied, a flicker of something unsaid behind his eyes.

Inez inhaled deeply, filling her lungs with the clean night air. "It's beautiful out tonight. Everything feels… fresh."

Zaire watched her for a moment before offering his hand. "Come with me. I want to show you something."

There was something about the way he said it, low, inviting, secretive. She hesitated only a second before placing her hand in his. His grip was firm yet gentle as he led her indoors, moving through the gathering hall and out onto the training field.

They continued walking until the landscape opened into a nearby lake, its waters calm and reflective beneath the moonlight. A dock stretched out over the surface, its weathered wood worn smooth from years of use.

"This is beautiful," she breathed, turning to face him.

"There's more," he said, holding out his hand once again.

Without hesitation, she took it, allowing him to guide her onto the dock. The wood creaked beneath their weight as they reached the edge.

"Lie down and look up," Zaire instructed as he reclined on the dock.

Inez hesitated. He was so mysterious to her, indecipherable in ways that only made him more intriguing. But curiosity won out, and she slowly lowered herself beside him.

As soon as she tilted her head back, she gasped.

The midnight sky was alive with stars, scattered like diamonds on a velvet canvas. They pulsed gently, twinkling against the darkness, each one a quiet message from the universe.

Zaire turned his head slightly, his gaze landing on Inez. The moon's glow illuminated her ivory skin, casting shadows over her delicate features. He watched her, mesmerised by the way the light danced in her eyes, by the gentle rise and fall of her breath.

And suddenly, all he wanted was to pull her close, to taste the warmth of her lips, to surrender to the unfamiliar but undeniable pull between them.

But he knew he couldn't.

He shouldn't.

"We better get back," he said, showing restraint.

Inez sat up quickly, her brows knitting. "Oh… okay. No problem." Her words were even, but there was a flicker of something else beneath them, uncertainty.

They walked in silence, the energy between them shifting, growing heavier. Inez's mind replayed the moment over and over. Did she do something wrong?

When they reached her door, she opened it quietly, stepping inside without a word. Zaire turned to leave, but something held him back.

"Inez," he called suddenly.

She appeared in the doorway again, eyes wide, expectant. "Zaire."

He hesitated, then softened. "Sleep well. See you tomorrow."

She nodded, watching as he turned and walked away, his shoulders tense as though something had been left unsaid. As the door clicked shut behind her, she exhaled deeply, pressing her forehead to the wood.

When he was back in his own room, Zaire sat on the edge of his bed, jaw clenched in frustration. Why did he act like that? The question gnawed at him, but no answer came, just the image of her under the stars.

20

Training in the Storm

Days had passed since Inez last spoke to Zaire. She saw him in passing, at meals, in the halls, but he avoided her at every opportunity, his presence fleeting and distant. The silence between them was deafening, a void she couldn't fill.

Today marked the beginning of her training. She needed to learn how to harness her powers, to channel them with precision and control. And who better to teach her than an upper rank? Yet, as she entered the training room, her stomach twisted. Zaire was there, standing alone, his posture rigid.

Her eyes darted around the room, searching for anyone else, but it was empty. "Your powers are unpredictable at the moment," Zaire said, his voice steady but detached. "So this is a private session."

Inez's lips pressed into a thin line. "So now you'll talk to me," she muttered under her breath, the bitterness in her tone undeniable.

Zaire rolled his eyes, his patience already wearing thin. "This is training," he replied curtly. "I've been ordered to train you, so I'll do my job."

His words cut deep, each one a blade to her heart. She had started to open up to him, to trust him, and now, here he was, cold and distant, hurting her all over again.

They stepped onto the mat, the tension between them palpable. "So what are we going to do?" Inez asked, frustrated.

Without warning, Zaire flicked his wrist, releasing a gust of wind so powerful it knocked Inez flat onto her back. She landed with a thud, the impact jarring her.

"Train," he said, the word dripping with sarcasm.

Inez groaned, pushing herself up from the floor. "Ow! Was that necessary?" she snapped, glaring at him.

"Yes," Zaire replied. "Other people won't go easy on you. You need to learn."

"What even is your power?" she asked, her irritation bubbling to the surface.

"You won't know your enemies," he shot back. "And you can't have a chit-chat with them."

"Fine," she muttered, her fists clenching at her sides. He was starting to wind her up, and he knew it.

Over and over, Zaire used the same manoeuvre, sending her sprawling onto the mat each time. Her frustration grew with every fall, her body aching from the repeated impacts.

"Do something else," she begged.

"Okay," Zaire said, his tone almost mocking. With another flick of his wrist, rain poured down from nowhere, drenching her in seconds.

"What the fuck!" Inez shouted, her anger boiling over.

"Okay, sorry," Zaire said, though his apology lacked sincerity. With another flick, the rain stopped, replaced by the scorching heat of the sun. The warmth dried her instantly, but it didn't stop there. The heat intensified, searing her skin.

"Stop! It's burning! Zaire, stop!" she cried desperately as she shielded herself.

Her scream tore through the room, raw and primal. She raised her arm instinctively, and a surge of power erupted from her, sending Zaire flying across the room. He hit the wall with a thud, the sun disappearing in an instant.

Inez's skin, burnt and flaky, began to heal before her eyes, the wounds closing as if they had never existed. She stood there trembling, her breath ragged.

Zaire pushed himself up, brushing off the dust as he made his way back to the mat. His expression was unreadable as he asked, "Ready to continue?"

Inez said nothing, her silence heavy with determination. She shifted her stance, her body poised for a fight.

With a flick of his wrist, Zaire unleashed the wind again, knocking Inez off balance and sending her sprawling onto the mat. She groaned, leaning over to push herself up, only to yelp in surprise as a sharp jolt of lightning zapped her backside.

"Seriously?" she muttered, rolling her eyes as she stood.

Zaire smirked, his stance relaxed as he prepared to knock her over once more. But this time, Inez was ready. She raised her hands, channelling her energy, and rebounded his force. The tables turned as Zaire found himself flat on his back, the wind knocked out of him.

Karma is a bitch, Inez thought smugly.

"Yes, it is," Zaire said aloud, clearly amused.

"What?" Inez froze. "What is?"

"It is a bitch," Zaire repeated, shaking his head as though trying to clear it.

"I… I didn't say anything," she stammered.

"You said it telepathically," he explained, his eyes betraying a flicker of unease. *Can you hear me?* Zaire asked silently, testing the connection.

Yes, Inez responded, her voice echoing in his mind.

Zaire's expression hardened as he stepped closer, gripping her arms firmly. "We need to be careful with this. Don't tell anyone, you understand me?"

"Yes, but why?" she asked.

"People won't like you in their head," he said, his voice low and serious. "And the boss… the boss will use you."

Inez pulled back, her brows furrowing. "Why would you care?"

Zaire hesitated, his gaze dropping for a short while before meeting hers again. "Something about you is different, Inez. But I'll end up hurting you. It's best to stay away from me."

"Don't you think I get a say in this?" she countered, stepping closer, her defiance sparking between them.

"No," he said firmly, closing the distance between them. The air grew heavy, their warmth mingling.

Suddenly, the doors burst open, shattering the moment. Instinctively, Inez raised her hand, sending Zaire flying across the room with the same force he had used on her earlier. He landed with a thud, groaning as he pushed himself up.

"Wow, she put you on your arse," Hunter said as he stepped into the room.

"Time for dinner," Nadia interjected, smacking Hunter's arm lightly. "Easily distracted, are we?"

Inez smirked, her eyes meeting Zaire's as he rolled his eyes and stood. She couldn't resist a final jab, zapping him on the backside as he had done to her earlier. He jumped, glaring at her.

"Enough now," he ordered, his voice firm.

Dinner came and went, and the days passed in a blur. The tension between Inez and Zaire simmered, growing hotter with each interaction. Despite his attempts to push her away, he found himself drawn to her, unable to resist the pull.

He took her back to the same spot by the lake on several evenings, their conversations growing deeper, their connection undeniable. They shared lunches in her room, their time together filled with quiet intimacy. Evening runs became a ritual, their footsteps echoing in the stillness of the night.

But every now and then, Zaire would retreat, his walls rising again. He didn't know how to let anyone in, how to trust, how to be vulnerable. Yet, he wanted to. He wanted to let her in, even if it terrified him.

The announcement came suddenly: Zaire, Nadia and Hunter had been assigned a mission. It was dangerous, unpredictable and could leave Inez alone for weeks. The thought of being apart weighed heavily on both of them, though neither dared to voice it.

21

The Morning Begins

The following day, Inez awoke to the soft glow of morning light filtering through her window. As she stretched, her gaze landed on something unfamiliar, a piece of paper slid under her door. Puzzled, she swung her legs off the bed, shuffled over and picked it up. The handwriting was unmistakably Zaire's.

Sorry to leave so suddenly. This happens with the missions sometimes. You'll be on the rota for chores now, and the others will explain how it all works. You have a combat class with Megyn if I'm not back on time. See you soon.

Inez read the letter twice with a sinking feeling in her chest. The abruptness of his departure was nothing new, but the absence left an ache she couldn't quite explain. She folded the note carefully and placed it on her chest of drawers, as if keeping it close would somehow bridge the distance.

Shaking herself out of her thoughts, she got undressed and stepped into the shower, letting the warm water soothe her tension. By the time she emerged, she felt refreshed, though the unease still lingered at the edge of her mind. Dressing quickly, she tied her hair up, ready for what promised to be her first full day in this strange new routine.

The morning air was crisp as she ventured outside, deciding to explore the green space before her tasks began. She found herself drawn to a quiet corner, settling on a worn wooden bench with her book. The garden around her was a masterpiece of nature, vivid hues of blossoms peeked from bushes, each one a burst of colour. The fountain in the centre, although slightly covered in moss, had a rustic charm that added to the tranquillity of the space. It was an oasis, a perfect spot to unwind and soak up the morning sun.

As she flipped through the pages, Inez caught movement out of the corner of her eye. A woman emerged from the building, her presence striking and confident. Her blonde hair, streaked with brown roots, was swept into a high ponytail, revealing piercing blue eyes framed by glasses. Tattoos danced along her arms, a tapestry of ink. She was dressed in a black strapless body con dress that hugged her figure, paired with chunky black ankle boots.

The woman seemed distracted, her eyes fixed upwards. Inez followed her line of sight but saw nothing but the clear morning sky. *It must be a bird,* Inez thought, *maybe something connected to her power.*

Wanting to introduce herself, Inez closed her book and stood. "Hello," she greeted, her voice light and friendly.

But before she could say another word, the woman spun around sharply, her movements almost predatory. In a blur, she caught the bird mid-air, cradling it carefully as it fluttered weakly in her hands. Without so much as a glance at Inez, she hurried back inside, leaving Inez standing there, stunned.

Was it something I said? Inez thought, baffled.

Deciding not to dwell, she returned to her room, her curiosity piqued. On the door was another piece of paper pinned with a small tack, a rota. She took it down and walked inside, setting her book aside before sitting on the windowsill. The day stretched ahead, promising new faces and challenges, but Inez couldn't shake the encounter from her mind. Who was that woman? And why did she seem so guarded?

Monday
AM, Breakfast Duty (25 Tokens)
PM, Free
Tuesday
AM, Free

PM, Cleaning Duty (35 Tokens)
Wednesday
AM, Breakfast Duty (25 Tokens)
PM, Dinner Duty (25 Tokens)
Thursday
AM, Garden Duty (50 Tokens)
PM, Free
Friday
AM, Cleaning Duty (35 Tokens)
PM, Free

*You may only collect two hundred tokens per week, maximum. You may request additional shifts or changes with your upper rank.

"I'm going to be late," Inez muttered, placing the letter hurriedly on her chest of drawers before darting out the door. Her feet pounded lightly against the hallway floors as she made her way to the dining hall, her nerves mounting.

"Breakfast isn't served for another hour yet," a woman behind the counter called out as Inez entered, slightly out of breath.

"I'm here for breakfast duty," Inez replied shyly, her voice small as she approached the counter.

The woman glanced up, her red eyes locking onto Inez with a piercing yet oddly warm gaze. "You must be the new one. Inez, right?"

"Yes," she affirmed, shifting under the woman's intense stare.

"I'm Lamia," the woman said, her lips curving into a gentle smile. "Cooking duties are simple. Make the food, serve it, clean up, and then you're done."

Inez nodded, taking in Lamia's striking appearance. Her short red hair framed her face in a straight-cut fringe, accentuating her piercing red eyes. Freckles dusted her nose and cheeks, and a small collection of nose piercings glinted under the overhead light. Mysterious but approachable, Lamia had an effortless presence that put Inez at ease.

They worked side by side, preparing breakfast in comfortable silence. By the time they finished and placed the food into the serving dishes, Inez felt a small sense of accomplishment.

"Anything else?" she asked, eager to ensure everything was complete.

"Nope, that's all," Lamia replied. "I'm going to grab some food and head to my room. See you around," she added with a parting smile before disappearing down the hallway.

Inez returned to her room, setting her apron aside and reaching for her book. Her morning had just begun, but she couldn't shake the sense that every encounter here was wrapped in layers of mystery. She decided to take her book with her, heading back to the hall to grab some food and settle in.

As she approached the serving area, her eyes caught sight of a familiar figure, the same woman she had seen earlier in the green. Determined to make amends for the awkwardness of their first encounter, she approached cautiously.

"I'm sorry about earlier," Inez said sincerely. "I didn't mean to startle you."

The woman turned quickly, her movements stiff and guarded. "It's no problem," she said, stuttering. Her piercing blue eyes darted away. "I thought I was alone."

"I'm Inez," she offered, her voice gentle. "I'm new here, and I just… I don't know anyone."

The woman hesitated, her demeanour softening slightly. "How are you new? You're an adult," she said, her words blunt but not unkind. "Sorry. I'm Kimmie."

Inez's brows knitted in confusion. "What do you mean by 'an adult'?"

Kimmie's eyes widened, panic flashing across her face. "Sorry, I have to go before everyone else gets here." She hastily began piling bacon and sausages onto her plate.

"I'm on a special meat diet," she added, her words rushed as she avoided eye contact. "Bye." Without waiting for a response, Kimmie clutched her plate and hurried out of the hall, leaving Inez standing there, speechless.

Inez balanced a bowl of warm porridge and a glass of water as she made her way to the central green. The morning sunlight filtered through the canopy of leaves, casting dappled shadows across the vibrant garden. Finding an inviting bench beneath a flowering bush, she settled in, placing

THE MORNING BEGINS

her book beside her.

As she ate her porridge, the peaceful surroundings worked their magic, helping her unwind from the previous day. She paused between bites, taking sips of water and letting her eyes wander over the lush greenery. The fountain stood at the centre, its moss-covered surface glistening under the light, its soothing trickle blending seamlessly into the quiet hum of nature.

Once she had finished her food, she leaned back against the bench, flipping open her book and losing herself in its pages. Time passed gently, the air carrying hints of floral fragrance as she read.

Out of the corner of her eye, she caught movement, a small creature darting between the bushes. Her gaze landed on a little grey cat, its fur a smoky hue that shimmered in the sunlight. "Hello there," Inez called softly, hoping not to startle him.

The cat paused, tilting its head inquisitively before cautiously approaching her. She reached out a hand, letting him sniff her fingers before gently stroking his sleek coat. "Aren't you just the most handsome thing?" she murmured affectionately, noticing the name tag around his neck. "Qita," she read aloud with a smile.

Inez reached for her glass of water, pouring a small amount into her hand and offering it to him. Qita sniffed at the liquid before licking it eagerly, his whiskers twitching. Satisfied, he jumped onto her lap without hesitation, his warm little body curling comfortably against her as he rubbed his face on her arm.

She chuckled, letting her hand glide through his fur as he purred contentedly. For a brief moment, she felt truly at peace, the weight of the day melting away.

But then Qita sprang up, his ears flicking as if he'd heard something in the distance. He leapt off her lap and darted away, disappearing into the bushes as swiftly as he had arrived.

Inez watched him go, a smile on her face as she returned to her book, the memory of their brief encounter a small, unexpected joy in her morning.

22

Not Like Them

Later that day, Inez wandered the halls, aimlessly at first, until she found herself in the training room. She paused in the doorway, observing Kimmie and a masked woman engaged in what looked like a sparring session. Their movements were sharp, practised, but graceful, the rhythm of combat. Just as she considered leaving, both women stopped, turning their attention to her. Before she could process it, Kimmie was suddenly beside her.

"You can come in. It's an open room," Kimmie said with a welcoming smile.

Inez startled, stepping back instinctively. One moment, Kimmie had been on the mat, the next, she was right beside her, as if reality itself had skipped a beat.

"Are you okay?" Kimmie asked, tilting her head.

"How did you do that?" Inez blurted out, still processing the impossible speed.

"Oh, have you not seen the book in the main hall?" Kimmie chuckled. "It's got everyone's name, powers and a photo. It's cool."

"No, I'd better get to that," Inez responded, still slightly dazed.

With that, she left the hall, allowing Kimmie and the masked woman to resume their training. As she strolled down the corridor, passing the dorms, she made her way to the main lobby, intent on finding the mysterious book

Kimmie had mentioned. Upon arrival, she took the time to admire the grandeur of the space, modern yet steeped in history. The lobby was an impressive balance between sleek innovation and old-world charm.

"May I help you?"

The voice startled her, and she turned to see Lamia sitting behind the desk, casually flipping through a document.

"Ohh, hi, Lamia," Inez greeted, relaxing at the sight of a familiar face.

"Hi! Long time no see." Lamia laughed, pushing a stray strand of hair behind her ear.

"Kimmie mentioned a book—"

"The one with everyone's photos?" she finished.

"Yes," Inez confirmed.

"I'll drop it in your room after dinner," Lamia assured her, smiling. "Are you free in the morning?"

"I have AM listed as free," Inez replied.

"Perfect. If you drop the book back, we can update it with your details," Lamia explained.

"Sounds good! See you later," Inez said before heading back down the hallway.

After grabbing dinner, she retreated to her room, eating alone as she lost herself in thought. Today had felt unusually long, stretched by the absence of Zaire. She hadn't expected to miss him so quickly, and this gnawed at her. She glanced at the time, an hour remained until the lights-out bell. That was enough for a run around the building.

By the time she returned, a book leaned against her door with a neatly folded note attached.

See you in the morning., Lamia

Inez exhaled, lifting the book in her hands.

That night, sleep eluded Inez as she flicked through the pages of the book, absorbing the details of those around her. Each profile revealed a piece of the puzzle, an intricate web of abilities and identities that shaped the world she had found herself in.

Nadia was gifted with speed and flexibility, traits that explained her effortless movement in combat. Hunter possessed impenetrable skin and remarkable strength, making him a formidable force. Zaire was an elemental, which clicked immediately; his command over the elements had been demonstrated in their training session. And then Kimmie, her ability to control portals suddenly made sense. That was how she had appeared beside Inez in the blink of an eye.

But it was Lamia's entry that made her pause. A shape-shifting siren. The words alone sent a ripple of surprise through Inez. She skimmed further, searching for the identity of the masked woman who had been sparring with Kimmie, but there was nothing. No entry, no name.

That mystery would have to wait.

As morning arrived, Inez made her way to the main lobby, the book tucked under her arm. Lamia greeted her with a soft smile as she accepted it.

"Thank you," Inez said.

"Did it help?" Lamia asked, but there was a flicker of something, an emotion beneath the question.

"Yes, I feel like I can start to learn some names now," Inez admitted. "Is everyone in that book?" The thought had stayed with her all night.

"Yes, as far as I know," Lamia replied, "except you."

Inez nodded, absorbing the information before glancing at the time. "Okay, thank you. I better run, have a training session." She turned but hesitated, stepping back towards Lamia.

"Your power seems cool," Inez said with sincerity. "I would love to see it sometime."

Lamia's smile was small but genuine, though there was an edge to it. "Thank you. No one has ever said that after reading that book. Their opinion usually changes."

"I'm not like everyone else," Inez said simply before walking away.

Lamia watched her go before muttering under her breath, "No, you are not."

23

The Untold Part

Inez stepped into the training hall, only to find it eerily empty. The stillness pressed against her, the only movement coming from Qita, who lounged lazily on a mat near the far side of the room.

"Hello?" she called out, her voice echoing against the walls.

No answer. She glanced around, then walked over to Qita, kneeling beside him and running her fingers through his fur. "Hi, handsome," she murmured with a smile.

Before she could react, a sudden force knocked her off her feet, sending her straight onto her back. A gasp escaped her lips as she hit the floor, pain radiating across her spine. She groaned, sitting up quickly and scanning her surroundings, but there was no one in sight.

Qita remained on the mat, calmly watching her as if nothing had happened.

"Who's there?" Inez shouted, tension creeping into her voice.

A voice echoed from the shadows, cool and unwavering. "Your guard should always be up."

Inez turned her head sharply, searching for the source of the voice.

"Close your eyes and sense me," the voice instructed.

"How?" Inez asked, frustration building.

"What have they been teaching you?" The voice scoffed before the woman finally stepped into the light. It was the same woman Kimmie had been sparring with the day before.

Qita wasted no time, bounding towards her and climbing effortlessly onto her shoulder.

"Who are you?" Inez demanded.

The woman didn't answer immediately. Instead, she fixed Inez with a calculating gaze before replying, "I asked you a question first."

Inez hesitated but then answered, "I have a session with Zaire, he's been helping me unlock my powers."

"So, no combat training?" The woman's tone was laced with disappointment.

Inez shook her head.

The woman sighed. "I'm Megyn."

Inez turned towards the mat, readying herself, but Megyn's voice cut through.

"No. We are going to the ring," she commanded, her tone firm.

Inez frowned. "Why? I thought I was developing my power."

"You expect to wield powers without basic combat training?" Megyn raised an eyebrow. "Can you even punch?"

"Yes, I can," Inez snapped back.

"You won't always have your powers," Megyn stated coolly. "You need to be able to fight."

Inez exhaled loudly. "Fine."

Megyn smirked. "And don't expect me to go easy on you like your darling Zaire."

Inez blinked, caught off guard. "What does that mean?"

"Oh, I see how you two look at each other," Megyn teased, crossing her arms.

"How? I've never seen you around," Inez countered, narrowing her eyes.

Megyn let out a quiet chuckle. "I have more than just one pair of eyes here."

Inez swallowed but stood her ground.

"Now get in the ring," Megyn ordered. "It's time you learned how to fight."

Inez stepped into the ring, an unsettling weakness washing over her almost immediately. She turned to Megyn, her brow furrowed.

"That's normal," Megyn said.

"So, why weren't you in the book?" Inez asked, curiosity overriding her discomfort.

"I transferred here from another camp," Megyn replied.

"Camp?" Inez echoed.

Megyn raised an eyebrow, her sarcasm cutting through the air. "Wow, do you not know anything about this place?"

Before Inez could respond, Megyn smirked. "Since you have hundreds of questions, let's make it interesting. Every time you successfully dodge, you get to ask one."

"Dodge what?" Inez began, but the words barely left her mouth before she was swept off her feet. Megyn had dropped to the floor, her leg spinning in a 180-degree arc that knocked Inez flat on her back.

Groaning, Inez sat up, glaring at Megyn, who extended a hand to help her up.

"You could have warned me," Inez snapped.

"We're in a ring. This is your warning," Megyn shot back.

They stood still for a moment, the tension thick in the air. Inez braced herself, expecting another attack, but Megyn remained motionless, her hands clasped behind her back and her eyes closed.

Taking the opportunity, Inez lunged forwards, aiming a punch at Megyn's face. Without opening her eyes, Megyn tilted her head to the right, effortlessly dodging the blow.

Inez froze, stunned. She tried again with her other hand, but Megyn leaned back, avoiding the strike with the same ease. Frustrated, Inez attempted a kick, only for Megyn to flip backwards onto one hand, landing gracefully in her original position.

"How are you doing this? I thought the ring removed powers," Inez asked.

"These aren't my powers," Megyn replied coolly. "I trained with the finest warriors known to man before being sent here."

"Do you have powers?" Inez pressed.

"Yes," Megyn admitted, though she offered no further details.

"How did you all get them?" Inez asked, her curiosity growing.

Megyn's expression shifted to one of shock. "Did Zaire not tell you?"

"No," Inez admitted. "We started talking about where he grew up, but then he had to leave."

Megyn scoffed. "You look so in love with him, yet you know nothing about him or this place. Maybe you should be asking him these questions, he's clearly not telling you everything."

"He probably didn't have time," Inez said defensively. "He had a mission."

"Grow up," Megyn retorted. "He's either scared of you or the power you possess."

With that, Megyn turned on her heel. "Well, the session's over. Maybe see you around, thoughhopefully not."

Qita leapt from the mat, scampering after Megyn and climbing onto her shoulder as they disappeared from view.

Inez stepped out of the ring, her legs shaking beneath her as she sank onto the bench at the edge of the training hall. She leaned forwards, burying her face in her hands, her mind swirling with emotions she couldn't quite untangle. The weight of Megyn's words and the revelations about Zaire troubled her, leaving her unsure of what to believe or how to proceed.

Out of nowhere, a soft, glowing box shimmered into existence beside her. Kimmie emerged from it with her trademark energy, her presence instantly lightening the room.

"That was intense. Are you okay?" Kimmie asked, her voice gentle but curious.

Inez peeked up from her hands, managing a small nod. "Yes… I just don't know what to think about everything."

Kimmie crouched beside her, nudging her lightly on the shoulder, her glasses sliding down her nose in the process. "Have dinner with me later, okay? You can ask me anything," she offered with a grin.

Inez felt warmth seep into her chest at Kimmie's simple act of kindness. She managed a smile, nodding.

"Okay."

Satisfied, Kimmie pushed her glasses back up with a quick motion, stood up and gave Inez an exaggerated skip as she vanished through a portal to her room, leaving a faint trace of glowing light behind her. Inez watched her go, her mind slowly quieting, as Kimmie's cheerful energy lingered. Perhaps dinner would bring the answers she desperately needed.

24

Access Denied

Inez spent the rest of the day alone in her room, finding solace in her painting. She was finally in the mood to create. But as her brush moved across the canvas, her memories began to surface, unbidden and relentless. Slowly, the image of the cell she had been imprisoned in began to take shape. Her strokes became more precise, her emotions spilling into the painting until it stood before her as a haunting masterpiece, a vivid and painful reminder of her past. She stared at it for a long while, conflicted, before finally stepping away.

Seeking comfort, she ran herself a warm bath. The heat eased the tension in her muscles and helped her unwind after the long, emotionally draining day.

When dinnertime came, Inez headed to the dining hall. She glanced around for Kimmie but couldn't see her. Shrugging it off, she made her way to the counter, grabbed a tray of food and sat alone at an empty table. Minutes later, Kimmie burst through the doors, slightly out of breath. She hurried to grab her food and plopped down across from Inez, her cheeks flushed.

"Hi, sorry I'm late. I had an issue with a flame," Kimmie said, panting as she fanned herself with a hand.

"No problem. The fire out?" Inez asked, a small smile playing on her lips.

"Yes, just a candle mishap," Kimmie replied, brushing it off with an embarrassed laugh.

Inez glanced at Kimmie's plate, curiosity sparking. "I thought you were on a special meat diet?" she asked.

"Oh, well, yes... I just didn't feel like it tonight," Kimmie stammered, looking away briefly.

Before Inez could press further, Megyn entered the hall. She grabbed some food, her gaze sweeping the room.

When her eyes landed on Inez, she immediately turned on her heel and left without a word.

"Ignore her. She's like that," Kimmie said with a wave of her hand.

"How well do you know her?" Inez asked, watching the doors Megyn had disappeared through.

"Probably better than anyone else here. She's been around for a few years now. She arrived with that cat from another camp, and I train with her most of the time," Kimmie explained, shrugging. "She doesn't talk much, though, just scoffs and makes sarcastic remarks."

"Qita," Inez said suddenly.

"What?" Kimmie asked, blinking in confusion.

"The cat. His name is Qita," Inez clarified.

"How do you know that?" Kimmie asked, her brows furrowed in surprise.

"I stroked him and saw his collar," Inez said casually.

"What?" Kimmie's voice rose in disbelief. "She let you near her cat? No one gets close to him! She'd never allow it!"

"Yeah, like she can control a cat," Inez said, her voice dripping with sarcasm.

"That's exactly what she does," Kimmie shot back.

"What?" Inez stared at her, puzzled.

"As well as being a badass ninja warrior, she's an animal manipulator," Kimmie explained.

Inez tilted her head, her expression sceptical.

"Right, this is all new to you," Kimmie realised, leaning in as she elaborated. "She can see through the eyes of any animal she chooses. And if she's bonded strongly enough with one, she can fully control it. That's why she was allowed to bring the cat."

"Qita," Inez corrected her again.

"Right, Qita. Sorry," Kimmie said quickly, nodding.

The bell rang, signalling the lights-out warning, cutting their conversation short. They agreed to meet in the library after breakfast for a study session before Kimmie got up and made her way to her room with a cheerful wave. Inez followed suit, walking to her own room.

The following morning, after a quick breakfast, Inez entered the library. Her mind was still occupied by thoughts of Megyn, Qita and the mysterious powers that surrounded her. Everything about this world was both fascinating and daunting, and she couldn't help but feel like she was only beginning to scratch the surface.

The grand hall stretched before Inez, its sheer scale leaving her breathless. Towering shelves reached high into the domed ceiling, crammed with books on every imaginable topic. She took in the sight, marvelling at the organised chaos that catered to every interest. Yet, her gaze paused on the restricted section, cordoned off and mysterious, its books housed behind iron gates.

Inez spotted Kimmie sitting at a table amidst the sprawling aisles. She approached her, whispering, "Hi."

"Why are you whispering?" Kimmie asked, blinking at her curiously.

"It's what you do in libraries," Inez responded, slightly baffled by the question.

"How would I know?" Kimmie said casually, leaning back in her chair.

Inez furrowed her brow. "You've never been in a library before?"

Kimmie gave a bittersweet smile. "I've been here my whole life, we all have. We're orphans."

Inez's face fell instantly, the revelation sinking in. Megyn had been right, Zaire, Nadia and Hunter had kept this from her. The realisation stung. Why wouldn't they just tell her? Were they truly her friends?

"You okay?" Kimmie asked, snapping Inez out of her thoughts.

"Yes… I just had no idea," Inez replied softly, her sadness evident.

"Ohh, I thought Zaire or Nadia would've told you. You spend so much time with them," Kimmie said, shrugging.

Inez forced a smile. "I would've thought so too. Anyway, what books are you looking for?"

"Well, I'm studying fantasy creatures, and this next section is all about dragons, anything about them, their habitats, diet, you name it," Kimmie explained excitedly.

They spent hours combing through the rows, but their search turned up empty. Eventually, Inez excused herself for her cleaning duty, leaving Kimmie behind to continue digging.

Just as Inez disappeared, Megyn's voice materialised from the shadows. "It's in the restricted section," she said simply.

Kimmie turned, surprised but grateful. "Thank you. How's Qita?" she asked politely.

"He's fine," Megyn replied, her tone guarded. "Just learning who I can trust."

"Am I one of them?" Kimmie asked cautiously.

"I wouldn't have got this book for you otherwise," Megyn said, handing over a battered book about dragon lore, its broken chain dangling ominously from its binding.

"So, why do you need this?" Megyn asked, suspicious.

"I don't need it," Kimmie said quickly. "I'm just fascinated. And, honestly, there isn't much else to do here, the games are getting a bit boring."

Megyn rolled her eyes at the response.

"Maybe you should get a PC too and join in sometime," Kimmie teased, trying to lighten the mood.

Megyn didn't reply, her expression stoic as she walked away. From the corner of the room, Qita emerged, leaping gracefully onto Megyn's shoulder, where he settled as they exited the hall together.

Kimmie smiled to herself, clutching the book tightly before diving into its secrets. She was determined to uncover every piece of lore about dragons, those rare creatures that fuelled her curiosity and sparked her imagination.

25

The Secret Shared

A few days later, Inez and Kimmie sat in the dining hall, their laughter filling the air as they recounted stories from their recent training sessions. The atmosphere was light-hearted, but it was quickly disrupted by the sound of the hall doors swinging open with force. Nadia strode in, her presence commanding attention.

She walked directly over to Inez, grabbing her arm and pulling her up from the chair before enveloping her in a tight hug. "Made some new friends, I see," Nadia said as she shot a glare at Kimmie.

"Yes, actually, we were—"

"We are back now, so you can go," Nadia said dismissively, waving Kimmie off like an unwanted guest.

Kimmie hesitated but offered Inez a small smile. "I guess I'll see you around," she said before leaving the hall.

"You're welcome," Nadia said smugly, letting out a laugh.

"Welcome? For what? Your rudeness?" Inez snapped, her anger bubbling to the surface.

Nadia raised an eyebrow. "Don't tell me, we leave for two weeks, and you make friends with the freaks?"

Inez stood abruptly, her chair scraping against the floor. "Aren't we all freaks in here? At least those 'freaks' tell me the truth," she retorted.

"What is going on? Why are you acting like this?" Nadia asked.

"Me? Why were you so rude?" Inez countered, glaring at her.

Nadia sighed. "I'm sorry for that. We just don't normally mingle here."

"And whose choice is that?" Inez shot back, and she turned to leave.

As she reached the doors, Nadia called after her, "Zaire is waiting for you."

Inez slammed the doors shut behind her, her emotions swirling in a storm of frustration and hurt. The sound echoed through the hall, ending the chatter of others as Nadia turned her attention to a nearby table. "What are you looking at?" she barked at the group seated there.

Meanwhile, Inez wandered the halls, torn between seeing Zaire or retreating to the solitude of her room. After some hesitation, she decided to head to her room, but just as she reached for the door handle, she paused, the sensation unmistakable, it was him.

Unable to resist, she turned and made her way outside, towards their familiar spot. The sight of him brought a momentary calm to her racing thoughts. Zaire sat at the edge of the dock, his jeans rolled up, feet dipping into the water below.

Inez stepped onto the grass, slipping off her shoes as she made her way to him. The soft fabric of her dress brushed against her legs as she walked down the dock. Without a word, she lifted her dress slightly and sat beside him, their silence speaking louder than any words could. The water rippled gently, reflecting the emotions neither of them dared to express out loud.

Their feet danced in the water, tracing aimless circles, the surprising warmth emanating from Zaire's subtle control over the elements. Inez tilted her head back, her gaze fixed on the infinite expanse of the cloudless night sky, the stars glittering like scattered diamonds.

She felt his eyes on her and glanced towards him. Her cheeks flushed instantly, and she quickly looked away, heart racing. Zaire noticed the goosebumps on her arms and reached out instinctively, his fingers brushing her skin as if to check if she was cold. Inez's eyes followed his hand, then lifted to meet his again. His hand slowly dropped to hers, their fingers intertwining.

After a pause, Zaire shifted uncomfortably, breaking the tension as he leaned away from her and cleared his throat. "So, how have you been?" he asked casually but with genuine concern.

"I've been well. I made some new friends," Inez replied.

"Well, I'm glad you were looked after," Zaire said, though his eyes fell to his lap, betraying a flicker of worry. He wondered if her new friend was someone more significant, a possibility that unnerved him.

Inez noticed the expression on his face and decided to shift the focus. "So, how well do you know Kimmie?" she asked lightly.

Zaire smiled faintly. "Yeah, I've known her for quite a while, but we're not close."

"Quite a while?" Inez tilted her head, giving him a curious look.

"Yeah," he added simply, shrugging.

She leaned in slightly, her playful tone returning. "Okay, so how was the mission? Are you allowed to tell me, or is it top secret?"

Zaire chuckled, appreciating her humour as he began recounting the story.

When Zaire, Nadia and Hunter had set out on their mission, the journey had been gruelling. Hours on the road left them fatigued, but they arrived at their destination, a modest hotel, where everything had been prepared for them. The room served as their base, and it was there that Zaire explained the mission details to Nadia and Hunter, relaying the briefing he'd received first-hand from the boss.

Another camp had reported a theft, a valuable artefact had been taken, one of great significance. The Ruby Quartz Crystal. Their task was to retrieve it. The mission required precision and patience; their first week was spent staking out the location where the artefact was rumoured to be hidden. They studied every detail, the building's layout, the rotations and habits of the guards, and every nuance of the floor plan provided in the briefing.

After their meticulous study, they had a few days to craft their plan, each step carefully designed before the final execution. Zaire's voice softened as he shared these details.

As his story unfolded, Inez listened intently, her curiosity and admiration for him growing with each word. The warmth of the water and the quiet of the night wrapped around them, a comforting cocoon as they shared this moment.

It was the night before their mission, the room was filled with the sounds of utensils clinking and casual conversation as Zaire, Nadia, and Hunter sat down to dinner. The air felt deceptively light for the gravity of the task ahead.

"How long are you going to avoid telling her the truth? I keep having to dodge her questions," Nadia said, turning her sharp gaze on Zaire.

He sighed heavily, pushing his food around on his plate. "I will. I just… don't know how. It's going to be a lot for her to process, and honestly, I don't trust her enough yet to tell her everything. Only the three of us even have an inkling of what's really going on," Zaire admitted, his voice low and troubled.

"Well, true," Nadia conceded, "but at least we can all sense something's off about this place."

She studied Zaire closely as he picked up his chopsticks, eating a mouthful of noodles in silence. Her lips curled into a sly smile as a thought came to her. "You like her, don't you?" she asked, leaning back in her chair with a knowing look.

Zaire froze for the briefest moment, then sighed again. "Yes… but the boss wanted her for a reason. If he didn't, he would've sold her by now. I just can't trust her," he said, a trace of sadness in his voice.

"If it's any comfort, I don't think she knows anything," Hunter interjected. "She's terrified half the time, and honestly, we barely even know what really happened to her."

"She was married," Zaire said suddenly, reaching into his pocket and pulling out a pair of rings. They gleamed under the faint lighting.

Nadia's eyes widened as she sat up straighter. "How do you have those? How do you even know that?" she demanded.

"She told me where she used to live," Zaire explained. "I got her furniture after clearing it with the boss. I found the rings there. I didn't know if she'd want them back, so I kept them."

"Wait," Hunter cut in, frowning. "Why would the boss let you leave for something personal like that?"

Zaire shook his head. "He told me to do anything I could to make her comfortable. He cares about her for some reason, but I can't figure out why."

Nadia and Hunter exchanged a brief, puzzled glance, neither of them having an answer for Zaire.

Finally, Nadia broke the silence. "We should get some sleep. Tomorrow's going to be a long day," she said, standing up and beginning to tidy the room. The others followed suit, the tension lingering in the air as they prepared themselves for the mission ahead. The unspoken questions weighed heavily, but none of them dared voice them as they turned in for the night.

26

Sunrise Glimpse

The morning sun barely kissed the horizon, painting the sky with hues of amber and rose, as the team geared up for what could be the most critical day of their mission. The objective was clear: retrieve the artefact and return it to their enigmatic leader, Raphael. Failure was not an option.

Arriving at the heavily guarded site, the team hoped to execute their plan without the need for their powers. The air buzzed with tension as they approached the entrance, only to be met with an unforeseen challenge, the shift change had come earlier than anticipated. Panic rippled through their ranks as they realised the timing was off. The door was closing, and they wouldn't make it. Thinking quickly, Zaire, the group's elemental prodigy, summoned a gust of wind to hold the door open. Nadia dashed forwards with her signature agility, catching the door just in time. "So much for no powers," Hunter quipped, his grin widening. But Zaire silenced him with a quick gesture, his expression stern.

Once inside, the trio moved with cautious precision, navigating a labyrinth of stark hallways. The air grew heavier as they descended a flight of stairs, each step echoing ominously. Their path ended at a high-tech handprint scanner guarding the entrance to the artefact chamber. Zaire stepped forwards, exhaling warm air onto the frosty device. The subtle shift in temperature tricked the scanner into granting them access.

Hunter stayed behind as the lookout, his sharp eyes scanning for any movement, while Nadia slipped into the room. The chamber was a symphony of danger, red laser beams criss-crossing the air like a living web. At its heart rested a glass case containing their prize: a glowing red gem that seemed to hum with otherworldly energy. Nadia moved with the grace of a gymnast, twisting and flipping through the lasers, her every movement calculated. Reaching the wall, she flipped a switch, disabling the lasers.

Zaire swapped places with Hunter, his body practically impervious to the heat radiating from the softened glass. He reached in and grasped the gem, its warmth pulsating against his skin. The operation was flawless, until they encountered a guard on their way out. "Hey, what are you doing?" The guard's voice cut through the silence like a knife.

Without missing a beat, Zaire replied, "We were instructed to relocate the artefact due to a malfunctioning scanner." The guard, seemingly convinced, nodded and walked away.

Their return to the hotel was unceremonious but filled with a quiet relief. Back at Sunstone Manor, Zaire wasted no time in delivering the artefact to Raphael. The room was dimly lit, with shadows dancing on the walls. Raphael stood by the window, his posture regal yet relaxed. "Enter," came his commanding voice. Zaire placed the gem on the desk and stood at attention.

Raphael turned, his face illuminated by the glow of the gem. "You've done well, Zaire," he said. Zaire nodded, his gaze drifting to the window where he spotted Inez, her figure framed by the morning light. She was reading, her expression serene. His heart ached with a sudden longing he hadn't expected.

"You are my most trusted follower," Raphael continued. "You may call me Raphael, not sir." Zaire bowed slightly, murmuring his thanks before retreating to his quarters. The weight of the mission lifted, he allowed himself a rare moment of peace, showering and sinking into a deep, dreamless sleep before the evening meal.

27

The Life I Lost

The moonlight shimmered on the lake's surface, casting a silver glow on the pair who sat side by side with their feet dangling into the cool water. The air was still, the calm contrary to the storm brewing in their hearts. Inez spoke, her voice steady yet filled with emotion. "So, the mission was successful then?"

"Yes, I would say so," Zaire replied, his tone reserved. He fidgeted with two rings he had kept hidden in his pocket, turning them over in his hand as he wrestled with his thoughts. Would this moment bring them closer, or drive them further apart? Before he could decide, Inez turned to him, her eyes piercing his soul.

"Why do you still lie to me?" Her voice cracked, revealing the sorrow that had been festering beneath the surface.

Confused, Zaire furrowed his brow. "What do you mean? The mission *was* successful," he responded, his defences rising instinctively.

"I don't mean the mission," she snapped. "I know you've been here your whole life. I know you're all orphans. Why didn't you tell me?"

Her words hit him like a wave, and he struggled to find footing. "That's not lying," he said, his voice softening. "It's just… not telling you everything." He exhaled deeply, guilt pressing on his chest.

Inez huffed, her frustration evident. "I'm an orphan too, if that helps," she said bitterly.

Zaire's eyes widened in surprise. "You are?"

She nodded, her expression a mix of resignation and pain. The revelation hung between them, begging to be unravelled. Why did only orphans have powers? Was this by chance, or was there something sinister rooted in the foundations of this place? The question sat heavy in the air.

"I'm sorry," Zaire said, breaking the tension. "I should have told you. When you asked about my life… This place… it's all I've ever known."

"I'm sorry too," Inez interrupted, her tone cutting through his apology like a blade.

"When I saw your life before and how beautiful it was, I panicked." Zaire froze.

"Saw my life before?"

"Yes, I'm the one who retrieved your belongings," he confessed. "I saw your home, it was wonderful."

His words ignited a fire in her eyes, anger bubbling to the surface. "So you can know everything about me, but I can't know anything about you?" She stood abruptly, her movements jerky as she fought to contain her rage. "How much do you know?"

"I… I saw the crib," Zaire admitted hesitantly. A single tear escaped her eye, tracing a glistening path down her cheek. Zaire reached out instinctively to wipe it away, but she slapped his hand, her fury erupting.

"No, you can't play the hero," she said, her words sharp as glass. She turned to leave, her steps heavy with anger and sorrow.

"Inez, stop!" Zaire called after her.

She stopped and turned, her expression unreadable. "What?"

"I have something for you," he said, stepping closer. He placed the rings in her hand and stepped back, watching as realisation dawned on her face.

Rage consumed her as she stared at the objects. "I left them for a reason," she spat. "That part of my life is gone. My husband is dead. My baby is dead. That isn't my life any more." Without hesitation, she flung the rings into the lake, the splash echoing like a final goodbye. Her hand struck Zaire's face, the sting physical and emotional.

"I wish I had never met you," she said, her voice trembling. "How could I start to fall for someone like you?" With those words, she turned and ran, leaving Zaire standing alone, his heart fractured.

"Inez," he called, his voice breaking. But she was already gone, swallowed by the darkness.

28

Return of the Siren

The night wrapped the dock in a gentle stillness, stars shimmering like distant lanterns in the inky sky. Zaire leaned back, his hands braced on the edge of the wooden planks, and let his eyes drift upwards. The stars provided a fleeting moment of peace. But the quiet was broken by a familiar voice, dripping with amusement and reproach.

"You always brought me here," it said like a ripple across the water. "This is your little hook-up spot, isn't it?"

Zaire jolted upright, his head swivelling towards the lake. His eyes adjusted to the dim light as he spotted the unmistakable glow of Lamia's crimson hair and fiery eyes. They seemed to smoulder against the moonlit backdrop, her silhouette in the darkness like a spectre from his past. She swam languidly towards the dock, her siren tail shimmering beneath the surface, catching the moonlight like liquid fire.

"How long have you been here?" Zaire asked, his voice tense, caught off guard.

Lamia rested her elbows on the dock, her presence both magnetic and haunting. "Long enough," she replied with a coy smile. Her words twisted the knife she so expertly wielded. "Long enough to see you mess things up with her. She's a nice girl, Zaire. She deserves better than you."

Zaire's lips tightened, a flicker of irritation flashing in his eyes. "Or maybe," he countered, his tone biting, "you just don't want anyone else to have me?"

Lamia's smile faltered, her expression hardening. The pain she'd carried for so long surfaced fleetingly before she masked it again. "How could you say that?" she said, her voice shaking with restrained emotion. "You know I'd want you to be happy… even if it's not with me."

Her words settled over them like a heavy fog. Their past hung between them, a bittersweet ghost of what once was. Lamia had been the first person Zaire could truly open up to, the one he trusted with his vulnerabilities. Together, they had built a bond forged through countless shared moments, her swimming under starlit skies as he sat on the dock, the two of them laughing, dreaming and learning to navigate their extraordinary powers. They had been inseparable, and for a time, it had felt like nothing could tear them apart.

But then Lamia had left. A secret mission had called her away for months, and just before she departed, she had ended their relationship. She hadn't explained why, and Zaire hadn't asked. The ache of her absence had been unbearable, a hollow void that left him clinging to Hunter and Nadia for solace. And now, just as he was finding himself drawn to Inez in a way that felt real and unshakable, Lamia had returned, unspoken truths glimmering in her eyes.

"I've got to go," Zaire said abruptly, rising to his feet. He couldn't stay here, couldn't let the past ensnare him when the future felt so fragile.

"Do you truly love her?" Lamia's voice stopped him in his tracks. It was a question, but it carried something more, a plea for honesty.

Zaire turned to face her, his expression softening. "I do," he said, a small smile tugging at the corners of his mouth. The certainty in his voice surprised even him.

Lamia's gaze stopped on him, her own smile tinged with sadness. "Then go get her," she said simply, her tone gentle yet resolute.

As Zaire turned and walked away, Lamia watched him go, her heart breaking. Once he disappeared from view, she sank back into the water, her tears mingling with the lake. She had never wanted to end things, but circumstances beyond her control had forced her hand. She had hoped

Zaire would find happiness in her absence, but seeing him move on was more painful than she had imagined. As her sobs were muffled by the water, she whispered to herself, "You'll always be my true love."

29

The Rings and the Loss

Zaire hesitated before knocking on Inez's door, his hand brushing lightly against the wood. He waited, the seconds dragging into an eternity. Silence. Her lack of response gnawed at his nerves. Was she simply ignoring him, or had she left? The uncertainty stirred a sinking feeling in his chest.

Determined to find her, Zaire stepped away and headed towards the green. It was her regular reading spot, a tranquil corner surrounded by nature's embrace. But as he approached, the space greeted him only with emptiness, the book she often held missing from its usual perch. Panic swelled within him. Where else could she be? His legs carried him quickly to the training room, his instincts telling him that perhaps she was there, channelling her anger into movement. Yet, as he entered, the room mirrored the emptiness of the green.

Each option slipped from his grasp, leaving him with no other ideas. Zaire found himself standing outside Nadia's door. He knocked, his urgency reflected in the force of the sound.

The door opened, and Nadia's concerned eyes met his. "What's wrong?" she asked, her voice gentle but firm.

"I messed up," Zaire confessed. "I told her everything… and I gave her the rings. She was so angry, furious, and now I can't find her. I have no idea where she's gone." His words poured out in fear.

Nadia stepped forwards, pulling him into a comforting hug. "Just give her some time," she said soothingly. "She's hurt, but we'll see her at breakfast tomorrow. You can talk to her then."

Zaire clung to Nadia as though she were an anchor, steadying him in the storm of his guilt and despair. "She was pregnant, Nadia. The baby and her husband both died. How could I have been so blind? What have I done?"

Nadia's arms tightened around him briefly before pulling away, her expression unwavering. "It will be okay, Zaire. I know this feels impossible right now, but she'll need time to process everything. You need to trust that she'll come around."

Her confidence seemed unshakable, and while Zaire appreciated the comfort, doubt still lingered in his heart. "Thank you," he murmured softly. "I'll… I'll see you in the morning, I guess."

Turning away, Zaire walked down the hall. His steps slowed as he passed Inez's door again, and he nearly raised his hand to knock once more. But Nadia's advice echoed in his mind, give her time. With a heavy sigh, he moved past, heading towards his own room.

Once inside, the events of the night dawned on him. The turmoil in his heart made sleep seem unattainable, but exhaustion quickly overtook him. As his head hit the pillow, his thoughts churned with memories of Inez, each moment between them playing out like fragments of a dream. His regret loomed large, but somewhere deep within, hope flickered. Tomorrow would bring another chance.

30

Wing on Her Shoulder

After Zaire broke the news to Inez, her emotions spiralled into confusion and pain, leaving her with only one instinct: to run. She ran aimlessly, her heart racing and her thoughts a chaotic whirlwind, until suddenly, she felt herself phasing through the walls of the manor, her powers activating without control. She didn't stop until she found herself standing inside Kimmie's room, trembling and teary-eyed.

"I'm so sorry to intrude, but I don't know what to do," Inez blurted out, her voice cracking as tears began to stream down her face. Her sudden appearance startled Kimmie, who stared at her in both shock and horror.

"Erm… Hi?" Kimmie said cautiously, unsure of how to react. Inez's gaze fell on the creature curled up on Kimmie's lap, its small form radiating an unusual energy.

"What… is that?" Inez asked as her tear-streaked face turned to curiosity.

"This is Kek," Kimmie replied awkwardly, her smile tight as she petted the creature protectively.

Recognition flashed across Inez's face. "That's what I saw flying in the green earlier! I thought it was a bird!" she exclaimed.

Kimmie shook her head, her expression growing serious. "No, he's a dragon," she said in a hushed tone. "No one knows about him, and I need to keep it that way. If they find out, they'll take him away to experiment on him. Please, don't say anything."

Inez nodded quickly, her face softening. "I won't say a word, I promise. Oh, that explains the meat I saw you sneaking out of the dining hall and your obsession with those dragon books," she added with a small smile.

Encouraged by Inez's calm reaction, Kimmie smiled back. "Do you want to pet him?" she asked.

Inez hesitated, her hand hovering uncertainly. "Can I?" she asked timidly.

Kimmie gave Kek a gentle nudge, rousing the dragon from his slumber. The little creature blinked a few times before padding across the bed towards Inez. When he reached her, he rubbed his scaled head against her outstretched hand, releasing a gentle purr that sounded like tiny bells chiming. Inez's heart melted at the sound, her earlier pain temporarily forgotten.

"How did you get him?" Inez asked.

Kimmie grew distant as she recalled the surreal event. "One night, I was asleep and had this bizarre, vivid dream about another world. It felt so real. When I woke up, I saw a portal closing right in the middle of my room. I think I must have opened it while dreaming. A few moments later, I noticed Kek climbing up onto my bed, and he's been with me ever since. I've been trying to figure out how to send him back home for months, but I don't even know where the portal led."

As Kimmie stroked Kek, the dragon stood at the edge of the bed, his sleek tail twitching. He stretched his wings, their translucent scales catching the room's light like fragments of a rainbow. With a sudden burst of energy, Kek took flight, circling the room with elegant ease. He landed gracefully on a shelf Kimmie had emptied for him, where his bowl of meat slices sat. Grabbing a piece of steak with his small teeth, Kek tossed it into the air and caught it effortlessly, his jaw snapping shut.

Inez chuckled, watching the dragon's antics. For the first time since her confrontation with Zaire, she felt a small sense of relief, an escape from the heaviness in her chest. Kek's presence, along with Kimmie's warmth, made her feel a little less alone.

"I love your room," Inez said as she perched on the edge of Kimmie's bed, her eyes scanning the eclectic space.

"Thank you," Kimmie replied with a grin. "I like pink, if you couldn't tell."

The room spoke volumes about her personality. The walls were a sleek grey, accented by a light black wire design that added a modern touch. Kimmie's bed was a luxurious grey velvet, topped with vibrant hot-pink bedding that popped against the muted tones. A black desk sat in the corner, housing a powerful gaming PC and an ergonomic chair. Above the desk, a pink neon dragon light glowed softly, casting a whimsical hue across the room. Gadgets, replicas and books filled every available space, each item a testament to Kimmie's unapologetic nerdiness.

As if on cue, Kek sneezed, sending a tiny ball of fire into the air. The flame fizzled out harmlessly, but the little dragon wasn't done showing off. He glided effortlessly to the light shade, hanging upside down as it swung gently under his weight. With a graceful leap, he landed in Kimmie's arms, nuzzling her affectionately before climbing onto her back and settling on her shoulder.

"I don't think he'd want to leave you," Inez observed.

Kimmie's smile faltered, replaced by a look of sadness. "Part of me doesn't want him to go," she admitted, stroking Kek's scales. "But leaving him here is unfair. If they find him, they'll hurt him. I can hide him for now, but not forever."

"How long have you had him?" Inez asked, her curiosity piqued.

"Four months," Kimmie replied wistfully.

The conversation shifted as Kimmie leaned forwards, her expression turning serious. "Oh, we got sidetracked. You came here for a reason, didn't you?"

Inez hesitated, her gaze dropping to her hands. "Yes, it's Zaire," she began, barely above a whisper. "He decorated my room... went to my home in the city."

"That's so sweet," Kimmie said, her eyes lighting up.

"Yes, but that was my old life," Inez countered, her voice growing heavier. "He saw Leo's crib and brought my husband's wedding ring to me."

Kimmie's eyes widened in shock. "You're married? And have a baby?"

"Not exactly," Inez said as tears welled up. "My husband was killed. They kidnapped me, and I lost the baby." Her words hung in the air, raw and painful. Unable to hold back, she began to cry.

Kimmie leaned forwards, wrapping her arms around Inez in a comforting hug. "I know he wanted to do something nice," Inez said through her sobs. "But it wasn't his place. It brings it all back, and it hurts like mad every time I think of them."

Her emotions shifted from sorrow to anger as she pulled away slightly. "He only told me when I confronted him about being here his whole life. Why wouldn't he just tell me?" she added, frustration creeping into her voice.

Kimmie leaned back, shrugging her shoulders. "And we had a moment," Inez continued bitterly. "I thought he was going to kiss me, but nope. He pulled away and decided to mention my dead baby. He's a jerk." Her eyes dropped to her hand again, her fingers tracing invisible patterns as she remembered Zaire playing with them on the dock.

"But you love that jerk, don't you?" Kimmie said, a smirk tugging at her lips.

"Yes," Inez admitted, her voice softening. "I think I do."

"Well, tell him it needs to be all honesty going forwards," Kimmie advised. "And then you'll be willing to try."

"You're right," Inez said, her resolve strengthening. "Thank you. You're an amazing friend."

Kimmie blushed at the compliment, her cheeks turning a light pink. "Thank you. You too. See you at breakfast?"

"Yes, definitely," Inez replied, standing to leave. She paused at the door, turning back to wink at Kek. "Also, your secret is safe with me."

Kek tilted his head at her, his curious gaze following her as she left the room.

31

The Smile That Stayed

Inez made her way to her room, her head swimming with emotions. As she walked down the dimly lit hall, she caught sight of Zaire heading in the opposite direction. Her heart skipped a beat, and for a fleeting moment, she considered running after him. But the previous day's events held her back. She needed rest, clarity and a fresh start. Tomorrow, she thought. Tomorrow, she would face him.

Once in her room, she undressed and stepped into the shower, letting the warm water wash away the tension clinging to her body. Afterwards, she curled up in bed with a book, hoping the familiar comfort of words would lull her into sleep. It worked, eventually.

The following morning, the manor buzzed with the usual energy of a new day. Everyone gathered in the dining hall for breakfast, the air filled with the clatter of plates and the hum of conversation. Inez sat with Kimmie, their bond strengthened by the secrets they now shared. As they ate, Inez discreetly wrapped some extra meat in a napkin and slid it across the table. "For Kek," she said with a wink. Kimmie grinned, her cheeks flushing as she tucked the napkin away.

Across the room, Megyn sat alone, her ever-watchful companion Qita perched on the chair beside her, scanning the hall with sharp eyes. Meanwhile, Nadia and Hunter shared a table, though Nadia barely touched her food. Her gaze kept drifting to Inez, guilt etched across her face. She hadn't been able to shake the events of the previous day, and it showed.

The atmosphere shifted when Zaire entered the hall. His presence was magnetic, drawing eyes without effort. Kimmie nudged Inez, tilting her head towards the door. "Go," she whispered.

"No," Inez replied, her voice steady. "I'll let him eat first."

But Zaire's focus was already locked on her. Every bite of his breakfast seemed mechanical, his attention divided as he stole glances in her direction. Inez felt his stare and decided it was time. She stood, her movement catching his eye. As she walked past him, he couldn't help but ask, "Where are you going?"

She turned slightly, a playful smile tugging at her lips. "Follow me and find out," she said, her tone light but inviting.

Zaire didn't hesitate. He followed her down the hall. She led him to the training room, its vast space empty and quiet. He stepped inside, looking around for her. "Can't find me, can you?" Inez's voice echoed.

"Where are you?" Zaire called out, spinning in place.

She stepped out of the shadows confidently. "I had some good training sessions while you were away," she said, a hint of pride in her voice.

"I can see that," Zaire replied warmly.

The playful energy between them shifted as Inez's expression grew serious. "We need to talk about yesterday," she said.

"I know we do."

"I know you were trying to do a nice thing, and I should have thanked you," Inez began, her words measured. "But that was my old life, Zaire. I've let it go."

"I overstepped," he admitted sincerely. "And I'm sorry."

"No, it was sweet," she said. "But I need to be straight with you. I do like you, but I hate that we're not honest with each other. I don't even know how you feel."

Zaire took a step closer, his eyes meeting hers. "I like you too," he said. "How about we go out on a date tomorrow?"

Inez raised an eyebrow, a teasing smile playing on her lips. "What, and walk around the green?"

"No," Zaire said, chuckling. "I'll take you out properly. I'll speak to the boss and get it approved."

"Will he do that?" Inez asked, sceptical.

"For me, maybe," Zaire said, though his tone betrayed a hint of uncertainty. "At least we can get to know each other properly."

"I'd like that," Inez said, her cheeks flushing.

"Good," Zaire said, a smile breaking across his face. "I'll let you know later if it's approved."

As he turned to leave, Inez called out, "Zaire."

He stopped and turned back to her, curiosity in his eyes. Before he could react, she flicked her wrist, sending him sprawling onto the floor.

"Karma," she said with a mischievous giggle, walking away as he lay there, stunned but smiling.

32

Barefoot by the Sea

Zaire stood in the main lobby, his eyes fixed on the grand staircase leading to Raphael's office. His thoughts churned as he prepared himself to make the request. After retrieving the artefact, surely Raphael would grant him this one favour. He took a deep breath, paced himself and then ascended the stairs, each step echoing in the quiet air.

Upon reaching the towering wooden doors of the office, he paused, inhaling deeply to steady himself. Knocking firmly, he waited.

"Enter," came the familiar voice from inside.

Zaire stepped forwards, closing the door behind him with quiet precision. As always, Raphael sat with his back to the room, his piercing gaze locked onto the landscape beyond the window. He rarely looked at the person speaking to him, his presence alone was enough to command respect.

"How can I help you, Zaire?" Raphael's voice was firm, unwavering.

"I was wondering," Zaire started, choosing his words carefully, "as we retrieved the artefact—"

Raphael cut him off with a swift wave of his hand. "Yes, you may go out and celebrate. You have my permission."

Zaire blinked, surprised at how easily Raphael had granted the request. "It's okay to leave?" he asked, wanting confirmation.

"Yes," Raphael replied, his tone final. "Now leave."

Zaire nodded, his posture straightening. "Thank you, sir—"

Raphael coughed pointedly.

Zaire quickly corrected himself. "Sorry. Thank you, Raphael."

With that, he left the office, closing the door behind him, his mind already drifting towards the evening ahead.

At dinner, Zaire shared the news with Inez, excitement flickering in his tone. Across the hall, Nadia and Hunter entered, choosing to sit at a different table. Inez glanced in their direction, her expression thoughtful.

"I need to speak to her," she said quietly.

"Go find her after dinner," Zaire encouraged, squeezing her hand with a smile. "I'll go for a run with Hunter."

Inez blushed slightly, glancing around the hall to see if anyone had noticed their closeness. But someone had, Lamia. Her stare lingered on them for a moment before she stood abruptly and left the dining hall, looking visibly shaken.

"She hasn't spoken to me in a few days," Inez murmured, watching Lamia disappear down the corridor. "I hope she's okay."

"Who?" Zaire asked, glancing around.

"Lamia," she replied.

Zaire exhaled, knowing honesty was part of their new arrangement. "Inez, we promised we'd be open with each other."

"Yes," Inez confirmed, her expression shifting to one of curiosity.

"Well…" Zaire hesitated. "Lamia and I were together for a few years until about eight months ago. She ended things before leaving for a long mission."

Inez pulled her hand away, absorbing the revelation. "Oh," was all she said, a mixture of emotions flickering in her eyes, surprise, discomfort and something else she wasn't ready to name.

Zaire saw Nadia and Hunter beginning to leave the hall. He turned back to Inez. "Go talk to her. We'll catch up tomorrow?"

"Yes, definitely," Inez said, nodding before standing.

Zaire and Hunter headed out for their run, their laughter and footsteps soon fading into the distance. Meanwhile, Inez hurried to catch up to Nadia.

"Can we talk?" she asked hesitantly.

Nadia's face softened, and she nodded. "Yes, I'd like that. Come in."

They entered Nadia's room, settling in as Nadia prepared hot chocolate for both of them. What started as a tense discussion gradually eased into understanding, shifting from serious to laughter. Inez explained how betrayed she had felt and admitted she'd unfairly taken it out on Nadia first, simply because she had walked in before Zaire. Nadia reassured her, explaining the reasons for keeping things from her and emphasising that Zaire had always wanted to tell her everything.

By the time their conversation wound down, the air between them felt lighter, as if the weight of the previous day had dissipated.

Their chat was interrupted when Hunter entered the room, his presence signalling the evening was drawing to an end.

"I should head out anyway," Inez said, standing and wrapping her arms around Nadia in a grateful hug. "Thank you."

Nadia hugged her back. "You're always welcome."

As Inez left the room, she smiled at Hunter in passing before heading back to her own quarters.

Once alone, Inez found herself pacing between her easel and the new book she had picked up earlier. Her thoughts swirled, replaying memories from the past few days.

She chose to paint.

For hours, she remained lost in brushstrokes and colour, the canvas filling with reflections of her past. First, she painted a double mini canvas, one depicting the warm familiarity of her front room in the city, the other capturing her late husband's office, untouched and frozen in time.

Then, she moved onto the third canvas. This one was different. Harder. The medical room. The place where she had become something else, something darker. A murderer.

She hesitated, staring at the half-formed lines. But the memories wouldn't let her go.

As the night stretched on, she kept returning to one thought, how she had thrown the last piece of her husband into the lake, letting it sink beneath the surface, lost forever.

Inez crept out of her room, her bare feet barely making a sound against the cold floor as she slipped through the corridors. The night air was crisp, wrapping around her as she stepped outside and made her way to the lake. Her heartbeat quickened with the uncertainty of her search. As she reached the water's edge, she crouched down, scanning the shoreline for any sign of the rings. Nothing.

She stepped onto the dock, its wooden planks cool beneath her skin, and peered into the lake. The surface rippled gently, reflecting the silvery light of the moon, and for a moment, she thought she saw something. Something glimmering beneath the water. She was readying herself to jump in when suddenly a voice interrupted.

Startled, Inez stumbled back slightly, clutching her chest. "Hi, you scared me," she breathed.

"I have that effect," Lamia said, laughing.

Lamia's amusement continued, her crimson scales catching the moonlight, shimmering like liquid fire beneath the water. "No, I mean because it's lights out," Inez added, recovering from her shock.

"I know, I'm kidding," Lamia said casually, eyes twinkling. "But hey, you're out here, why can't I be?"

Inez considered this. "That's fair," she admitted.

Lamia tilted her head. "I'm here because there's nowhere else to swim. Why are you here?"

Inez hesitated, her eyes dropping to the water. "Yesterday, I got mad and threw two rings into the lake. I wanted them back."

Lamia reached out her hand, revealing two rings resting in her palm. "You mean these wedding rings?" she asked.

Inez gasped, relief washing over her. "You found them," she whispered, her voice barely containing the gratitude flooding her.

"I was here yesterday," Lamia explained. "I heard you and Zaire. I saw you throw them, and I just knew you'd regret it."

Inez's throat tightened. The realisation that someone had looked out for her, even unknowingly, struck her deep. "Thank you," she said.

Lamia smiled and motioned towards the manor. "Come on, let's go in."

She stepped out of the water, her transformation instant. The shimmering scales faded, replaced by smooth skin as she grabbed a hidden towel. Inez watched in awe. "That is incredible," she breathed, mesmerised by the effortless shift.

Lamia smirked, shaking the water from her hair before turning to Inez. "I wanted to speak to you, actually." Inez gently took Lamia's hand.

"About what?" Lamia raised an eyebrow.

Inez swallowed hard, gathering her thoughts. "Zaire told me about you two today," she said cautiously. "And… he asked me out. I just wanted to make sure that nothing would change between us."

Lamia studied her for a few seconds before breaking into a soft smile. "You're sweet for asking," she said. "But no, nothing will change."

Inez exhaled, some of her tension dissolving. With quiet understanding between them, the two made their way back to their rooms.

Once inside, Inez gently placed the rings in the lower section of her jewellery box. She didn't need to see them, but she liked having them close. A silent reminder of the past, one she was slowly learning to make peace with.

Slipping into her pyjamas, she crawled into bed and let sleep claim her, her thoughts filled not with sorrow, but with a quiet sense of clarity.

33

The Outfit and the Past

The morning sunlight streamed through the windows as Inez paced her room, her nerves bubbling over. She had no idea what to wear or how to prepare for her date with Zaire. The thought of making a wrong impression gnawed at her, so she did the only thing she could think of, she ran to Nadia for help.

Inez banged on Nadia's door with urgency, the sound echoing down the hall. The door swung open, revealing Hunter. "Who's dying?" he asked, raising an eyebrow.

"Me, if I don't get Nadia's help," Inez replied frantically.

"I'm here," Nadia said, stepping into view as she tied her hair into a casual bun. "What's wrong?"

"I have a date with Zaire, and I don't know what to wear. I need your help," Inez said, her words tumbling out in a rush.

Hunter smirked and gestured for Nadia to leave. "Go," he said, pushing her gently towards the door.

The two women made their way to Inez's room, which looked like a tornado had swept through it. Clothes were draped over every flat surface, creating a chaotic sea of fabric. Nadia took charge, sorting through the mess with a discerning eye. After much deliberation, they settled on the perfect outfit.

Inez hopped into the shower, letting the warm water calm her nerves.

Meanwhile, Nadia dried and styled her hair, creating effortless beach waves that framed her face beautifully. She then worked on Inez's makeup, adding her signature cat-wing eyeliner and a bold red lipstick she had found tucked away in Inez's makeup box.

When Inez emerged, she slipped into the chosen outfit: tight blue ripped jeans paired with a sheer black silk shirt layered over a fitted black vest. The ensemble hugged her figure perfectly, accentuating every curve. Nadia completed the look with her own black zip-up ankle boots, adding an edge to the outfit.

Inez stood in front of the mirror, her confidence slowly building as she took in her reflection. She felt ready, more than ready, to face the evening ahead.

The two tidied up the room, folding clothes and wiping down surfaces until everything was back in place. Just as they finished, a knock sounded at the door.

Nadia swung the door open, her expression playful. "You are not Inez," Zaire said, surprised as he took in the sight of Nadia standing there.

"Great eyesight, jackass. We were having girl time," Nadia replied with a smirk.

"Oh," Zaire said, shaking his head as if to clear his confusion. "Inez, Zaire's here for you," Nadia called over her shoulder.

In the bathroom, Inez placed her hands on the sink, staring at her reflection. "A new life," she whispered to herself, her gaze dropping to her hand where her rings had once rested. The memory tugged at her heart, but she pushed it aside, taking a deep breath. She turned and walked out, her steps purposeful.

Zaire stood in the hallway, adjusting his shirt nervously. When he heard the door open, he looked up, and froze. His jaw dropped as his eyes took in Inez, from her perfectly styled hair to the bold red lipstick that made her look both elegant and striking. She was radiant, every detail of her appearance meticulously crafted yet effortlessly stunning.

All Zaire could think about was how perfect she looked, how much he wanted to reach out, pull her close and kiss her, smudging that lipstick in the process.

Nadia glanced over at Zaire, breaking the silence in the room. "She looks great, doesn't she?" she asked, her tone light yet pointed, as if trying to disarm the tension.

Zaire inhaled deeply before nodding, his gaze flickering to Nadia briefly before returning to Inez. His voice was sincere as he said, "You look perfect."

Inez looked up from the floor, a shy grin spreading across her face as she adjusted the strap of her bag on her shoulder. "Are you ready to go?" she asked.

Zaire nodded, walking to the door and holding it open for her. Before stepping through, Inez turned to Nadia and pulled her into a quick hug. She leaned in close and whispered, "Thank you. I needed this."

Nadia's face eased into a genuine smile as she hugged her back. The words hung in the air, warm and grounding. In that moment, Nadia knew she'd made a friend for life. "Anytime, Hun," she replied warmly.

The car ride was quiet at first, with the sound of the engine humming in the background. Inez sat in the passenger seat, her head turned towards the window as she watched the world pass by. The scenery shifted from the familiar streets of the manor to sprawling landscapes, but no matter how much she wanted to ask where they were heading, she held her tongue. Zaire seemed focused, his hands steady on the wheel, and she didn't want to interrupt.

Her thoughts strayed, and she found herself wondering what was going through his mind. The temptation to reach out with her powers and investigate was strong, but she stopped herself. She hadn't mastered that skill yet, and even if she had, it would feel like a betrayal of trust.

Twenty minutes passed before Zaire reached over to turn on the radio. The sudden sound filled the car, causing Inez to perk up. Her favourite song played through the speakers, its melody instantly lifting her mood. Without thinking, she reached for the volume knob, her hand colliding with Zaire's as he moved to do the same.

The brief touch startled him, and he quickly pulled his hand back, placing it firmly on the gear stick. Inez glanced at him, a small giggle escaping her lips as she turned up the volume herself. The tension that had filled the car melted away.

The car ride grew increasingly enjoyable as the awkward silence dissolved, replaced by laughter and the shared appreciation for music. Each song seemed to bring them closer, as though the melodies were weaving a connection between them. Before they knew it, they arrived at their destination, back where it all began. The abandoned casino.

Zaire stepped out of the car and walked around to open the door for Inez, his gestures thoughtful and unhurried. He held it open, allowing her to step out first. The casino looked different now. Gone were the layers of dust that had once blanketed the room; the rags covering the windows had been removed, and the skylight now illuminated the space with natural light. Sunbeams poured in, reflecting the azure expanse of the ocean just beyond. For the first time, the building felt more alive than abandoned.

He led her upstairs, their footsteps light against the worn carpet. They arrived at the room where they had first met, and for a while, they simply stood there, soaking in the memories. Zaire broke the quiet, his voice tinged with emotion. "This shouldn't have been how we met," he admitted, his eyes drifting to the floor before returning to her. "This is where it happened, but I would have rather it been… I don't know, something normal. A walk along the beach. Sharing an ice cream."

"Sharing? I want my own," Inez teased, a giggle bubbling up as she crossed her arms mock-defensively.

Zaire chuckled, the sound soft and warm. He raised his hand, his fingers brushing a strand of her hair from her face. His touch paused briefly, his thumb grazing her cheek in a tender, almost hesitant motion. Inez caught his hand in hers, stopping him. Her voice quavered slightly as she asked, "What is this? What are we doing?"

Without answering, Zaire placed his other hand gently on the opposite side of her face. He leaned in, closing the space between them, and kissed her. It was a kiss that carried every unspoken word. Every longing glance had built to this. Time seemed to stand still as they lost themselves in each other, the kiss leaving them both breathless.

THE OUTFIT AND THE PAST

When it ended, Inez's gaze dropped to the floor, her thoughts swirling. She felt overwhelmed by the cascade of emotions surging through her, love, compassion, lust, friendship, loyalty. It was everything she had ever wanted, everything she hadn't known she was missing. As her eyes met Zaire's again, the truth crystallised in her mind. She didn't even feel this way with her late husband after their first kiss as husband and wife. Somehow, this was different. It was more.

Everything in her life had led her to this moment, to Zaire. Though she wished their journey had unfolded under better circumstances, she couldn't imagine not having him at all.

Zaire seemed to sense her thoughts, his hand still resting lightly against hers. Smiling, he gently took her hand and led her back downstairs and out onto the beach. The air smelled of salt, and the sound of waves lapping against the shore was a melody all its own.

They found smooth stones along the shore, and Zaire began to skim them across the water. His skill was undeniable, the stones bouncing across the surface before disappearing into the distance. Inez, on the other hand, hadn't done it before. Her first few attempts were clumsy, sending stones plopping straight into the water. She groaned playfully, pretending to pout.

Zaire laughed, his joy infectious. "Try this one," he said, handing her a perfectly flat stone. Inez tried again, and though the stone managed a single skip before sinking, she felt a rush of accomplishment.

"I think you're sabotaging me," she teased, narrowing her eyes at him.

"Me? Never," he replied with mock innocence, his grin giving him away.

They spent the next hour like that, laughing, teasing and marvelling at the ripples that spread across the ocean's surface. The sight of the shimmering water struck a chord in Inez. As she stood there, watching the ripples fade into the endless expanse, she felt something stir within her. She wanted to draw.

"Can I borrow your phone?" she asked suddenly.

Zaire handed it over without hesitation, curious. She began snapping photos, of the stones, the ripples, the waves catching the light just so. Each picture captured the serenity of the scene, a memory preserved in pixels.

Zaire watched her, his chest tightening with emotion. She looked happy, truly happy, and he realised there was nothing he wouldn't do to keep her smiling like that.

The wind swept through Inez's hair, tangling it across her face. She brushed it aside with a flick of her hand, her eyes drifting back towards the car. For the briefest moment, she froze. A figure, faint, ghostly, leaned against the hood. Her breath caught in her throat as recognition struck her like a wave. Lucian. She blinked, her heart pounding, and when she looked again, the figure was gone. But his face lingered in her mind, vivid and unshakable.

She handed Zaire's phone back to him, her fingers trembling slightly, and returned to skimming stones. Yet, the guilt began to creep in, wrapping around her like a cold tide. Memories of the last time she stood on this beach flooded her thoughts. It had been after her escape, when everything she'd lost had nearly consumed her. She remembered staring out at the water, the pull of the ocean calling her to walk deeper and deeper until the seabed disappeared beneath her feet. She had wanted to let the waves take her, to surrender to the exhaustion and the pain.

But then, another memory surfaced, one of warmth and light. Her honeymoon with Lucian. She could almost feel the sand beneath her feet as they walked along the shore, their laughter mingling with the sound of the waves. She remembered the way he had grabbed her waist, pulling her close for a kiss that sent butterflies fluttering through her chest. It had been perfect. This moment with Zaire, it was more. More intense, more real, more alive.

Zaire, oblivious to her inner turmoil, searched the beach for the perfect stone. When he found it, he stepped behind her, gently placing it in her hand. His other hand rested firmly on her waist, steadying her, while his fingers lightly guided her wrist. He leaned in close, his voice a soft murmur in her ear as he explained the technique for the perfect skim. The warmth of his breath against her neck sent a shiver down her spine, and his hand on her waist ignited a longing she couldn't ignore.

She threw the stone, and it skipped across the water, bouncing several times before sinking. A triumphant laugh escaped her lips as she jumped for joy. Without thinking, she turned and grabbed Zaire, pulling him into a kiss. It was impulsive, electric and all-consuming. The world around them faded, leaving only the two of them, lost in each other.

The spell was broken by the sharp ring of Zaire's phone. He pulled away reluctantly, his breath still uneven, and answered the call. It was Raphael, as commanding as ever, asking for an update. Zaire played it off, his tone casual, but his eyes never left Inez. As he hung up, a small smile tugged at his lips. Whatever Raphael had said didn't matter. Being here with her was all that mattered.

The afternoon unfolded with a playful ease as Zaire and Inez strolled up to a quaint ice cream parlour. Zaire ordered two Cornetto ice creams, each topped with a Flake, and handed one to Inez. She ate hers carefully, ensuring not a single drop of ice cream smeared her face or clothes. Zaire, on the other hand, was a mess, his face, shirt and jeans were streaked with melted ice cream, resembling a child who had just discovered the joy of dessert. Embarrassed but laughing at himself, he excused himself to find the nearest restroom to clean up.

While waiting outside, Inez's attention was drawn to the claw machines lined up against the wall. She studied the teddies inside, sceptical. "No one ever wins these," she muttered to herself. As she leaned closer to inspect the prizes, she caught Zaire's reflection behind her in the glass.

"Move out of the way, and I'll show you how it's done," Zaire teased, nudging her gently aside.

Inez raised an eyebrow. "What do you want?" he asked, scanning the teddies.

"The green dragon," she decided, pointing to the vibrant plush toy nestled among the others.

"It's yours," Zaire declared confidently. He inserted a pound coin, which granted him four attempts. The first three tries were close but unsuccessful, and Inez smirked, ready to tease him. But on the final attempt, Zaire's precision paid off, the claw grabbed the dragon and dropped it perfectly into the prize chute.

He retrieved the toy and turned around, his smirk widening as he noticed a small crowd had gathered to watch his feat. The spectators clapped lightly, impressed by his skill, and Zaire basked in the attention for a few seconds before handing the dragon to Inez. "Told you I'd get it," he said, his grin infectious.

They continued their afternoon with a leisurely walk along the beach. Inez held the green dragon close, examining its features. "It looks just like Kek but green," she said, laughing.

"Kek?" Zaire asked, puzzled.

"Oh, it's a character from Kimmie's game," Inez stammered, her voice faltering.

Zaire narrowed his eyes playfully. "You're lying. You can tell me anything."

Inez hesitated before grabbing his hand. "You cannot say anything. Promise me," she pleaded.

"I promise," Zaire said reassuringly.

Taking a deep breath, Inez spilt the truth. "Kimmie accidentally opened a portal, and a baby dragon came through. She's been trying to get him home, but she has no idea where he's from."

Zaire's eyes widened in shock. "She has a dragon?"

"Yes, and he's adorable," Inez replied, her smile returning.

"You've seen it?" Zaire asked, still processing the revelation.

"Yes. He let me stroke him, but you cannot say anything," Inez insisted.

As the sun dipped below the horizon, painting the sky orange and pink, they decided it was time to head home. Zaire opened the car door for Inez and shut it firmly behind her. He sighed deeply, his mind racing. He wanted more, more time, more moments like this.

Sliding into the driver's seat, Zaire glanced at Inez, her face glowing with happiness. He couldn't bring himself to end the day just yet. Without a word, he took a detour, driving further down the beachfront to a secluded area. The road was quiet, the ocean stretching to the horizon beside them.

He parked the car and leaned back in his seat, letting out another sigh. Inez turned to him. Slowly, she reached out and placed her hand on the inside of his thigh. The gesture caught Zaire's attention immediately. Her smirk was playful, her shoulder lifting in a cheeky shrug.

Zaire shifted in his seat, his posture stiffening. Inez noticed the change and pulled her hand back, suddenly unsure. She leaned back in her chair, her gaze drifting out the window, the moment hanging between them like an unfinished sentence.

Zaire stared ahead, his thoughts briefly lost in the quiet of the night. But the pull was too strong to ignore. He turned back to Inez, his eyes locking onto hers with an intensity that made her breath hitch. Without hesitation, he reached out, his hands gently cradling her face as he tilted it towards his own. His lips met hers in a kiss that was deep, meaningful and filled with every ounce of passion he had been holding back.

The world seemed to fade away, leaving only the two of them in their shared bubble of warmth and connection. When the kiss ended, they didn't pull apart completely. Instead, their foreheads rested against each other, their breaths mingling as they let out simultaneous sighs. The tension melted into quiet laughter, their giggles soft and intimate as their eyes met again.

Unable to resist, Zaire leaned in for another kiss, his body shifting closer to hers. The space between them disappeared, and it felt perfect, the culmination of everything that had brought them to this point. But just as the world seemed to pause for them, the sharp sound of Zaire's phone ringing shattered the silence.

34

Visor Memory

Raphael's name flashed on the dashboard, and Zaire's demeanour shifted instantly. He grabbed his phone, muttering a quick apology, and stepped out of the car. The cool night air greeted him as he walked a short distance to the wooden fence lining the beach. Leaning against it, he answered the call, his voice steady but tense.

Inside the car, Inez exhaled deeply, trying to collect herself. She adjusted her top, brushed her hair back into place and flipped down the sun visor to check her makeup. As the visor opened, something slipped out and landed in her lap.

Curious, she glanced down and froze. It was a photograph, a candid shot of Zaire with a young boy. Who was this child? Why did Zaire have this photo tucked away? She quickly looked up to see if Zaire had noticed, but he was still facing the ocean, his finger raised to signal he'd only be a minute longer.

When he turned back towards the car, Inez hurriedly slipped the photo back into the visor and snapped it shut. She composed herself just as Zaire opened the car door and slid into the driver's seat.

"I'm so sorry about that," he said genuinely.

Inez offered him a small smile, letting him know it was okay. Zaire started the car, buckled his seatbelt and glanced at her. "I'm sorry, I need to get you back," he said regretfully.

Inez nodded slowly, her sigh barely detectable. She turned her gaze to the window, watching the world blur past as they drove in silence. The magic of the evening felt like it was slipping away, leaving her with a bittersweet ache.

When they arrived back at the manor, Zaire walked her to her room. He hesitated, his eyes searching hers as if he wanted to say more. Instead, he simply said, "Goodnight," his voice warm but restrained.

"Goodnight," Inez replied, her heart sinking slightly as she closed the door behind her.

The quiet didn't last long. A loud knock echoed through the room, and Inez's heart leapt. For a fleeting moment, she hoped it was Zaire, returning to pick up where they had left off. But when she opened the door, she was met with a very different energy.

"Tell me all the details!" Nadia exclaimed, practically bursting into the room. She shut the door behind her and grabbed Inez by the arm, dragging her to the edge of the bed. "Sit," she commanded, pulling over a chair for herself. She plopped down, crossing her legs and resting her elbows on her knees, her face cupped in her hands. Her eyes sparkled with anticipation.

Inez sighed, a smirk tugging at the corners of her lips. She looked down briefly, then up at Nadia with softened eyes. "Well," she began as she stared at the wall, a dreamy smile spreading across her face. She bit her bottom lip, unable to hide her excitement.

"Oh my God, just tell me already!" Nadia leaned in closer, practically vibrating with curiosity.

"It went well," Inez started, but before she could elaborate, Nadia cut her off.

"Did he kiss you?" she demanded, her voice rising with excitement.

Inez stopped biting her lip, her smile growing impossibly wide. Her eyes sparkled with a glow that said everything. She nodded quickly, her giggles bubbling up uncontrollably.

Nadia shot to her feet, grabbing Inez by the arms and pulling her into a tight hug. "I knew it!" she squealed, spinning her slightly before letting her go. The room filled with their laughter, the tension of the evening melting away in the warmth of their friendship.

The knock at the door startled both Inez and Nadia, their laughter and chatter abruptly silenced. Inez took a deep breath, trying to calm herself and Nadia before cautiously opening the door. The hallway appeared empty at first glance. She stepped out, her eyes scanning left, nothing. Then she turned right, and there he was. Zaire stood a few steps away, his expression soft as he turned towards her and rushed over.

"I'm not disturbing you, am I?" he asked gently.

His gaze drifted past her into the room, catching sight of Nadia. "I am interrupting," he said quickly, his voice full of regret. "I'm sorry, I'll go."

As he began to turn away, Nadia's phone rang, breaking the moment. She glanced at the screen and smiled. "It's Hunter. He's made dinner and is waiting for me," she said. She turned to Inez, squeezing her shoulder affectionately. "Bye, girl," she said, her grin playful. Then, with a quick nod to Zaire, she added, "Later, Zaire," before walking out and shutting the door behind her. But not before giving Inez a cheeky look.

Zaire turned back to the door, ensuring it was shut securely. He locked it, then faced Inez with a smirk. From behind his back, he revealed the green dragon teddy. "You left this in my car," he said. "I thought I'd return it to you."

Inez took the teddy from his hands, her fingers brushing against his briefly. She looked down at the toy, a smile spreading across her face. When she looked back up at Zaire, her heart swelled with a realisation that hit her like a wave. She had fallen for him, deeply, completely, in a way she hadn't thought possible.

35

The Tempest and the Silence

Without hesitation, she tossed the teddy onto the bed and wrapped her arms around his neck, pulling him close. Zaire responded instantly, his hands finding her waist as their lips met in a kiss that was nothing short of electric. It was passionate, raw and filled with every feeling they had been holding back.

As the kiss deepened, Zaire gently guided her towards the bed. He lay her down, his body hovering over hers as he continued to kiss her, each second more intense than the last.

He began to feel a strange mix of emotions, love, care and a deep desire not to rush anything. He leaned in for one more long, tender kiss before attempting to get off the bed. But Inez wasn't ready to let him go. She grabbed his arm and gently pulled him to the other side of the bed, wrapping herself around him. They lay there, holding each other, their bodies fitting together like puzzle pieces.

Time seemed to slow as they talked for hours. They shared stories, dreams and secrets, their connection deepening with every word. Inez rested in Zaire's arms, her leg draped over him as they faced each other. The world outside the room faded away.

Inez leaned in to kiss him, her lips hovering just inches from his. But Zaire pulled back, a mischievous giggle escaping him. She blinked in surprise, her brows furrowing slightly. She tried again, leaning in closer, only for him to pull away once more, his laughter growing.

"Are you serious?" she asked, her voice a mix of shock and amusement. She tried a third time, and again, he pulled back, his grin widening. Frustrated, she sat up, crossing her arms as if to give up entirely.

"No, no, no," Zaire said quickly, reaching for her hand. "I'm just messing with you. Do it again, I promise I won't pull away this time." His voice was playful, but his eyes were sincere as he pulled her back into his arms.

Inez hesitated, her lips curving into a small smile. She leaned in one final time. This time, their lips met in a soft kiss filled with unspoken promises.

Zaire pulled her back into his arms, holding her close as if he never wanted to let go. Inez hesitated again before leaning in for a final kiss. Their lips met, and the kiss was tender, filled with a quiet intensity.

With a playful glint in her eye, Inez suddenly pushed Zaire onto his back and climbed on top of him. She leaned in as if to kiss him again, her lips hovering just inches from his. But just as he leaned in to meet her, she pulled away, a mischievous smile spreading across her face.

Zaire blinked in surprise. "It's not nice when it's done to you, is it?" she teased.

Her little game ignited something in him. Zaire, caught up in the moment, couldn't resist. He reached up, his hands gently cradling her head, and pulled her in for a kiss that was anything but playful. It was deep, passionate and filled with the kind of energy that made the world around them disappear.

The tension between Zaire and Inez grew heavier, thick like the air before a storm. He placed her gently onto the bed, his hands lingering just a second too long. Every thought, every urge, every desire clawed at him, but he forced himself to think of her instead. What she needed. What was right.

"We really shouldn't," Zaire said, his voice barely above a whisper, but his words hung between them.

"Okay," Inez said, her gaze unwavering. "We won't. We don't have to."

But then, after a beat, she tilted her head ever so slightly, studying him as if searching for the answer deep within him.

"But do you want to?" she asked, challenging him.

He leaned in, his fingers threading gently through her hair as he cradled the back of her head. Then, after some deliberation, he kissed her, deeply, fully, as if he was pouring every unuttered word into his touch.

"Does that answer your question?" he murmured against her lips, his breath warm.

She pulled back just enough to look into his eyes, her eyes glowing with something more than just desire. A slow, knowing smile spread across her lips, the corners of her eyes crinkling with quiet joy.

Without another word, she grabbed his collar, tugging him closer, pulling him back into the kiss, this time with even more fervour, more urgency, as if she never wanted to let go.

36

Unseen Reflection

The following morning, Inez was jolted awake by the sound of a phone ringing. Groggy, she rolled over to grab her phone, only to freeze as her eyes landed on Zaire lying beside her. For a moment, she thought the events of last night had been nothing more than a wonderful dream. But there he was, a reminder of their perfect evening.

She quickly grabbed her phone and saw Nadia's name flashing on the screen. Without hesitation, she hung up and sent a quick text, promising to call later. Letting out a deep sigh, she placed her phone on the bedside table and turned her attention to Zaire. The memory of their date washed over her, filling her with warmth. They hadn't slept together, but the night had been magical nonetheless.

Inez lay back down, wrapping her arm around him. Zaire stirred, letting out a deep breath as he reached for her hand, guiding her to squeeze him tighter. Together they drifted back into a peaceful sleep.

As the morning wore on, Inez began to toss and turn, her bladder urging her to get up. She opened her eyes, staring at the ceiling with a reluctant sigh. The comfort of the bed was hard to leave, but nature called. She slipped out quietly, heading to the bathroom. When she returned, she was met with disappointment. Zaire was gone.

Though she understood he likely had things to attend to, the emptiness of the room tugged at her heart. She made herself a warm cup of hot chocolate and settled by the window, the steam curling softly into the air. As she gazed out at the world, her thoughts drifted back to the night before. Every detail replayed in her mind, the laughter, the connection, the way he made her feel. She couldn't help but smile.

Her daydream was interrupted by the sound of Zaire's voice. "How did you do that?" he asked, his tone curious.

Startled, Inez turned to face him, her confusion evident. "Do what?" she replied, her brows furrowing as she tried to understand.

Inez sat up, rubbing the sleep from her eyes as she turned to Zaire. "Where did you go?" she asked, her voice still groggy.

Zaire placed a tray on the bedside table, the scent of fresh food filling the room. "I just got us breakfast," he said casually, pulling out a chair. "Let's eat. But first, can you tell me how you did it?"

Inez blinked, confused. "Did what?"

Zaire studied her for a while before answering. "It's another power," he said, both intrigued and amused. "Your thoughts, your memories, were reflecting out of you like a projection. I saw what you were thinking."

Inez stiffened, her heart skipping a beat. "What did you see?" she asked nervously.

Zaire smirked, clearly unfazed. "I saw you and me last night," he admitted. "It's okay. At least now I know we're both on the same page. And honestly?" He leaned back with a small chuckle. "I can't stop thinking about it either."

Inez swallowed, still processing his words. She hadn't even realised she was projecting anything, but the idea of Zaire seeing her thoughts, especially ones so personal, perturbed her.

Zaire reached for a plate, handing one to her. "Now, let's eat," he said, flashing her a reassuring smile. "And after that? We train."

37

The Portal and the Plea

One crisp morning, Kimmie was fresh from her shower when a firm knock shattered the quiet. Wrapped only in a soft towel and her vulnerable thoughts, she tiptoed to the door. Peeking through the narrow opening, she saw two guards standing in formation, their uniforms impeccably neat and their eyes guarded. One of them broke the silence with a measured, professional tone, "May we enter? We have been asked to conduct a routine search."

Her pulse quickened, and a flush crept along her cheeks as she hesitated for a while before asking, "May I get dressed first?" Their eyes diverted downwards, and she clutched her towel a little tighter.

The reply came without hesitation. "Yes, of course, no problem, miss." With a racing heart, she quickly shut the door behind her and dashed into her room. The urgency in her mind was not just about the imminent intrusion; she was also worried about Kek. She knew that her secret was at risk.

In the midst of her rising panic, a single clear thought emerged: there was one person she could trust. Steadying herself, Kimmie summoned her inner resolve and activated a portal, a shimmering gateway, to Inez's room. With a voice barely above a whisper, she called out, "Inez, are you there?"

Her plea was both a lifeline and a prayer, and Inez's calm reply resonated from the other side: "Yes, come in." Settling into a chair with her usual poise,

Inez's presence offered a promise of safety. "I can't, they are searching my room. Please, take Kek and look after him," Kimmie pleaded, her words hurried as she carefully passed the little creature through the portal.

Heart pounding, Kimmie composed herself and returned to the door. "Sorry for the wait. I am suitably dressed now," she announced, attempting a casual tone that belied her inner turmoil. As she opened the door wider to let the guards in, resignation and determination welled up within her. Once inside, she stepped back into the corridor and pressed herself against the cool wall, watching in dismay as the search began in earnest.

One of the guards methodically ripped aside her duvet cover and scattered her pillows on the floor, exposing her private sanctuary with clinical precision. The other moved with equal force, flinging books off the shelf, their pages rustling and tumbling to join the chaos. In what seemed like a rehearsed routine, they then knocked down the meticulously arranged replicas that adorned the room. The intrusion wasn't limited to the common spaces; one guard stormed into her closet, tossing her carefully kept clothes about as if they were nothing more than scraps, while his partner invaded the bathroom, the latter even removing the bath panel and peering behind the mirror, his search methodical.

As Kimmie absorbed the disarray, confusion and dread mingled inside her. This wasn't a simple routine check; it was a thorough inspection that threatened to unravel every secret she guarded. Then, breaking through the silence, one of the guards strode back into the hall. He halted in front of her, his expression hardening into one of frustration. "Where is it?" he demanded.

Startled and bewildered, Kimmie managed to ask, "Where is what?"

His anger escalated, and he roared, "The creature!" The air in the hall thickened as his voice reverberated, prompting residents from nearby rooms to stir and gather in the corridors, their murmurs betraying a growing alarm.

In that charged moment, every second stretched like an eternity. Kimmie's heart pounded not only with fear of being discovered but with the crushing betrayal and uncertainty. The routine search had morphed into something invasive, and she realised that the stakes were far higher than she had ever imagined.

Kimmie's voice shook as she tried to maintain her composure. "I don't know what you are on about," she said, her tone laced with worry.

The guard's expression remained stern as he replied, "We had a report to confirm that someone had seen it." His gaze shifted towards Megyn, who had just stepped out of her room, her presence adding an air of tension to the hallway.

"Room sweep done. It's clear," the other guard announced, stepping out of Kimmie's room and signalling the end of their search.

Kimmie seized the opportunity to plead her case. "See, there is nothing. I'm not hiding anything," she said.

The guard nodded curtly. "You may enter your room now," he said before turning away and walking down the hall with his partner.

Kimmie stood in the doorway, her heart sinking as she surveyed the wreckage left behind. Her once orderly room was now a mess, with books, clothes and personal items strewn across the floor. As she tried to process the scene, Megyn approached her. "Do you need a hand?" she offered.

Kimmie's frustration boiled over, and she turned to Megyn with a fiery glare. "No, not from you. This was your doing, wasn't it?" she snapped, stepping closer to Megyn in a confrontational stance.

Megyn's brows furrowed in confusion. "What are you on about?" she asked defensively.

"You thought you could sense something, and, of course, you had to be a good slave and report it. Maybe everyone was right, no one liked you in your previous camp, and you had to move," Kimmie retorted, her words cutting. Her anger was palpable, and Megyn recoiled, her face reflecting shock and hurt.

"Wow, that's just cold," Megyn replied in disbelief.

"Just fuck off. You've done enough," Kimmie said as she turned away and stomped into her room, slamming the door behind her. The sound echoed through the hallway, leaving Megyn standing alone.

Inside her room, Kimmie took a deep breath, trying to calm the emotions swirling within her. She opened a portal to Inez's room, her hands trembling as she reached through to retrieve Kek. "Thank you for that," she said, her voice strained.

Inez immediately noticed Kimmie's distress and asked gently, "What's wrong?"

Kimmie's frustration bubbled to the surface again. "Megyn. She's a bitch," she replied bluntly.

Inez hesitated for a beat before responding. "She can be a bit closed off and weird, but I wouldn't call her a bitch," she said, attempting to defend Megyn.

"She sensed Kek with her animal manipulation and reported it. They searched my room, looking for him," Kimmie explained, her volume rising with indignation.

"Oh, that is terrible. I'm sorry I tried to defend her. Do you need help tidying it up?" Inez offered, concerned.

"No, I'm just going to do it myself. I need some time alone. Thank you for being such a good friend," Kimmie said, managing a small smile. Inez nodded her understanding as Kimmie closed the portal and began the arduous task of restoring her room to its former state.

Kimmie closed the portal and sank to the edge of her unmade bed, cradling little Kek tightly against her chest. Tears streamed down her face as she sobbed, the agony of nearly losing him overwhelming. In that moment, her heart ached with the unbearable notion that she could ever be without him. Every fibre of her being screamed that she would let Kek down if she abandoned him, even the selfish idea of opening a portal to send him home seemed unthinkable. As if sensing her distress, Kek nuzzled his small, warm face against her cheek and let out a gentle clicking sound from his throat, a quiet, reassuring murmur that echoed his affection. Kimmie wiped away her tears, pressed a gentle kiss on his head and managed to whisper, "I'd better tidy the room then."

Despite her grief, Kimmie summoned the strength she needed while Kek flitted around her feet, eager to help. He jumped onto the scattered pillows and began fluffing them back into shape, his tiny paws working with admirable skill. With equal enthusiasm, he gathered some of her carefully arranged replicas and meticulously put them back in order. When it came to the heavy gaming chair that lay abandoned on the floor, Kek attempted to lift it by flapping his wings with all his might. His earnest efforts, however, could only muster a few feeble gusts of air, and the chair refused to budge. Smiling at his valiant attempt, Kimmie walked over and hoisted the chair herself. "You are a good boy," she praised him warmly, and Kek chirped happily in response.

Elsewhere in the manor, Inez was still reeling after her conversation with Kimmie. Megyn's betrayal, reporting Kek, had left her incredulous and hurt. Wanting to unravel the tangled web of secrets, Inez made her way quietly to Megyn's room. With measured steps, she knocked on the door, and upon hearing a flat "Yes," she said, "It's about Kimmie."

Megyn's tone softened as she responded, "Come in," and Inez stepped inside, finding herself in a space that was the antithesis of disorder.

Megyn's room was minimalist, with a floor bed dressed in cool blue duvets, a few samurai swords arranged neatly on one wall and a cat climbing frame crafted for Qita, who lay curled up on a ball atop the bed.

Seating themselves on simple chairs, the tension in the room quickly gave way to a hesitant conversation. "Did you say something about a creature?" Inez asked.

Megyn's eyes flicked up momentarily before she replied, "Dragon, and no."

The reply, curt and almost dismissive, caught Inez off guard, prompting her to echo, "Dragon?" in disbelief that Megyn even knew of such a thing.

Megyn's response was firm as she said, "Don't play dumb, I know you know."

Confused and anxious, Inez pressed on. "How do you know?" Her voice quivered as she sought answers.

"Kimmie was right. I can sense him, but I wouldn't have reported her." Megyn's words sank in as Inez looked down at her hands, realising with a sinking heart that this was more than a simple misunderstanding. It dawned on her that sharing the secret had been a grave mistake, a secret that was not hers to reveal. Sensing the remorse and hurt in Inez's eyes, Megyn's expression hardened as she asked quietly, "You told him, didn't you?" Inez could only nod in silent contrition. With a heavy sigh and an uncomfortable tap on Inez's shoulder, Megyn said, "I'm sorry. No one can truly be trusted here."

Inez left Megyn's room with a heavy heart, her footsteps echoing in the quiet hall. Every step felt laden with uncertainty. Should she confide in Kimmie immediately, or wait until she confronted Zaire? The secret was tangled within her thoughts, pulling her in different directions.

When Inez reached her own room, the familiar surroundings did little to ease her inner turmoil. Resting on her unmade bed was the dragon teddy that Zaire had won. Picking it up, she marvelled at its delicate craftsmanship, feeling the soft fabric and intricate details under her fingertips.

After a long pause, Inez gently set the teddy back onto the rumpled bed and steeled herself. She needed to speak with Kimmie to share what she'd learned, even if it meant exposing a betrayal. With resolute steps, she made her way down the hallway to Kimmie's room and knocked lightly on the door.

Kimmie opened the door with a hesitant smile that quickly faded when she saw the sombre expression on Inez's face. "Come in," Kimmie said, her tone betraying a guarded warmth.

Once inside, Inez's voice trembled with conflicted urgency. "Sit down, we need to talk. I spoke to Megyn."

Kimmie's eyes flashed with anger. "That wasn't your place."

The words stung, and Inez looked down at her clasped hands, feeling the acrimony bite. "You are right, but it wasn't her…" Inez started.

"Who then?" Kimmie demanded sharply.

"Me, indirectly," Inez confessed, her admission coming out in a quiet, pained moan.

The air around them crackled with tension. Kimmie's face hardened. "What? Get out!" she exclaimed, rising to her feet.

"Let me explain, please," Inez pleaded, stepping forwards with desperate eyes.

But Kimmie was too wound up for an explanation. With a curt dismissal, she said, "No, I don't want to hear it, get out." In an abrupt movement, Kimmie summoned a shimmering portal that led directly to Inez's room, an otherworldly doorway that hovered in the charged silence. Reluctantly, Inez stepped towards it, the glowing edge illuminating the conflicted lines on her face.

Even amidst the escalating tension, little Kek, ever perceptive, sensed the unease. He clambered onto Kimmie's back, nestling beneath the silky strands of her ponytail in a plea for comfort.

As Inez passed through the portal, she called back, "Megyn does know, but it wasn't her." Once safely on the other side, Inez turned, and the portal snapped closed behind her, ensuring that no further words would travel back to Kimmie's room. The door sealed off the exchange abruptly, leaving behind only the echo of secrets that now loomed large between them.

38

Catastrophe Training

After they finished their breakfast, Inez indulged in the soothing warmth of a shower, letting the water calm her mind before her anticipated training session with Zaire. She dressed in gym leggings, a snug sports bra and a loose-fitting T-shirt that allowed her freedom of movement. Gathering her hair into a high ponytail, she mentally braced herself and made her way to the training hall.

As she stepped into the expansive space, the muffled echoes of activity greeted her. Zaire turned at the sound of her entering. "You ready?" he asked, his tone neutral, though with an underlying excitement. Inez nodded, her response betraying none of her apprehension. Without hesitation, Zaire surveyed the room and ordered everyone else present to leave. The gravity of the moment weighed heavily as the hall fell silent, leaving just the two of them.

Both prepared to start, Inez's inner turmoil churning violently. She feared what Zaire might uncover, not just about her, but about her abilities, which she barely understood herself.

The introductory session began with Zaire adopting a curious yet patient demeanour. His questions came quickly, trying to get to the crux of her power: "What were you thinking when it happened?" "How did you feel?" "Do you have any idea how you did it?" Each struck deep, rattling Inez's resolve. She was overwhelmed, but Zaire sensed it and gently reassured her. "We can slow down if you need to."

His fascination with her abilities was obvious. Inez hesitated at first but gradually opened up. She spoke of her yearning to relive the critical moment, to see, feel and absorb every detail as though she were right there once more. Her words painted vivid images in Zaire's mind. He recalled the inexplicable happiness that had engulfed him during their last encounter.

Zaire encouraged her to attempt to summon another memory. Inez nodded, determination flickering in her eyes. She drew a deep breath, the air steadying her pulse, and let a smile form as she closed her eyes. Concentrating deeply, she began to reach into her mind, pulling out fragments of their car journey. Bit by bit, the memory started to materialise, giving fleeting glimpses of the skimming stones.

But it wasn't complete. Zaire's confusion grew as he noticed the disjointed projection, it was like watching a fractured reel of film. His gaze narrowed when Inez's attention shifted to her feet, and recognition dawned as he spotted Nadia's shoes. A sick realisation sank in: she was projecting last night's journey, the one he deliberately hadn't disclosed to their boss. Anxiety overtook his composure as the stakes became abundantly clear. If Inez showed even a fragment of his face from that memory, it would spiral into madness.

"Inez, stop!" Zaire's urgent voice thundered through the hall. His commanding tone broke her focus instantly, the projection vanishing as swiftly as it had appeared. He couldn't afford to let the boss see this memory, one he'd kept buried. As silence returned to the room, the tension between them became a tangible force.

Breaking abruptly from the projection, Inez's mind reeled, disoriented and consumed by confusion. She couldn't understand what had happened or why Zaire had reacted with such urgency. Her unease deepened as she saw the alarm in his eyes, and soon, she began to feel the familiar sting of dread creeping up inside her, an echo of the night her husband had died.

Inez instinctively stepped back from Zaire, her breathing ragged as panic took hold. Memories she had worked so hard to bury began to resurface. She felt her chest tighten, her pulse quicken, and suddenly, she was consumed by the terror of that night. Before she could comprehend what was happening, she became overwhelmed, triggering a powerful and uncontrollable projection that engulfed the entire room.

The memory spilt out of her, vivid and visceral. Shadows and fragments of that night materialised around her like a storm, filling every corner of the training hall. Overcome, Inez fell to her knees and let out a gut-wrenching scream. Her cry reverberated through the building, a sound so haunting that it shook the windows and blew the training room doors wide open.

Nadia, alarmed by the commotion, burst into the room. When her eyes landed on Inez, she was hit by the raw, unfiltered projection, an overwhelming onslaught of emotions and imagery from that fateful night. Through the projection, Nadia saw everything: the mayhem, the heartbreak, the terror. But what struck her most was the paralysing sense of loss that Inez had experienced. It hit Nadia so deeply that she, too, became trapped within the projection, unable to escape its powerful grip.

Nadia tried to approach Inez, desperate to reach her and pull her back from the brink. Yet, every time she got close, the ripples emanating from Inez pushed her away with force. The cries of anguish pouring from Inez drowned out every attempt Nadia made to call out to her.

Meanwhile, Zaire, who had been frozen in place, watched the memory play out in horrifying detail, unable to move or intervene. He was completely caught in the projection, experiencing Inez's pain as if it were his own. Every sound, every emotion, assaulted him until he was overwhelmed.

With a surge of energy, Zaire broke free from his trance and charged towards Inez, his body propelled by sheer urgency. But the projection reached its peak as Inez relived the moment her husband was shot. The pain was unbearable, ripping through her like a tidal wave. She screamed, a sound of pure agony, and the intensity of it caused a sudden blackout in the room. The force of the projection flung Zaire across the hall with such strength that he collided with a pillar, rendering him unconscious.

Inez crumpled to the ground, her body giving up as she passed out from the emotional and physical toll. The room fell eerily silent, save for the echoes of what had just unfolded. Nadia, shaken but still conscious, ran over to Zaire to check his condition. She called out for Hunter.

39

The Breakaway

When Inez stirred awake, the soft light filtering through the curtains greeted her, but the cuffs on her wrists quickly pulled her back to reality. Hunter sat beside her, his expression one of concern and awkwardness. She tried to sit up, but the restraints held her back. "Really?" she asked in disbelief.

Hunter shrugged apologetically. "I'm sorry, they needed to," he muttered.

Inez chuckled, her amusement breaking through the tension. Without hesitation, she phased through the cuffs, her abilities rendering them useless. "Where is Zaire?" she asked. "Is he okay?"

Hunter nodded reassuringly. "He's in his room, resting," he replied, before his gaze shifted to her arms. "Is that a new one?" he asked, gesturing to the faint marks that adorned her skin. Inez glanced down, a small smile tugging at her lips as she nodded in confirmation.

Before the conversation could continue, Nadia appeared in the doorway, her head poking through cautiously. "All good?" she asked gently. Inez hesitated, looking down at her lap as she shook her head. The recent events hung heavy in the air. Nadia, sensing the need for privacy, tilted her head towards the door, instructing Hunter to leave. He complied without protest, closing the door behind him as Nadia stepped into the room.

She settled at the foot of the bed, her presence grounding. "Are you okay?" Nadia asked. Inez took a deep breath as she struggled to find the right words.

"I saw what happened," Nadia continued, her tone filled with empathy. "I'm sorry."

Inez looked up, her eyes meeting Nadia's. "It's the past," she said, her voice firm yet vulnerable. "It made me who I am now. But I need to see him, please, Nadia," she pleaded.

Nadia hesitated, her protective instincts battling against Inez's will. Finally, she relented, a sly smile forming on her lips. "If you can phase through the wall, I'll let you go," she challenged.

Inez smirked, her confidence returning. "Piece of cake," she replied. Without another word, she sprang into action, phasing through wall after wall with ease. Her determination carried her through the building, past the main lobby and up the stairs. When she finally reached Zaire's room, she paused at the threshold, her heart pounding in anticipation.

As she stepped inside, her breath caught in her throat. The sight before her was unexpected, and the reality of Zaire's condition hit her like a wave. The room was quiet, save for the sound of his breathing, and Inez stood frozen as she took in the scene.

40

Among the Trees

As Inez entered Zaire's room, a heavy sense of dread washed over her. The sight before her was both alarming and heart-wrenching. Zaire lay unconscious on the bed, surrounded by an array of machines. Wires and tubes connected him to beeping monitors and a white IV dripping steadily into his veins. Inez felt her stomach churn, taking in his ashen skin.

"Zaire," she whispered, her voice trembling as she moved closer. She gently took his hand, her fingers curling around his, seeking any sign of life or recognition. But there was nothing, no movement, no response. Her chest tightened, fear prickling her mind.

The sudden creak of the door snapped her out of her thoughts. She turned as Hunter entered, his expression shifting from confusion to surprise when he saw her. "How did you get in here?" he asked.

"I phased through the walls," she replied bluntly, her focus already returning to Zaire. Her eyes traced the lines of his body, searching for visible injuries, trying to piece together what had happened to him. "What's wrong with him? Why isn't he waking up?" she asked desperately.

Hunter walked over, placing a reassuring hand on her shoulder. "When he went flying into the pillar, he damaged his spine. It's serious, but he'll heal, it'll just take time," he explained. His tone was steady, but Inez could sense the worry lurking beneath the surface.

"How do you know?" she pressed, suspicious. She glanced at the white IV bag, its contents slowly dripping into Zaire's system.

"The IV." Hunter gestured towards it. "It's infused with a regenerative solution. It's designed to heal anything, even injuries as severe as this." His words were meant to comfort, but they had the opposite effect.

Inez's heart skipped a beat as a memory surfaced, a white IV, just like this one, connected to her own arm during her captivity. The room seemed to tilt for a moment as the memories clawed at her mind. She took a shaky breath, forcing herself to stay present.

Days passed, and despite the promising effects of the IV, Zaire remained unconscious. Inez knew she couldn't let herself fall apart. Her training resumed, and she threw herself into it with renewed purpose.

Combat training with Megyn proved to be both challenging and enlightening. Megyn taught her to rely on her senses, to listen to her surroundings, to feel vibrations through the ground, to anticipate movements even when one sense was taken away. Blindfolded, Inez honed her ability to detect subtle cues. With soundproof earbuds, she relied on visual details. Even with her hands tied, she learned techniques to defend herself and fight effectively. The intensity of the sessions left her exhausted, but she could feel herself improving rapidly.

Alongside her combat training, Inez worked with Nadia to refine her abilities. They experimented with different techniques, attempting to extend her control and explore the limits of her powers. Nadia emphasised the importance of emotional regulation, something Inez struggled with. Her emotions were the key to her powers, but they could also make her lose control. Talking to Kimmie helped her find some balance, Kimmie had a way of grounding her, of making her feel understood.

Everyone pitched in to support her in their own ways. Hunter rarely left Zaire's side, keeping watch over him and monitoring his progress. In the evenings, Inez found solace by the dock. She would bring a book to read, but more often than not, she ended up staring at the water, imagining Zaire sitting beside her, talking to her, laughing with her. During the day, she painted, letting her emotions flow onto the canvas. She added new pieces to her collection, capturing memories of the guard, her new room and even Kimmie, carefully excluding Kek.

Noticing Inez's mounting stress, Nadia invited her on a special outing. They ventured into the woods behind the manor, wandering for hours beneath the canopy of towering trees. The tranquillity of the forest offered a sense of reprieve, and as they walked, Inez found herself opening up about her experiences. Nadia listened intently, the bond between them strengthening with every word. She could feel the echoes of Inez's pain from the projection, and though it was overwhelming, she wanted to support her friend.

Their journey through the woods brought them to an unexpected discovery, a majestic waterfall cascading into a serene lagoon. The sun filtered through the trees, casting a golden glow on the water. Inez's breath hitched as she took in the sight. "This is beautiful," she murmured, her voice filled with awe.

Nadia was equally stunned. "Yes, it is. I didn't know it was here," she admitted.

Inez turned to her, eyebrows raised. "Wait, have you not been here before?"

"I have," Nadia replied, her expression puzzled, "but I've never seen this."

The two women exchanged a look, their curiosity piqued by the mystery of the place. Inez broke the contemplative silence with a playful smile. "Should we go for a swim?"

Nadia laughed, the sound light and free. "Of course," she agreed without hesitation.

They shed their outer layers, stripping down to their underwear before plunging into the cool, clear water. The lagoon was surrounded by lush bushes and towering pine trees, the waterfall's roar creating a soothing backdrop. Inez felt a glimmer of peace.

After their refreshing swim, Inez and Nadia returned to the manor, their spirits lifted momentarily. The manor was alive with activity as the evening dinner was prepared. They joined Hunter at a table in the grand dining hall. Despite the warmth of the setting, Inez's thoughts remained clouded with worry. It had been weeks since the accident, and Zaire still hadn't regained consciousness. She felt uncertainty pressing down on her. Her appetite diminished despite the enticing spread before them.

As they ate, an unfamiliar sensation rippled through Inez. It wasn't a sound or a touch, it was something deeper, an undeniable connection. *Inez,* a voice called softly in her mind. She froze, the fork slipping from her fingers onto the plate with a quiet clatter. Her heart raced as she recognised the voice. It was him. She didn't say a word, her mind consumed with a single thought. Standing abruptly, she bolted from the hall, leaving Nadia and Hunter bewildered.

"Inez?" Hunter called after her, but she was already gone, moving with an incredible speed that left even Nadia astonished. They exchanged confused glances. "She was just here. What just happened?" Hunter asked, clearly perplexed.

"She's fast," Nadia remarked, her brow furrowed in concern. They both quickly stood and ran after her, knowing exactly where she was headed.

Meanwhile, Inez reached Zaire's room, her chest heaving with anticipation. She didn't waste time with doors, she phased through the solid wood with ease. Her heart pounded as she crossed the threshold, spotting him on the bed, his body still connected to the machines. "Zaire," she gasped as tears welled in her eyes. She rushed over to him, emotions flooding her as she leaned down and wrapped her arms around him tightly.

The sudden pressure elicited a whimper of pain from Zaire, and Inez immediately pulled back, guilt flashing across her face. "I'm sorry," she said quickly, her voice thick with emotion.

"It's okay," Zaire said weakly, his lips curling into a smile. "How long has it been?"

"Two weeks," Hunter answered, walking into the room. He had finally caught up, Nadia close behind him.

She wasted no time running over to Zaire, wrapping him in a warm hug. "I missed you," she said, her voice breaking with relief.

Inez, still overcome with emotion, grasped Zaire's hand gently. She closed her eyes and reached out to him mentally. *Are you in pain?*

A bit, Zaire responded, his voice echoing in her mind.

I'm sorry, it's my fault. I wish I could take it away, Inez thought, her fingers brushing against his hand to comfort him.

Suddenly, Inez felt a sharp pain in her arm. She winced, the sensation spreading as her veins began to darken, turning a deep midnight blue. "What's happening to your arm?" Nadia asked urgently.

Zaire's eyes widened as realisation struck. With effort, he pushed himself into a sitting position. "You took my pain away," he said in awe.

Inez's breathing steadied as the pain subsided. The eerie blue of her veins began to fade, returning to their normal appearance. She stared at her arm in disbelief, the moment sinking in. "Wow, that's pretty cool," Hunter remarked, his astonishment breaking the tension in the room.

The air hung heavy with relief and wonder as everyone absorbed what had just happened. Inez glanced at Zaire, her emotions still raw but steadied by the bond they shared. She had taken his pain, she didn't know how, but she was determined to figure it out.

41

The Lake Remembered

It was a perfect day, the kind that felt like a reward after the chaos of the past week. Zaire, now fully healed, radiated his usual confidence, while Inez seemed to glow with newfound mastery over her powers. The sun blazed in the sky, making it the warmest day of the year, and the group knew they had to find a way to cool off. Inez and Nadia exchanged a knowing glance, their thoughts perfectly aligned. "The lake," they said in unison, grinning.

With a sense of adventure, they packed a picnic and headed into the forest. The journey was filled with laughter and light-hearted teasing. Hunter and Nadia walked hand in hand, their connection clear in every shared glance. Meanwhile, Zaire took Inez's hand, his touch gentle yet firm. He smiled at her, and she couldn't stop herself from blushing. As if drawn by an invisible force, he leaned in and kissed her softly. The gesture was sweet, but Nadia's playful voice broke the spell. "Come on, lovebirds," she called, rolling her eyes.

The group soon arrived at the waterfall, its surging waters sparkling in the sunlight. The boys, eager to show off, climbed to the top and leapt into the lake below, their laughter echoing through the trees. The water was cool and refreshing, a perfect contrast to the heat of the day. For Zaire, Hunter and Nadia, this was a rare moment of freedom, a chance to escape the confines of the manor and simply enjoy life.

As they swam and splashed around, Zaire couldn't help but steal glances at Inez. There was something magical about the way she moved, and her laughter was like music to his ears. He led her to a hidden alcove behind the waterfall, a secret spot where the world seemed to fade away. Inez hesitated as they passed through the curtain of water, but Zaire's reassuring presence gave her courage. She wiped the droplets from her face and looked up at him, her heart racing as he gently placed his hands on her waist. "I love you, Inez," he said, his voice barely above a whisper.

Her cheeks flushed, and she wrapped her arms around his neck. "I love you too," she replied, her voice trembling with emotion.

They continued to kiss, their lips intertwining as Inez straddled Zaire, wrapping her legs around his waist. She could sense him getting harder between her legs. They were completely immersed, their senses engaged in a rhythm. Time seemed to slow as they basked in the purity of their shared experience. It felt as though the universe itself conspired to ensure that nothing, absolutely nothing, could shatter this spellbinding harmony. In that fleeting yet infinite moment, it was just them, invincible and untouchable, caught in the brilliance of an emotion that defied words.

Their moment of intimacy was interrupted by Hunter's sudden appearance, his mischievous grin making them jump. "Come on, lovebirds, let's eat," he said, laughing as he splashed water in their direction. Zaire rolled his eyes but couldn't suppress a smile. With a flick of his hand, he used his powers to send a playful wave that sent Hunter sprawling.

As they emerged from their hidden spot, Zaire shielded Inez from the waterfall's spray. "You couldn't do that when we went in?" she asked, playfully swatting his chest.

"I wanted to see you wet," he replied with a smirk, his eyes twinkling with mischief.

The group gathered on a blanket spread out on the grass, their picnic a feast of simple pleasures. Nadia reclined with her head on Hunter's lap, her laughter ringing out as he fed her grapes and strawberries like a queen. Zaire, ever the romantic, offered Inez a grape with a flourish. "A grape for my lady," he said, his tone mock-serious.

Inez giggled, playing along. "Why thank you, kind sir," she replied, her eyes sparkling with amusement.

Nadia, not to be outdone, tossed a handful of berries at them. "Jerks," she said, laughing as the group dissolved into fits of laughter.

As the day turned to dusk, they made their way to the edge of the forest, the manor visible in the distance. The sky transformed into a canvas of stars, and they spread their blankets on the field to stargaze. Inez nestled in Zaire's arms, the warmth of his embrace making her feel safe and cherished. Hunter and Nadia eventually wandered off, leaving Zaire and Inez alone under the vast expanse of the night sky. Their kisses grew more passionate, the world around them fading into insignificance. In that moment, nothing else mattered but the love they shared and the stars above.

Nadia reclined with her head on Hunter's lap, her laughter ringing out as he fed her grapes and strawberries like a queen. Zaire, ever the romantic, offered Inez a grape with a flourish. "A grape for my lady," he said, his tone mock-serious.

Inez giggled, playing along. "Why thank you, kind sir," she replied.

Nadia, not to be outdone, tossed a handful of berries at them. "Jerks," she said as the group dissolved into fits of laughter.

Inez stood up, her eyes locking with Zaire's. "Follow me," she said, her voice filled with promise.

"Anything you say," he replied, standing up and taking her hand. Together, they disappeared into the night.

42

Dawn Mission

They made their way to her room. Inez turned and locked the door with a quiet click, the cool brass brushing her fingertips. When she turned back, Zaire was close—so close she could feel the warmth of him, the quiet intensity in his gaze. She leaned gently against the door, her breath catching as he stepped forwards and kissed her, slow and deep.

His hands found her waist, steadying her as she tilted her head back, surrendering to the moment. Their kiss lingered, full of longing and quiet urgency. He drew back slightly, his eyes searching hers before he pressed a tender kiss to her neck, then down to her collarbone. She shivered beneath his touch.

With a glance for permission, he lifted the hem of her dress. She raised her arms to help, and he slipped it over her head, letting it fall softly to the floor. He continued to kiss her skin, each touch sending a ripple through her. Inez ran her fingers through his damp hair, then reached for the hem of his shirt, pulling it off and adding it to the growing pile.

She kissed him again, guiding him gently towards the bed.

In one fluid motion, Zaire turned her and eased her down onto the mattress. He leaned over her, brushing her cheek with his lips before trailing soft kisses along her neck and shoulders. Their breathing grew heavier, the air between them charged with quiet anticipation.

He paused, his voice low. "Are you alright?"

She nodded, her cheeks flushed, her eyes bright with trust.

They moved together slowly, exploring each other with reverence and care. Every touch was deliberate, every kiss a promise. Their bodies pressed close, the rhythm of their connection building gradually, tender and intense.

Zaire whispered her name, and she responded with a soft moan, her fingers gripping the sheets. He held her close, his movements gentle but sure, attuned to her every breath. They found a rhythm that felt like poetry—unspoken, instinctive, and deeply felt.

When the moment came, it was quiet and powerful, a shared release that left them breathless and still. They lay together, hearts pounding, the silence between them filled with warmth.

"That was..." she began.

"Amazing," he finished, brushing a strand of hair from her face.

She smiled, her expression soft. "Yes."

Later, after rinsing off the day's adventures, they stepped out of the shower, the warmth of the water still clinging to their skin. Inez wrapped herself in a towel, her cheeks tinged with colour as she turned to Zaire. "Would you like to stay here tonight?" she asked, hopeful.

Though his room was just upstairs, the thought of being close to her was too tempting to resist. "I'd love to," Zaire replied with a gentle smile. "Let me go and get changed." He dressed quickly, and after a final glance at Inez, he left to head to his room. The air between them was thick with quiet anticipation.

But when Zaire opened the door to his room, he found Raphael seated on the edge of the bed, the soft light casting shadows across his furrowed brow. Surprised, Zaire offered a respectful greeting, though his voice betrayed his unease.

"Sir."

"Why are you so sweaty? Where have you been?" Raphael asked, his tone sharp.

Zaire hesitated. "I was with Inez..." The words came out in a rush.

Raphael's eyes narrowed. "So why are you sweaty?"

Zaire faltered, cheeks warming. "We... well..." he stammered.

Raphael sighed and stood. "Oh, I see."

"Raphael—"

"That's 'sir' to you," Raphael corrected, his voice cool.

Zaire's heart sank. He'd crossed a line, and the privilege of familiarity had been revoked. Guilt settled over him like a weight.

"I have some information for you," he said quietly, lowering his gaze.

"About what?"

"It's about Kimmie," Zaire replied, his voice heavy. "She opened a portal… and she has a dragon." The words felt like a betrayal, and he hated himself for saying them.

"How do you know this?"

"Inez saw him. In her room."

Raphael was silent for a long moment, then simply said, "Very well," and left the room, leaving Zaire with a troubled conscience.

Seeking comfort, Zaire dressed and made his way through the quiet corridors to Inez's room. The cool evening air brushed his skin as he approached her door. When she opened it, her expression shifted from concern to relief.

"Sorry I was delayed," he murmured.

Together they stepped inside—their sanctuary.

Later that night, the world outside faded away. They lay wrapped in each other's arms, sharing soft whispers and gentle laughter. When dawn arrived in hues of gold and rose, Zaire stirred to the sound of footsteps. Inez entered with a tray of breakfast, her smile bright and full of promise.

"Morning," she said warmly.

"Morning, gorgeous," Zaire replied, stretching and savouring the moment.

Over breakfast, they shared quiet conversation and contented smiles. But soon, duty called—Raphael had given him a mission, one that would take him away for a few days. With a final lingering glance and a promise woven into his farewell, Zaire left Inez's side, stepping into the day with quiet resolve.

43

The Passage Within

Kimmie paced in her room, her mind racing. She didn't know what to think. Why would Inez betray her trust like that? Her chest tightened as the thought settled. She ran through every conversation, every moment they had shared, searching for clues she might have missed. Guilt crept in, she should have let Inez explain herself. But what would that change? The damage was done. Shaking her head, she sighed. She owed Megyn an apology; there was no avoiding it.

"What should I do?" she asked, barely above a whisper. Kek, her dragon companion, tilted his head at her from his perch on the shelf. His bright eyes held a glimmer of understanding that comforted her.

"I'd better apologise," Kimmie said, determination pushing through her hesitation. "Stay hidden, okay? I'll be back as soon as possible." Kek flapped his wings and landed on a fluffy pillow, curling up as if to say, *I'll wait.*

The hallway felt colder than usual as Kimmie made her way to Megyn's door. With every step, her stomach churned. She knocked gently. The wait was agonising.

The door creaked open, revealing Megyn. Her eyes narrowed, and her lips curled into a sarcastic smile. "Hi. Come to swear at me some more?"

Kimmie winced at the words. She deserved that. "To apologise, actually," she replied.

Megyn raised an eyebrow, sceptical. "Inez told you it was Zaire then?"

"Zaire?" The name hit Kimmie like a lightning bolt. Her confusion was written all over her face. "What are you talking about?"

Megyn sighed, her expression softening. "Come in," she said, stepping aside to let Kimmie through.

They sat down, and Megyn took a deep breath and began to explain. She recounted how Inez had told her about the date with Zaire. The memory of Zaire winning a dragon teddy at the carnival, one that reminded Inez of Kek, was vivid. Megyn detailed how Zaire's curiosity had led to questions and, eventually, promises of no more secrets between them. Yet, it seemed Zaire had broken that promise. She could only assume he had reported what he learned.

Kimmie listened intently, her shock growing with each revelation. Had she misjudged Inez completely? Her heart sank, realising how quickly she had let her anger take control.

"Can I see him?" Megyn asked hesitantly, pulling Kimmie from her thoughts.

"Of course," Kimmie said, flicking her wrist. A shimmering portal appeared, revealing her room on the other side. But Kek was nowhere to be seen.

"Kek," Kimmie called, her voice echoing through the portal.

A second later, a small shadow darted from the top shelf. Kek leapt through the portal with a graceful swoop and landed in Kimmie's arms. She smiled, cradling him close.

"This is Megyn," Kimmie said, introducing her dragon companion. "This is Kek."

Kek tilted his head curiously before climbing onto Megyn's lap. He bowed his head, a gesture of respect that took Megyn by surprise. She hesitated before mirroring the gesture, earning a light purr of approval from the dragon.

The tension between the two girls eased as they talked about Kek, his origins, his quirks and what they should do moving forward. Slowly but surely, the rift between them began to mend, leaving space for understanding and trust to grow again.

Kek and Qita darted around the room, their playful energy filling the space. They took turns chasing one another, leaping onto the climbing frame and tumbling into a pile of soft cushions. Kimmie watched them, her thoughts clouded. She and Megyn had just made an important decision, they needed to inform someone about Kek. Her hands fidgeted as she wrestled with her anxiety.

Megyn noticed her unease and leaned closer, placing a reassuring hand on Kimmie's shoulder. "I'll be with you," she said firmly. "No one will hurt him. I won't allow it. I can feel the bond between you two, it reminds me of us." She smiled and glanced at Qita, who paused his play to nuzzle against Megyn's leg.

Taking a deep breath, Kimmie nodded. They gathered Kek and Qita, preparing for what lay ahead. As they walked down to the main lobby, Qita padded silently beside Megyn, his tail swishing with each step. Kek perched on Kimmie's shoulder, his small claws gripping her shirt for balance. Kimmie could feel her heartbeat quickening, each step bringing a wave of doubt and panic. Her face turned pale, her breathing unsteady.

Megyn stopped, noticing the fear etched across her friend's face. Without hesitation, she took Kimmie's hand, squeezing it gently. "You've got this," Megyn whispered. The simple gesture calmed Kimmie enough to keep moving.

They approached the front desk. The receptionist looked up, her eyes widening as her gaze landed on Kek. "Is that a dragon?" she stammered.

"We need to speak to the boss," Megyn replied. It wasn't a request, it was a command.

The receptionist, still staring at Kek in disbelief, scrambled to pick up the phone. After a quick exchange, she looked back at them. "Please go up," she said, gesturing to the stairs.

Climbing the stairs felt like an eternity to Kimmie. Her legs felt heavy, her mind running through worst-case scenarios. What if they took Kek away? What if they didn't understand? At the top, they paused before the heavy wooden door. Kimmie hesitated, but Megyn gave her hand another encouraging squeeze.

Megyn knocked firmly. A deep voice called out, "Enter."

The room they stepped into was grand, with tall shelves filled with books and artefacts. Behind a large desk sat the boss, his sharp eyes taking them in. "How may I help you, ladies?" he asked, his tone even.

Kimmie swallowed hard, summoning her courage. "I'm here to confess," she said, her voice trembling but resolute.

The boss leaned back in his chair. "I know about the dragon," he said calmly, surprising both girls. "I always have. I saw him flying in the green, a remarkable creature."

"You knew?" Megyn blurted out.

"Yes," he replied, folding his hands in front of him. "I've been waiting for someone to report him or for you to confess."

"But why?" Kimmie asked.

"Because he will be a great asset to the team, once he is big enough," the boss said with a small smile. "You, too, have a special bond with him, a bond that is rare and valuable."

The tension in the room began to lift as his words sank in. "Is there anything else?" he added.

Kimmie hesitated before speaking again. "Just to confirm," she said slowly. "I can keep him? You don't want me to try sending him back? And no one will take him?"

The boss nodded. "No, he is all yours, as Qita is Megyn's. No one will touch him. But know this: I had to search your room to show I act on what I am told."

Kimmie's heart sank at the intrusion, but was quickly soothed by his final words. "Also, for your peace of mind," he said, "yes, it was Zaire."

"Thank you, sir," they said in unison, relief washing over them as they turned to leave the office.

As they descended the stairs, Kimmie glanced at Kek, who chirped softly on her shoulder. She felt a renewed sense of hope, they had faced their fears, and now, together, they could move forward.

44

Click Without Closure

Later that evening, Kimmie and Megyn sat down for dinner together in the bustling hall. Laughter and chatter filled the room, but their table was the centre of attention. Qita happily licked his bowl clean, savouring the salmon and rice meal prepared just for him. Kek sat primly at the table, his small, gleaming bowl of chicken in front of him. His presence drew wide-eyed stares from everyone around. Whispers rippled through the crowd as people tried to comprehend the sight of a dragon dining among them.

Unbothered, Kek dove into his meal with gusto, but it didn't take long for the little dragon to finish and glance around, his hunger still not quite satisfied. With a flutter of his wings, he launched into the air, gliding over to the counter. The room collectively held its breath. Inez stood there, calm and unshaken. She smiled warmly and handed him a tender piece of steak. Kek chirped in gratitude before flying back to the table, meat firmly in his claws. He landed gracefully, devouring the steak in seconds.

From across the room, Inez's gaze caught Kimmie's. She smiled at her, an expression that held a mix of understanding and regret. Kimmie hesitated, her emotions swirling, before turning back to her conversation with Megyn. She wasn't ready to face Inez, not yet.

The following morning, the two friends ventured into the woods behind the building. The air was crisp and filled with birdsong. Sunlight filtered through the trees, casting dappled patterns on the ground. Kek soared above them, his wings slicing gracefully through the air as he explored his newfound freedom. Below him, Qita darted between tree roots and bushes, leaping over fallen branches and clambering onto stumps with agile precision. Their exuberance was contagious, and Kimmie and Megyn couldn't help but laugh as they watched.

As they wandered deeper into the woods, the roar of a waterfall reached their ears. Following the sound, they soon came upon a cascading stream tumbling into a crystal-clear pool. Kek landed on a moss-covered rock by the water's edge, dipping his snout to drink the cool, fresh water. Nearby, Qita sniffed cautiously before finding a dry patch to sit on, keeping his paws well away from the damp ground.

The journey became a daily ritual for the group. They returned to the woods each day, allowing Kek to practise his flying and hone his skills. As the days passed, Kimmie noticed subtle changes in him, his wings grew broader, his movements more confident. Freed from the confines of her room and with unlimited food to fuel him, Kek was growing rapidly.

Kek quickly developed a fondness for the water. He took to flying up to the top of the waterfall, pausing only briefly before diving gracefully into the pool below. His splashes sent ripples across the water, scattering startled fish in every direction. With a predator's instinct, he would snag a fish mid-swim before surfacing triumphantly. More often than not, he shared his catch with Qita, dropping the fish at the cat's feet. But Qita's aversion to all things wet sent him leaping backwards, fur bristling, when the slippery fish splashed against him.

Through these shared moments, Kimmie and Megyn's bond deepened. They talked for hours, their conversations weaving a tapestry of trust and understanding. Meanwhile, Qita and Kek formed an unlikely but inseparable friendship. Together, they explored, played and napped, always finding comfort in each other's company.

Unbeknownst to them, the boss watched from afar. His sharp eyes tracked Kek's growth and progress. Every flap of his wings, every display of strength and every interaction was meticulously noted and filed away. He saw potential, remarkable, untapped potential, and quietly waited for the day when that potential would be fully realised.

The team returned from their mission, their chatter fading as their eyes turned to the sight before them. A dragon, a real dragon, was soaring gracefully above the green. Gasps echoed among them; no one had expected such a thing. Zaire stood frozen as he tried to process what he was seeing. He hadn't shared anything about this with Hunter or Nadia. How could he? He barely believed it himself. But as the dragon banked sharply in the air, sunlight glinting off its iridescent wings, one thought consumed Zaire's mind: Inez.

Without another word, Zaire left the group and made his way to Inez's room. His knuckles rapped lightly against the door. For a moment, there was no response, and then it opened. Her expression was unreadable as her eyes locked onto his.

"You're back," she said simply.

"May I?" Zaire asked, gesturing towards the room.

Inez hesitated briefly before stepping aside. "Yes, come in." She walked over to sit on the edge of her bed. Zaire took his usual place in the reading chair, his posture tense.

They sat in silence, the air between them charged. Finally, Inez broke it. "So, you reported Kimmie?" The accusation hung heavily in the air.

Zaire flinched. "Wow, okay, yes, I did," he replied, surprised at her bluntness.

"Why?" Inez demanded, her eyes narrowing.

"I had no choice," he said defensively.

"No choice?" she echoed, disbelief creeping into her voice. "How did you have no choice?"

Zaire exhaled heavily, rubbing the back of his neck. "He found out about us. He didn't approve, and I had to give him something."

Inez's lips pressed into a thin line. "So you turned in a friend," she said, her voice filled with quiet anger. "You promised me, Zaire."

Her words hit him like a slap. "I'm sorry," he said earnestly. "I didn't know what else to do."

Inez pulled her hand away as he reached for it. "You should have spoken to me," she snapped. "You had plenty of time."

"When?" Zaire countered, his frustration bubbling over.

"Oh, I don't know," Inez shot back, sarcasm dripping from her words. "How about the times you were trying to win me over with sweet words and empty promises?"

Zaire's face softened, guilt written across his features. "I messed up," he admitted. "But I care about you, Inez. That hasn't changed."

Her gaze dropped, the fire in her eyes dimming slightly. "I need time, Zaire," she said quietly. "I can't just forgive this."

"I understand," he said, rising from the chair. His usual confidence was replaced with an uncharacteristic humility as he moved towards the door. "I'll see you later."

Inez didn't respond as the door clicked shut behind him. She sat there, staring at her easel across the room, lost in thought. Her heart was a tangle of emotions, betrayal, anger.

45

The Break Went Deeper

Later that day, the training hall buzzed with energy. Megyn and Kimmie practised together, guiding Qita through an intricate series of agility drills while Kek soared above them, practising sharp turns and dives. Across the room, Hunter and Nadia were sparring, their movements synchronised. Everything felt normal, until the door swung open.

Zaire strode into the hall, his presence instantly shifting the atmosphere. Kimmie's heart lurched at the sight of him, and her body tensed. The memory of nearly losing Kek was still fresh, and anger surged through her. Kek perched on her shoulder, sensing her emotions. He let out a piercing screech, the sound slicing through the hall and bringing all activity to a halt.

Every pair of eyes turned towards them, following their line of sight to Zaire. The stares didn't faze him; he met them with his usual calm confidence. But Megyn saw what was brewing in Kimmie and stepped in front of her, hands raised in a gesture of caution.

"Don't do it, Kimmie," she said imploringly. "It's not worth it."

Kimmie's eyes burned with fury. She gently pushed Megyn aside and shouted across the hall, "Zaire!"

He paused mid-stride, looking around to ensure no one else had spoken. "What?" he asked guardedly. Deep down, he already knew what was coming.

"Why did you do it?" Kimmie began to walk towards him. Megyn stayed close, her hand brushing Qita's fur as the cat trotted at her side.

Zaire folded his arms, his expression indifferent. "I am an upper rank. I don't need to explain anything to you."

"What is going on?" Nadia cut in, her sparring session forgotten as she approached with Hunter.

Kimmie's jaw clenched. The fury she'd been holding back spilt out in her next words. "Your upper rank reported a baby dragon to the boss," she said, her words dripping with contempt. "Didn't realise your head could get any further up his arse, Zaire."

A flicker of discomfort crossed Zaire's face, but he masked it quickly. "You reported it?" Nadia asked, her tone laced with shock. This wasn't the Zaire she knew.

"He did," Kimmie confirmed, her voice rising. "Almost cost me Kek."

Hunter and Nadia exchanged a glance. They knew Zaire wouldn't act without reason, and though his actions puzzled them, their loyalty was unwavering.

Zaire took a step towards Kimmie and Megyn, his posture stiff. Hunter and Nadia flanked him. The tension was palpable, the air thick with the unspoken challenge.

"Are we going to do this?" Zaire asked, his voice low and almost dangerous.

Kimmie's hands balled into fists. "All you have to do is apologise," she said, daring him to deny her.

"I'm not apologising for doing my job," Zaire shot back.

"Your job?" Kimmie laughed bitterly, the sound devoid of humour. "How is this a job? We are orphans, captives. We can't leave because of our powers. He is the enemy, and you're helping him!"

Zaire's eyes narrowed, and his voice was cold but measured when he said, "He is not the enemy. What would you have without him?"

The room fell silent, everyone holding their breath as the two faced off. The clash of ideals and loyalties between them had reached its boiling point, and their confrontation hung heavy in the air.

Kek screeched again, his piercing cry reverberating off the walls of the training hall. His small frame bristled with defiance as he glared at Zaire. Unfazed, Zaire raised a hand, summoning a gust of wind that sent Kek tumbling off Kimmie's shoulder. Kek managed to steady himself mid-air, but the act had already lit a fire in both Kimmie and Megyn.

Kimmie's fists clenched at her sides, her anger bubbling to the surface. Megyn, always attuned to Kimmie's emotions, immediately stepped forwards, placing herself between Zaire and her friend. Her stance shifted instinctively, one hand rested on the hilt of her katana, the other poised in readiness. The blade gleamed faintly in the light, a silent warning.

Nadia and Hunter exchanged a glance, the question passing between them. "We're doing this," Hunter said grimly, stepping into position.

Megyn was outnumbered two to one, but she didn't falter. Her determination burned brighter than her fear. She moved with precision, her movements fluid and calculated as the fight began. Nadia's agility made her a difficult target, her flips and spins keeping her just out of reach. Megyn struck at her opponent relentlessly, but every punch missed its mark. Nadia was like a shadow, always there but impossible to touch.

Hunter came at Megyn from the other side, his fists swinging with brute strength. She ducked under his strikes, her reflexes keeping her one step ahead. As his arm swung past her once more, she used the momentum to her advantage, delivering a well-timed sweep that sent him crashing to the ground.

Meanwhile, on the other side of the hall, Kimmie faced off against Zaire. It was a battle of raw emotions and unbridled strength. Kimmie launched herself at him, her punches landing hard and fast. Zaire stumbled back, blood trickling from a cut on his cheek. Fury flashed in his eyes, and he retaliated by summoning a bolt of lightning. The strike shot through the air, arcing towards Kimmie.

But Kimmie was ready. With a swift motion, she opened a shimmering portal above her, redirecting the lightning to the other side of the room. The bolt struck the ground dangerously close to Nadia, who leapt back in alarm.

Megyn, seeing an opportunity, called out, "Kimmie, Qita!"

Without hesitation, Kimmie opened another portal, this time connecting to Megyn. Qita, sensing the urgency, jumped through. What emerged on the other side was not the small cat everyone was familiar with but a sleek, formidable grey panther. The transformation was startling, and the power radiating from Qita was undeniable.

Qita prowled to Megyn's side, his golden eyes fixed on their adversaries. A low, guttural growl rumbled from his throat, sending chills down the spines of everyone in the room. Even Nadia hesitated, her confidence failing.

"You get her. I have him," Megyn said firmly to Qita.

"My pleasure," Qita responded, his voice deep and smooth, sending a ripple of shock through the room. No one had expected him to speak.

Nadia, her agility no match for the imposing panther, made the only choice she could. She turned and bolted for the door, disappearing into the woods with Qita in pursuit.

Megyn turned her attention back to Hunter. He rose to his feet, but there was no mistaking the uncertainty in his eyes. Megyn gripped her katana tightly, its edge infused with a rare, glowing metal designed to cut even the toughest skin. She advanced, ready to end the fight.

Kimmie and Zaire continued their fierce battle, the tension between them crackling like electricity. Kek soared above them, his wings cutting through the smoke-filled hall. With a sudden, guttural roar, he unleashed a stream of fire down on Zaire. The flames engulfed him, and for a moment, everyone froze, unsure of what had just happened. As the smoke cleared, Zaire stood unharmed, encased in a shimmering air bubble that had shielded him from the blaze. His expression was calm, but his eyes betrayed the storm brewing within.

Suddenly, Qita burst into the hall, his sleek panther form streaked with blood. His golden eyes glinted dangerously as he growled low and deep. Hunter's gaze locked onto him, fear flashing across his face. "Zaire," Hunter said with barely contained rage. "If she's hurt…" His words trailed off, but the threat was clear. Without waiting for a response, Hunter turned and bolted out of the hall, disappearing into the woods.

Kek landed gracefully on Kimmie's shoulder, his claws gripping her tightly as he spread his wings wide. He let out a screech so powerful it rattled the windows, the sound reverberating through the hall like a war cry. Megyn stepped forwards, her katana glinting in the dim light, its blade stained with blood. She stood beside Kimmie, her stance unwavering. Behind her, Qita prowled, his growls growing louder, his muscles coiled and ready to strike.

"I'm sorry," Zaire whispered.

"Speak up," Qita snarled.

"I'm sorry!" Zaire shouted, his voice cracking under the guilt. Qita's form trembled, and with a flash of light, he shifted back into his smaller feline form. The tension in the room eased slightly, but Zaire didn't wait for further confrontation. He turned and fled, his footsteps echoing as he ran out of the hall and into the field.

Outside, Zaire stopped abruptly as he saw Hunter emerging from the woods. In his arms lay Nadia, her body limp and lifeless. Zaire's heart sank, dread pooling in his stomach. From the hall windows, Kimmie and Megyn watched the scene unfold, their expressions grim.

Hunter carried Nadia to the infirmary, his movements urgent but careful. Zaire followed closely behind, his mind racing with questions and worries. Inside, the doctor worked quickly, hooking Nadia up to an IV filled with a strange white liquid, the same substance Zaire had been given once before.

After stabilising Nadia, the doctor turned to Hunter and Zaire, shooing them out of the infirmary with a stern look. The door clicked shut behind them, and the hall fell silent. But the quiet didn't last long.

Hunter grabbed Zaire by the scruff of his neck, slamming him into the wall with enough force to leave a dent. His eyes burned with fury as he leaned in close. "If she's hurt," Hunter growled, "you will feel it too."

46

Silent Hallway

Inez stepped into the hallway just as the tension reached its breaking point. Both figures turned to look at her: Zaire, fuming but silent, and Hunter, his jaw clenched in barely contained rage. With a sharp motion, Hunter released Zaire, his eyes narrowing.

"What's happened?" Inez asked, concerned.

Hunter's glare didn't falter as he spat, "Ask your boyfriend." Without waiting for a response, he stormed off, his heavy footsteps echoing against the walls.

Confusion etched across Inez's face as she turned back to Zaire. "What happened?" she repeated, firmer now. Before Zaire could answer, their attention was drawn to the sound of retreating figures, Kimmie and Kek disappearing around the corner. Seconds later, Qita and Megyn emerged from the hall, Megyn's katana glinting ominously as she casually wiped it clean of blood. Hunter's blood.

"What the fuck happened?" Inez snapped, slicing through the air like a whip as she stared Zaire down.

His expression hardened. "They told me to apologise for the dragon thing," he said defiantly. "But I refused."

"And?" Inez pressed, her worry mounting. "That blood on Megyn's katana, what's it from?"

Zaire hesitated, then admitted, "We all fought. And... Qita attacked

Nadia."

Anger surged through her. "Why couldn't you just apologise?" she demanded, heavy with disappointment. Her gaze bore into him, but Zaire only let out a frustrated huff and turned on his heel, walking away without another word.

Frustrated and disheartened, Inez headed to the infirmary. The sterile smell hit her as soon as she pushed open the door. Spotting Nadia lying pale and motionless on a bed, Inez hurried to her side, only to be intercepted by the attending doctor.

"You cannot be in here, miss," he said curtly.

"I can help," Inez insisted, brushing past him to grab Nadia's hand. As her fingers curled around her friend's, a strange energy surged through her. Her veins shimmered, shifting colours in a mesmerising yet alarming display. Inez let out a pained whimper as the energy coursed through her, transferring the agony she felt from Nadia. The moment was brief but intense, and then, as quickly as it started, the pain ceased. The colourful glow faded from her veins.

The doctor stood frozen in shock. But then, to his amazement, Nadia's eyelids fluttered. Her lashes lifted slowly as she blinked and focused on the face smiling down at her.

"Can you hear me?" Inez asked softly.

"Yes," Nadia murmured.

"Just rest. I'll get Hunter," Inez reassured her, giving her shoulder a gentle squeeze before turning to leave the room.

She found Hunter in the gym, his fists pounding into a punching bag with ferocity. The sound of leather against leather reverberated through the space. "She's awake," Inez announced, breaking his focus.

Hunter froze, his eyes snapping to hers. "What? How?" he asked, his expression one of both shock and hope.

"I healed her," Inez explained simply.

In an instant, Hunter closed the gap between them, pulling her into a tight, almost desperate embrace. "Thank you so much," he said.

Later, as Inez went to relay the news to Zaire, she could sense him nearby.

He was in his room, but he wasn't alone. She went back to her room and decided to look for him later, when he was by himself.

47

The Still Building

Raphael was with Zaire, his fury palpable as he berated Zaire for his failure. As an upper rank, Zaire had responsibilities, and Raphael was appalled that he had allowed things to spiral so far out of control.

"You've disappointed me," Raphael said coldly. "You should have prevented this."

The consequences were swift and harsh. Raphael temporarily stripped Zaire of his rank, appointing Lamia as his replacement. The message was clear: Zaire needed to earn back his position and prove he was worthy of the trust placed in him.

That night, the day's events settled over the building like a suffocating fog. As punishment, or perhaps as a means to let emotions cool, everyone involved was confined to their rooms. The halls, usually filled with conversation, were eerily quiet.

Megyn sat cross-legged on the floor, diligently wiping the crimson streaks from her katana. She carefully cleaned not only the blade but also Qita's face, removing the remnants of the earlier confrontation. Across the building, Kimmie lay curled up in bed, pressed against Kek's warmth, seeking comfort in his presence.

Nadia remained in the infirmary, her injuries keeping her tethered to the sterile space. Hunter, unwilling to leave her side, had been allowed to stay. He sat at her bedside, watching over her as she rested, his fingers absent-mindedly tracing patterns on the sheets beside her hand.

Inez refused to let anyone go hungry. Despite the tension, she ensured everyone had food. Moving through the quiet corridors, she placed trays of carefully prepared meals outside each door, knocking gently before walking away. There were no conversations, no shared glances, just an offering of nourishment.

When she reached Zaire's door, she knocked and waited for a response. None came. She sighed, shifting the tray in her hands. "I have some food for you," she said through the closed door. The silence stretched between them. With a quiet shake of her head, she set the tray down and walked away, leaving him to his solitude.

Back in her room, Inez sought comfort in the only thing that made sense, art. She pulled out her paints and, under the dim glow of her lamp, set to work. Every stroke was painstakingly precise. This wasn't just any painting, it was him. Her husband. She memorised every contour of his face, every shadow and highlight, every expression that had once been hers to witness. The canvas soon held the most intricate design she had ever created, a perfect rendition of the man she loved.

As the paint dried, exhaustion pulled at her. She set the brush aside, letting out a slow breath. Without another thought, she crawled into bed, her mind in the past as sleep finally claimed her.

48

Untouched Tray

When Inez awoke the next morning, her heart sank. He was staring at her again. That same piercing gaze, heavy with unspoken words. A lump formed in her throat as she quickly turned away, shoving the canvas behind the others, hiding it from view. The sight of it was unbearable now.

It was still early, so she made herself a hot chocolate, wrapping her hands around the mug for comfort. She needed space, needed air, so she slipped out to the green, her book tucked under her arm. As she settled onto the damp grass, she found herself wondering whether she would see Kimmie and Kek. But they never turned up.

Disappointed and restless, she returned to her room, slipping the book back onto the shelf before changing into something more practical. The scent of food wafted through the air as she made her way to the dining hall, where she silently took her place at the serving station. Her mind drifted elsewhere as she ladled out portions for each approaching guest. Once she finished, she grabbed a plate for herself and sat alone at a table, waiting for everyone else to arrive.

When Kimmie finally entered, Kek was by her side. They settled far across the room. Then Zaire walked in. He barely acknowledged her presence, going out of his way to sit as far from her as possible, as if she carried some disease he needed to avoid. The quiet ache in her chest deepened.

UNTOUCHED TRAY

Megyn arrived next, Qita trailing beside her, taking a seat near Kimmie. Time dragged as the tension lingered in the air. Eventually, Nadia stumbled in, her balance off. Hunter was there, his arms around her, guiding her towards their table. The sight was bittersweet.

Then Lamia entered, her brows furrowed at the undeniable division in the room. Though she had expected some fallout after her conversation with the boss, the reality of it was striking. She grabbed her food, intending to leave, but Zaire's voice called her back.

She hesitated, then walked over to him, sliding into the seat across from him. Inez watched as they leaned in, their voices hushed, their hands intertwined. The way they looked at each other was intimate, familiar, and undeniable.

Her stomach twisted violently.

He wasn't in his room last night.

The air in the dining hall suddenly felt suffocating. She pushed herself to her feet and hurried out. The moment she reached the bathroom, she collapsed over the sink, the nausea overwhelming her. Her stomach heaved, and she barely managed to steady herself before vomiting.

She gasped for breath, gripping the edges of the sink as she stared at her own reflection. How could she have been so stupid?

The urge to run nagged at her, hanging over her like a thousand voices screaming for escape. But that's all she ever did, run. She hated it. But this time, it felt unavoidable.

With trembling legs, she made her way upstairs to the upper-rank quarters, her eyes searching out Zaire's door. The tray of food she had left for him was still there, untouched. Confirmation of her worst fears.

She didn't think. She just ran.

Out of the building. Into the woods.

49

The Water Rippled

Back inside, Kimmie couldn't shake the feeling in her gut. Inez hadn't shown up for their gardening duty, and after witnessing the scene in the dining hall, worry gnawed at her. She found Megyn and filled her in, and together, they prepared to search.

Just as they reached the exit, they nearly collided with Nadia and Hunter.

"Where are you rushing off to?" Hunter asked, his brows knitting together.

"Inez is missing," Kimmie explained hurriedly. "She didn't show up for duty, and she's not in the building."

"We're heading into the woods to look for her," Megyn added.

"We'll come with you," Nadia said firmly, bracing herself against Hunter.

"You're not strong enough. You stay here and find a way to tell us if she returns," Kimmie replied.

"They're right," Hunter agreed, gripping Nadia's arms. She hesitated, then nodded.

"I'm sorry," Megyn said, her voice quieter now. "It wasn't all our fault. Zaire should have just apologised."

Nadia shook her head. "It's okay. What's done is done."

Kimmie glanced at the door. "We'd better go."

Nadia paced anxiously in Inez's room, arms wrapped around herself as she fought off the unease clawing at her chest. "I'll stay here until she returns," she murmured to Hunter, who nodded before heading off. He refused to sit still, he needed to be doing something. He spent the morning making rounds, checking every entrance, every shadowed hallway, hoping to catch a glimpse of her returning.

Meanwhile, Megyn and Kimmie ventured deep into the woods. Kimmie glanced at Kek before whispering, "Go. Find her."

With a powerful thrust of his wings, Kek soared above the treetops, scanning the terrain below.

Megyn reached for Qita, her fingers glowing as she unleashed her power. His form shuddered, shifting seamlessly into a sleek panther. His muscles tensed, golden eyes flickering with newfound predatory instinct. "Locate her," she commanded.

"I'll do what I can," he growled in response before sprinting into the dense forest.

Kimmie and Megyn followed on foot, their hearts hammering with urgency.

Suddenly, a deep, echoing roar split through the trees.

"That's him!" Megyn called, breaking into a run.

They reached the edge of the forest and found Qita standing rigid, eyes locked onto the waterfall beyond. "There," he instructed, flicking his tail towards the top of the cliff.

Inez sat curled on a rock, arms wrapped around her knees as silent sobs wracked her body. Kek had landed beside her, watching with quiet concern.

Inez lifted her tear-streaked face. "What are you doing here?" she whispered.

Kek tilted his head, then shifted his gaze down to the figures waiting below.

Something in Inez shifted. She inhaled sharply, straightening her posture. In one swift movement, she stood, then launched herself from the rock, descending towards them in a graceful burst of energy.

Kimmie's eyes widened. "Whoa, new power?"

Inez landed effortlessly, her expression devoid of emotion. "Yes. Just managed to do it," she responded flatly.

Qita's panther form shimmered, dissolving back into his normal size as he leapt onto Megyn's shoulder.

Kimmie wasted no time. She opened a portal back to Inez's room, stepping through with ease. "We have her, and we're on our way back," she informed Nadia, who let out a sigh of relief. "She wants to walk."

Closing the portal, they began their journey back, heading towards the green. As they approached the lake, Kimmie came upon a scene that made her blood boil.

Zaire and Lamia, together.

The rage in Kimmie bubbled over. She strode straight towards them, her voice cutting through the air like a blade. "What the fuck is your problem?" she spat, venom lacing every syllable. "You injure your so-called friends, cheat on your girlfriend and don't even notice that she goes missing? You're a scumbag."

Zaire stiffened, his jaw tightening, but he said nothing.

Kimmie exhaled, grabbing Inez by the arm, ready to drag her away from him.

"Inez," Zaire called.

She turned slightly, but Kimmie tightened her grip, pulling her forwards before she could look back.

"Stop," Lamia's voice rang out, power rippling through the air in waves. Her siren command forced them to a standstill.

They turned towards her, confusion etched across their faces.

"Let them talk," she urged.

Inez's gaze darkened. "I don't want to talk to him. I don't trust him," she said coldly. "I'll only talk to you."

Lamia nodded. "You two go in," she told Kimmie and Megyn. "I'll meet up with you for dinner."

Zaire dawdled for a moment, looking at Inez, before silently stepping away, leaving the dock and walking past her without another word.

Inez turned to Lamia, watching as the water rippled around her form.

"So why do you want to talk to me?" Lamia asked.

"Because you've never lied to me," Inez answered firmly. "And I want to hear your side."

Inez sat on the dock, her legs dangling in the cool water, ripples forming with every slight movement. The sun was beginning to set, casting a warm orange glow over the lake. She turned to Lamia. "Did you two spend the night together?" she asked, her eyes searching for answers.

Lamia took a deep breath, her expression calm but bathed in sadness. "Let me explain everything," she said softly. She began recounting the events of the previous night. The boss had demoted Zaire, replacing him with Lamia, a decision that had shaken everyone. Concerned for him, Lamia had gone to check on Zaire, but he wouldn't answer the door. Worried, she wandered to the dock and found him there, sitting alone, his shoulders hunched and his face streaked with tears. He had been crying, overwhelmed by the weight of his mistakes.

Zaire had confessed to Lamia how his behaviour had nearly cost him everything, his relationships with Nadia and Hunter and, most painfully, his bond with Inez. Lamia assured Inez that nothing had happened between them beyond words. She had opened up to Zaire about her own struggles, and in the morning, she had thanked him for listening and apologised for burdening him with her thoughts.

As Lamia finished her explanation, Inez felt a wave of guilt wash over her. She realised she had been wrong to jump to conclusions. "Thank you," she whispered. Then, without another word, she stood up and ran, her heart pounding in her chest.

She reached Zaire's room and pounded on the door. When he opened it, his face was a mix of surprise and concern. "What's wrong?" he asked.

"I'm sorry," Inez blurted out, tears welling in her eyes. "I should have trusted you." Before he could respond, she threw herself into his arms, wrapping her arms tightly around his neck. Their lips met in a long overdue kiss.

50

Watching Moon

After a few days, things had finally settled. Nadia had made a full recovery, and Zaire reclaimed his position as an upper rank. Life resumed its rhythm until he was summoned for a private meeting with the boss.

The assignment laid before him was unlike any before. A new mission, one that would test them all. And this time, he was ordered to bring Inez along. They wanted to see how she handled pressure, how she adapted to the field.

Standing on the wooden stage in the gathering hall, Zaire raised his voice so everyone could hear him. "This week's mission log: Myself, Nadia, Hunter and Inez."

The moment her name was spoken, the hall shifted. Eyes turned towards Inez, scrutinising her, questioning her readiness. She swallowed hard, scanning the faces around her. But then, Megyn dipped her head, a silent reassurance. Inez exhaled. She had trained for this. She was ready.

As the meeting adjourned and the crowd dispersed, Zaire caught her arm. "Wait," he said, his voice low.

Inez turned swiftly, startled. The hall emptied, leaving only the two of them behind.

He stepped closer, his gaze locked onto hers. Without hesitation, he cupped her cheek, his touch warm and grounding. Then, he kissed her, just

WATCHING MOON

long enough to steady them both.

"Are you up for this?" he asked, his thumb grazing her skin.

Inez hesitated, searching his eyes. "Do I get a choice?"

"If you don't want to go, I'll make an excuse for you," he offered, his fingers brushing along her cheek.

Her brows furrowed. "Why would you do that?" She tightened her grip around his hand.

His expression softened. "I won't put you in a situation you don't like. Why would I do that when I love you?" The words spilt out before he could second-guess them.

A spark lit up in her eyes, mischievous yet sincere. "I love you too," she admitted, her lips curling into a playful smile.

They rested their foreheads against each other, laughter spilling between them before their lips met once more. Then, hand in hand, they exited the hall, heading towards their rooms to prepare.

Today was Inez's first day in the field. The four of them had been tasked with recovering another gem, this one locked deep within a vault inside a secluded science lab. The facility, nestled in the heart of the forest, was heavily secured. For the last three days, they had observed every detail: guard rotations, security protocols, hidden entry points.

Everything had been mapped out.

This should be simple.

And yet, as Inez fastened her gear and steadied her breath, she knew, missions like these were never as simple as they seemed.

The team returned late that night, the forest shrouded in darkness, with only the faint glow of moonlight filtering through the dense canopy. They had spent days observing the lab's security patterns, and their plan was meticulously crafted. Four guards patrolled the perimeter: one stationed at the front entrance, another at the back and two patrolling the east and west sides of the building. Each team member had their assignment.

Hunter moved first, his steps silent as he approached the guard at the back entrance. His movements were calculated, like a predator stalking its prey. In one fluid motion, he lunged forwards, wrapping his arm tightly around the guard's neck while his other hand pressed firmly against the back of the man's head. The guard struggled briefly before succumbing to unconsciousness. Hunter wasted no time, binding the man's wrists and ankles with rope before retreating into the shadows.

Nadia, ever the charmer, took a different approach. She sauntered towards the west side, her posture relaxed. Leaning against the wall with one leg propped up, she began to play with her nails, her demeanour casual yet alluring. The guard noticed her immediately. "Are you lost, miss?" he asked in a gravelly voice.

Nadia tilted her head, a coy smile playing on her lips. "Can you help me?" she replied sweetly, her voice dripping with innocence. As she stepped closer, her hips swayed with calculated rhythm, drawing the guard's attention. In a swift and unexpected move, she reached for his stun gun, pulling it from its holster and pressing it against his side. The guard crumpled to the ground, and Nadia smirked, satisfied with her handiwork.

Meanwhile, Inez approached the east side, her heart pounding as she activated her newfound ability. Her form shimmered and vanished, rendering her invisible as she crept towards the guard. She moved with caution, but her concentration faltered. As she reached the guard, her invisibility faded, leaving her exposed. Without hesitation, she grabbed the man by the scruff of his neck, her hands sparking with electricity.

The guard convulsed briefly before collapsing, and Inez quickly secured him to a nearby pipe with rope.

Zaire, tasked with the front entrance, moved with equal determination. His approach was stealthy, but the guard spotted him, raising his stun gun in defence. Zaire reacted instantly, summoning a gust of wind that knocked the man off balance. He closed the distance, grabbing the guard's wrist to prevent him from using the stun gun. The guard, however, was skilled and managed to flip Zaire onto his back, pinning him down. The stun gun hovered dangerously close to Zaire's face, its crackling energy a stark reminder of the stakes.

Zaire considered his options. He could summon lightning to incapacitate the guard, but the risk of fatality was too high. Rain could neutralise the stun gun, but it would also leave him vulnerable. As he struggled, Nadia's voice came through his earpiece. "I'm on my way," she said, her urgency palpable.

Before Nadia could intervene, Inez appeared behind the guard. Her hands sparked with electricity as she pressed them against the man's back. He collapsed instantly, and Inez stepped back, blowing imaginary smoke from her fingertips. "Piece of cake," she said with a smirk. "For those who have stun guns for hands."

Nadia rolled her eyes. "Show off," she muttered, shaking her head.

The team regrouped, their mission progressing smoothly. The lab's defences had been neutralised, and the path to the vault was clear. But as they moved forwards, the weight of the unknown remained, success was never guaranteed, and the night was far from over.

The four of them regrouped at the entrance as they prepared to infiltrate the premises. Hunter stood tall, his eyes scanning the surroundings for any signs of movement. Without a word, they entered the building, their footsteps quiet against the cold tiled floor.

Nadia took the lead, heading straight for the reception desk where the CCTV monitors displayed a live feed of the entire facility. The screens showed every corner of the building, including the vault where the gem was secured. Nadia pulled out a USB drive, her fingers deftly plugging it into the computer. Within moments, the cameras began looping old footage. Yet, something was off, the footage inside the vault wasn't displaying correctly. Hunter stood guard over Nadia, his stance protective as she worked her magic on the system.

Meanwhile, Zaire moved cautiously through the corridors, his back pressed against the wall as he peeked around a corner. A guard stood just ahead, his posture alert. Nadia's voice crackled through the earpiece, providing updates on the guards' positions. She had managed to disrupt their communication mics, leaving them isolated and unaware of the team's presence.

Inez activated her invisibility, her form flickering as she vanished and reappeared behind the guards. The power was a game-changer, allowing her to move undetected. One by one, she stun gunned the guards from behind, their bodies crumpling to the floor. Zaire followed closely, dragging the unconscious guards into a nearby closet, locking them away to ensure the path remained clear.

But Inez wasn't content with stealth alone. She decided to test her combat skills, engaging a few guards head-on. Her movements were swift and precise, a kick to the head here, a calculated strike there. She left them dazed, their injuries minor but enough to incapacitate them for days. Her training with Megyn had paid off, and she relished the opportunity to prove herself.

At last, Inez reached the locked vault, her pulse quickening as she waited for Zaire to catch up. "Take your time," she teased, a smirk tugging at her lips. Zaire rolled his eyes.

As Inez stood before the vault, an odd sensation came over her. It was as if the air around her had shifted, charged with an unfamiliar energy. She could feel something, or someone, alive within the vault. The sensation was disconcerting, yet it drew her closer.

Zaire arrived, his hand reaching for the keypad. "Wait," Inez said urgently. She explained the feeling, the presence she couldn't quite identify. Without hesitation, Zaire contacted Nadia through the intercom, instructing her to code the door. The vault hissed open, revealing its contents.

Before Zaire could step inside, Inez had already teleported into the room. The gem sat on a pedestal, its glow pulsating with an otherworldly light. As she approached, the glow intensified, consuming the room in a brilliant flash. When the light faded, Inez found herself transported to an entirely different world.

The sky above was a fiery orange, helicopters slicing through the air, their searchlights piercing the dense grey smoke. The ground tremored as explosions erupted behind her, the sound deafening. She turned to see soldiers advancing, their weapons trained on fleeing civilians, adults and children alike. The scene was chaos, the screams of the innocent echoing in her ears. The air was thick with the acrid smell of burning flesh.

The people under attack were not human. Their features were flawless, their symmetry almost ethereal. Yet, humanity was the aggressor, slaughtering them without mercy. Inez's heart sank as she watched the senseless violence unfold. Her gaze was drawn to a young girl, her cries piercing through the commotion. The child knelt beside her parents' lifeless bodies, shaking them desperately, pleading for them to wake up. She was too young to understand the finality of death.

Inez crouched beside the girl, a small comfort amidst the horror. Her eyes scanned the area, taking in the theft of the gems, the very lifeblood of this alien race. The crowns of the girl's parents lay discarded on the ground, a symbol of their fallen royalty.

The girl's trembling hand reached out, gripping Inez's arm with surprising strength. Her eyes, filled with tears, met Inez's. "Help us," she pleaded.

51

The Gem Glowed

"Inez!" Nadia's voice rang through the earpiece, pulling Inez back to reality. She winced, clutching her arm as a sharp pain radiated through it.

Zaire stepped closer, concern etched across his face. "Are you okay?" he asked.

Inez nodded, her expression resolute. "Yes. Let's just do this and get out of here," she replied. She placed her hand on the glass encasing the gem, her fingers phasing through it as if the barrier didn't exist. The gem pulsed as she pulled it free, its glow dimming in her grasp.

Zaire took the gem from her, carefully placing it into a briefcase equipped with a fingerprint lock. "Let's move," he said.

As they headed towards the exit, Inez suddenly stopped. "Wait," she called out. Without explanation, she teleported to the locked closet where the guards were confined. She unlocked the door, allowing them to escape, before teleporting back to her team. "Let's go," she said. Together, they left the premises unscathed, except for Zaire, who bore a few bruises.

The van hummed softly as they drove back to base. Zaire turned in his seat to face Inez, who sat in the back, cradling her arm. "What was that?" he asked.

Inez hesitated, her gaze distant. "The stone glowed, and I saw… I don't know what I saw," she admitted, her voice faltering.

THE GEM GLOWED

Zaire frowned, his confusion deepening. "I didn't see it glow," he said.

Nadia leaned over, nudging Inez playfully. "Well, we did the mission, and it went great, especially for your first," she said, her attempt at lightening the mood.

52

Remaining Pain

Back at base, Zaire wasted no time. He sought out Raphael, the boss, to deliver the gem. "Did it go smoothly? Any hiccups?" Raphael asked, his tone brisk.

"No, it went smoother than expected," Zaire replied, exhaustion creeping in.

Raphael's eagle eyes caught the swelling on Zaire's cheekbone. "You've got a shiner coming in. Go get some IV, I'll send for it. Need you healed quickly," he said. Zaire nodded, placing a hand on his cheekbone and hissing in pain. He made his way to the infirmary, eager to recover.

Later that evening, the team gathered in Inez's room, their curiosity driving them to uncover the truth. Inez sat on the edge of her bed, her expression troubled. "The gem… it gave me this feeling. It glowed when I looked at it, and I saw things, horrible things," she said. She recounted the vision, the little girl's plea and the burning pain in her wrist.

Nadia leaned forwards, her eyes wide. "Can you show us?" she asked.

"It's not pleasant. You'll feel what they felt," Inez warned.

"Show us," Zaire said firmly.

Inez closed her eyes, projecting the vision for them to see. The room fell silent as the horrors unfolded before them, the screams, the bloodshed, the senseless violence. The weight of humanity's actions.

When the projection ended, the silence lingered. Each of them struggled to process what they had seen. "Our kind knew," Zaire said finally, his voice barely above a whisper. "And instead of communicating, we chose to destroy."

The team exchanged glances, their thoughts aligning. The red gem had given them all powers, but Inez's connection to it was stronger. It had shown her its history, its truth.

Inez winced, clutching her wrist as the burning pain returned. "What is it?" Hunter asked, filled with concern.

"Didn't you feel it in the projection? When the little girl grabbed me?" Inez asked, her voice strained.

They shook their heads. "It's like it's burning my skin," she added.

"Show me," Zaire demanded.

Inez rolled up her sleeve, revealing the mark burned into her skin, a perfect imprint of the little girl's hand, like a tattoo. Nadia gasped. "Let's go to the infirmary now," she said urgently.

"No, she can't," Zaire interjected. "If we take her there, he'll know. He'll have questions. We have to handle this ourselves."

Inez frowned. "Why can't I go? It needs to be checked."

Zaire turned to Hunter. "Go to the infirmary and tell the doctor I need an IV for Project Axis. He'll hand it over," he instructed. Hunter nodded and left the room.

When Hunter returned, he handed the IV bag to Inez, its contents a milky white liquid that shimmered under the light. "This will heal us; it'll be okay," he reassured her.

Zaire stepped forwards, taking the IV from Inez. He gently grabbed Inez's arm, tapping it lightly to make a vein appear. "Hold still," he murmured. With practised precision, he inserted the needle, allowing the liquid to flow into her bloodstream. Inez winced slightly but remained silent, staring at the mark burned into her skin.

Fifteen minutes passed, the room quiet except for the hum of the IV. When the bag was empty, Zaire carefully removed the needle and inspected her arm. The burn mark, however, remained untouched, its edges dark. He frowned, his concern deepening.

Zaire turned to Nadia and Hunter. "We should tell her," he said, his voice low.

Nadia nodded in agreement, her eyes flicking to Inez. Hunter, however, hesitated, his face twisting into a grimace. "I guess the majority rules," he said with a shrug.

Zaire turned back to Inez. "Inez, we have to tell you something. Soundproof your room."

Inez raised an eyebrow. Without a word, she closed her eyes and lifted her hands. A faint shimmer filled the air as a forcefield enveloped the room, sealing them in. Hunter glanced around, impressed.

"Neat trick," he said with a wink. "Bet you and Zaire use that a lot."

Nadia burst into laughter, the tension in the room momentarily broken. Zaire rolled his eyes but couldn't suppress a small smile. Inez, however, remained focused, her gaze shifting between them. "What is it?" she asked.

53

The Mission Was a Lie

Inez sat in silence, absorbing every word as Nadia, Zaire, and Hunter explained their secret mission. Their loyalty to Raphael wasn't real, it was a façade, a carefully orchestrated deception to dismantle the organisation from the inside out. Every mission, every choice, was a calculated step towards their ultimate goal: taking down the boss and putting an end to the horrors that had plagued them for too long.

"So, who is Raphael?" Inez asked.

"The boss," Nadia responded. "He runs the organisation."

Inez's mind raced as a name she had buried in her grief resurfaced. "He is the one who killed my husband?" she whispered. "His name is Raphael?" Her eyes darted from one person to the next, searching for confirmation, for something, anything, that made this revelation less devastating.

Zaire leaned in, his voice gentle. "Are you okay?"

Inez inhaled sharply, grounding herself. "Yeah. Just in shock," she admitted. Then, she steeled herself. "Who else is involved in this?"

"Just us three," Hunter answered.

The moment pressed down on her. They wanted her to be a part of this, to fight with them. There was no hesitation in her response. "I'm in," she said firmly.

Still, a thought tugged at her. "Why did you only ask me now?" she questioned, her eyes narrowing slightly.

The three exchanged glances. "We weren't sure if you could be trusted," Zaire admitted.

Inez scoffed. "So, we are whatever we are, experiments, and you couldn't trust me?" she asked, incredulous.

"It was me," Hunter interjected. "I didn't trust you. But after you helped Nadia, you won me over."

That settled it. She was one of them now.

The conversation shifted as they revealed their next target, a man who worked closely with the doctor. If they could get to him, they would be one step closer to the truth.

Inez reacted instantly. "The Yin-Yang bandana," she said.

Zaire's eyes locked onto hers. "You've seen him?" he asked.

"Look." Without hesitation, Inez projected the memory of when she was dragged out of the van in cuffs. The image flickered to life in the room, replaying the scene exactly as she had experienced it.

Nadia glanced at Zaire, urging him to comfort her. "Are you okay?" he asked softly.

Inez managed a small smile. "It's the past."

Before anyone could process it further, Hunter interrupted. "Inez, show us that again, but focus on his right wrist."

Confusion rippled through the group. They exchanged puzzled looks before turning back to Inez, waiting.

She replayed the projection, shifting the focus as Hunter requested. The reaction was instant, gasps filled the room, and eyes widened in shock.

"What is it?" Inez demanded.

Nadia's face paled. "It can't be him."

Zaire's voice was grim. "It's him."

Inez's brows furrowed as she analysed the projection again. "All I see is a shark tooth."

But the others saw something more, something far worse.

Zaire took a deep breath before speaking. "He was an orphan here, too."

Inez's brow furrowed. "And what happened to him?"

Zaire hesitated, but Hunter answered instead, his voice heavy with regret and disbelief. "He went on a mission one day and never came back. Raphael told us he died on duty."

Silence fell over the room as the truth struck them. They knew it had to be Xander, he would never have left without that bracelet. It had been a part of him, his most personal token.

"So, Xander is the doctor's helper now," Nadia murmured. "But why? And where does he go next?"

"He won't find the doctor," Inez interjected.

Hunter, Nadia and Zaire turned to her in confusion. "What? How do you know that?" Nadia asked.

"Because I killed him," she admitted without hesitation. "He took my child. I had a way to escape... and I took it."

Hunter stared at her in disbelief. "You killed him?"

Inez held his gaze. "Yes. He made me angry... and I was going to die there otherwise. So I did what was necessary."

Nadia glanced between them, processing Inez's words. "But how are you here?"

Inez let out a dry chuckle. "You lot brought me here."

Zaire shook his head. "No. They mean that Raphael kills anyone who disrupts his plan. So why spare you?"

Inez shrugged, genuinely at a loss. "No idea."

"Maybe your powers are too important," Nadia offered, trying to make sense of it.

Zaire's expression darkened as he prepared to share something he had kept hidden for far too long. "In Raphael's office, he once left a hologram open on his desk... it was a tracking board," he admitted. "It had everyone's location, the entire camp. Exact positions."

Nadia's eyes widened, and Hunter stiffened. The revelation hung thick in the air.

"And you never told us?" Hunter's voice rose in anger as he abruptly stood, moving towards the window, his hands clenched into fists.

Nadia's voice was colder, calculated. "What about all the times we told you we wanted to run? You stopped us. Is this why?"

"Yes."

Hunter turned slightly, his eyes shifting towards Inez. "I thought we couldn't trust her, not you," he muttered.

Zaire sighed, running a hand through his hair. "I'm sorry… but the mission has to go on. We need to work together. Without Inez, we wouldn't have found out who Xander is. And without Raphael trusting me, I wouldn't have known how to get his location."

The tension in the room remained heavy and unforgiving. But now, the truth was out, and there was no turning back.

54

Minutes Remain

As Zaire stood at Raphael's desk, frustration gnawed at him. He had expected to find some obvious mechanism, an inconspicuous button under the desk, perhaps, but the hologram remained sealed. Every item he shifted had to be placed back with precision, leaving no trace of his intrusion.

Nadia's looping of the camera bought them time, but not endless amounts of it. Inez, watching from the security feed, noticed his hesitation. She decided to join him, slipping into the office with swift, practised movements. The moment she crossed the threshold, however, something felt off.

A scent, something familiar, clung to the air, and she froze for a fraction of a second. The subtle mix of sharp citrus and a deeper musky note rattled her, stirring a memory she couldn't quite place.

"Inez?" Zaire's whisper cut through her thoughts. "Are you going to help then?"

Snapping herself back into focus, she nodded and moved towards the desk. They didn't have time for distractions, not when the mission, their freedom, and their futures hung in the balance.

Her gaze flickered across the surface, absorbing every detail. Then she saw it. A groove along the edge of the desk, nearly imperceptible unless someone was looking for it.

"Here," she said, running a finger along the ridge. "This could be something."

Zaire leaned in, heart pounding. He knew this was it, whatever lay beyond, whatever files Raphael had kept locked away, they would be one step closer to revealing the truth.

55

The Names Held Ghosts

Inez focused her ultra-vision, her eyes glowing blue with the power, scanning every inch of Raphael's office for something hidden, something the naked eye couldn't detect. Zaire instinctively stepped back, giving her space to work. Her gaze sharpened as she spotted the telltale outline of a concealed drawer within the desk's structure. Without hesitation, she opened the top right drawer, reached beneath it and pressed a discreet button.

A soft hum vibrated through the desk, and suddenly, the hologram sprang to life before them. Nestled beside the hidden button was the USB drive they needed. Inez extended her hand, and Zaire placed the drive in her palm. A data transfer initiated, the countdown ticking, three minutes until they had everything.

While the files were uploaded, Inez took the opportunity to sift through Raphael's open desktop. His emails sprawled across the screen, each one coded in a cypher. Yet one message stood out, a name burned into her memory. Lucian Clarke.

Raphael had sent him an email the day before he died.

The words chilled her:

Lucian, please forgive me. I need you with me on this. There is so much you don't know, but I can show you. It has more power than we ever imagined. Please meet me tonight, I'll explain everything. I cannot discuss this via email. Your family will need you around.

Inez's chest tightened. Had Raphael tried to warn Lucian? Had Lucian ignored him? Had they met that night?

Zaire noticed her sudden silence. "Are you okay?" he asked gently. She nodded but couldn't shake the unease in her bones.

Zaire's phone interrupted the moment, Raphael. Everyone instinctively held their breath as Zaire answered. He listened intently before responding, "Yes, sir. Is that all?" Then he hung up, exhaling deeply.

"His meeting is running late."

But something else had caught Inez's eye, a board displaying hundreds of names. Confusion flared in her expression. "There are more names than orphans here. Who are the others?"

Zaire leaned in, eyes scanning the board. He shook his head. "I have no idea."

"What does it mean?" she pressed, but Zaire was already focused on their escape.

"I don't know. We have to go."

With the USB in hand, they evacuated quickly. Zaire descended the stairs, reuniting with Nadia and Hunter, while Inez hung back for one last check. The receptionist was returning to her post, but she stayed just long enough to activate her ultra-vision once more. And then she saw it, a safe behind a framed painting on the wall.

The painting it was hers. Her first-ever painting of the coffee shop. How did Raphael have this?

From the safe, a red glow pulsed. And then, a vision. The girl. The one from an alien planet, the one who had begged for help. But this time, she didn't transport Inez away. She transported herself there.

Inez reached out, but before she could react, the girl disappeared.

Swallowing her shock, Inez turned invisible and slipped down the stairs. She tapped Nadia's shoulder, signalling her safe escape.

"Thank you for your help," Nadia said to the receptionist, a signal for the others to leave. As they walked out, Nadia discreetly leaned over the counter and retrieved her USB.

THE NAMES HELD GHOSTS

Back in Nadia's room, the group plugged the USB into her laptop. The file was enormous, it couldn't be loaded all at once. Nadia had to break it down into sections, a painstaking process that would take time.

For now, they had to act normally. Inez joined Nadia and Hunter for training. Zaire continued running errands. A full day passed before every file had been successfully downloaded.

When it was finally time, they all gathered in Nadia's room. Inez reinforced the walls, ensuring no sound could escape.

What they uncovered chilled them.

A folder labelled *Influential People* contained names of those in the manor and beyond. Some were marked deceased. Others were still active, tracked through the same system Raphael had used.

Then, another folder. *Relatives.*

Among the images, one face stunned Inez. Lucian.

Zaire gasped beside her.

But then, Inez froze.

Her eyes darted to another image, her pulse hammering.

"Wait, her," she murmured.

"What about her?" Nadia asked.

"That's Lara," Inez breathed. "I was imprisoned with her."

And just like that, the truth unravelled before them.

After an exhaustive search, their efforts paid off, and they found Xander, a mere thirty-minute drive away at a modest hotel. Wasting no time, Zaire and Inez piled into their car while Nadia and Hunter sped off on their motorcycle.

As they approached, Inez activated her new ability, her glowing blue eyes piercing through the walls of Xander's room. She saw him sitting alone, an unmistakable red aura emanating from his body. The glow was mirrored in her companions, it had to be the gem. This cemented their approach. Xander wasn't an enemy; he was one of them. Violence wasn't an option, they needed to reach him with understanding, not force.

Hunter took the lead, rapping his knuckles on the door while expertly concealing the peephole. They heard the shuffle of hesitant steps on the other side before the door creaked open. The moment Xander laid eyes on them, panic overtook him. He slammed the door shut with a forceful thud.

Unfortunately for Xander, he underestimated Hunter's strength. With a casual flick of his fingertip, Hunter stopped the door mid-slam, holding it ajar. He turned to Nadia with a weary smirk, muttering, "Every time."

Hunter's voice softened as he addressed the frightened man inside. "Xander, we just want to talk."

Xander hesitated before retreating into the farthest corner of the room, his whole body trembling. "I'm not going back," he stammered.

As Zaire, Nadia and Hunter cautiously stepped inside, Xander's wide eyes flitted between them, recognition dawning. "Wait," he said, voice faltering. "I remember you. Hunter, Nadia… Zaire. You were in the manor with me." His gaze then landed on Inez, confusion marring his features. "You weren't there, but you… look familiar."

Inez stepped forwards, her demeanour calm yet resolute. "I'll show you why," she said, projecting her memories to him, sharing pieces of her past that would explain the connection.

As the memories flooded him, Xander's terror melted into sorrow. He sank onto the edge of the bed, his head falling into his hands. "I'm sorry," he whispered, broken. "I'm so sorry. I never wanted to do any of it, but I didn't have a choice."

His words hung in the air. Inez and the others exchanged glances, their resolve strengthening. Xander wasn't their adversary, he was another victim, another piece of the intricate puzzle they were trying to solve. Now, they just had to convince him to join them.

56

She Saw the Words

They began interrogating him, their voices sharp and relentless. He explained, his tone heavy with regret, that he never wanted to hurt anyone. His eyes darted to Inez, searching for understanding. "You have a child, right?" he asked hesitantly.

Inez stiffened, her anger bubbling to the surface. "No, I don't have a child, because you dragged me in there, and they took him from me—" Her voice cracked, her loss threatening to consume her.

Zaire stepped in. He gently took Inez by the arm and led her to the bathroom, his voice low and soothing. "He's done some crappy stuff, but we all have. He didn't take him from you, remember that."

Inez took a deep breath as she gripped the edge of the sink. *I can do this*, she told herself, forcing her emotions aside to focus on the bigger picture.

Back in the room, Xander's voice cut through the silence. "Wait, did you say you had a boy?" he asked cautiously.

Inez nodded, her gaze fixed on the floor. The weight of her grief was unbearable. "He's alive," Xander said, his words hanging in the air like a lifeline.

Inez collapsed, her knees giving way as the shock overwhelmed her. Nadia and Zaire rushed to her side, their arms steadying her before she hit the ground. Hunter stepped forwards, his fury igniting like a flame. He grabbed Xander by the collar, his face inches from his. "He's alive. Tell us."

Xander stammered as he recounted the story. He explained how he returned to the facility sometime after Inez escaped. The doctor had given him a job to deliver a baby to a brown-haired woman in the middle of nowhere. "If I saw her again, I'd remember her," Xander said, tinged with guilt. "I was the delivery boy, the errand boy. They said drive, I drove. They said kill, I killed."

Inez's voice halted his confession. "How do you know it was my baby? There were other women there."

Xander hesitated, his brow furrowing as he tried to recall. "I thought it was just you," he admitted.

Inez shook her head. "It wasn't my baby. It was probably one of theirs."

Xander looked to the floor, his shoulders slumping. He continued in a whisper. He was there the day Inez escaped. He had loosened the strap, following the instructions of a mysterious woman who told him to leave it loose. He admitted that Inez never killed the doctor. "I went into the building and found him lying there, alive. So I finished the job. After everything he made me do, I couldn't let him live."

Inez exhaled, her relief palpable. *I'm not a murderer*, she thought, the realisation washing over her like a wave. The happiness was overwhelming, a rare moment of solace.

Zaire stepped forwards, his voice firm yet compassionate. He managed to convince Xander to return to the manor, emphasising the importance of secrecy. "None of this can be mentioned to anyone. We can't trust anyone else."

The story unfolded as Xander returned to the manor. Hunter, during his weekly checks of the premises, spotted Xander and brought him in. The group reconvened, their emotions raw and unfiltered.

As the day wound down, Nadia and Hunter retreated to their room. Inez, however, was restless. She paced her room, her thoughts consumed by her little boy. *Was it Leo that Xander delivered? Where is he? Who is he with?* Her mission had shifted; she was determined to find him. The vision of the little girl who had lost her parents haunted her, a stark reminder of how baby Leo must have felt.

A knock at the door pulled her from her trance. Zaire stood there, his expression soft and understanding. "How are you?" he asked.

Inez shrugged, her emotions too complex to articulate. Zaire stepped inside. "We will find him. It's our end goal. If he's out there, then it's time to reunite Leo with his mum."

The words broke through her defences, and she hugged him tightly. The floodgates opened, her tears spilling out in a torrent. Zaire led her to the bed, lying down beside her and holding her close. He knew she hadn't slept in days. His presence was a balm, a source of comfort in the madness.

As the night deepened, they fell asleep together, her head resting against his chest. For the first time in days, Inez found a sliver of peace.

After Inez woke up, her mind still foggy from restless dreams, she showed Zaire a peculiar rock she had found in Raphael's office. The stone was unlike anything she had seen before, its texture rough but drawing her in, with foreign words etched across its surface. "It's not English," she murmured. "We need to translate it."

Intrigued, Zaire shared the discovery with the others, and they convened in the library, the space cloaked in the scent of aged books. Days stretched into weeks as they combed through texts, analysing the cryptic markings on the stone. The closest they came to a translation was: *On the Eighteenth year, beast shall hide; fire and anger shall spread through the realm.* Yet even this eerie verse left them perplexed, the meaning just beyond their grasp.

They endured long, sleepless nights as they worked tirelessly to decode the message. The library became their sanctuary, a place of shared purpose and growing camaraderie. The weight of their task pressed upon them, but their resolve never faltered.

One evening, Hunter made his way to Zaire's room, where the group of four had gathered. The atmosphere was thick as they sat around the table. Nadia, ever the nurturer, brought steaming cups of tea and coffee for everyone. The warmth of the drinks was a small comfort amidst the growing tension.

The conversation shifted to the next steps of their plan. Xander, once the doctor's helper, had revealed chilling truths about his past role. The doctor, now deceased, had been a pawn in a larger, more sinister game. The hierarchy was clear: next in line was the boss's right-hand man, Zaire. And then, at the top of the chain, the boss himself, an enigma they had yet to confront. For Inez, however, her focus had narrowed. Her end goal was no longer revenge, nor justice for her husband, who was beyond saving. Her mission now was Leo, her baby boy, lost and alone in a world too cruel for someone so small.

They agreed to regroup every Wednesday at noon, a time when the boss was occupied with meetings and conference calls. The library, safe from searches, would be their clandestine headquarters.

One afternoon, as Inez studied the mysterious stone alongside Zaire and Xander, Kimmie entered the room. Her bright, lively aura was a stark contrast to the gravity of the moment.

"Hey, how was your first mission?" Kimmie asked cheerfully.

Inez glanced up, offering a faint smile. "Yeah, it went great. Thank you."

Kimmie's gaze shifted to the rock on the table. "Ooo, what is this fancy little thing?" she asked, picking it up with nimble fingers. Her expression changed in an instant, her eyes widening with fear. "What is this?" Her voice trembled, her usual confidence shaken.

Zaire responded, his voice steady, "A rock from another world."

Kimmie's hands quivered as she held the stone. "I know this," she said. "It looks so familiar." Her eyes darted across the carved words, her face pale. "And this writing, I've seen it before."

Before Kimmie could say more, Xander interjected. "We've already translated it," he said, his tone clipped. But the room had shifted, a ripple of unease spreading among them.

What had Kimmie recognised? And how would her knowledge shape the path they were on? The questions hung in the air.

Kimmie held the stone in trembling hands, her eyes scanning the translated text. "You have it wrong. *On her twenty-fifth birthday, the lost princess shall return and retake her throne. She shall restore the power to the realm and break the Lunar curse.*" Her voice wavered, as if the words carried weight far beyond their surface meaning.

The group exchanged puzzled glances. "The girl I saw, it's her," Inez said, barely above a whisper but filled with conviction.

Kimmie snapped to Inez, curiosity etched across her face. "What girl?" she asked, suspicious.

Inez hesitated, glancing at the others before quickly deflecting. "Just a photo we found on a mission. Nothing special," she said, forcing a casual tone that didn't quite mask the tension in her voice.

Xander leaned forwards, his brow furrowed. "What language is this, anyway?"

"I don't know," Kimmie admitted. "I didn't even know I could read anything other than English." Her fingers traced the carvings absently, her mind beginning to spiral into fragmented memories. The room seemed to fade around her as she became lost in her own world.

"Kimmie!" Inez's voice was sharp, snapping her back to the present. Kimmie blinked, startled and turned to Inez.

"Yes?"

"Are you okay?" Inez asked, concern softening her voice.

"Yes. I... I'd better get going," Kimmie stammered. Without waiting for a response, she opened a portal, the shimmering edge illuminating the room. She stepped through, disappearing into the comfort of her own space.

Inez exhaled, rubbing her temples as guilt clawed at her. She hated lying to her friend. "We can't tell anyone, you know that," Zaire said, his gaze locking onto her.

"She just helped us. Why can't we trust her?" Inez countered, her voice carrying both anger and desperation. She searched Zaire's face for any sign of agreement.

Zaire sighed, his expression firm yet empathetic. "We just can't. Not now. Be patient. Once we've sorted the main problem, everyone will be free."

His words offered little comfort. Inez clenched her fists, her heart heavy. She couldn't shake the feeling that she was being forced to pick sides again, a battle she thought she had left behind. But this time, the stakes felt impossibly high, and the threads of trust she clung to seemed to be unravelling.

57

The Leap and the Feeling

After weeks of torment and heartache, Inez learned there was a possibility her son was still alive. The news hit her like a storm, how could she focus on the mission when every fibre of her being ached to hold him in her arms?

Her obsession consumed her. It was as if her mind had been rewired to function on a single frequency, one that blotted out all else. She forgot the small things, like charging her phone or ensuring her toast didn't burn. Even in moments of relative quiet, her thoughts twisted into a whirlpool of 'what ifs', leaving her distracted and increasingly agitated.

The only person she could confide in was Nadia. Inez found solace in her presence, opening up to her in ways she couldn't with Zaire. While Zaire shared her desire to reunite with Leo, his primary focus was on Raphael. There was a quiet determination in his eyes whenever the subject came up, one that often felt like it pulled him further away from her.

Nadia, on the other hand, became her anchor. Whenever Inez unravelled, Nadia would be there, piecing her back together. Nadia's freedom to leave the manor made her invaluable. She chased every lead, no matter how improbable, and reported back to Inez. More often than not, those leads turned out to be dead ends, but her resolve never faltered. She did everything in her power to bring Leo back to his mother, as though the fight were her own.

THE LEAP AND THE FEELING

"Why are you helping me?" Inez asked one evening.

"I'm an orphan, remember?" Nadia replied, her lips curling into a bittersweet smile. "I would give anything to meet my parents or even know who they were. If I can help someone else reunite with their family, I will."

"Well, I'm thankful for all your help," Inez said, her lips curving into a rare, genuine smile. For a brief moment, the heaviness in the room lifted.

Meanwhile, Zaire tried to distract Inez from her anguish. He offered to take her out of the manor on countless occasions, suggesting walks, sparring, or even mundane errands. Each time, she rejected his offers, her mind firmly fixed on Leo. Eventually, Zaire managed to coax her into walking through the forest, though her focus never left her goal. Even amidst the serene beauty of the woods, all she could think about was finding her son.

One day, during a training session, Inez's emotions got the better of her. Her movements on the mat were erratic, her mind clouded with thoughts of revenge. Zaire, noticing her distraction, reverted to his old tactics. He struck her with a bolt of lightning, not to harm her, but to jolt her out of her reverie. Inez instinctively responded with a rebound spell, her magic crackling in the air. Then, unexpectedly, the room began to tremble. Vibrations coursed through the ground, growing stronger by the second.

Fear flashed across Inez's face. Zaire saw it and immediately rushed to her side, his protective instincts taking over. In that instant, as he shielded her, Inez realised how much she had neglected him. She had already lost her husband, and yet here was someone willing to stand beside her, someone who truly cared. Her heart raced, not just from the vibrations, but from her feelings for him.

Without thinking, she grabbed his face and kissed him. The world seemed to stop as he pulled back, his eyes searching hers. Then he leaned in, returning her kiss with the same intensity. The vibrations escalated, and a glow began to envelop them. The light grew blinding, and Inez felt herself being pulled into it.

"Don't let me go," she pleaded.

"I'll never let you go," Zaire promised, gripping a nearby pillar with one hand and holding her tightly with the other.

Hunter and Nadia burst into the room, drawn by the commotion. They tried to approach Inez and Zaire, but the glow repelled them. Forced to shield their eyes, they could only watch helplessly as the light consumed the couple. When they looked again, the glow had vanished, and so had Inez and Zaire.

When Inez awoke, the world around her was unfamiliar. She pushed herself off the ground, her heart pounding as she scanned her surroundings. She was in a vast, open field, the air thick with the scent of wildflowers. Before panic could take hold, she felt a hand grasp hers firmly.

"I said I wouldn't let you go," Zaire said reassuringly.

Inez turned to him, her fear melting into relief as she saw his face. He tightened his grip on her hand, as if to ensure she wouldn't slip away again. A grin spread across her face, and she squeezed his hand in return.

They wandered in circles for what felt like an eternity, the landscape offering no clues to their whereabouts. The sun overhead seemed to mock their disorientation, its heat harsh as the minutes dragged on. Inez, frustrated and weary, cursed under her breath. She didn't have her phone, it had been left behind during training, and Zaire's phone was a useless, shattered relic, having borne the brunt of their sudden journey through the light.

"There's a rock up ahead," Zaire pointed out, his voice breaking the silence. "Might give us some perspective if we climb it."

Inez nodded, her energy dwindling but her will unshaken. They trudged towards the large rock, the crunch of their footsteps against dry grass the only sound. But as they walked, an unnerving realisation began to creep over them, the light was fading. It had been ten in the morning when training started, and they hadn't been here that long. Yet, the golden glow of the day was slipping away into an unnatural darkness.

"What time is it?" Inez murmured, glancing at Zaire, though neither of them could answer.

They reached the rock just as the last rays of daylight kissed the horizon. Zaire climbed up first, his movements swift and agile. Reaching the top, he froze, his expression unreadable.

"You have to see this," he called down, urgency lacing his tone. His outstretched hand beckoned her.

Inez climbed up with his help, her heart pounding not just from exertion, but from a creeping sense of dread.

When she reached the top, the scene before her stole her breath. Stretching out as far as the eye could see was a field of golden wheat, the stalks bending slightly in the growing breeze. Darkness licked at the edges of the horizon, slowly swallowing the light. And far in the distance, barely discernible, was the outline of a forest.

"What is this place?" Inez whispered. The scenery was hauntingly familiar, yet undeniably alien.

"Give me your phone," she said suddenly, urgency sharpening her voice.

Zaire raised an eyebrow. "You know it's broken. What's the point?"

"Just give it to me," she insisted, her hand outstretched. With a reluctant shrug, he pulled it from his back pocket and handed it over.

Inez cradled the phone in her hands, her expression shifting into intense focus.

"What are you doing?" Zaire asked, leaning in as if proximity might offer answers. "Is something supposed to be happening?"

She opened one eye and shot him a look. "Shh."

Zaire watched, alarmed, as she closed her eyes, inhaled deeply and tilted her head side to side in an almost trance-like motion. For a second, he thought she was having some kind of fit. Then, without warning, the phone vanished from her hands.

"Did it work?" she asked, her eyes snapping open.

"Work? What do you mean, did it—" He stopped, his confusion deepening as Inez gestured for him to check his pocket. Frowning, he reached into his back pocket. His fingers brushed against something, and his eyes widened in disbelief as he pulled out his phone, now perfectly intact.

"It's… working," he said, staring at the screen as though it held all the answers to their predicament.

Inez allowed herself a small, triumphant smile. "I've been practising with

Nadia. I've learned to teleport items, not just through space, but through time. I sent it back to before it broke."

Zaire gave her a look that was equal parts awe and exasperation. "You didn't think to mention this sooner?"

"I didn't think it would work," she admitted with a shrug. "Let's see where we are."

Using the location app on the newly restored phone, they discovered something shocking, they were still at the manor. Or rather, a version of the manor. What had they stepped into?

As the last of the light faded, they decided to find shelter. Nearby, they spotted a tree with low-hanging branches, its silhouette stark against the deepening dusk. As they approached, an uneasy familiarity washed over them. This was *their* tree, the one near the lake with the dock where they had shared countless quiet moments. But the lake and dock were missing, and the surroundings felt… wrong.

They settled under the tree, deciding to take turns keeping watch through the night. Zaire took the first shift, his eyes scanning the open field for signs of danger. Inez leaned against him, her exhaustion finally catching up to her. She rested her head on his shoulder, seeking the comfort and stability he had always provided.

She was asleep within minutes, her breathing soft and steady against him. Zaire wrapped an arm around her, his grip protective as though he could shield her from whatever lay ahead. His gaze remained on the horizon, the questions in his mind swirling like the wind rustling through the wheat. One thing was certain, they were far from home, and the journey back would be anything but easy.

Before they knew it, morning arrived. The sun crept over the horizon, its golden light warming their faces and gently rousing them from sleep. Inez stirred first, squinting as the bright rays broke through the wheat stalks.

When she turned to Zaire, she noticed he had fallen asleep too, despite his promise to stay awake for his shift.

She sighed, shaking her head with a mix of amusement and frustration. They stretched, shaking off the grogginess, and decided to explore further, though they were careful not to stray too far from the tree. The field around them seemed endless, its uniformity almost disorienting.

As they walked, Inez's foot suddenly caught on something, and she stumbled forwards, barely catching herself.

"Ouch!" she yelped, rubbing her toe as Zaire burst out laughing. "Don't be a jerk," she snapped, grabbing a handful of wheat and tossing it at him. "It hurt my foot."

Still chuckling, Zaire teased, "Maybe the wheat was fighting back."

Ignoring him, Inez turned to investigate what she had tripped over. She bent down, brushing aside the golden stalks, and tilted her head at what she saw. "What is this?" she called to Zaire.

He joined her, kneeling to clear more of the wheat away. Beneath the stalks lay a utility hole cover, incongruous in the middle of the vast field. The two exchanged bewildered glances.

Zaire leaned in closer, running his fingers over the edges. A wheel was affixed to the top, and he began to unwind it. The sound of clanking metal echoed through the quiet field, mechanical and strange against the natural backdrop. After a few minutes, he grunted in frustration. "It's welded shut."

He stretched his hand towards the cover, concentrating as the heat of the sun gathered in his palm. The metal began to melt under his focused energy. With a triumphant smirk, he tried again to lift the cover, but it refused to budge. He frowned. "It's too heavy. We'll need—"

"Move," Inez said firmly, cutting him off.

"Don't be ridiculous," Zaire replied, but she was already stepping in.

With surprising ease, she bent down and heaved the cover upwards, lifting it like it weighed nothing. She straightened, tossing the heavy lid to the side. "Tada," she said with a sarcastic smile.

Zaire raised an eyebrow, pretending to be unimpressed. "Show-off."

Inez peered into the dark opening beneath the cover. "So, who's going first?" she asked, her tone light but her posture tense.

"I'll be the gentleman," Zaire offered, giving her an exaggerated bow. Inez rolled her eyes, lifting her hand to summon a glowing orb of light that floated beside her. The soft glow spilt down into the pit, illuminating a ladder leading into the unknown.

They descended slowly, the orb lighting their way. When Inez reached the last rung, she slipped, her foot missing the step. She yelped, but Zaire was already there, catching her around the waist. For a moment, their eyes met, the tension lingering in the space between them.

"Thanks," she murmured, stepping down onto solid ground.

"Anytime," he replied warmly.

The room they entered was pitch black, save for the faint light of the orb. They fumbled around, searching for any indication of what this place was. Inez found a light switch and flipped it, but nothing happened. Zaire wandered off and eventually discovered a fuse board. With a pull of the red lever, the room came alive with a low hum, and fluorescent lights flickered to life.

They found themselves in an office, out of place in such a remote location. The air was clean, the surfaces free of dust, suggesting it was still in use. Filing cabinets lined the walls, and several desks sat neatly arranged.

Inez wasted no time, rifling through the desk drawers with little concern for tidiness. She sent pens and papers clattering to the floor as she searched for anything of value. Zaire, meanwhile, opened the filing cabinets, his movements more considered.

"Look at this," he said suddenly. He held up a folder, his eyes scanning the contents intently.

"What is it?" Inez asked, abandoning her search to join him.

"These look like the files we pulled from Raphael's system, but in paper form," Zaire explained, holding up a photo of a woman with the word 'DECEASED' stamped across it.

Inez frowned, taking the folder from him and flipping through the pages. She pointed to the photo. The name below it read *Mary Ford*.

Zaire leaned over her shoulder, reading aloud. "*Medical records from October 21, 1951. Tests, experiments...* What do you think happened to her?"

"I don't know," Inez replied, her mind racing. "But if these files are here, it means this place is connected to Raphael. We might be closer to answers than we thought."

This field, this hidden office, it was no accident. Whatever they had stumbled upon, it was part of a bigger puzzle. And they were determined to solve it.

58

Lost in Time

They continued to comb through the room, but their search yielded nothing further. Frustration hung in the air as they turned their attention to the door at the far end of the office. It led into a long hallway, barely illuminated by a single flickering bulb struggling to stay alight. The place seemed to amplify every sound, their footsteps, the hum of the dying light, the rustle of their clothing.

Zaire reached for the nearest door and pushed it open. Inside was an empty room, barren except for a metal bed and chair bolted to the floor. Across the hall, Inez opened the opposite door and found an identical setup, cold, sterile and lifeless.

"It's the same thing in every room," Zaire muttered as they moved from door to door. The monotony was unsettling, each identical space raising more questions than answers.

At last, they reached the final door at the end of the hallway. Unlike the others, this one exuded a sense of danger, its presence heavy with unspoken secrets. Inez stepped forwards, her hand outstretched to open it, but suddenly she froze in place.

"What's happening? I... I can't move," she said, her voice laced with panic.

"What?" Zaire responded, rushing to her side. Before he could reach her, Inez's entire body began to shake violently. Zaire grabbed her shoulders, trying to steady her, but a sudden force sent him flying backwards. He hit the wall hard, the impact knocking the air from his lungs.

Inez gasped, her breathing erratic as she tried to centre herself. And then, without warning, her surroundings dissolved. The hallway vanished, and she found herself back on that planet, the one from her visions. The little girl stood before her, her expression hauntingly calm despite the carnage surrounding her. Dead bodies littered the ground, the remnants of a brutal war that had finally ended.

"I need help," the girl said quietly.

"I want to help you. Please, tell me how," Inez pleaded, her heart breaking at the sight of the child amidst such devastation.

"You are on the right path," the girl replied, her tone cryptic but resolute. "If I tell you, you won't be able to help."

"What do you mean?" Inez asked, her confusion mounting.

"You are the key," the girl said slowly. "But you are stronger together."

Before Inez could respond, the girl's expression twisted into fear. She screamed as invisible hands dragged her backwards. Inez watched helplessly as the child was pulled into a plane, its engines roaring to life. It took off, disappearing into the sky and leaving Inez alone.

The burning sensation in Inez's arm returned, pulling her back to reality. She found herself standing before the door once more, her hand still outstretched. This time, she was able to push it open.

Zaire, groaning, picked himself up from the floor and rushed to her side. "What happened?" he asked.

"I saw her again," Inez replied.

"The girl from that planet?" Zaire asked, his brows furrowed in concern.

"Yes," Inez confirmed. She rubbed her temple, trying to make sense of the vision. "She said I'm the key, but we are stronger together. I don't know what that means."

Zaire placed his hands gently on her cheeks. "It will be okay. We'll figure this out."

Inez shook her head, dread rising in her chest. "I don't know what to think. I don't know how to act or what to do. We have no idea where we are or how to get back." Her words tumbled out in a frantic rush.

Zaire cupped her cheeks again, pulling her closer. "It will be okay," he repeated, his voice firm yet tender. Then he kissed her, the gesture grounding her. For a moment, the uncertainty and fear melted away, replaced by the warmth of his presence.

After Inez calmed down, her breathing finally normal, she and Zaire resumed their cautious journey through the eerie, dimly lit halls. The flickering bulb above cast jittery shadows, heightening the unease that gripped them both. Eventually, they reached the final room. Inside, the space resembled an office, filled with more filing cabinets and a desk topped with computer monitors.

Curiosity overtook them as Zaire tapped the keyboard. The dormant screens flickered to life, illuminating the room with their glow. Camera feeds filled the monitors, showing various parts of the property. Two of the cameras revealed the world above, the sea of golden wheat.

Inez froze, her eyes fixed on the screens. Her expression shifted from curiosity to dread, and she gasped audibly.

"What's wrong? What did you find?" Zaire asked, moving to her side.

Tears welled in her eyes, spilling onto her cheeks. "We are definitely at the manor," she whispered in disbelief.

"What do you mean?" Zaire pressed, concern etched into his face.

She pointed to one of the screens, her finger shaking. Zaire followed her gesture, and as his eyes took in the date displayed in the corner of the feed, his heart dropped. The year was 2002. Horror consumed his expression as he absorbed the implications.

"We're… in 2002?" Zaire's voice barely rose above a whisper.

Inez shook her head, tears streaming now. "What are we supposed to do? How do we get back?" she pleaded.

"I don't know… I don't know…" Zaire stammered.

"Leo," Inez whispered, her voice breaking. "I need to get back to find Leo. How do we get back? How do we fix this?" Her desperation intensified, her hands trembling as she clutched her temples.

"Inez!" Zaire said firmly, grabbing her wrists. "Calm down. We'll figure it out." He held her gaze, his own anxiety simmering beneath the surface,

LOST IN TIME

but he knew he needed to stay strong for her.

"How did we even get here?" she asked.

Zaire gently but firmly repeated, "Inez, calm down."

She finally let out a shaky breath and nodded, her tears still glistening but her panic momentarily subdued. They moved to the chairs in the room, sitting down to collect themselves.

"So... time travel," Inez said after a beat. "We time-travelled?"

"Seems like it," Zaire replied, running a hand through his hair. "I didn't even know time travel was possible."

Inez gave a humourless laugh. "I didn't think any of this was possible, powers, other planets, visions. And yet, look at us now."

Zaire chuckled softly at the absurdity of their situation. "Yeah, you're not wrong."

Her smile faded as the enormity of their predicament returned. "How are we going to get back?" she asked.

Zaire sighed, shaking his head. "I honestly don't know."

Silence settled between them. After a few moments, Zaire broke it with a smile. "If I'm trapped in another time with someone, I'm glad it's with you."

Inez raised an eyebrow, a small grin tugging at the corner of her lips. "Yeah, but... I don't think it would be *too* bad if Nadia were here," she teased.

Zaire smirked. "Not funny."

"Well, I think it's a little funny," she shot back, nudging him playfully.

After a shared laugh, Zaire straightened up, determination forming in his features. "Let's keep searching. Might as well do something while we're stuck here."

Inez nodded, the flicker of hope in his voice giving her a shred of courage. "You still have a battery on your phone?" she asked.

"Yeah, why?" Zaire asked, pulling it from his pocket.

"Take photos of everything," Inez instructed. "When we get back, we can analyse them properly."

Zaire hesitated. "Who's to say the photos won't disappear when we go back?"

Inez shrugged. "I don't know. But it's worth a shot."

Zaire meticulously searched through the filing cabinets, snapping photos of anything that seemed remotely significant. His desire to gather every possible piece of evidence burned brightly as he tried to make sense of their impossible situation. Meanwhile, Inez focused intently on the monitors, scanning the CCTV footage. She cycled through camera feeds, her brow furrowing as she noticed something peculiar, a blurred figure on one of the screens. Stranger still, one of the rooms appeared faded, as though it wasn't fully there. Her heart raced as she continued scanning. The footage revealed parts of the facility they hadn't seen yet.

There had to be more doors somewhere, hidden from view.

"I'll check the other rooms again," Zaire offered, stepping out to retrace his steps. But after a thorough search, he returned empty-handed. "Nothing. No hidden doors, no secret passages. Try that... viewing thing you do," he suggested, motioning to her.

Inez nodded and closed her eyes. When she reopened them, her vision transformed, the world around her taking on a surreal glow. Zaire radiated his familiar red aura, vibrant and stable. She turned slowly, her enhanced perception revealing a glowing outline, a false door concealed behind the book cabinet.

"There," she said, pointing.

Zaire didn't hesitate. He walked to the cabinet, his strength evident as he dragged it aside, the legs scraping loudly against the floor and leaving deep marks. Behind it was a hidden passageway, just as Inez had seen.

They stepped through the doorway and into the unknown. Inez's heightened senses picked up a red glow in the distance, small but unmistakable. "There's something ahead," she whispered.

As they approached the source, they found themselves in a chillingly sterile room. Zaire froze as he took in the sight before him. Women, strapped to chairs, unconscious, with their arms tethered to glowing red intravenous. The setup was disturbingly familiar, it mirrored what Inez had once endured in her cell.

But there was something different. As Inez scanned the room, she noticed that the women themselves weren't glowing. Instead, the glow emanated from the unborn children in their wombs. The intravenous connecting the woman to the machines also pulsed with the same eerie light.

"Zaire," Inez said, her heart racing.

"What is it?" he asked, his eyes shifting from her to the women.

"They're pregnant. The babies have glows like us," Inez said, her voice tinged with both awe and horror.

Zaire's jaw tightened as he processed the information. This wasn't just experimentation, it was something far darker.

On the side of each chair, there were folders neatly arranged. Inez picked one up and flipped through it. The files contained detailed information about each woman, their names, ages and due dates. The sheer coldness of the documentation sent shivers down her spine. Despite the information at their fingertips, they were no closer to understanding what was truly happening.

"We can't just leave them like this," Inez said.

"Okay," Zaire agreed. "Let's take out the IVs and untie them. But I don't know when, or even if, they'll wake up."

Together, they moved through the room, carefully removing the glowing intravenous and loosening the straps that bound the women. Once their task was complete, they stepped back, waiting for any signs of movement.

While Zaire stayed behind to keep watch, Inez's curiosity drew her to a door at the far end of the room. "I'm going to check this out," she told him.

"Don't go too far," Zaire warned.

Inez pushed open the door and stepped inside, her breath catching as she took in the sight before her.

Suspended in a tank filled with liquid, a mermaid floated, her body perfectly still, as if frozen in time. Her long tail shimmered in the pale light, and her webbed fingers rested against the glass. It was an otherworldly sight, made all the more startling by the swell of her abdomen. She was pregnant.

"Zaire, you need to see this," Inez called out.

Zaire entered the room, his eyes widening as they landed on the mermaid. He approached cautiously, studying her features. "Is she like Lamia?" Inez asked, referring to the shapeshifting siren they had encountered before.

"No," Zaire said, shaking his head. "She looks different. She has gills and webbed fingers." He reached for a folder attached to the side of the tank and began reading aloud. *"Pure-bred mermaid. No powers."*

"So she's different. Lamia is a siren, a shapeshifter," Inez remarked, her gaze never leaving the mermaid.

"She's not like Lamia," Zaire confirmed. Then he stopped, his expression darkening as he read further. *"Captured from Planet X,"* he said, his voice low. "She's not just different, she's from another planet."

"From another planet?" Inez repeated, her mind reeling. "Is she... is she all alone?" Her voice faltered.

Zaire closed the folder, his expression troubled. "I have no idea."

The room seemed to grow colder as they stared at the mermaid, their questions multiplying. Who had brought her here? Why was she pregnant? And what connection, if any, did this have to the glowing children and the women in the other room? The mysteries of this place were deepening, and the answers felt farther away than ever.

They returned to the filing cabinet, intent on uncovering more details about Planet X, they assumed it had to be the mysterious world Inez had seen repeatedly in her visions. Zaire rifled through folders while Inez scanned for any useful clues.

"Here, I got it!" Zaire exclaimed. Inez moved closer as he began to read aloud. *"Planet X... The planet's surface is approximately 95% water, with breathable air. Three mermaids captured, one died during transit, one died due to inadequate water levels, and the third is currently... in testing."*

Zaire's voice trailed off.

"What are they testing?" Inez asked, frustration and confusion etched into her face. "I don't understand."

"Neither do I," Zaire replied grimly, shaking his head.

"So... is all of this still under the manor?" Inez asked, her voice wavering.

"Well, when we get back, we'll look," Zaire said. Though his words were meant to reassure her, they offered little comfort.

Suddenly, a voice broke the silence: "Help me." It was weak but clear, coming from the direction of the room filled with women. Inez and Zaire exchanged a worried glance before rushing back.

One of the women had begun to stir, her movements slow and disoriented. "Are you okay?" Inez asked gently, bending down to meet the woman's gaze.

The woman flinched, her eyes wide. "Who are you?" she asked.

"I'm Inez, and this is Zaire," Inez answered quickly. "What is going on here?"

"I… I was kidnapped one day," the woman began. "I've been here ever since. The doctors… they do checks and give us intravenous for the babies, but… we can't leave." Her voice cracked, the fear and despair palpable.

Inez's heart twisted painfully. She knew too well the torment this woman was describing, it mirrored her own experience. She glanced at Zaire, sorrow swimming in her eyes. He nodded subtly, an acknowledgement of their shared resolve to help.

59

The Emotional Collapse

Over the next hour, the other women began to wake, groggily pulling themselves to their feet. Inez and Zaire guided them as they paced the room, their movements shaky. But freeing them was only part of the problem, they needed to escape, and quickly.

"I'm going to check the utility hole we came through," Inez said. She hurried to the entrance, her pulse quickening when she found it closed and locked from the outside. Panic rising, she sprinted to the camera room, scanning the screens. Her stomach sank as she spotted guards making their way down a hall.

"We have to go, *now*," Inez said sharply, her urgency pulling Zaire's attention. "The entrance is locked, so there *must* be another way in."

Inez closed her eyes and reopened them, searching for any sign of an alternative exit. Her enhanced vision revealed pathways glowing ahead, guiding them deeper into the facility. "Follow me," she told Zaire and the women, her voice steady despite her mounting dread.

They passed by the tank with the mermaid, her motionless figure eliciting gasps and murmurs from the group. Inez swallowed hard and pressed forward, leading them down a winding path. At last, they reached another utility hole cover that led to an empty sewage line. One by one, the women climbed inside, their fear barely contained. Inez stayed behind, ensuring everyone made it through safely.

As she turned back for a final check, something caught her eye, a vibrant glow, pulsating faintly at the edge of the hall. Her heart clenched, and she knew she couldn't ignore it.

"Zaire," she called. "Follow the pipe. Take a right at the T-junction and then head up the slope."

"What about you?" Zaire asked.

"I need to do something. I'll catch up," Inez replied.

"I'm not leaving you," Zaire snarled, his jaw tight.

"Trust me," Inez said softly, her eyes locking onto his with quiet intensity.

He exhaled heavily, frustrated. "You have ten minutes, and then I'm coming back for you," he said, determined.

Inez nodded, watching as Zaire led the women into the sewage line. She turned back towards the glow, her heart pounding as she prepared herself for whatever awaited.

Inez crept towards the locked room cautiously. Through the small glass panel on the door, she spotted the source of the glow, the red crystal, pulsing as though alive. It seemed to beckon her, and she reached out instinctively.

"Don't," a voice said from the corner of the room.

Inez jerked back, her heart leaping. She spun towards the voice and saw the little girl standing there, her expression grave.

"Why not?" Inez asked.

"You need to go before it's too late. Get to him," the girl said cryptically. Before Inez could ask more, the girl vanished, fading into the air like a whisper.

Her mind reeling, Inez turned away from the crystal and phased back through the locked door. She was immediately met with danger, a guard stood right in front of her. Without hesitation, she activated her invisibility and bolted, her footsteps light as she sprinted towards the utility hole cover.

Knowing she couldn't risk being spotted climbing inside, Inez phased through the cover, dropping onto the floor below. She landed in a crouch, her muscles tensed, and quickly took off running. Activating her thermal vision, she scanned the area, locating Zaire and the women up ahead.

But then she heard it, the sound of boots pounding against the ground.

She turned, her breath hitching as she spotted six guards sprinting towards her. Panic surged, and she pushed herself harder, her legs burning as she raced down the tunnels glowing red from the flashes of the security system.

The tunnel echoed with the wailing alarm, the noise blaring in her ears and disrupting her focus. She needed quiet to think, to plan. Suddenly, the alarms stopped. The oppressive ringing in her head faded, leaving her in eerie quiet. Inez paused briefly, realising she had somehow stopped the alarms without meaning to. She had no time to dwell on how, it was an advantage, and she needed to use it.

Picking up her pace, she caught up with Zaire and the women, who were huddled near the end of the path. But as she reached them, her stomach sank, they were at a dead end. Inez stared at the solid wall, hopelessness creeping over her. "No, this cannot be the end," she whispered, her voice shaking.

Zaire noticed her fear and leaned closer. "What is it?" he asked, squinting in confusion. He tilted his ear towards her as if trying to hear her better.

Inez raised an eyebrow, her sarcasm breaking through her anxiety for a brief moment. "Why am I speaking into your ear?"

"I can't hear you over the alarm," Zaire admitted, though the alarm was only a distant hum to him now.

Inez shook her head, realisation dawning on her. "I stopped it, for me," she said quietly, her words almost lost in the chaos.

One of the women stepped forwards, her presence commanding despite the tension. "There is magic here, I can feel it," she said confidently. Her voice was calm, almost regal. "Inez, put your hand on the wall and drain it."

"What? How?" Inez asked, bewildered.

"How is not important right now," the woman replied firmly, her poised demeanour leaving little room for argument.

Inez stepped forwards hesitantly, spreading her fingers and pressing her palm flat against the wall. A tingling sensation immediately shot up her arm, causing her to wince. The wall began to glow green, the light growing brighter as the magic seeped into her.

Zaire, who had been keeping watch, turned towards the sudden illumination. The green glow captured his attention, drawing him closer to Inez. "How are you—" he began, but the woman interrupted him with a subtle head bow, her calm demeanour silencing him.

Her noble bearing struck Zaire as strangely out of place. Both he and Inez exchanged a brief glance, wondering who she truly was.

The glow intensified as Inez drained the magic, and with a quick burst, the wall dissolved into a doorway. The abrupt release left Inez stumbling back, the tingling in her arm spreading to her fingers.

Zaire moved forwards, gripping the door handle. As he twisted it, a blast of energy shot through him, sending him flying backwards. He slammed into the opposite wall with a sickening thud, collapsing limply onto the floor.

Inez's heart seized as she rushed towards him, anguish written on her face. But the woman intercepted her, raising a hand. "I have him. Don't worry. You need to get us out of here."

Reluctantly, Inez turned back to the door, her hand trembling as she grasped the handle. This time, she focused, pulling in the magic and neutralising the energy. Her thoughts returned to what the little girl had said: "Get to him before it's too late." Was she talking about Zaire?

Inez hesitated, glancing over her shoulder at the women, who were watching her with wide eyes. She could hear the alarm blaring again, its pulse reverberating through their bodies. But she also heard what no one else could, the guards' footsteps growing louder, their pace quickening as they closed in.

She steeled herself, knowing their time was running out.

Inez's gaze snapped back to the door, determination igniting in her chest. She poured every ounce of energy she had into draining the magic from the handle. It pulsed against her fingers, resisting, but she pushed harder, her body shaking with the strain. Finally, the handle gave way, the magic snapping apart like a broken chain, and the door swung wide open.

She staggered back, motioning frantically for the women to flee. Her eyes darted to Zaire, fear clawing at her stomach. He was still out cold.

The regal woman, steady but urgent, turned to Inez. "We need to get him out!" she shouted with an uncharacteristic edge.

Inez didn't hesitate. Leaping forwards, she raised her hands, channelling an unfamiliar energy. A shimmering silver glow surged from her fingertips, expanding outwards like ripples in water. Within seconds, a translucent crystal dome formed around them, locking them inside a fragile sanctuary.

Then, the guards arrived.

A dozen men rounded the corner, their laser guns already raised. Their fingers hovered over the triggers, ready to fire.

"Get him out!" Inez shouted, her voice raw from the effort.

The regal woman wasted no time. She laid Zaire carefully on his back, slipped her arms under his shoulders and dragged him towards the open doorway. "He's clear, hurry!" she called, her composure cracking.

Inez's arms shook as the energy in the dome wavered. The guards, sensing its weakening structure, adjusted their approach. They swung their laser rifles back, unclipping handguns in perfect unison.

Their weapons were now aimed directly at her.

Gritting her teeth, Inez lowered one hand to prepare her escape. The dome splintered at its seams, fragments of crystalline magic cascading to the ground as bullets bounced off its surface. She took a single step back, then sprinted towards the door.

Behind her, the dome shattered entirely, dissolving into shards of light and glass. A blast of wind rushed past her as the door slammed shut behind her with a flick of her wrist.

Inez landed hard, face-first into the grass. The earth was cool beneath her palms, and she pressed her weight into it, gasping for breath.

The regal woman crouched beside her, resting a hand on Inez's back. "You are not made for this magic," she said gently. "You need to purge it from your system before it consumes you."

Inez, still disoriented, lifted her head and frowned. "What do you mean?"

"Place your hands on the grass," the woman instructed. "Close your eyes."

Inez obeyed, laying her fingers flat against the ground.

"Now, spread them, feel the roots below," the woman continued. She inhaled slowly, guiding Inez through the process. "Give your power to the earth."

Inez took a deep breath, focusing on the pulse beneath her fingertips. The moment she let go, magic surged from her skin, sinking into the soil. The ground glowed, first faintly, then brightly. Flowers of every imaginable colour erupted around them, stretching towards the sky like they had been waiting for her touch.

Gasps of awe rippled through the group. The women, weakened but standing, observed the spectacle in silence.

Inez exhaled, her breath shaky as she lifted her head. "Did I..." She turned to the regal woman, her voice barely above a whisper.

"Yes," the woman confirmed, a bittersweet pride in her gaze. "This is magic from my land. It was stolen, taken for cruelty instead of restoration. It is what heals my world. It *needs* an outlet."

Inez felt a strange chill settle over her. "Your *world*?" The words barely escaped her lips.

The woman bowed her head in acknowledgement. "I know you have questions, but I am needed elsewhere."

Before Inez could speak, the woman lunged forwards, slipping through an opening between two trees. In a blink, she vanished through an invisible portal.

"No!" Inez's voice cracked as she reached forward, but the woman was already gone.

Zaire, groaning, pushed himself up from the grass, his movements sluggish but determined. He limped to Inez's side, placing an arm around her. "We have to go," he said quietly, nodding towards the group of women.

Inez's mind raced. They couldn't stay here, not with the guards searching for them. Then, an idea struck her.

Kimmie. Her powers.

If Kimmie could open portals, maybe *she* could, too.

She focused, stretching her energy outwards. A shimmering portal flickered into existence before her, revealing the inside of a hospital.

"This is our way out," Inez said breathlessly.

One by one, the women stepped through, their freedom finally within reach.

The moment the last woman passed through, Inez stumbled back, colliding into Zaire's chest. The connection to the other side snapped shut instantly.

Then, just as the portal sealed, another force took hold.

A wind tunnel formed around them, violent, overwhelming. In an instant, they were ripped from the ground, sucked into the vortex.

Spiralling through the madness, Inez and Zaire could only hold on to one thought:

They had no idea where they would land.

60

Vault of Forgotten Names

Inez opened her eyes slowly, blinking against the soft glow of the white light that illuminated the immaculate ceiling above her. Her vision sharpened gradually, and she began to take in the soothing surroundings. A shadow moved into focus, and she recognised the figure of Zaire, who stood at her bedside. His expression was filled with warmth as he gently offered his hand, helping her rise to a sitting position.

As she surveyed the room, it struck her as serene and meticulously designed, everything exuded elegance. The double bed, perfectly made with crisp white linens, anchored the space. The walls, painted a flawless shade of white, seemed to radiate light. Her gaze wandered to the bookcase that stretched vertically along one wall, crammed with volumes of every size and colour. It spoke of a life steeped in knowledge and imagination. Opposite the bed, a plush blue fabric sofa beckoned, complemented by an oak coffee table that lent a natural charm to the ensemble.

Inez inhaled deeply, absorbing the calm yet unfamiliar ambience. "Where are we?" she asked, tentative but curious.

Zaire's smile widened, his happiness tangible. "We are back," he answered. "You are in my room." He sat beside her on the edge of the bed, his hand holding hers securely, as though to anchor her to this new reality.

Relief washed over her, and her chest swelled with emotion. "We are home," she murmured, her voice carrying a quiet conviction. Zaire's nod was gentle, his eyes filled with reassurance. Tears welled up in her eyes and spilt down her cheeks, a release of all the pent-up tension and fear. She smiled through her tears, and without hesitation, Zaire leaned closer, enveloping her in a comforting embrace.

As she relaxed into his arms, her emotions gave way to a different sensation. She pulled back slightly, her eyes drawn to the outline of his lips, full and inviting, framed by the stubble that added to his rugged charm. Her heart quickened, and she bit her lip, battling the temptation that surged within her. The ache to feel his lips on hers was undeniable, yet she held herself back, savouring the profound connection they already shared. The moment hung delicately between them.

He cupped her chin gently, his thumb and forefinger cradling her face as he tilted her head upwards. His gaze locked onto hers, as though he was searching for something hidden deep within her soul. She felt her heart race, her thoughts swirling with uncertainty and longing. Was this the right time? Was kissing him what she truly wanted? Her mind begged for answers, but her heart already knew.

I just want to kiss her, Zaire thought, his emotions raw and unguarded. *She is extraordinary, and I want her to be mine.* The thought lingered in his mind as he lowered his hand from her face, his fingers brushing against her skin one last time before he sighed, the weight of his feelings pressing down on him.

Inez leaned forwards, her movements quick and decisive, as though propelled by an invisible force. Her lips met his in a fleeting kiss before she pulled back to gauge his reaction. Her eyes searched his face as she waited for his response.

Zaire's expression shifted, his desire unmistakable. He leaned in, his arms wrapping around her lower back with a firm yet tender grip. The world around them seemed to dissolve as he kissed her deeply, his embrace filled with longing and passion. The kiss stole her breath, leaving her utterly captivated by the intensity of the moment. It was as though time had stopped, and nothing else mattered but the connection they shared.

Their lips met in a tender collision of passion. A soft, measured moan escaped her as she reciprocated the kiss, each sensation unfurling like a delicate symphony of emotions. She felt his gentle approach, a careful caress as his tongue inched towards her lips, inviting her into a dialogue of desire. In response, she parted her lips with graceful vulnerability, and together they embarked on an intimate dance.

61

The Broke Silence

Zaire changed into his fitness gear before heading out to meet Hunter for their run. As he stepped out, the door clicked shut behind him, and in the weak glow of the hallway light, something flickered in the corner of his vision, a dark shadow. He froze. Turning slowly, he found himself face to face with a tall, imposing figure shrouded in the half-light.

"Follow me," the man commanded, his voice low and authoritative, resonating like a distant rumble of thunder. Without waiting for a response, he turned and strode down the corridor towards his study. Zaire hesitated before trailing cautiously after him.

The tall man reached the study door and stopped, his hand resting lightly on the frame as he waited. His gaze bored into Zaire as he stepped inside. "Sit," the man ordered curtly, moving to the window, his silhouette framed against the shifting light outside. For a moment, he stared out, as if lost in thought, before speaking again.

"Tell me everything. Going from there to here, what was it like?" His voice was steady, but there was an undercurrent of something darker, fear, perhaps, or suspicion.

Zaire sat quickly, his posture stiff, his mind calculating what he could and couldn't divulge. Carefully, he recounted the events he was willing to share: the mission, the team's covert plans, the mysterious enemy they were working to dismantle. He chose his words carefully.

"Is that everything? You don't remember anything else?" The tall man's voice betrayed a crack in his composure.

"No," Zaire replied firmly. "Like I said, I was knocked out and came around just as I was being dragged through the portal. After that, I was back here."

The man inhaled deeply, his broad shoulders rising with the effort, before exhaling in a long, slow breath. Straightening his stance, he continued to stare out the window, his reflection in the glass appearing almost spectral. "And the place you were in… worn-out papers, an abandoned building… You mentioned a staircase?"

"Yes," Zaire confirmed. "It was dodgy. I fell through and hit the ground hard. That's when I blacked out. I'm not sure what else you're hoping to hear. I could bring in Inez—"

"NO!" The man's voice exploded like a gunshot. He spun around, his expression hard, though his eyes flickered with regret almost instantly. "No," he repeated, softer this time. "I apologise. I shouldn't have reacted that way."

"Sorry, sir. I didn't mean to—"

"It's not you," the man interjected. "Inez… her abilities… I'm still uncertain how far they'll evolve. I cannot afford to have her this close to the office."

Unbeknownst to him, Inez had already been in that very office, her keen eyes scanning every hidden document, every locked drawer, unravelling the secrets he so desperately sought to keep.

"You may see yourself out; I have paperwork to do. Keep Inez close, I need to be informed of any new powers that evolve," the boss said in a measured tone, his hand sweeping towards the door, motioning for Zaire to leave.

Authority hung in the air, his commanding presence unwavering even as he sank into the deep cushions of his armchair.

"Sir…" Zaire hesitated, his brows furrowing.

"What, Zaire? I'm occupied." The boss's voice was harsher now, impatient.

"How long has this place been here?" Zaire ventured cautiously, his voice barely more than a whisper.

The boss sighed deeply, steeping his fingers as he peered into the distance. "Far too long. Longer than even I know. Is that all?"

"Yes. Thank you, sir," Zaire replied curtly, retreating.

The heavy oak door groaned as Zaire shut it, the latch clicking into place with finality. He paused in the dimly lit corridor, his thoughts churning like a restless tide. Slowly, he descended the stairs that led to the library, a sprawling sanctuary of faded tomes and secrets untold.

At the entrance, Zaire stopped. Through the crack in the door, he spotted Kimmie and Inez locked in an intense exchange, their hushed voices carrying an air of urgency. He pushed the door open fully, his arrival startling the pair.

"Hi," Zaire greeted coolly. He turned towards the nearest aisle without waiting for a response.

Before he could immerse himself in the labyrinth of bookshelves, a door materialised before him, shimmering faintly. From the threshold stepped Inez and Kimmie, their expressions full of mischief and defiance.

As the door vanished behind them in a glow, Zaire exhaled, levelling a look at the two women.

"Really?"

"What are you doing here?" Inez snapped, crossing her arms as she stepped closer.

"I'm researching," Zaire shot back tersely, brushing past them without further explanation.

The library seemed alive in that moment, charged with unspoken questions, the three figures navigating its depths like players in a precarious game.

Tightening her hand into a fist, Inez halted Zaire mid-step, her grip firm enough to make him wince. "Wait," she said sharply. She glanced over her shoulder at Kimmie. "Give us a second, please."

Without hesitation, Kimmie nodded and disappeared down the nearest aisle, her footsteps fading into silence. Inez released her hold on Zaire's arm, and he immediately drew in a deep, shuddering breath, his chest rising and falling as he steadied himself.

"Was that really necessary?" he asked irritably as he rubbed his arm.

She merely shrugged, her lips curling into a mischievous smirk. "Maybe not. But it was fun," she replied, a glint of amusement in her eyes. "Now, care to enlighten me? What's going on?"

Zaire exhaled slowly, visibly composing himself. "I asked him how old the building was. He doesn't know."

Her expression darkened instantly, her smirk replaced by a frown. "You spoke to him? How many times do I have to tell you? We cannot trust anyone."

"Listen to me," Zaire said firmly, holding her gaze. "I didn't betray anything. I asked a simple question. That's all."

He paused, letting the tension settle. "I'm trying to find blueprints for this place. Do you want to help, or not?"

Inez's stance relaxed, and the corner of her mouth lifted into a reluctant smile. "Where should we start?"

Kimmie came back around the corner, brushing a strand of hair behind her ear, her brow furrowed with curiosity. "You need any help?" she asked, trying to keep her tone casual.

Inez hesitated, her eyes darting to Zaire like an SOS. There was a flicker of uncertainty in her expression, equal parts hope and nervousness, as though she were asking for permission more than guidance.

Zaire leaned back against the wall, arms folded, and exhaled through his nose. He didn't need to speak for his impatience to be known. "Fine," he muttered with a resigned sigh, waving a hand. "Sound bubble and tell her."

Without another word, she motioned for Kimmie to follow, leading her swiftly down the hallway to her bedroom, the tension threading tightly between them. Inez raised her hand, the shimmer of the soundproofing field flickering into place with a soft hum, cloaking their voices in silence.

As the door clicked shut behind them, Inez turned, opening her mouth to begin the explanation, only to freeze as a knock echoed from the hallway.

Kimmie opened the door cautiously, revealing Megyn standing on the threshold with arms crossed and a knowing glint in her eye.

"If you can trust me," Kimmie said firmly, stepping aside to let her in, "you can trust Megyn."

Inez studied both women for a moment. Trust wasn't something she offered lightly, especially not now. But something in Kimmie's voice anchored her.

With a small nod, Inez snapped her fingers. The shimmer reappeared, stronger this time, sealing the room in silence. Whatever was about to be revealed, it wasn't leaving these walls. She ushered them in, closing the door behind them.

62

Veins of Colour

Hours later, the once-pristine table was littered with books, papers and exhaustion. A dull light flickered above. Everyone sat slumped in various degrees of frustration, their energy drained after hours of relentless searching.

"Nothing," Megyn said, slamming a stack of books onto the table with such force that Hunter flinched. "We've found absolutely nothing!"

Hunter's startled expression shifted into a smirk as he turned to Inez. "If only we had someone with amazing vision," he said drily as he fixed her with a knowing look.

"No," Zaire interjected abruptly, his voice cutting through the mounting tension.

"I agree," Nadia said gently. She rested a comforting arm around Inez's shoulders.

"We can't let her powers be exposed, not yet. But do we have any other choice?"

Kimmie chimed in from Inez's other side, her expression warm and empathetic. "Don't do anything you're not comfortable with," she said softly.

Inez's gaze moved between them all, her chest tightening as conflicting emotions warred within her. She wanted to help, but the thought of disappointing Zaire was at the forefront of her mind. "I need to think," she murmured as she sank into a chair, overwhelmed.

Just as the room fell into an uneasy silence, a voice emerged from the doorway, smooth and melodic. "You already know what you want to do. Don't worry about bothering him."

The woman stepped into view, her glowing red hair cascading like waves of fire. Her presence was magnetic, her voice as striking as her looks.

"Lamia," Inez breathed, rising to her feet instinctively. Her hesitation dissolved as she turned to Zaire. "I'm sorry, but I can help."

Inez shut her eyes tightly, blocking out the team behind her. She needed to clear her mind, to focus. Deep breaths slowed her racing heart as she centred herself, seeking anything that might reveal their next move.

Opening her eyes, Inez concentrated. A glimmer of red illuminated her pupils, the glow growing steadily stronger.

"Her eyes!" Kimmie gasped, stepping back instinctively.

"It's fine," Nadia assured her gently, placing a hand on her shoulder. "She's done this before."

The glow flickered briefly, then dimmed. Inez's shoulders sagged as frustration seeped into her voice. "Nothing. I see nothing."

Lamia stepped closer, her heels clicking on the tiled floor. "Look around," she prompted in her smooth, commanding tone. "At everything."

Inez obeyed, sweeping her eyes across the group. Her focus hovered on each of them for a moment before coming to rest on Kimmie.

"Why is she looking at me like that?" Kimmie asked nervously, shifting under Inez's scrutiny.

"You're not glowing," Inez responded bluntly.

Kimmie's eyes darted anxiously to the others. "Not glowing? What does that mean?"

"We've found that everyone with powers has a red glow surrounding them," Zaire explained to the group. "It's linked to the power we were given, or however it was bestowed on us."

"So, why don't I have it? Is there something wrong with me?" Kimmie's voice cracked with concern.

Hunter leaned back against the wall, arms folded. "Use your power," he suggested, his tone almost challenging.

Reluctantly, Kimmie lifted her hand and created a portal across the room. The shimmering vortex created patterns of light on the walls, its edges pulsating with otherworldly energy.

"Oh my God," Inez breathed. "What's happening?"

Kimmie's panic surged as she looked down at her arms. "What is it? What's wrong?"

"Your veins…" Inez said, her voice quivering. "They're glowing, a rainbow of colours. Blue, purple, pink, red, green… There are so many." Her eyes were wide, the sight unlike anything they'd seen before. She looked over to Megyn and Lamia, noticing the same thing, but their auras were nowhere near as strong as Kimmie's.

"We need to stay on task," Zaire interjected. "We'll figure this out later."

"Right," Lamia chimed in, her words dripping with sarcasm. "Yes, boss."

"Okay, sorry," Inez said, shaking her head to refocus. She turned away and strode purposefully down an aisle. The others followed at a distance, peeking around the corner cautiously, their watchful eyes tracking her movements.

Inez's arm rose, her finger pointing towards a bookcase on the far wall. "There," she said firmly, interrupting the heavy silence.

No one moved.

Inez stepped forwards confidently. She removed three worn books from the shelf, revealing an almost invisible flap beneath. Gently, she pressed the small, concealed button.

"I'm pretty sure in all the movies, pressing the big red button is a terrible idea," Kimmie muttered, clinging nervously to Megyn's arm.

Megyn rolled her eyes and scoffed. "You'll live," she said, tugging her arm away.

As if in defiance of Kimmie's fears, a hidden door slid open with a mechanical hum, revealing a spiralling staircase descending into the void. The blackness beyond was absolute, and the smell of damp earth wafted up from the abyss.

Inez shut her eyes momentarily, extinguishing the red glow, before reopening them. Her gaze was steady as she stepped onto the staircase. "Let's go," she commanded.

One by one, the others followed her down. The door slammed shut behind them with a deafening clang, plunging them into darkness.

"Ouch! You're on my foot," Lamia snapped, her pitch rising sharply.

"Sorry!" Nadia replied, exasperated. "If you haven't noticed, we can't see anything."

The group stumbled forwards cautiously, the stairs stretching endlessly into the depths.

63

The Dreams are True

A few moments later, beams of light flickered to life beneath their feet, glowing through the grates of the staircase. The illumination climbed gradually, the light casting eerie shadows as it ascended. The faint hum of the system activating echoed through the confined space.

"Well, that solved the problem," Hunter remarked sarcastically. He tilted his head to watch the lights reach the ceiling, bathing the staircase in a cold, artificial glow.

"Let's go," Inez said firmly as she resumed her descent. She moved with purpose, her footsteps echoing against the metal stairs. The rest of the group followed, cautious but determined.

At the bottom of the spiral, they found themselves standing before a lone blue door. Its paint was chipped and faded, and the frame was lined with rust. The air around it was heavy with dampness, each breath pervaded by the scent of decay.

"Come on," Megyn said with a sigh, crossing her arms. "It's not like it's going to be open." Her tone was blunt, her expression sceptical.

Inez ignored her and reached for the doorknob. It turned smoothly, and with a gentle push, the door creaked open. The sound was loud and jarring in the otherwise silent corridor.

"Well," Hunter said, his lips curling into a smirk as he glanced at Megyn. "Looks like someone was wrong. It was open."

Megyn rolled her eyes and shoved his arm playfully, though it didn't faze him in the slightest. He simply grinned down at her.

Without waiting for them, Inez stepped into the room. Darkness engulfed her, but the familiar smell hit her immediately, stagnant water, old paper and layers of undisturbed dust. It clung to her senses like a ghost of memories past.

"Zaire, we've been here."

Zaire stepped in behind her and scanned the room. His eyes landed on a wall near the corner, where his memory guided him. His fingers brushed over the surface until they found the familiar switch.

Fluorescent lights buzzed to life, flooding the room in stark brightness. The walls were lined with shelves of forgotten artefacts, papers and strange objects that seemed to hum with power.

And there it was, what they'd been searching for.

Inez stepped into the room first, her gaze sweeping across the space as memories flooded back. The sight stopped her cold, everything was just as they had left it. She couldn't tear her eyes away from the haunting familiarity.

One by one, the others followed her inside, their expressions shifting as they took in the scene. Nadia froze near the door, her eyes widening in disbelief. "It's just as you described," she said in awe.

Lamia, however, wrinkled her nose in disdain and stepped back instinctively, clutching at her scarf. "What is this dump?" she muttered.

Ignoring Lamia's remark, Inez moved purposefully towards a door in the far corner of the room, her heart pounding with urgency. She pushed it open, revealing the smaller chamber where she and Zaire had freed the women in 2002. The stale air hit her immediately, the memories rushing back like an unstoppable tide.

Zaire joined her and turned towards Lamia, his voice heavy with the past. "Inez and I travelled to the past," he began sombrely. "We found the crystal that gave us our powers. We found pregnant women being experimented on, and we set them free."

Inez's shoulders stiffened suddenly, her hand flying to cover her mouth in horror. Her eyes darted to the tank at the back of the room, its contents unchanged save for time's cruel toll. The mermaid was still inside, her once-glimmering form now reduced to a grotesque, mummified carcass. The water level had dropped significantly, leaving behind murky puddles of decay. But there was no sign of a baby.

"All but one," Inez whispered as tears pricked at the corners of her eyes.

Lamia stepped closer, drawn inexplicably to the tank. Her movements were slow, as if caught in a trance. She leaned towards the glass, her eyes brimming with unshed tears. "I've seen her in my dreams," Lamia said quietly as a single tear streaked down her cheek.

Inez's instinct took over. She stepped forwards and rested a gentle hand on Lamia's shoulder, her touch steadying even as she struggled to keep her own composure. The room was suffused with grief, their shared histories hanging over them.

Then Kimmie's voice broke the silence. "She has the same last name as you," she said, addressing Lamia.

All eyes turned towards her. Lamia's gaze shifted, her mind trying to connect the dots as Kimmie's words settled over the group. The room seemed to hold its breath.

"She's my mum."

The words hung in the air like a thunderclap, reverberating through the room. For a moment, no one spoke. The group exchanged glances, their expressions shifting between shock, disbelief and understanding.

Hunter's brow furrowed as he turned towards Lamia. "How old are you?" he asked cautiously.

Lamia hesitated, her eyes dropping to the floor as she wrestled with her thoughts. "I… I'm twenty-four," she said softly.

Zaire stepped forwards, his face pale. "That's impossible," he said. "If she's your mum and we travelled to the past… that would mean she—"

"Died before I was born," Lamia finished for him, her voice trembling as fresh tears welled in her eyes. She turned back to the tank, the mummified remains of the mermaid staring at her like a grim echo of the truth she was only now uncovering.

Inez placed a hand on Lamia's arm. "We don't know everything yet," she said gently, her own voice thick with emotion. "There might be more to this than we realise."

Hunter folded his arms, his face a mask of scepticism. "So what? Are we saying that this... creature was experimented on and somehow gave birth to Lamia? That doesn't make any sense."

"We know it doesn't make sense," Kimmie interjected, her tone sharper than intended. "But nothing about what happened here has ever made sense, has it?"

Lamia turned to Kimmie suddenly, a flicker of resolve shining through her tears. "She's the reason I have the dreams," she said with conviction. "All my life, I've seen her face. I thought it was just... random. But now I know she was trying to tell me something."

"It's more than just dreams," Nadia said, stepping closer. Her expression was thoughtful, her gaze flicking between the tank and Lamia. "The connection is too strong. You share her last name. Maybe your powers, your dreams, all of it, it's tied to her."

"We're not going to figure this out by staring at her," Zaire said firmly. "If this place was experimenting on her, there might be files or records somewhere. Something that explains what happened."

"Fine," Hunter said, throwing his hands up. "But let's make it quick. This place gives me the creeps."

The group began to search the room, each step heavy with the weight of their discovery. Lamia lingered near the tank for a moment longer, her fingers brushing against the cold glass. "I'll find out the truth," she whispered, more to herself than anyone else.

With a deep breath, she turned and joined the others, the promise of answers urging her forward.

64

Lady of Lunathira

"They found a way to preserve the foetus. They wrote notes and needed to wait until a certain year to bring her into the world. There was a prophecy, and she was needed for it," Megyn read from a folder nearby. Inez could see the pain in Lamia's eyes and wanted to help. Inez placed her hand on the glass, and the water began to fill and become less murky. The mermaid was filling with life, becoming less of a mummy.

"Lamia, look," Kimmie said, holding her hand.

Lamia opened her eyes, and tears flooded her eyes. "Mum." Lamia placed her hand on the glass and closed her eyes, starting to mumble something in a language no one else could understand. She opened her eyes. "She told me to say that to her if I ever found her."

The mermaid started to breathe and flail around in the water. She took a big breath and opened her eyes. "My Lamia, you found me." Lamia started to cry more. "Thank you for waking me. Can someone drain the tank?" The mermaid looked at Inez. Once again, Inez placed her hand on the glass, but rather than fill it, she emptied it.

Seconds later, the mermaid sprouted legs, and a loose gown appeared. She was flawless with the voice of an angel. "Are you a mermaid or a siren?" Zaire asked.

"I was a mermaid until they experimented on my daughter, and she made me part human. I am a Lunaric lady and a sea folk representative of Lunathira. My name is Kaitora, but you can call me Kai. My beautiful Mayaielia, we shall go home and rejoin our family and retake our place as representatives of the sea."

Lamia smiled at her mother. "Where is Lunathira?"

Kai smiled at all the puzzled faces in front of her. "It is a world far away from here, full of magic, happiness and love."

"Sorry, Kai, but how long has it been since you were there?" Megyn asked.

"Well, that would depend entirely on what year it is here," she said softly but sternly.

"It's 2026," Lamia responded.

Her mother's face dropped. "That is far longer than I had expected. We shall have to get a move on. Where is the crystal? It must return."

Everyone looked at each other. "The red crystal, it's not from here," Kimmie said.

"Of course not, dear. You remind me of a woman I once knew. The eyes are rare." Kai smiled at Kimmie.

Everyone looked at each other, not knowing who should tell Kai the difficult truth. Nadia stepped forwards, taking a deep breath. "You can't leave this room," she said firmly.

Kai's reaction was immediate, her face contorting as if she had been slapped. She pulled Lamia protectively to her side. "I am Lady of Lunathira, you do not command us," she hissed, her voice filled with authority and indignation.

Nadia stood her ground. "You are on Earth now. I'm sorry, but being Lady means nothing here. We need you to stay hidden. There are other people in control, and they cannot see you," she responded, her tone apologetic but resolute.

Kai's grip on Lamia's wrist tightened. "They are right, Mum," Lamia said, trying to soothe her mother. "I will come and spend every second I can with you, but you cannot go upstairs." She held her mother's hand, her eyes pleading for understanding.

"I have an idea," Inez interjected. "Kimmie, open a portal to the lake out back. Lamia and Kai can go through it, and we will continue to search."

"Are you sure?" Lamia asked, her voice tinged with concern.

Inez nodded and looked at Kimmie, who concentrated and opened the portal. "You are not from here, young one. We will talk about it once you are done down here," Kai said to Kimmie, both curious and commanding. They walked through the portal, and the door closed behind them.

The rest of the group continued down the hall to the room on the left, where they found chairs with restraints. "This is horrible," Nadia said.

"This is what they do," Inez snapped back bitterly.

"What were they doing here?" Hunter asked, his usual sarcasm absent for the first time that day.

"Making us," Zaire responded, lowering the brown file he was reading. The group looked at him in horror.

"*Foetus experiment 1, talking to animals, successful,*" Megyn read aloud. Everyone looked at her, then at Zaire.

"*Experiment 2, strength, successful,*" she continued, and they turned to Hunter.

"*Experiment 3, time reversal, failed,*" she read, and everyone took a deep breath.

"So, the ladies you helped escape were our parents?" Nadia asked.

"I think so," Zaire responded, continuing to read more details from the file.

"*Chair 203, foetus with impenetrable skin.* This was Hunter. *The captor escaped. Chair 218, foetus with weather control.* This was Zaire. *Captor deceased on escape. Chair 126, foetus with flexibility.* This was Nadia. *The captor deceased at birth. Tank 101, foetus with shapeshifting abilities.* This was Lamia. *Captor safe. Chair 209, foetus with flight.* This was Xander. *Captor deceased on escape.*" The list continued, revealing that most had died during their escape attempts, but three had survived.

"She was there. I left her behind, and she died," Zaire said, his voice trembling with guilt and sorrow. He felt sick to his stomach, his actions pressing heavily on him. Inez was at his side in seconds, wrapping her arms around him in a comforting hug. Zaire held her shoulders and pushed her away slightly, looking deeply into her eyes. "Take me back," he begged. "I can save her this time, save all of them." He glanced over her shoulder at the others, seeking their support.

Inez felt a pang of guilt. "I can't, and you know that. We cannot go back and change things. We don't know what it will do. What happened before was always meant to happen. I'm sorry," she said, filled with regret.

"She is right, mate. We don't know the effect it will have." Hunter tried to comfort his friend, his tone gentle.

"It's okay for you. Your mother is still out there somewhere," Zaire snapped back, his frustration boiling over.

"Stop. Mine is gone, and I know we cannot do this. Go back to your room and cool down, Zaire. You are not thinking straight," Nadia interjected. She looked towards Kimmie, who nodded and opened a portal to Zaire's room.

"Fine, I see how it is." Zaire stormed through the door, not looking back.

Inez felt heartbroken that the one thing he had asked for was something she couldn't help with. The group gathered as much paperwork as possible, trying to focus on the task at hand despite the emotional turmoil.

Kimmie's portal led everyone back to their rooms, where they could regroup and process the day's events.

65

The Siren's Grief

Inez sneaked out early, went to the canteen to grab dinner and returned to her room unnoticed. She sat at the desk in her room researching, doing everything she could to uncover the truth. As she delved deeper into her investigation, she started to panic. If they were doing these experiments on the babies, was that what they had tried to do to baby Leo before he was taken from her? She had to figure it out.

Inez discovered that they were breaking the crystal fragments, turning them into dust, adding a chemical compound into a liquid and injecting this into the mother's bloodstream to reach the babies. These powers were not transferred to the mother, and there had to be a reason for that. She was deep in thought, trying to piece together the puzzle, when she heard a knock at the door.

Startled, Inez quickly folded all the papers and placed them under a magazine on the table. She stood up but lost her balance after sitting on her foot for so long. She stumbled to the door and opened it, shocked to see Megyn standing there. "Hi, you alright?" Megyn asked seriously.

Inez shook her head slowly, a dull ache pulsing behind her eyes. Her movements were heavy, as though gravity itself had turned against her. Shadows clung beneath her eyes, and her shoulders sagged with the weight of too many fruitless hours. The search had worn her thin, mind, body and spirit fraying at the edges. She was tired of chasing echoes, of grasping at pieces that never fit. Every step forwards felt more like a stumble through fog.

"I need to talk to you," Megyn said, her expression grave.

"Come in," Inez replied, opening the door wider for Megyn to enter her room. As she went to close the door, Qita sneaked in. "Sorry, Qita, I didn't see you there." He lifted his head and walked in, ignoring her.

They walked over to the sofas by the bookcase and sat down. Qita sprawled out next to Megyn. "So, what do you need to tell me?" Inez asked, trying to break the ice.

"I know more about the testing," Megyn said, shocking Inez. "I didn't grow up here. I grew up in a land far away from there, where I lived in a temple with other powerful people," Megyn continued to explain. There were other locations like this one. Sunstone Manor was the main operation, and they expanded over time. Very few knew of the others, but Megyn was the best in the temple, and they needed her elsewhere.

She learned how to fight in the temple and use her powers. The training was strict, with scheduled classes. If they failed a test, they were punished severely. They were hurt, bones broken, beaten black and blue, and then healed with a magical white glowing liquid, only to feel the pain again. Megyn was treated differently there; she had such strong powers and skills that they trained her to be a warrior. They would break her bones repeatedly until she couldn't feel the breaks any more.

"There is more than just here, than just us," Inez said, in disbelief. "I'm so sorry that happened to you."

Megyn bowed her head slightly. "I'm sorry too. I should have told you all sooner."

"No, you don't have to tell us anything," Inez reassured her. "I do have some questions, though."

"Of course, anything." Megyn lifted her head, ready to answer.

"How strong is your connection with Qita?" Inez asked, looking at his bright orange eyes.

"I feel what he feels, and he feels what I feel," Megyn said, stroking under his chin, causing him to purr.

THE SIREN'S GRIEF

"If you ever want to talk about it, we can. I'm here."

"I appreciate it, but now isn't the time," Megyn replied. She continued to explain the main details about the other locations and how long this project had been going on. After their long talk, Megyn went back to her room with Qita, and Inez decided to go for a walk.

The rest of the team was in the hall having dinner. They were laughing and joking, which was shocking considering what they had found out today. The room began to quiet when it started vibrating. The team looked at each other in fear. The glasses shattered on the table when Kimmie opened her eyes. "Lamia," she whispered urgently. She opened a portal and jumped through before anyone could follow. Kimmie couldn't believe her eyes.

Kai floated motionless on the surface of the lake, her limbs adrift, hair fanning out like ink in water. The light danced around her pale skin, eerily serene, as though the world hadn't just fractured.

Lamia didn't hesitate. With a cry that broke the silence, she leapt into the lake, her form warping mid-air, the smooth transition into her siren self as natural as breath. A haunting scream tore from her throat, raw and primal, splitting through the afternoon air. Windows trembled. Glasses cracked in the manor. The lake itself seemed to shudder beneath her grief.

On the shore, Kimmie strode forwards, her steps firm despite the nerves clawing at her. Her voice cut clean through the chaos. "Come out of the water. Bring her over."

Lamia obeyed, gliding through the water with unnatural speed. She cradled Kai's body, careful yet urgent, and delivered her to the edge where Kimmie waited, arms already extended. Kneeling, Kimmie slid her hands beneath Kai's limp arms and pulled her gently up onto the wooden deck, water pooling around them.

Lamia stepped out next, her transformation slipping away with the water dripping from her skin. She dropped to her knees beside her mother.

Kimmie rose unsteadily to her feet, backing away as her gaze locked onto Kai's unmoving chest. Her thoughts spiralled, fragments of anxiety and strategy tumbling over one another. Without a word, she summoned a portal with a flick of her wrist, tearing the air apart with violet light, and reached through. With a sharp yank, she pulled Zaire out from wherever he had been, dropping him onto the deck beside them.

"Was that necessary?" Zaire asked, straightening his top. Kimmie just looked towards Lamia, crouching on the floor. He could see Kai's lifeless body in her arms and walked towards her. He placed a hand on her shoulder, and she looked at him with smudged makeup streaking down her face.

"She's gone," Lamia whispered, her voice breaking.

Zaire closed Kai's eyes gently, placing her on the floor. He stood Lamia up and hugged her tightly, feeling her still-wet hair against his T-shirt. He looked towards Kimmie. "My room," he said. Kimmie closed her eyes and opened a portal leading directly to his room. Zaire and Lamia stepped through, leaving Kimmie behind.

66

Lake that Held Her

Inez stormed into the canteen and stood at the end of the table where the team was gathered. "You won't believe what I just saw," she said, filled with fury. She glanced around and noticed the broken glass on the table. "Why is there smashed glass?" she questioned in a calmer tone.

"Lamia smashed them somehow, but we don't know why or what happened," Nadia answered, looking at Hunter for confirmation.

"I can tell you what happened, Lamia was busy having a moment out by the lake with Zaire!" Inez exclaimed, her anger intensifying. She was furious that Zaire wouldn't talk to her but would embrace Lamia.

Hunter and Nadia tried to comfort her, but before they could say much, Kimmie walked in, leaning on Megyn for support. The others scooted down the bench to let them sit. "What happened?" Inez asked with concern.

"I have used too much power today; it's draining me," Kimmie responded, her voice weak. "Kai's dead, she was shot," she informed the team. They all gasped, and Inez looked down, feeling a wave of guilt wash over her.

"I feel terrible," she said, looking towards Nadia.

"How were you to know?" Nadia responded, embracing her friend. "She saw them hugging at the lake when she went for a walk," Nadia explained to the others.

"I'm going to take Kimmie to her room and turn in for the night," Megyn said, helping Kimmie up. Qita followed them as they exited the hall.

Inez held her head in her hands. "I feel terrible. I'm going to go to my room," she said, standing up.

Nadia grabbed her hand. "Do you want me to come with you?" she asked gently.

Inez shook her head and exited the hall, leaving Nadia and Hunter alone.

67

The Faulty Door

Inez walked down the hall to her room, her footsteps echoing softly against the polished floor. As she approached her door, a sudden realisation struck her, she didn't want to return to her room; she wanted to see Zaire. Her heart pounded with anticipation as she turned and crept up the stairs towards his room, ensuring she wasn't heard or seen. The house was quiet, the only sound being the creak of the wooden steps beneath her feet.

She reached Zaire's door, her hand trembling slightly as she closed her eyes and faded through it. When she opened her eyes, the horror hit her. Lamia was lying in Zaire's arms in his bed, wrapped in a towel, both of them sleeping peacefully. Inez felt a sickening twist in her stomach and stepped back, accidentally knocking into a bookcase. The sound of books shifting was loud in the silence, and she turned quickly to ensure she didn't drop anything. When she turned back, Zaire's eyes were on her, wide with surprise.

"I'm sorry, I should have knocked, I'm going to go," Inez stammered. She phased back through the door and ran to her room, confused and hurt.

Zaire looked at Lamia, his expression full of guilt and concern. He hadn't meant to fall asleep. "Lamia," he said, gently shaking her. She stirred, looking up at him with sleepy eyes before realising the situation and jumping up, clutching her towel tightly.

"Oh, I'm so sorry," Lamia said, embarrassed.

"It's fine, but I must go. I need to find Inez," Zaire replied, getting up from the bed and quickly putting on his shoes. "You can grab something clean from my wardrobe."

Lamia smiled at her friend for his support, secretly missing his touch. Zaire left the room, and Lamia grabbed some shorts and a baggy T-shirt from his wardrobe, getting changed quickly. She sneaked out of his room with her wet hair, holding her dirty clothes, hoping to avoid any awkward encounters. As she turned around, she saw Nadia standing there, her expression unreadable.

"It's not what it looks like," Lamia said defensively, trying to explain herself.

"So, it's not Zaire comforting you and telling you that you stink after being in that lake?" Nadia responded sarcastically.

"Okay, it's exactly as it looks, but can we not mention this to anyone? I don't want to upset Inez." Lamia giggled nervously, hoping to lighten the mood.

"Your mum just died, and you care about someone else? Maybe you have changed, but I still don't like you after what you did to Zaire. I am sorry about your mum, though," Nadia said, her voice softening as she smiled at Lamia and walked away.

Zaire made his way to Inez's room, his heart heavy with concern. He knocked gently at her door. "Let me in, please." He waited, but there was no response. He could feel her presence, the emotional turmoil she was experiencing. "Please let me in," he begged again, resting his forehead against the door. After a moment, he heard a click and pushed the door open.

Inside, Inez was lying in her bed, curled up and crying. The sight of her in such distress pained him deeply. He walked in and closed the door behind him, locking it to ensure they wouldn't be disturbed. He approached her slowly, his heart aching with every step. "You did this," she said, choked with tears.

"What?" Zaire responded, confused and hurt by her accusation.

THE FAULTY DOOR

"You don't like seeing me like this, but you did it," she replied, her words cutting through him.

"You read my mind?" he asked, still trying to understand.

"Just go," she begged him, her voice breaking.

"Never," he responded firmly.

Zaire removed his shoes and climbed into her bed, instantly feeling the warmth from her body. He hugged her tightly, trying to offer some comfort. "Her mum just died, she was covered in algae from the lake, and she needed someone. I told her to shower, and I comforted her. We must have fallen asleep. That's it, I promise," he explained, gentle and sincere.

Inez turned around and looked up at him with her puffy, tear-stained eyes. He smiled at her, a soft, reassuring smile, and slowly leaned in, waiting for her to complete the connection. She did, closing the gap between them. Inez took a deep breath, her emotions still raw. "I shouldn't have just come into your room. I am sorry for that. I guess I don't even know what this is," she admitted.

She placed her hand on his chest, feeling his heart rate elevate under the fabric of his T-shirt. The steady beat was comforting, a reminder of his unwavering support. Zaire held her close, his arms providing a safe haven from the storm of emotions swirling around them.

Zaire gently cupped Inez's chin with his finger and thumb, lifting her head until her large, expressive eyes locked onto his. "I want everything with you, Inez; I love you," he declared, his voice filled with sincerity and warmth.

Despite her best efforts to contain it, a radiant smile spread across her face. "I love you too," she responded, her smile widening until it seemed to light up the room.

"I won't let anything happen to you. I will always protect you and look after you," Zaire promised.

Inez's expression shifted, a playful glint appearing in her eyes. "I'm stronger than you, and faster, and more talented…" she teased, a sarcastic smile playing on her lips.

Before she could continue, Zaire leaned in and captured her lips in a deep, passionate kiss. "That's enough," he murmured out of the corner of his mouth.

"And smarter," she added cheekily, unable to resist the playful jab.

In response, Zaire's hands moved to her waist, and he began to tickle her mercilessly. "I'm sorry, I'm sorry, please stop!" Inez pleaded between fits of uncontrollable laughter, her protests mingling with the sound of her joyous giggles.

68

Rules Were Written

A week had passed, and no one had seen Lamia or heard from her. The group had begun to worry, and Zaire decided it was time to see the boss. He stood outside the doors to the boss's office, straightened his shirt and prepared to knock. Just as he raised his hand, he hesitated. He didn't want to face the boss and get questioned about Inez. Before he could decide, a voice from inside called out, "Enter."

Zaire pushed the door open and stepped inside. The boss was standing by the full-length window, his back turned to Zaire. A red-headed lady was sitting in the chair opposite the window. "Sorry to disturb. I will come back later," Zaire said to the lady. She turned around, and to his surprise, it was Lamia.

"We have been looking for you. We have all been worried about you," Zaire said, his voice filled with relief.

"That is all, Lamia. Thank you ever so much for the information. You are granted leave."

Lamia stood up, walked over to Zaire and placed her hand on his shoulder. "Good luck. You should have chosen me." She walked away, leaving Zaire gobsmacked. She was dressed in tiny leather hot pants, a black graphic T-shirt with red Chinese symbols and knee-high boots.

"Zaire, sit," the boss commanded, breaking Zaire's daydream. Zaire sat down, feeling anxious but curious. He had never heard the boss speak to him in such a way before. "Our dear departed friend told me about your little adventures. You found the old research centre?" The boss turned around and looked deep into Zaire's eyes, making him gulp with fear.

"Yes, we did," Zaire responded, trying to keep his voice calm.

"This 'we'? Is that Nadia, Hunter and Inez?" the boss asked.

"Yes, sir," Zaire replied firmly.

"Anything else to tell me?" the boss enquired with a hint of menace.

"No, sir," Zaire said, gripping the arms of the chair tightly.

"That is all," the boss said, turning back to look out the window. Zaire stood up to leave, but the boss coughed, stopping him in his tracks. "Hand the leaflets on my desk out to the people living in my house," the boss instructed. Zaire leaned forwards and grabbed the letters.

"And Zaire, STAY AWAY FROM INEZ. I SAID TO KEEP AN EYE ON HER, NOT BED HER. SHE IS NOT YOURS. DO YOU UNDERSTAND?" The boss slammed his fists on the desk.

"Yes, sir," Zaire said, jumping at the shock of the boss's reaction.

"DISMISSED," the boss barked, watching Zaire intensely as he left the room.

Standing at the top of the stairs, leaning on the bannister, Lamia played with her nails. Her eyes glinted with amusement and defiance. "Oh, honey, that didn't sound pleasant?" Lamia smirked, her voice dripping with sarcasm.

Zaire's face contorted with anger as he took a step towards her, his fists clenched at his sides. "I cannot believe you. How could you do this to us?" His voice was a low growl.

Lamia's smirk widened as she met his gaze, unflinching. "I could have told him so much more," she said casually, almost as though she were bored. She leaned in, her lips brushing against his in a brief, mocking kiss. Then, without another word, she picked up her bag and walked down the stairs, her heels clicking against the wood with each step.

Zaire stood there, frozen, watching her leave. His eyes fell to the leaflets scattered on the floor, and he huffed in frustration, running a hand through his hair. The house seemed to echo his sense of loss and confusion.

He walked into the centre garden where the group sat having lunch in the sun. The atmosphere was light, filled with laughter and the clinking of glasses. Nadia looked up from her plate, her eyes narrowing with concern. "Did you find out where she is?" she asked.

"Yes," he replied bitterly. "She screwed us all over. She made a deal with him, and he let her leave." His gaze shifted towards the long blacked-out glass panel that dominated one side of the garden. The panel seemed ominous, an observer to their conversation.

Kimmie's eyes widened in fear as she clutched Kek closer to her. "He is watching us?" she asked, barely above a whisper. The group fell silent, the revelation hanging over them like a dark cloud. The sun continued to shine, but the warmth seemed to have been replaced by a cold, creeping dread.

"He always watches," Zaire responded, looking down at the leaflets in his hand.

"What's that?" Inez asked, grabbing his arm in an attempt to see the papers. Zaire pulled away from her defensively. He handed a letter to each group member.

"I have to go and distribute these," he told the group, indicating that there was no room for discussion.

"I'll help," Inez offered.

"I don't need your help," Zaire said sharply, his words suspended in the air as he walked away. The group watched him leave, a heavy silence settling over them.

Inez looked around the group in shock, her stomach churning with unease. "What was that about?" Nadia asked.

Inez shrugged in response, unable to find the words. "I think it's to do with this," Megyn added, shaking the paper in the air. The group turned their attention to the letters they had been given.

Dear Residents,

Effective immediately, all social activities must be requested at the reception, and I will personally grant permission for each. This policy includes the following:

- **Sparring Sessions**: *Any physical training or combat practice must be*

scheduled and approved.
- **Study Sessions**: Group study meetings require prior approval.
- **Group Activities**: Any organised group events need to be authorised.
- **Social Lunches**: Any social lunches that are not located in the food hall must be approved.

Additionally, please adhere to the following rules:

- **Bedrooms:** No other person is allowed in each other's bedrooms; they are designated for individual use only.
- **Pets and Creatures**: No pets or creatures of any kind are to be kept on the grounds.

Failure to follow these rules will result in punishment.
Thank you for your cooperation.
Sincerely,
Raphael

69

The Mission Fractured

Kimmie stood up abruptly, her heart pounding in her chest, and she ran inside, her eyes searching frantically for Kek. She found him hovering near the window, and without a second thought, she threw her arms around him, hugging him tightly. Megyn, not far behind, chased after her with Qita striding close by, his eyes alert.

Nadia and Hunter exchanged a glance, their hands finding each other's in a silent agreement, and they walked inside together, fingers intertwined, seeking comfort in their shared presence.

Inez, standing alone outside, looked up at the glass panel above her. Her face twisted in a scowl, and she hoped he would see her reaction. Frustration bubbled up inside her, and she scrunched up the paper in her hand, throwing it into the nearby fountain with a splash. She looked back up, the glass almost clear with the sunlight beaming on it, and for a moment, she swore she saw a ghostly figure. She stepped back in shock, accidentally knocking a cup off the table. When she looked back, the figure was gone. Was it him? Was it really Lucian?

Inside, Megyn knocked on Kimmie's door. "I know you're in there, it's me," she announced.

From the other side, Kimmie's voice came, sharp and defensive. "Go away. I'm busy."

Megyn wasn't deterred. "Let me in," she insisted. Suddenly, the door opened, and Kek was hovering in the doorway.

Kimmie turned to him, her eyes narrowing. "Traitor," she muttered. Qita, seising the opportunity, darted inside and tried to swat Kek from the air. Kek ducked and dived, narrowly avoiding Qita's swipes.

On Kimmie's bed lay a suitcase, hastily packed with the nearest clothing she could find. Megyn's eyes softened with concern. "You cannot run; he will find you," she said gently.

Kimmie's eyes flashed with determination. "Not if I run to where Kek is from. He won't be able to get there," she retorted.

Megyn shook her head, grabbing Kimmie's hand. "You don't know where that is. You're not thinking," she said.

"Well, what are you going to do?" Kimmie asked, challenging her.

"Go back to the Opal Temple. You can come with me. I already spoke to Raphael, and he approved, but we cut contact with everyone here and leave at midnight tonight," Megyn explained, looking at Kek and Qita for their reactions.

Kimmie looked to Kek, who had perched on the arm of the desk chair. He bowed his head at her in approval of the plan. "We leave tonight," Kimmie said, her voice resolute.

Megyn smiled, relieved. "I could use your doorway to move all our stuff over," she suggested.

Kimmie nodded. "Of course."

Meanwhile, Nadia and Hunter returned to their room, their minds racing with the implications of the night's events. They shared a room, and their relationship added another layer of complexity to their situation. As they stood in the doorway, Zaire appeared, his expression unreadable. "Hunter, you're upstairs, second door to the left," he said, tossing a set of keys to him. Hunter caught the keys, his face a mask of confusion.

"How can you allow this... be okay with this... This affects all of us, including you... What about the mission?" he demanded, his voice rising.

Zaire met his gaze steadily. "The mission is dead," he said simply, turning on his heel and walking away, leaving Hunter and Nadia to grapple with the weight of his words.

At dinner, the atmosphere in the hall was tense. Silence hung heavily over the room, as if the very air was weighed down by the unresolved conflict. The tables were filled with people, yet everyone seemed isolated, divided by invisible barriers of mistrust and resentment. No one dared to break the silence, their eyes cast down or staring blankly at their plates.

The door swung open, and Zaire walked in, immediately drawing the attention of everyone in the hall. Heads turned, and eyes filled with disgust and anger followed his every move. He ignored the hostile stares, his expression one of indifference, and made his way to the food counter. He grabbed a tray, filled it with food and walked to an empty table, sitting down alone.

Inez, seated at the far end of the hall, looked up and locked eyes with Zaire. Without a word, she stood up and walked out of the hall. Zaire stood abruptly. "Inez!" he shouted. But she didn't stop, didn't even turn around. He wanted to run after her, to explain, to beg for her forgiveness, but his eyes flicked to the cameras in the corners of the hall. He knew they were watching, recording every second. On the other side of the room, Raphael sat, a cruel smile playing on his lips as he watched the pain he had caused unfold.

Later that night, Zaire lay in bed, staring at the ceiling, unable to sleep. His mind was a whirlwind of thoughts and emotions, all centred around Inez. He longed for her presence, for the chance to explain everything, to feel her warmth in his arms. Frustrated and restless, he jumped out of bed and headed to the shower, hoping the hot water would tire him out. But instead, it only made him more awake. He changed into his shorts and was towel-drying his hair when he walked back into the bedroom.

To his shock, Inez was sitting on the edge of the bed, her eyes soft and understanding. Zaire's heart skipped a beat, and he smiled, shaking his head in disbelief. *Is she really here?* he wondered. "Yes, I'm here. I can read you, remember?" Inez replied, her smile warm and reassuring. Zaire's face lit up with joy, and he ran over to the bed, grabbing her in his arms. He buried his hand in her hair, holding the back of her head as he kissed her deeply, pouring all his emotions into that one kiss.

Inez laughed, pulling away gently. "Let me breathe," she said, her eyes sparkling with amusement. Zaire chuckled, his heart lighter than it had been in days. "None of us is giving up," Inez said firmly, tossing him a shirt.

Her words were a promise, a vow that they would face whatever came their way together.

Seconds later, a portal opened in Zaire's room, and the team stepped out, their faces a mix of determination and concern. Zaire was taken aback; he hadn't known this was the plan. They hadn't anticipated Raphael's reaction, but they had all sacrificed so much for this moment. Kimmie and Megyn could now conduct more research at the Opal Temple, a remote location that would be safer for Kek. Nadia and Hunter could pretend to be angry at Zaire, creating a diversion, while Inez would be out of harm's way.

"There is something else," Kimmie said, her voice serious as she turned to Zaire. She opened another portal, and Lamia walked through, her expression playful yet sincere.

"Sorry, honey, when have I ever called you that? Come on, Zaire, you should know when I'm messing with you," Lamia teased. Zaire's confusion deepened, but he listened intently. "We had to let Raphael know something was going on. Now he will focus on me. He'll increase security in the library and forget about everywhere else. Plus, we all know his name is Raphael now," Inez explained, her eyes meeting Zaire's with a reassuring gaze.

"I hate you all," Zaire said, looking around his room at the team. Despite his words, there was a hint of gratitude in his voice.

"We will meet up every three weeks with Kimmie and Megyn from the Opal Temple. We will all meet up at least twice, but Lamia, this is where we leave you for now," Inez added.

Lamia walked around the group, hugging everyone tightly. When she reached Zaire, she held him a little longer. "I'm sorry, but I cannot be here. I need to be on my own," she said. She walked back through the portal, not turning back, leaving Zaire with a sense of loss.

"We better get going," Megyn said, her voice breaking the silence. She and Kimmie hugged the team goodbye, their embraces filled with unspoken promises. Nadia and Hunter pulled Zaire into a mini group hug before they

THE MISSION FRACTURED

too left the room.

Now, Zaire and Inez were alone. The room felt different, quieter, yet charged with the energy of their shared mission. "I cannot believe you all tricked me," Zaire said, grabbing Inez's hands.

"We weren't tricking you; we were tricking him," Inez replied, tilting her head and looking into his eyes with a soft smile. Zaire leaned in and kissed her, the tension melting away.

"You are lucky you are cute," he murmured, resting his forehead against hers, feeling the warmth and strength of their bond.

70

Two Doses Left

Days later, Zaire was summoned to Raphael's office. The atmosphere was tense as Zaire approached the door, his heart pounding with anticipation. He knocked firmly and waited for an answer. Silence greeted him. He knocked again, this time with more urgency, and pressed his ear against the door, straining to hear any sign of movement. Still nothing.

Zaire took control of the wind, channelling his power to blow the door open. The door swung wide with a gust of air, revealing Raphael slumped in his chair, motionless. "Sorry for the intrusion," Zaire muttered as he rushed to Raphael's side. He shook him voraciously, hoping to elicit a response.

Zaire listened intently to Raphael's chest, but there was no heartbeat.

Without hesitation, he placed his finger on Raphael's chest, summoning the lightning within him. The electricity pulsated through his body, shocking Raphael back to life.

Raphael gasped, his eyes snapping open in shock. He looked at Zaire, bewildered. "You saved me," he whispered, his voice filled with gratitude and disbelief.

"I guess I did," Zaire responded, stepping back to give Raphael space. He watched as Raphael stood up, adjusting his shirt and blazer, trying to regain his composure.

"You may continue to train Inez, but only in the battle hall unless you make the request," Raphael instructed, authoritative despite the recent ordeal. "You may start now. Go," he added, shooing Zaire away with a wave of his hand.

The door closed with a resounding thud, and Raphael immediately clutched his chest, his breaths coming in short gasps. His vision blurred as he staggered towards the wall, each step feeling like an eternity.

With trembling hands, he reached behind the art piece Inez had painted and fumbled with the hidden safe. The combination lock clicked open, revealing a small vial of red liquid labelled 'L'.

Raphael's hands shook as he extracted the nearly empty vial and a syringe. He carefully inserted the needle into the vial, drawing out the precious liquid. His heart pounded in his ears as he injected the substance into his arm.

Almost instantly, a wave of relief washed over him. The colour returned to his pallid face, and his breathing steadied.

"Thank you, brother," he whispered to the empty room. He stared at the vial, noting with growing concern that there was only enough for two more doses. The questions that had haunted him for weeks resurfaced: How long would this last? What was happening to him?

Raphael's mind raced as he tried to piece together the fragments of his condition. The mysterious ailment that plagued him was relentless, and the red liquid was the only thing keeping him alive. He knew he had to find answers, and quickly. The dwindling supply of the elixir meant time was running out, and he couldn't afford to waste a single moment.

71

The Breaking Point

Zaire knocked at Inez's door, his knuckles tapping lightly. The door creaked open, revealing Inez's face, which lit up with a smile at the sight of him. However, her expression quickly shifted to one of alarm, her eyes widening with fear at the thought of being caught.

"What are you doing here? I cannot let you in," Inez roared, her voice loud enough for anyone nearby to hear. The urgency in her tone was unmistakable.

"I am under instructions to continue training with you again in the hall only," Zaire responded, matching her volume to ensure their conversation sounded official. He let out a small smirk, a hint of defiance in his eyes, and turned to walk down the hallway towards the fighting room.

As he approached the room, he saw Hunter and Nadia occupying the ring. Nadia was effortlessly running circles around Hunter, delivering swift kicks that left him struggling to keep up. They both paused their sparring to look at Zaire as he entered, followed closely by Inez.

"Ready?" Zaire asked Inez, who nodded in response.

"Sparring time is over. You are not winning, Hunter," Zaire shouted towards them. Nadia darted past them, her movements causing Inez's loose strands of hair to flutter in the air.

"What are you doing?" Nadia whispered to Zaire.

"Training. We are under orders, not that I have to answer to you," Zaire replied, his tone cold and dismissive as he looked down his nose at her.

Hunter walked over, his shoulders squared and chest puffed out in a challenging stance. "Do you want to get out of her face, or else we can spar without the ring, Zee?" Hunter questioned Zaire, provoking him.

Zaire rolled his eyes and walked away, not interested in engaging further. Nadia glanced at Inez, who shrugged her shoulders in response, a silent acknowledgement of the tension.

"Inez, let's not waste time," Zaire shouted impatiently from the mat.

"I'll talk to you at dinner," Inez said to Nadia, grabbing her hand as she walked away.

They entered the ring, and Zaire wasted no time. With a rapid motion, he blew a gust of air towards Inez, sending her sprawling onto the ground. "Dick," she muttered under her breath. She quickly jumped up, brushing the dirt from her backside, and fixed her gaze on him. With a mischievous wink, she vanished from sight.

Zaire looked around, dazed and confused. Suddenly, snow began to fall, blanketing the ring and revealing her footprints. Inez reappeared, tilting her head thoughtfully as she considered her next move. Lightning crackled above her, and just before the strike, she crouched down, enveloping herself in a protective bubble. Zaire smiled, genuinely impressed by her quick thinking.

"Meeting tonight. Are you still attending?" Inez questioned Zaire, her voice steady despite the intensity of their training. He simply shook his head in response.

Inez stood straight, her eyes locked onto his as he began to float. She turned invisible once more, causing Zaire to panic. He knew that while floating, his aim would be off, rendering his powers ineffective. Suddenly, she dropped him, and he landed hard on his back. Inez reappeared above him, a knife forged from ice in her hand, pressed to his throat.

"No weapons," Zaire said, his voice firm. He leaned up, examining the icy blade. "Okay, that's allowed," he conceded, recognising the weapon as an extension of her powers.

Inez reached out and helped Zaire to his feet. She blew on her hand, causing the ice to crack and break off, leaving her undamaged. Their eyes met, and a moment passed between them, filled with mutual respect.

Suddenly, the sound of clapping broke their gaze. Nadia and Hunter stood at the side of the room, applauding their performance. The interruption brought them back to reality, and the tension in the air dissipated.

72

Lightning Struck

Later that night, Inez made herself invisible and silently slipped into Zaire's room. She reappeared, but Zaire was not there yet. They had scheduled to meet in twenty minutes, and she hoped they could have some alone time first. As she looked around his room, her eyes fell upon an open book on his bedside table. Curiosity piqued, she picked it up and began to read. To her surprise, she realised it was not just any book, it was his diary. He noted everything meticulously. Feeling a pang of guilt, she put it back, wanting to respect his privacy.

She wandered over to his bookcase and noticed it was filled with similar books, chronicling his life from childhood to the present. The temptation to read them was strong, but she knew that all she had to do was ask him, and he would tell her anything she wanted to know.

Meanwhile, Zaire knocked at Inez's door, unaware that she was upstairs in his room. When there was no answer, he knocked again, and the door creaked open. He stepped inside, looking around for her, but there was no sign of her presence. His attention was drawn to the easel in the corner of her room, where her latest painting of Kek and Qita stood. He walked over and began to flick through the finished pieces leaning against the wall under the window. Each artwork brought a smile to his face, as they depicted the many places they had visited together.

At the back of the pile, a smaller canvas covered with a fabric sheet caught his eye. Zaire picked it up and placed it on her table, removing the fabric. He stepped back in shock, unable to believe what he saw. It wasn't possible. His emotions surged uncontrollably, and outside, rain and lightning began to strike all over the manor's grounds.

Sensing the storm, Inez reached out telepathically. *Where are you? I am in your room waiting for you.* Within seconds, the storm ceased, and Zaire came crashing through the door.

"What is this?" he demanded, holding up the canvas.

"That is… was my husband," Inez replied, her eyes filling with pain.

"Your husband?" Zaire was taken aback, struggling to process the revelation.

"You went through my stuff?" Inez's face was flushed with anger.

"I didn't mean to. I was observing the art and saw it, and I guess I snooped. I'm sorry," Zaire said as he walked towards her and handed her the canvas, now covered again with the fabric.

"Why did it make you so mad?" Inez asked, more curious than accusatory.

"It didn't," Zaire replied, but Inez gave him a look that demanded the truth. "I just saw art of where we had been and then saw a random man, and I got jealous."

Inez placed the fabric on his bed and walked over to him. She hugged him tightly and kissed him. "There is only you now. I love you," she said softly.

"I love you too," Zaire replied, but doubt still lingered in his mind.

A glowing portal opened in Zaire's room, and Kimmie and Megyn sat at a table, their expressions serious.

Kimmie waved her wrist, and another portal materialised, allowing Nadia and Hunter to step through.

"What was that about, bro?" Hunter asked Zaire, his tone curious and concerned.

"You made a storm. You never lose control," Megyn added, worried.

"Can we leave it, please, and get on with the meeting?" Zaire said, giving everyone a scolding look. The room fell silent as everyone turned to face Megyn and Kimmie.

"Well, we haven't been here long enough yet. It's a big adjustment," Kimmie said, hinting at the challenges they faced.

"We don't have access to the archives here yet. Kimmie still needs to show her loyalty to the clan before she gets to read any secret texts," Megyn added.

"They're mean here," Kimmie interjected, but Megyn shot her a look.

Inez looked over at Zaire, her eyes filled with concern. "Has there been anything new?"

"Yes, there is. He is ill," Zaire replied. "I was called to his office, and when I went in, he was unconscious. I had to shock him back to life," Zaire told the team.

"You saved him," Megyn said, shocked.

"We were trained to save, so yes, I did," Zaire added matter-of-factly.

Suddenly, there was a bang at the door through the portal. "Got to go, sorry," Megyn said hurriedly, and Kimmie closed the portal, smiling at the team.

"How are we all meant to get out of here now?" Nadia asked, frustrated.

Inez held out her hand, and Nadia took it. They both went invisible, the door opened and closed, and they were gone.

"Meet me later. I need to talk to you alone," Zaire told Hunter.

"Sparring mat," Hunter responded, understanding the need for privacy.

The door opened, and Inez reappeared. "That is sick," Hunter said, high-fiving her. Inez rolled her eyes but held her hand out to Hunter.

"Don't come back yet. I have a meeting with Raphael," Zaire told Inez.

"Okay, well, I'll find you later," she said, tapping her ear, signalling him to listen for her voice. *I love you*, she told him telepathically, and then she went invisible and left his room.

73

The Stones Were Grief

Zaire took a deep breath and went to sit on the edge of his bed but realised the canvas was still there. He picked it up, feeling a surge of frustration, and stormed out of the room. His footsteps echoed through the hallway as he made his way to Raphael's office. Without hesitation, he blew the door open and slammed it behind him, startling Raphael, who was engrossed in his work.

"Zaire, how dare—"

"Who are you? What is this?" Zaire demanded, holding up the canvas and removing the fabric that covered it. His eyes were fierce.

Raphael glanced at the canvas and responded with a hint of sarcasm, "It's an incredible portrait. Where did you get it? I should hang it in here somewhere."

Zaire's grip tightened on the canvas. "Inez did it. How does she know you? Why did she paint you? She said this was her husband…"

Raphael's face dropped, his expression shifting from surprise to sombre. "One question at a time," he said, trying to calm the situation.

"She met me once but didn't know who I was. That is not me. It was her husband," Raphael answered in a gentle tone, his eyes reflecting a deep sadness.

"Why does he look like you?" Zaire asked, his voice trembling slightly.

Raphael chuckled to himself, though there was no humour in his eyes.

"Funny thing about identical twins..."

Zaire's face dropped, the pieces of the puzzle finally coming together. The canvas slipped from his hands, landing softly on the floor as he stared at Raphael, the truth sinking in.

"Does she know about you?" Zaire asked.

"No, he left our family and the business behind," Raphael replied bitterly. "Any other questions? After you leave this room, I never want to speak about it again," Raphael added firmly, drawing a line in the sand.

Zaire hesitated for a moment before asking, "Are you dying?" He sat down in the chair at the desk.

"Yes, but I was able to prolong it," Raphael admitted. "Lucian had a deal. I let him leave and live his life if I got blood when I needed it. But then he died, and all that is left is a little vial in the safe. A blood relative would do the job, but unfortunately, I'm in short supply of those." As he spoke, Raphael pulled a bloodied rag out of the drawer and coughed into it, the sound harsh and unsettling.

Zaire stood up, feeling a mix of emotions. "Sorry, sir," he said quietly.

Raphael stopped him as he was about to leave. "Please look after Inez," he said, his eyes filled with genuine sadness.

Zaire nodded in acknowledgement and walked out the door. The information was overwhelming, too much for him to handle. He ran outside and jumped into the air. Using the wind's power, he blew himself across the field in seconds, the landscape blurring around him. He entered the forest and screamed, letting out his frustration. Lightning bolts shot from his hands, hitting the ground around him, and one struck a nearby tree, causing a loud cracking noise.

He sat down on a rock near the water, his energy spent. He began skimming stones across the surface, each splash a small release of his pent-up emotions. As he watched the ripples spread, he thought about what to do next, Raphael's request and the revelation about Lucian pressing heavily on his mind.

There was a deep cracking noise from the tree Zaire had struck. It toppled over, its massive trunk heading straight towards where Zaire sat on the rock. Panic surged through him as he tried to use the wind to push it off course, but the tree was too big and heavy, and he had used all his energy. He closed his eyes, bracing for impact, and wondered if death was peaceful.

Suddenly, he heard grunting. When he opened his eyes, he saw Hunter in front of him, holding the trunk with immense strength. "You want to move?" Hunter said through gritted teeth, his muscles straining under the weight.

Zaire quickly moved out of the way, and the ground shook when Hunter threw the trunk off his back, sending it crashing to the side.

"What is wrong? I saw the lightning. You said you wanted to talk alone," Hunter said, sitting on the trunk.

Zaire sat next to him. "How long do you have?" he asked.

"As long as you need, brother," Hunter replied, tapping Zaire's shoulder reassuringly.

Zaire took a deep breath and began telling Hunter everything. He recounted the conversation with Raphael, the revelation about Lucian and the request to look after Inez. Hunter listened intently, his mouth open in shock, unsure of what to say next. He was speechless, and Zaire couldn't think straight either.

After a moment, Hunter spoke up. "He is obsessed with Inez, right? Can we use that to trap him?"

Zaire looked at Hunter, the gears in his mind starting to turn. "Yes, we could use that. But we need to be careful. Raphael is dying, and we don't have much time."

Hunter nodded, his expression serious. "We'll figure it out. Together."

The two brothers sat in silence for a while, the weight of their conversation hanging in the air.

74

Portal Held Her Hand

Weeks later Raphael was in his office, staring at the almost empty vial of Lucian's blood. His phone rang, breaking the silence. He picked it up swiftly. "How long until you can get me more blood?" he asked the stranger on the other end.

There was a pause, and Raphael's expression darkened. "What do you mean you can't?" His voice grew louder, filled with frustration. "He's gone? How could you let this happen?"

The person on the other end tried to explain, but Raphael cut them off. "Find him. I don't care what you have to do." He slammed the phone down, the sound echoing through the room. His hand gripped the phone tightly, knuckles white with anger.

The phone rang again. Raphael snatched it up, his patience wearing thin. "What?" he shouted into the receiver.

"Sorry, sir, I don't mean to disturb you," came the hesitant voice of Zaire. "Inez ran away, and she broke my leg. I cannot drive, and she is now unconscious. She used too much power. I need you to get us."

Raphael's expression shifted from anger to concern. "Give me a minute, and I'll be on the way. Ping me the address," he replied, more controlled now. He hung up and quickly injected himself with the remaining contents of the vial. Almost immediately, his colour returned, and he felt a surge of energy.

He grabbed his keys from the drawer to his right and left the office, determination etched on his face.

He parked outside the abandoned airport hangar and cautiously entered the open space. The vast, empty area echoed with his footsteps as he approached Zaire, who was lying on the floor, clearly in pain.

"Zaire?" Raphael called out, crouching next to him. His eyes scanned the area, anxiety creeping into his voice.

"Where is Inez? She cannot see me, can she?"

Before Zaire could respond, a voice came from behind. "Behind you."

Raphael turned around just in time to see Hunter's fist flying towards his face. The punch landed with a sickening crunch, breaking Raphael's nose. He staggered back, clutching his face, blood seeping through his fingers.

Hunter, looking down at him with a mix of fear and surprise, said to Zaire, "He should be knocked out with a punch like that." The terror in Hunter's voice was palpable as he realised Raphael was not as easily subdued as he had hoped.

Zaire stood up and asked Raphael, "You have powers?"

"My brother and I were the first experiments, but he was healthy. I was the problem." He spoke through his hands, clicking his nose, and seconds later, the bleeding had stopped.

"That's why you need his blood, but he's dead," Zaire added.

"It has been at least a year. How have you survived?" Hunter asked.

"I told you I wouldn't speak about it again," Raphael replied curtly.

Hunter distracted Raphael while Zaire struck him with lightning, knocking him unconscious. "Tie him up as tightly as possible," Zaire instructed Hunter, who began to lug over the thick chains like it was nothing.

Zaire picked up his phone and said, "Come now," before putting his phone back in his pocket. A portal opened, and Kimmie and Megyn came through with Kek and Qita.

"He's getting big," Hunter remarked, looking at Kek. Kek snorted his nose at Hunter, steam coming out. He shadowed over Kimmie and Megyn, his neck and wings stretched. Kek filled the hangar.

Zaire looked at Kimmie and commanded, "Now." Kimmie waved her hand and opened another portal. Nadia walked through, holding Inez's hand behind her.

"What are you all doing..." Inez gasped. "Lucian... What are you all doing to him?" Inez pulled away from Nadia and ran to Raphael. She recognised the smell, the same smell from the night he died. She stepped back in shock.

"What is going on?" she asked, looking around at everyone.

Zaire strode across the dimly lit room, the floorboards creaking under his weight. With a firm but cautious grip, he shook Raphael's neck, jolting him out of his restless slumber. Raphael's eyelids fluttered open, his gaze darting around the unfamiliar surroundings, clouded with confusion. His disoriented mind barely registered the faces around him until his eyes found Inez. Fear flickered in his expression, a deep tremor that sent shivers down his spine. "Inez," he whispered, the name carrying a thousand emotions.

Inez's lips curved into a faint smile, though her tone was tinged with disbelief. "Lucian," she uttered softly, her voice faltering, "I thought you were dead."

Raphael's heart sank. He looked past her, his eyes landing squarely on Zaire, who stood silently like a sentinel. His face hardened, frustration simmering beneath the surface. "You think I'm Lucian?" Raphael's voice cracked, and his next words were a bitter accusation aimed at Zaire, "You didn't tell her."

"She needs to hear it from you," Zaire replied simply, his words settling heavily in the room. There was a quiet intensity in his tone, an unspoken demand.

Inez's brow furrowed, her confusion growing as she turned back to Raphael. The recognition in her eyes was undeniable, yet something didn't fit. "I am Raphael," he confessed, his voice stable despite the turmoil inside him, "Lucian's identical twin."

The revelation hit Inez like a blow. Her breath hitched, and she stumbled backwards, her world tilting off its axis. Nadia was there in an instant, catching her before she could collapse entirely. Nadia's presence grounded Inez just enough to still her trembling frame.

"You were there when he died, weren't you?" Inez's voice rang out, sharp and accusing as her anger flared. Each word was a dagger thrown at Raphael, whose face fell further with every syllable. "It was you."

The words spilt out of him. "It was me in the coffee shop. You were always meant to be with me," Raphael admitted, leaning forwards as far as the chains binding him would allow. His voice faltered under the weight of his confession. "I didn't know he left the business for you… or I would never have let him."

The room stood still, emotions sparking like electricity in the air. Inez took another step forwards, her anger mixing with sorrow in a volatile cocktail. Raphael sat frozen, his chains rattling as he shifted, every movement reminding him of the helplessness of his situation.

"Do you want to know everything? From the start?" Raphael's voice was measured, but there was something beneath it, something raw.

"Yes," Inez whispered.

And so, he told her.

75

The Truth Broke Her

The moment he saw her, he fell harder and faster than he thought possible. But love wasn't supposed to be part of his story. He was dying, clinging to life by a fragile thread, and Lucian had refused to give him more blood. Desperate, Raphael sought him out.

That was when everything changed.

Lucian was angry. Raphael was furious. And then came Inez, unexpected, unexplainable. A complication he hadn't prepared for. When she became pregnant, it was an out, a justification for his next action. He killed Lucian and took everything he could from him, every last drop of blood, to keep himself alive.

For months, it worked. But survival demanded sacrifice, and Inez was the price.

They took her to the lab, hoping to create more gifted children. Every experiment failed. And then there was Lamia, the girl trapped in the cell next to hers, whom Inez knew as Maris. Lamia had carried Zaire's child, but the baby hadn't lived beyond an hour. Raphael discovered something chilling: gifted people couldn't have children together. It was impossible.

And Inez, she was never supposed to be gifted.

He hadn't planned it. Hadn't wanted it. But fate was cruel, and mistakes had consequences. He had left the car outside the facility for her, knowing she would escape. He had followed her, watched every step she took. Yet still, he hadn't realised the depth of her power until Zaire mentioned a dream, until he told him to recruit her.

By then, it was too late.

She was stronger than he had imagined. More dangerous than he could have foreseen. When she uncovered the chamber beneath the facility, she saw too much. She knew too much. And Raphael had done what he always did when faced with a problem, he eliminated it.

He had killed Lamia's mother.

Now, standing before Inez, his voice carried the burden of years of choices, of sins he had tried to justify.

But could they ever truly be justified?

Inez screamed, her voice echoing like a battle cry, and thrust her hands forwards with all her might. The force of her blow sent Raphael hurtling across the room, crashing into the wall with a thunderous impact. Dust and debris rained down as the room seemed to shudder under the force. Hunter, unfazed, strode over with a calm intensity. With a single, effortless motion, he hoisted Raphael, chair and all, off the ground, his muscles taut with power.

But Raphael was no longer bound. The chains that had once restrained him clattered to the floor, useless remnants of a futile attempt at control. He rose to his feet with an eerie grace, every movement charged with an unnatural power. His eyes burned with a dangerous, almost inhuman light, something ancient and unstoppable.

Without hesitation, he flicked his fingers against Hunter's neck. The motion was so quick it barely registered, but its effect was catastrophic.

Hunter's body was wrenched backwards, lifted him off his feet as if struck by an unseen hammer. His spine arched unnaturally as he crashed down onto the unforgiving ground, the impact reverberating through his bones with a sickening crunch. Air exploded from his lungs in a strangled gasp, his head snapping back and colliding with the floor. A searing pain splintered through his skull, white hot and disorienting.

Agony rippled through his limbs, his right shoulder bore the worst of it, wrenched out of place as he instinctively tried to brace for the fall. His fingers twitched involuntarily, his breath shallow, his chest rising and falling in erratic, uneven heaves. His vision blurred, edged in darkness, as shock overtook his senses.

The silence that followed was suffocating.

Raphael exhaled slowly, surveying the wreckage with unsettling calm. This fight was over, but the real nightmare had only just begun.

Raphael smirked, his voice dripping with disdain. "So much potential," he mused, almost pitying, "but he never knew how to use it fully."

He stepped forwards, surveying the motionless body with something that resembled detached curiosity. The fight had been swift, too swift for a warrior with such promise. Hunter had once been fierce, unrelenting, brimming with energy. But in the end, it hadn't been enough. His strength had failed him, his body had given out, and now he lay as nothing more than a broken relic of what he had once been.

The echoes of battle had long faded, leaving only silence. A silence that swallowed the space whole. No movement, no breath, no resistance. Only stillness.

Raphael exhaled slowly, shaking his head. "Wasted," he murmured, before turning away, uninterested in lingering over the inevitable.

Before Raphael could revel in his triumph, Nadia became a blur of motion. A guttural scream tore from her throat as she hurled herself across the room, fuelled by sheer desperation. Her fist connected with Raphael's face, a strike driven by fury, by heartbreak, but the impact was jarring, like slamming into solid stone. Pain shot through her knuckles, but she barely registered it. She didn't care. She couldn't care.

Hunter was there, motionless.

She saw him sprawled across the ground, lifeless, unmoving. Her heart clenched, a suffocating pressure constricting her ribs. No, this wasn't happening. It couldn't be happening.

Her movements became frantic, reckless. She launched a flurry of punches, her limbs a whirlwind of rage and grief. Every attack was wild, driven by the unbearable ache threatening to consume her, but Raphael evaded each strike with supernatural ease. He moved with a terrifying grace, slipping through her fury like a shadow.

Tears blurred her vision, turning Raphael into a hazy spectre. She didn't even realise she was sobbing, the sound broken, choked. Hunter... her Hunter... he couldn't be gone.

She tried to reach him, tried to break past Raphael, but suddenly, an iron grip coiled around her throat.

A gasp escaped her lips as Raphael's arm tightened, cutting off her air. Her legs kicked wildly, hands clawing at his grip, but she couldn't break free. Darkness crept at the edges of her vision, swallowing her screams.

Her last thought before everything faded was his name.

Hunter.

Megyn tightened her grip on the black and blue hilted samurai swords, their gleaming edges catching the flickering energy in the air around them. The battlefield pulsed with an unseen force, a ball of power ready to erupt. Her gaze locked onto Qita as his feline form shifted, sinewy muscles rippling beneath his fur, preparing for the clash.

A simple meow had escaped him moments ago, but now twisted into something primal, a deep, resonant roar that sent vibrations through the earth beneath their feet. In an instant, his sleek grey body elongated, limbs stretching with a supernatural fluidity. His paws morphed into formidable claws, each talon sharp enough to carve through steel. His transformation into a panther was complete, his eyes burning with a fierce determination that promised devastation.

Then, he moved.

Explosive speed turned his form into a blur, a dark streak across the battlefield, too fast for even the most skilled eyes to track. Air whipped past Megyn as she steadied herself, sensing the imminent collision. Raphael, reading the urgency in Qita's movements, darted towards Hunter, his hand pressing against him in a fleeting gesture before he pivoted. Qita sprinting back to Megyn's side. His breathing was steady, his form controlled, but what had just transpired floated between them.

The atmosphere was electric, a moment balanced on the razor's edge of fate. The clash was inevitable, but who would strike first?

THE TRUTH BROKE HER

"He has power absorption, but he can only hold one at a time!" Kimmie's voice rang out beside Kek, slicing through the chaos like a blade.

"Don't let him touch Inez!" Zaire's warning was fierce, anticipating the looming disaster.

Kimmie reacted instantly, instincts overriding thought. Her fingers carved patterns in the air, weaving an intricate spell. A shimmering portal unfurled beneath Inez just as she started to resist, light swallowing her whole. In the blink of an eye, she vanished, reappearing in the manor, her body landing gently on the bed. Safe. For now.

But outside that sanctuary, the battle raged on.

Raphael's grip tightened around the chain, its metallic clink echoing like a whispered omen. Without hesitation, he hurled it at Zaire with brutal force, sending him crashing to the ground, unmoving. The room seemed to inhale, holding its breath in eerie anticipation.

Then Raphael turned, rage burning in his eyes, zeroing in on Qita.

A fluid motion, a ruthless strike, his boot connected hard, the impact sending the feline-like creature skidding across the floor. The sound of the collision was visceral, bone and muscle giving way under sheer force. Megyn gasped, clutching her side, as though the pain had transferred from Qita to her.

This was no longer just a fight. It was a storm, spiralling towards something far worse.

In a flash of light, Qita reverted to his cat form, his small body trembling. Megyn, her hands shaking, rushed to him, cradling him gently. Her voice was barely a whisper as she said, "I need to get you to Kimmie." Her eyes darted to Kimmie, who was already at the portal, her hands weaving the shimmering edges of the gateway into stability.

"Kek, go!" Kimmie commanded. The creature hesitated, its glowing eyes locking onto hers, before leaping through the portal. Kimmie took a step forwards, ready to follow, when Raphael's voice cut through the air.

"You can't leave," he said, his tone low and dangerous. "We need to talk, sister."

Kimmie froze, her hand hovering over the portal's edge. She turned her head slightly.

"Look after Kek," she said softly, her words directed through the portal. With a swift motion, she closed it, the shimmering light collapsing into nothingness. Behind her, Megyn let out a scream filled with despair.

Kimmie turned slowly to face Raphael, her eyes narrowing. "Sister?" she asked in disbelief.

Raphael's lips curled into a bitter smile. "Oh yes, well, half-sister," he said, his words dripping with venom. "Our mother was in love with my father. She left your father behind for him and got pregnant with Lucian and me. She was powered; my father wasn't. That's how we survived, but her power was split between us. Lucian got more, and I was left weak, a disappointment to my father. He blames me for her death."

Kimmie's mind was reeling. Tears welled up in her eyes as she whispered, "She's dead?"

Raphael's expression darkened. "Her last words after giving birth to Lucian and me were to keep you safe. It was for the greater good. She didn't even care about us, only you." His voice rose, anger seeping into every syllable. "Do you know what that does to a child? To know you're nothing but an afterthought?"

Kimmie shook her head, her tears falling freely now. "I didn't know," she murmured, her voice breaking.

Raphael's eyes glinted with something dangerous. "Your blood was no good for me," he said coldly. "I tried and failed. When Father caught me testing on you, he went crazy. So I slit his throat with a scalpel and took over the business. And you know what? I think I ran it better."

Kimmie stared at him, her face a mask of horror. "You're insane," she said.

"Not insane," Raphael corrected, eerily calm. "But you gain a certain clarity when you know you're going to die."

76

All Forgotten

Inez burst into the room, her presence electrified by a newfound power that seemed to radiate from her very being. Her eyes glowed with an ethereal light, and sparks of energy crackled around her fingertips. Without hesitation, she seized Raphael and propelled them both into the sky with a force that defied gravity.

"Goodbye, Raphael. Your darkness will no longer plague this world," she declared, resolute and filled with purpose. As they ascended, the air around them shimmered with magical energy, creating a dazzling display of colours. Higher and higher they soared, the air growing thinner and colder as she poured every ounce of her strength into ensuring his end.

The sky erupted in a blinding glow of white light, a moment of sheer intensity that seemed to freeze time itself. The light was so bright that it illuminated the entire landscape below. The energy around them reached a crescendo, and the very fabric of reality seemed to crumble.

And then, silence. The light faded, and the world returned to its normal state. Inez hovered in the air, power still radiating from her. She began to descend, her expression one of determination and relief.

From below, Kimmie watched the figures plummet from the heavens, her heart pounding. Acting quickly, she conjured a portal, guiding their descent into the hangar. They landed with a thud, and Inez lay motionless, her energy completely spent.

He, however, was a grotesque sight. The colour drained rapidly from his face as he began to cough violently, blood spewing from his mouth and staining his hands as he tried to stifle it. His voice, though weak and gurgling, carried a venomous finality. "You are not special," he spat, his words dripping with malice even as his strength ebbed away. Collapsing to the floor, his body convulsed briefly before going still. Blood pooled around him, and the light in his eyes dimmed until it was no more.

The room was heavy with the aftermath, the air thick with the weight of what had just transpired. Kimmie's gaze shifted between Inez's unconscious form and the lifeless body before her.

Inez wandered through the barren desert, a place ravaged by war, where the air seemed heavy with despair. Her eyes caught sight of the young girl once more, a haunting figure amidst the turmoil. The girl was being dragged towards a plane by her mother and a captor. Her father, dying to intervene, followed closely but was mercilessly shot by a guard.

In a moment of raw emotion, the little girl broke free from her mother's grasp and ran to her fallen father. Her mother, driven by instinct, chased after her, only to meet the same tragic fate. The girl stood there, her cries piercing the air as grief consumed her small frame.

The man, cold and unyielding, seized the girl and placed her by the plane's window. Meanwhile, two guards carried the lifeless body of her mother onto the plane, laying her on a table as though she were cargo. The plane ascended into the sky, and the girl's tear-streaked face pressed against the window. Below, her father's lifeless form grew smaller and smaller, a reminder of the life she had just lost.

But then, something shifted. The girl's tears abruptly ceased, as if a switch had been flipped. She turned to the man, her voice steady yet hollow. "How long until we are home?"

Inez, watching this surreal scene unfold, felt a wave of confusion. The girl's behaviour changed again, her volume rising into a scream as she locked eyes with Inez. "I need to get back home," she cried, her words echoing. "This is all forgotten."

The juxtaposition of grief and detachment left Inez questioning the reality of what she had just witnessed. What did the girl mean by 'forgotten'? And what was 'home' to her now? The desert, once a backdrop of war, now seemed to hold secrets far more profound.

Inez stirred awake, her eyes fluttering open as she took in the sterile white walls surrounding her. The hum of hospital equipment filled the air, and as she tried to sit up, a throbbing pain shot through her head. She winced, lifting a hand to her temple. For a fleeting moment, she wondered if it was all a bad dream. Perhaps, if she closed her eyes again, she'd wake up somewhere else, somewhere safer.

The sound of the door creaking open pulled her back to reality. Zaire stepped in, his familiar figure a stark contrast to the clinical environment. He wasn't alone, a nurse followed behind him, a clipboard in hand. The sight of them made the truth sink in. This wasn't a nightmare she could wake from. It had all been real. And if it was real, it meant she'd lost almost everything that mattered to her. Almost.

The nurse smiled warmly as she approached, performing routine checks. "You're in perfect condition," the nurse assured her. But the words felt hollow to Inez, her mind swirling with everything she'd endured.

Zaire pulled up a chair next to her bed and sat down, his dark eyes filled with an emotion she couldn't quite place. Gently, he reached out and took her hand in his, his grip firm yet comforting. "He's gone," Zaire said softly. "Dead. You did it, Inez. Everyone is free because of you."

Inez stared at him, the enormity of his words passing her by. She wanted to feel victorious, to celebrate the liberation she had fought so hard to achieve. But instead, a pang of emptiness settled in her chest. "Why am I in the hospital?" she asked. "Did I not heal?"

She could see the hesitation in his expression. Finally, he said, "Your powers... they're gone."

The words hit her like a physical blow. Gone. Her powers were all she'd had left after losing Lucian and Leo. Now they were stripped away too. A tear escaped her eye, followed by another, until she was silently weeping.

Zaire tightened his hold on her hand, his voice a quiet anchor in the storm. "You have me," he reminded her.

She looked at him then, truly looked at him, and saw the devotion in his gaze. It wasn't enough to erase her pain, but it was something to hold onto.

Hours later, with her discharge papers signed, Inez found herself stepping into the outside world once more. The hospital's automatic doors slid shut behind her, and Zaire guided her towards a waiting car. The drive was quiet, save for the occasional instructions from the GPS.

They were heading to a new safe house, their lives uprooted once again. Deep down, Inez knew it was only a matter of time before another organisation came after them. But for now, she leaned back against the car seat, letting herself find solace in Zaire's presence. Whatever came next, they would face it together.

77

The Ember and the Echo

As they turned onto the narrow dirt road, the car jostled over small bumps and dips, eventually coming to a stop outside a charming, rustic house nestled in the middle of an endless field. A thin plume of smoke drifted lazily from the back garden, curling upwards into the blue sky.

Zaire squinted and shook his head with a knowing smirk. "Lamia is doing a barbecue… her first one," he muttered with a hint of scepticism, already anticipating the culinary disaster that awaited them.

With a gentle but firm hand, he helped Inez out of the car. She still moved cautiously, her strength not fully restored, but determination sparkled in her eyes. Together, they made their way through the quaint house, each step bringing muffled bursts of laughter and the tantalising aroma of grilled food.

In the back garden, vibrant sunlight illuminated the scene of joyful disorder. Lamia, armed with tongs, stood by the barbecue with a proud, slightly nervous grin, flipping something that may or may not have been sausages. As they stepped onto the patio, Lamia caught sight of Inez. Without hesitation, she rushed over, throwing her arms around her in a fierce hug that seemed to say a thousand words.

"See? Told you she was a fighter," Lamia said as she glanced towards Zaire. The sound of sizzling food punctuated his words, the aroma of grilled vegetables and charred spices drifting through the warm evening air.

At the far end of the garden, a small boy played with a ball, his movements fluid and effortless. He caught it with ease, his body already accustomed to the rhythm of the game. Then, as if sensing something beyond the ordinary, his attention snapped towards the newcomers. He turned, his wide eyes searching for Inez, and suddenly, the world tilted.

The resemblance was staggering, a living echo of Lucian standing before her. His features, delicate yet unmistakably familiar, stirred something deep and aching within her, a bittersweet feeling of love and longing.

"Mum!" The boy's voice shattered the moment, breaking into an excited shout as he bolted towards her, his small legs moving so fast he seemed seconds away from tripping. Yet sheer willpower kept him steady, his feet drumming against the earth with purpose.

Zaire, ever the watchful guardian, raised a hand in gentle warning. "Take it easy. She just got out of the hospital," he said.

"I missed you so much," Inez choked out as she knelt, opening her arms.

Leo collided into her with a force that spoke of all the days, weeks and months they'd spent apart. His arms wrapped tightly around her, squeezing with everything his small body could offer. Tears spilt from Inez's eyes as she cradled him, her fingers threading through his hair in disbelief, gratitude and overwhelming love.

"How?" she whispered, barely able to form the word, her gaze lifting towards Zaire in search of answers.

"Lamia," he responded simply, his gratitude unspoken but evident in the way he looked at her.

Inez turned her attention to Lamia, who stood watching from across the garden. There was something knowing in the way she smiled, small, understanding, touched with quiet triumph.

"Thank you," Inez whispered.

Lamia gave a slight nod, no words necessary.

And as if afraid to let go, Inez pulled Leo into another embrace, shielding him against her, as if she alone could ward off the world's cruelty.

As the clatter of plates and silverware faded into the background, Inez found her voice, though the question felt like glass in her throat. "How is he so grown up?"

The words hung in the air, delicate yet heavy, the question that had been circling all night finally spoken.

Lamia set her fork down gently, her movements composed, thoughtful. "You were human," she began, meeting Inez's gaze. "Lucian had powers. So Leo survived."

Her voice carried a history too vast to be unpacked over dinner.

Zaire, always the one to offer clarity, leaned forwards slightly, his expression serious. "Leo's power is healing, rapid, intense. That's why he ages so quickly. His cells mature at an accelerated rate."

The explanation hovered over the table, logic intertwining with something almost mystical.

Zaire shifted in his seat, sitting a little straighter now. A deep breath filled his lungs before he spoke.

"Lamia isn't staying," he announced firmly, his protective instincts kicking in. "This is our home now, with Leo. I'm staying to protect both of you."

Inez nodded, relief washing over her like a tide. "Good," she murmured, her voice calm despite the tempest of emotions. "I want you here. With both of us."

And as the evening stretched on, the house grew quieter.

Lamia packed her things with quiet efficiency, slipping away into the serenity of the beach house. It was a goodbye, but not forever.

Later that night, Inez cradled Leo in her arms, feeling the warmth of his small frame pressed against her. She hummed a soft lullaby, the melody weaving through the dim glow of the night. His breathing slowed, deepened, until sleep finally took him.

She tucked him into bed gently, brushing a kiss against his forehead.

Then, slipping into their new room, she turned to Zaire. The question tumbled from her lips before she could stop it.

"Where are Nadia and Hunter?"

Zaire hesitated, his expression shifting as he prepared to break the news. Hunter was gone.

The words hit Inez like a punch to the gut.

She swallowed hard, struggling to speak past the grief pressing into her chest.

"Nadia?" she managed.

"She woke up," Zaire responded, his voice measured. "She took off on his bike. No one has seen her since. Lamia's going to look for her."

Silence stretched between them.

Eventually, exhaustion won out.

Inez climbed into bed beside Zaire, the day dissolving as she felt him beside her.

She whispered a quiet goodnight.

And together, they drifted into sleep, bound by love, protection and the hope of whatever tomorrow might bring.

78

World holding its breath

A year had passed, and the world seemed quieter, perhaps too quiet for Lamia's liking. She had spent months trying to make sense of the void that Nadia's sudden disappearance had left behind. The silence was disturbing, a constant reminder of the unknown dangers lurking just out of sight.

Then, without warning, a shimmering portal erupted into existence before her. The air crackled with energy, and a sense of foreboding filled the room. Out of the spinning energy stepped Kimmie, drenched in blood, her face etched with fury. Fire roared behind her, casting an ominous glow that danced across the portal's edges, illuminating the room in a sinister light.

"We need you," Kimmie gasped. "Come to the temple. Bring who you can."

Her words were sharp, cutting through the air like a knife. The urgency gave Lamia chills.

Before Lamia could respond or even process Kimmie's words, the portal snapped shut, vanishing as abruptly as it had appeared. Lamia was left frozen in place, her heart pounding in her chest. The room felt still, eerily quiet, as if the world itself had paused to absorb what had just happened. All that was left behind was a piece of parchment that floated before landing on the floor.

The shock slowly gave way to a deep, gnawing dread. Whatever Kimmie needed, it was no trivial matter. The blood, the fire, the desperation in her eyes, all pointed to a danger far greater than Lamia had ever faced. She could feel the dread clawing at her, threatening to overwhelm her.

Lamia knew she had to act, but the uncertainty of what lay ahead was paralysing. She took a deep breath, trying to steady herself. The decision she faced was monumental, and the stakes were higher than ever. She had to gather her strength, and her allies, and prepare for whatever awaited them at the temple.

With fear gripping her heart, Lamia began making plans. She knew that time was of the essence, and every second counted. The world had been quiet for too long, and now, the storm was about to break.

79

BONUS CHAPTER - Maris (Lamia)

I was head over heels in love with Zaire; we were inseparable. Every moment spent together felt like a dream, as if the universe had conspired to bring us together. His laughter was my favourite melody, and his touch felt like home. I couldn't imagine my life without him. But little did I know, one small mistake would unravel everything we had built.

It started with a feeling of sickness and nausea that clung to me like a shadow. At first, I brushed it off, blaming stress or a fleeting bug. But when I missed my period, the realisation hit me like a ton of bricks. I was pregnant. The emotions that surged through me were a whirlwind — joy, fear, hope and dread, all tangled together. This new life growing inside me was a miracle. It was also a storm that would change everything.

Zaire and I had been tasked with a mission, one that was far from ordinary. We were to collect a vial of liquid from a high-security lab. But this wasn't just a simple collection. It was a break-in. A theft. The stakes were impossibly high, and the risks were too great. I couldn't jeopardise my baby's life. Desperate to find a way out, I turned to Raphael, hoping he would understand my predicament. His piercing gaze bore into me as he questioned my sudden reluctance. I had no choice but to tell him the truth.

His initial reaction was fury. A tempest of anger that left me trembling. But then, as the storm within him subsided, his demeanour shifted. He saw the gravity of the situation. The fragility of the life I carried. Raphael explained that my powers — abilities I had always relied on — would become volatile and uncontrollable during the pregnancy. For my safety and the safety of those around me, I needed to be monitored.

I was confined to a concrete room. Stark and unyielding. With only a tub of murky water to keep me company. It felt like a prison. A place where time stood still and hope was a distant memory. The days blurred together, each one heavier than the last. And then, the contractions began. The pain was unlike anything I had ever known. A relentless wave that threatened to drown me. Fear gripped me as I fought for my baby's life, praying for a miracle.

When I finally gave birth, the world seemed to hold its breath. My baby was beautiful. A tiny, perfect being who had already stolen my heart. But heartbreakingly, their life was fleeting. They passed away within twenty-five minutes, and I never even got to hold them. The loss was a chasm that swallowed me whole, leaving me hollow and broken. I was sent back to the room to heal. But the wounds were more than physical. They were etched into my soul.

One night, Raphael visited me. His expression unreadable. He told me someone would be coming to see me and instructed me to tell her that my name was Maris, not Lamia. Confused and weary, I nodded. Too drained to question him. I thought I was alone in this desolate place. But one night, I heard a voice shouting down the hall. It was faint, but it was there. A lifeline in the darkness. I tried to shout back, but she couldn't hear me. Summoning my siren voice, I reached out to her through the wall, weaving my words into a melody that carried my message.

Her story was as heartbreaking as my own. A mirror of pain and resilience. I couldn't leave her to face this place alone. Together, we plotted our escape, clinging to the plan Raphael had shared with me. But deep down, I knew I wouldn't be leaving with her. My path led back to the manor. Back to a life where I had to pretend that nothing had happened. I had to bury the pain and the memories, locking them away in the shadows of my mind.

The experience changed me in ways I couldn't fully comprehend. The love I had for Zaire. The loss of my baby. The confinement in that concrete room. All left scars that would never fade. But I had to keep moving forward, even as the weight of my past threatened to pull me under. I had to survive. For myself, and for the memory of the life I had lost.

80

BONUS CHAPTER - Lamia

I stood in the dimly lit room, my thoughts tangled in the aftermath of everything that had happened. Inez had every right to react the way she did. Seeing me in Zaire's bed was a betrayal she couldn't stomach. But none of it mattered any more. Not after what I found in the lake. My mother's lifeless form, drifting in the water like a cruel echo of everything I had lost. That night, I lost her and Inez in one breath.

I couldn't stay here. Not when every shadow reminded me of the way my world had shattered. I told Inez I needed space. Needed air that wasn't suffocating with the weight of grief. But how does one escape when the walls close in tighter every time you try to move?

Inez summoned the team, and together we crafted a desperate plan. I would trade information to Raphael for my freedom. A calculated move. A deal with the devil himself. But it was my only way out. When I confronted Raphael, he accepted the trade without hesitation. What he didn't know was that I had no intention of stopping there.

Back in my cell, I turned my power against the doctor, ensnaring him in my siren song and forcing the truth from his lips. Leo wasn't dead. He was alive, hidden away in the Opal Temple, training for something I didn't yet understand. That revelation set my course, sharpening my resolve. If I was going to break free, I was taking Leo with me.

The night I escaped, I made my way straight to the temple. The enormous

BONUS CHAPTER - LAMIA

doorway loomed before me, its dragon-head door knocker glaring like a sentinel. I knocked, my heart a steady drumbeat of defiance.

A boy answered. Young, with piercing blue eyes and dark brown hair. His resemblance to Raphael was uncanny. He told me he was Leo, but before I could respond, a tall man with dark hair stepped in front of him, katana drawn, ready to strike.

I didn't flinch. Instead, I parted my lips and let my song unfurl, winding through the air and wrapping around the guards like a serpent. Their weapons lowered. Their bodies went rigid. Their minds bent to my will.

I slipped past them, finding Leo curled at the bottom of an oak wardrobe covered in green dragon carvings. His eyes were wide, filled with something too raw to name.

"I'm a friend of your mother's," I whispered.

Without hesitation, he reached for me, his small hand clasping mine. And together, we ran.

Later that night, I met Zaire, showing him Leo and demanding answers. What now? Raphael was dead. Inez lay in a hospital bed. Nothing felt real. Hunter was dead and Nadia had gone. Zaire was by Inez's side, and it was Leo and I left to set up their new house.

Leo sketched out his room himself, carefully selecting each detail like it was his lifeline. And then, we waited.

The moment Inez arrived, everything else faded. The instant her eyes landed on her son, the child she'd been robbed of, her face contorted with something deeper than joy, deeper than grief.

She had never been allowed to hold him. Never been given the chance to be his mother.

But now, at long last, here he was. And Inez, frail, tired, broken, collapsed into his arms like the weight of the universe had finally released her.

Afterword

Book playlist:
Arcade - Duncan Laurence
Hurts so good - Astrid S
Borderline - Tove Lo
Karma - Taylor Swift
Boys will be boys - Dua Lipa
Amo Soltanto Te - Andrea Bocelli (ft. Ed Sheeran)
One thing right - Marshmello & Kane Brown
Radioactive - Imagine Dragons
Run - Leona Lewis
Undo - Naughty Boy, Calum Scott & Shenseea

About the Author

Kimberley S Basham is a fantasy author with a passion for crafting immersive worlds and compelling characters. Her debut novel, *Blood of the First Flame*, is a thrilling blend of magic and mystery. She holds a certificate in creative writing, which has deepened her love for storytelling and helped shape her voice as an author. When she's not writing, she enjoys crafting and cooking, always finding new ways to bring creativity into everyday life.

You can connect with me on:
- https://kimberley-basham.com
- https://www.tiktok.com/@kimberley_basham

Printed in Dunstable, United Kingdom